LEGAL
ASYLUM

PAUL GOLDSTEIN

LEGAL ASYLUM

A COMEDY

ANKERWYCKE

Cover design by Elmarie Jara/ABA Design.
Interior design by Betsy Kulak/ABA Design.

Printed in the United States of America.

20 19 18 17 16   5 4 3 2 1

ISBN 978-1-63425-611-7

Discounts are available for books ordered in bulk. Special consideration is given to state bars, CLE programs, and other bar-related organizations. Inquire at Book Publishing, ABA Publishing, American Bar Association, 321 N. Clark Street, Chicago, Illinois 60654-7598.

www.ShopABA.org

For Jan

SUNDAY

ONE

Every one of the 37 men on State's law faculty was in thrall to Dean Elspeth Flowers, from George Cruikshank, who was well into his seventies, to young Benjamin Hubbell, the dean's most recent and brilliant hire. For the gay Bucholz twins, Garry and Larry, the dean's Galliano fashions and carmine-painted nails were a bright beacon against the austere New England horizon. If the faculty's seven women were somewhat less rapturous, they were nonetheless in craven debt to Elspeth for protecting their five-hour workweeks and four-month summer holidays against the overwhelmingly male legislature's insisting question: What do these professors *do* with the rest of their time?

But Elspeth feared that she was losing her powers. All men are really 11-year-old boys, as riveted by a girl's curves today as when they were adolescents, and Elspeth knew that if she let her wondrous glow dim for even a moment these boys would abandon her like a worn-out catcher's mitt. Just this morning, a United States senator who ordinarily jumped at her smallest demand kept Elspeth waiting for two hours, causing her to miss the noon flight home and making her late for her meeting with University President Rawleigh Bartles.

And when on the ride to the airport she called the usually submissive president to persuade him to postpone their budget meeting until Monday, Rawleigh demurred. "You're not the only person on my calendar, Ellie. I already made one exception, letting you plead your case on Sunday, of all days. I'm not going to make another."

The wooded New England landscape sped by outside her car window as Elspeth struggled to reassure herself that the senator's delay and the president's intransigence were only small lapses. She would prevail in her budget requests, even though it would require her to reverse in Rawleigh's mind the trammeling force of the university's history. Founded in 1871 as an agricultural college, State's academic embrace had, in the educational heyday of the 1950s, been broadened by a politically ambitious governor and a compliant legislature to take in not only the social sciences and the humanities, but the professions as well. Yet origins persist, particularly in the barnyard, and even today the Food Science Department and the Meat Lab consumed great chunks of the university budget, and classes like Poultry Economics and Swine Systems Management still ruled the curriculum.

Turning into the circular driveway of the president's house, Elspeth realized that she was betting her school's future, and her own, on the hope that President Bartles, a soils scientist who had clawed his way up through the ranks of the Ag School, was smart enough to understand the university's trajectory as well as its history: that in the future the shine on his institution's apple was not going to come from beef and grain. State's future glory was going to emanate from the newer schools, the Law School first among them, or so the dean prayed.

President Bartles himself came to the door, in chinos and a pink tennis shirt that deepened the natural flush of smooth cheeks to which lemony cologne had been liberally applied. "The loveliest of my deans!"

Elspeth quickly reviewed the possible responses before deciding on, "Is Mrs. Bartles home?"

"No, she's upstate visiting her sister." The president's color deepened a shade or two before he turned back into the house.

Again, Elspeth debated strategy as she followed the president through a succession of darkly furnished public rooms.

"Well here we are. *Sanctum sanctorum.* My man cave. No one is allowed in here but the housekeeper."

And not recently, Elspeth thought. A greasy film of dust covered every surface in the small, low-ceilinged study. Except for the massive television screen hanging on the opposite wall, the room looked as if it had been furnished by the state dormitory authority. There was a pole lamp, and the couch was little more than a slab of foam rubber on a wooden frame. Paperbacks and magazines were piled on bookshelves made of rough-cut pine boards. Below the shelves was an algae-clogged aquarium. Two listless tropical fish glanced at the president and his visitor, gulped, and moved on. The curtains on the den's single window were drawn, and there was a mustiness about the room that reminded Elspeth of the canvas army tent her father brought on their long-ago camping trips in the Maine woods.

A collection of family photographs occupied the top, mahogany-stained shelf, but it was a framed picture apart from the others that drew Elspeth's attention. She looked a second time and suppressed a cry. The photograph was of Rawleigh in black tie, his tuxedoed arm thrown around the bare shoulders of none other than Elspeth herself.

The president must have seen her reaction, for again his color deepened. "Don't you remember last year's reunion, Ellie? In June?"

The alumni event explained Rawleigh's formal attire and Elspeth's low-cut cocktail dress, but not the picture's presence here, set apart from the family photos like an icon in a shrine. Elspeth's sexual adventures had exposed her to the full spectrum of carnal eccentricity—and she also had appetites and fantasies of her own—but they were light-years removed from anything as creepy as this. Her thoughts must have been evident, because the president said, "I imagine the housekeeper moved the picture the last time she cleaned."

The lucite frame, when Elspeth lifted it to examine the picture, exposed a gleaming strip of varnished wood. The shelf hadn't been dusted for months. In the photograph, Rawleigh's eyes glowed red, probably from the photographer's flash, but oddly Elspeth's did not. A jury could debate whether the expression on the president's face was a smile or a leer, but no one would dispute that Rawleigh's eyes were aimed precisely, like a rifle at a rabbit, at what Elspeth in conversations with herself referred to as her "glorious cleavage."

The president took the picture from her hands and returned it to the shelf, where it disappeared behind the others, then looked at his watch. "I think you wanted to talk about your budget." He glanced at the watch a second time. "You should know, Ellie, I don't have time for any of your tricks."

Women had no trouble remembering Elspeth's given name, but men were powerless to call her anything but Ellie. The reason was transparently clear. The diminutive was meant to diminish her, to remove her as a threat. Yet, as much as she resented it, the dean never let on, for to do so would be to let these men believe that they had won; that she had capitulated. "No tricks," she said, raising her hands as if to demonstrate that she had nothing lodged up her sleeves.

The president deposited a few dusty granules from a small canister into the fish tank. "Then maybe you can tell me how, in a fiscal year in which the legislature has slashed the university budget twenty percent, a year in which I have been forced to ask every school and department to do the same, you have the temerity to deliver a budget to my finance office proposing a ten percent increase. I know where you get your ideas from, Ellie, but this isn't Yale. It's State."

State. No one had ever accused Elspeth of possessing delicate sensibilities, but her insides clenched at the brutish word. *Yale*, on the other hand, her alma mater—what a glorious, if slightly dissolute, champagne bubble of a name. Or *Harvard*, two plump syllables to melt elegantly on the tongue like a slice of *foie gras* or Perigord truffle, rich with the savor of history. *Stanford*. Elegant in its own way, and beautifully lacquered with the sun-speckled patina of the western frontier. Even *Chicago* and *Columbia* evoke delight as they toss urban grit into the machinery of highbrow intellectualism; and so many syllables! But *State*. A name for rubes and yokels, hayseeds with cow pies clinging to their boots.

Say "State" and half the locals in College Station think of pigs and pigskin, while the other half think you mean the Metropolitan State Hospital for the Criminally Insane, across Wiscassett Parkway from the university.

Elspeth watched Rawleigh screw the top back on the canister of fish chow. As usual, she found herself hoping to discover a rind of dirt beneath the soils scientist's fingernails, but of course, the flesh was pink, the nails neatly manicured. "I didn't ask for ten percent," she said. "I asked for twelve. And it's a bargain, Rawleigh. I know how concerned you are about the other schools and departments. That's why I whittled my request down from fifteen percent. But don't waste your breath trying to get me any lower. At twelve percent, we're hitting bone."

"And you think that, at a time when everyone else is tightening their belts, you should get an extra helping because something exceptional about the Law School entitles you to the largest offices on the campus, the highest faculty salaries—"

"The football coach makes more. The Director of Athletics."

"They're not faculty."

"Then the surgeons at the Medical School—"

"Only the ones doing heart transplants. Do you realize that a full professor of English makes less than half what you pay your most junior assistant professor? Closer to a third."

"We have to compete in the marketplace, Rawleigh. How many English professors do you know who have job offers to engage in the practice of literature? Law firms would pay my faculty three times what I do." In theory this was true. Rawleigh didn't need to know that, with one exception, there was not a member of her faculty who wouldn't pee his or her pants at the prospect of actually facing a client or arguing a case.

Elspeth reached out for the president's hand, surprising him, and drew him onto the couch next to her. Inches away from him, she could feel his heart pumping. This was good. In spite of her earlier concerns, she still possessed some of her magic. "What have you always wished for Santa to bring you, Rawleigh, but, come Christmas morning, it was never under the tree?"

"An electric train set."

A picture flashed through Elspeth's mind of the fleshy, balding president in his usual three-piece suit, seated on Santa's lap, asking for the Lionel Streamliner. "No, I mean now. Today."

"That's ridiculous, Ellie. Grown men don't believe in Santa Claus."

"How can you expect Santa Claus to believe in you if you don't believe in her?"

The president extracted his hand and edged down the couch. "What are we talking about here, Ellie?"

The president's distance worried her. "Close your eyes, Rawleigh, and make a wish." This was going to be a critical test of her power, and Elspeth scraped the hard floor of her consciousness for every last particle of will so that, laser-like, she could concentrate her intentions on the president. "Make the biggest, grandest wish you can."

Rawleigh's eyelids dropped for a full five seconds. When they opened, he said, "Well?"

"When was the last time *U.S. News & World Report* ranked one of State's schools in the Top Five?" Elspeth knew the answer: never. State's last brush with academic prominence occurred decades ago, when it successfully recruited the podiatrist Sheldon Lustig, for many years rumored to be short-listed for the Nobel Prize in Medicine. The Nobel never materialized, but as a consolation Lustig had been appointed the university's first, and so far only, Distinguished University Professor.

But that was State's sole encounter with academic glory and, as Elspeth expected, a pilot light flickered on in the president's gray eyes. "It hasn't happened once since you've been president," Elspeth said. "In fact, it's never happened, has it?"

Watching the play of greed and pride across the round, small-featured face made the dean suddenly queasy, as if she had consumed too many cups of coffee. But it also confirmed that her powers, even at reduced voltage, had not entirely deserted her.

"What are you trying to tell me, Ellie?"

"Give me my budget, and I promise you that when *U.S. News & World Report* publishes its rankings of American law schools next March, State will be among the Top Five." This would be the case but, in Elspeth's mind, only conservatively so. She had told no one, not even Associate Dean Jimmy Fleenor, but she was certain that she could catapult the Law School—*State!*—not only into the *U.S. News* Top Five, but into the Top Three, displacing Stanford or Harvard or—why not?—the perennial Number One, Yale itself. "But if I am to be able to do this, I need money. Real money. A twelve percent budget increase."

"How is money going to make a difference for *U.S. News?*"

This time, she aimed the narrow beam of her intentions squarely between the president's eyes and read his mind. "I promise you, no one is going to be bribed. But other than that, Rawleigh, you don't want to know."

Nor was there any need for him to know, for the light in his eyes that moments ago had been merely a speculative gleam had now transformed into a zealot's blaze. For the president of a former state agricultural college that possessed neither the athletic hegemony of the Big Ten nor the scholarly and research clout of a university system like California's, for a man long condescended to by his presidential counterparts in the American Association of State Colleges and Universities, the prospect that his institution, even if only a single school, would have its name in *U.S. News*'s sanctified and topmost tier possessed the same compelling allure that Olympic gold has to a farm boy vaulting a barnyard fence.

Elspeth knew that the moment she left his house, Rawleigh would be on the phone to the university controller, no matter that it was Sunday, ordering him to shift funds from other departments, most likely in the humanities, to the Law School. Even a soils scientist understood that in a single year the *U.S. News* rankings received more than a thousand times the attention of a century's worth of little poetry magazines, peckish history journals and experimental theatre combined.

"How are your applicant numbers, Ellie?"

When she was in practice, Elspeth loved doing battle with the law's fierce warriors, hawk-faced men with neck veins that bulged like tendons, their talons bared to shred her arguments to confetti, demanding that she respond with a thrashing ferocity of her own. Even on those few occasions that these adversaries beat her, the exhilaration was life-sustaining. To her chagrin, it was the mama's boys, flabby, pink and porcine like Rawleigh, whose blunt probes and easy lobs as often as not defeated her. "Our applicants' GPAs and LSATs are higher than they've ever been."

"No, I mean the number of applications. I saw on the news that law school applications are down all across the country."

The dean knew what he meant the first time. It was a child's rubber-tipped arrow, but it had found its target. She had no choice but to mislead. "Our application numbers are more robust than ever, Rawleigh."

"You know, that's been a problem at the Veterinary School. Applications are off by a third. Strictly between you and I, we've had to start thinking about shutting it down."

"I can assure you, Rawleigh—"

"What if I give you the money and you don't make it to the Top Five?"

"I'll resign my deanship."

Elspeth had been plotting her path to the deanship, and ultimately her escape from the university, even before she arrived at State 11 years ago. She had accepted or declined committee assignments, first in the Law School and later in the university's upper reaches, with an eye to those that would best display her capacity for leadership and for solving other people's problems, all the while keeping the 11-year-old boys who ran the place firmly under her control. For three years running, she chaired the Law School's personnel committee, keeping an eye out for recruits who would reshape the school's mission to better fit the objects that voters in the *U.S. News* poll regularly applauded and, no less important, who would support her in advancing that mission when she took over the school's helm.

Rawleigh didn't need to know that when the Law School made it into the *U.S. News* first tier, Elspeth's plan was to resign as dean in any event, and to take the next step on her life's path to be *"of the people, but above them too."* This had been Elspeth's personal striving since as a schoolgirl she read a biography of John Marshall, the greatest Chief Justice of the United States ever, a man who singlehandedly upended the American system of government by placing the federal judiciary on top, a man who, as described by his biographer, was *"of the people, but above them, too."* It was none of Rawleigh's business, or the business of anyone else at State, to know where the next rung on her career ladder would take her.

Rawleigh rose from the couch. "What about your visit from the ABA accreditation committee? Doesn't that start this week?"

"Tonight." The committee, if it kept to its schedule, had already arrived in College Station for its three-day visit to decide whether the Law School deserved re-accreditation, and its members awaited her now at the welcome reception at her associate dean's home, for which she was horrendously late. "Why should the visiting committee matter?"

"Because it would be a huge black eye if you don't get re-accredited. No one would care if we got into the Top Five."

Elspeth admired the asymmetry of presidential rhetoric. If the Law School makes it to the Top Five, it's *we*. But if the school doesn't get re-accredited, it's *you*. "You have no reason to worry on either count, Rawleigh."

"And you're sure you can do it? The Top Five?" Pride makes a potent cocktail. Awe dripped from the president's words like gravy.

"Absolutely."

"Then why don't we make it a round number," the president said. "Your budget increase. Don't you think fifteen percent has a nicer ring to it than twelve?"

"Only to someone who is a born leader," the dean said, rising. "I'll let myself out."

Elspeth's flame-red Mercedes raced through the back roads to Associate Dean Jimmy Fleenor's reception for the ABA visiting committee, and dusk descended in layers over College Station's hills and hollows, all laden with the melancholy of a late Sunday in autumn. Absorbed in her reflections on the meeting with the president, Elspeth almost missed the sign for the College Station exit. (The town's name was an artifact from the days when the university, five miles back, was still just an agricultural college and a railroad ran past it.) Estate-sized properties dotted the winding road off the parkway, mansions built a century ago by long-gone insurance and banking barons, and by the industrious captains of the carpet mills and shoe factories that once flourished on the banks of the area's many rivers. Today, merchants from the gray and rusting downtown occupied these properties, along with tradespeople, university types and local schoolteachers. And joining them this evening, if you believed the local lore, were dryads and nymphs, goblins and leprechauns sprung from their hiding places in the area's deep caves and dark hedgerows for Witches' Sabbath.

The landscape drummed the rhythms of an elegy for Elspeth. She had spent her entire life so far in New England—growing up in Maine and attending college there, and then law school in New Haven and practice in Boston before taking her first teaching job at State. On long nights, awake and alone, she would catalogue all that she would miss when the time came for her to make her move: the life-affirming textures and fragrances not only of autumn, but of all the seasons; the verdant trees, the neat town squares; the local residents, flintier and less welcoming to outsiders even than their popular reputation. It came as no surprise to her when, at a cocktail reception in New Haven before he retired, Supreme Court Justice David Souter confided his longing to return to New Hampshire. Even so, this daughter of Maine knew that she was made of sterner stuff, and that when the day came, she would leave without hesitation.

Elspeth shrugged off her self-congratulation for the budget victory over the president and concentrated on the ABA committee visit, an event that befalls each accredited law school in America once every seven years. Just the prospect of one of these visits has been known to plunge icicles the size of stalagmites into the bowels of the haughtiest law school dean. Few schools flunk the review outright, but just to be placed on probation by the ABA, as some schools have, means consignment to a purgatory from which it is impossible to recruit students, faculty or donors. After all, what college graduate in his right mind would invest $200,000 and the next three years of his life in a berth on a ship that is not only leaky, but sinking?

Elspeth herself had felt the tickle of that icicle, and not only because this was her first visit from an ABA committee since becoming dean. Three weeks ago, an acquaintance who now worked high in the ABA bureaucracy discreetly passed on to her the names of two of the three members of the committee that had been appointed to visit State, and the news could not have been worse. One, Warren Bioff, was the law librarian at a school 31 places below State in the *U.S. News* rankings. It wasn't the expected resentment of the underclass toward their *U.S. News* superiors—a resentment the dean understood all too well—that worried Elspeth, but rather her role in what must have been the deepest humiliation in Bioff's career as a law librarian, if not in his entire life. The presence on the committee of its second member, Herschel Fairweather, the Feckles Professor of Legal Philosophy at Columbia Law School, was even more vexing, if that were possible.

Within an hour of learning the identities of these two miscreant committee members, the dean delegated the task of researching Bioff's vulnerabilities to State's law librarian, Lee Brown, and retained a private investigation firm in Manhattan to vacuum up any dirt it could on Fairweather. That left her free to deal with the troublemaker at the American Bar Association who was making these disastrous assignments to her visiting committee, and to ensure that the final appointment, of the committee's chair, would be a lawyer of her own choosing, not the ABA's.

The ABA rogue, it turned out, was a Delaware securities lawyer whose second wife was suing him for divorce. From that discovery to persuading the securities lawyer to designate the dean's own choice as committee chair consumed no more than a handful of telephone calls around the country: to the man's divorce lawyer (a dead end); to the wife's divorce lawyer (ditto); to the chair of the man's law firm (who proudly emailed the dean a list of the securities lawyer's clients); and, finally, to the general counsel of several of these clients to which the lawyer was beholden. (*Bingo!*) One of these general counsel, of a large New York investment bank, confided to the dean that he would kill, if that was what it took, for his son, whose intellectual aspirations ranged no farther than the surface of his skateboard, to be admitted to State, even though the boy's college GPA and LSAT scores fell deciles short of the Law School's skyrocketing admission standards (one of the dean's proudest achievements). "There's no need for you to kill anyone," the dean told the general counsel. "All you have to do is drop a note to your securities lawyer, asking him to take my call. For my part, I would be honored to instruct my admissions officer to be on the lookout for your son's application and to see that it receives the careful attention that it deserves."

Two days later, Dan Gidron, a former federal prosecutor and rising star in the Chicago trial bar, was appointed chair of the ABA committee charged with reviewing State's accreditation. With Gidron's appointment, the dean's concerns about Bioff and Fairweather evaporated. Dan Gidron was a smart and forceful lawyer. Adept at extracting plea bargains from the most hardened felons, and at bringing judges and juries into alignment with his own view of the facts and law, Dan would have no trouble controlling a mere law librarian and law professor. But that was not the extent of Dan's accomplishments. A bear of a man, Dan had the stamina and moves of a world-class soccer player, moves that could cause carmine-painted fingernails to score an oaken headboard or rake a muscled back. The dean knew this because, for the last year and a half when their schedules meshed, Dan Gidron had been the dean's most ardent and virile lover.

Intercourse with men—any intercourse, in the bedroom or in the courtroom—was the pulsing engine that powered Elspeth's dominion over the 11-year-old boys in her life. Although the LSAT prep manual counseled a good night's rest before the day of the law school entrance exam, Elspeth spent the sleepless night fornicating with her college's second-string quarterback and received as close to a perfect LSAT score as any law school applicant that year. Later, at Yale, while her classmates crammed for first-year exams, Elspeth made her way systematically through the men's lacrosse team and as a result scored the second-highest grades in the class. (The fellow who ranked first refused to tell her his secret.) Other post-coital successes followed with stunning regularity: third-highest score on the state bar exam; a U.S. Supreme Court argument that resulted in a 9-0 decision for her client; the delivery and defense of a paper on real property law's Rule Against Perpetuities that won her an offer to join the Yale law faculty. So if she didn't get laid tonight, she might as well resign the deanship.

But the dean was going to get laid. And how! A last-minute houseguest almost wrecked her plans, but she had put the keys to her condominium under the mat and filled the refrigerator for him. For herself and Dan she had reserved a suite (king-size bed; in-room Jacuzzi) at the Shangri-La Resort and Spa in Beaver Falls, one town over from College Station. Less than a minute after hanging up, she called back to reserve a room on either side of the suite to forestall noise complaints from neighboring guests. Elspeth calculated: in an hour's time, she would have briskly greeted the colleagues gathered at Jimmy Fleenor's home; charmed two of the three members of the ABA's visiting committee; and escaped to the Shangri-La with its chairman. In two hours, the Boston Air Route Traffic Control Center was going to have to reroute all flights over Beaver Falls.

At the sight of her associate dean's rambling colonial home with its faded white clapboard and trim green shutters, Elspeth suffered for a moment the same small frisson of panic that she did before faculty meetings: that no one would be there; that her colleagues had seen the flimsy fabric of her authority for what it was; and, through that fabric, had seen Elspeth Flowers for what *she* was: a needy woman as crazy for some version of animal congress as a detoxing addict for his first hit, and in the same bottomless quantity. She was that desperate to overdose on Dan Gidron.

Elspeth turned off the engine of the Mercedes and switched on the vanity light to examine herself in the rearview mirror. She drew in her lower lip and bit down on it hard, then did the same with the upper lip. She dug around in her purse for a lipstick and, gazing into the mirror in a sort of ecstasy, applied gloss to the bruised, but now pouty lips. Next she removed the cap from a vial hardly larger than a matchstick and dabbed behind each ear the tiniest drop of the costly scent that, mixing barely detectible notes of musk, attar, and the locker room, never failed to enchant the little boys in her life.

TWO

Jimmy Fleenor sometimes thought that he loved his house even more than he did the Law School. He treasured the high ceilings (Jimmy was a gangly 6'4" and didn't like to be crowded); the white walls hung with colorful contemporary prints; the oak plank floors burnished gold by time; the Navajo throw rugs—one or two of them possibly genuine—that he and his wife Millicent had collected on trips through the Southwest. He delighted in how the blazing hearths, one in the living room, the other in the adjacent parlor, drew lively clusters of guests to their crackling illusion of warmth, and he loved how his colleagues fit as comfortably into the spacious rooms as the old and carefully selected furniture. Above all, for without it the rest would be meaningless, Jimmy loved the order that suffused every corner of the house. (The family motto, *Alles in Ordnung,* had accompanied his grandfather Theo Fleenor when he emigrated from Bavaria to America to open a branch of the family precision tool and die business, *Fleenor und Söhne.*) All that was missing was the dean. She was always late, but never this late.

Millicent was an indifferent, even negligent hostess who, left on her own, would let their guests forage through the cupboards for cheese spread and crackers, finding drinks where they might. Knowing this, the dean had called Jimmy to her office early in the week, and together they had organized the party's every beat, the dean specifying the smallest details, from the brand of frozen canapés to instructions on when to pop them into the oven (5:45 P.M.) and for how long (20 minutes at 350 degrees). She had also prescribed the wines, beers and spirits to be served (middle of the shelf; no Sam's Club vodka, but no Grey Goose, either) and in what quantities. "Hire a bartender you can trust, and make sure he pours generously for the committee members, Bioff and this philosopher from Columbia, Fairweather. I want you to have your camcorder ready. If they make fools of themselves and you have it on tape, they'll think twice before they put anything bad in their report."

"And the committee chairman—this fellow Gidron?"

"He doesn't drink."

Jimmy started to ask how she knew the chairman didn't drink, but the dean was already busy highlighting several faculty names in yellow marker. "I want the bartender to water their drinks and cut them off after three. We can't afford any of Heidi Hoehnemann-Mueller's whacked-out tirades. Or Poets or Quants throwing canapés at the Bog Dwellers."

All faculty who were not away on travel had come to the reception and, after picking up name tags at the door, had predictably divided the living room and parlor into the three camps. "Poets," "Quants" and "Bog Dwellers" were the catchwords the dean had affixed to the law faculty's three warring factions, like labels on jarred preserves. As a central tactic in her campaign to thrust the Law School into the *U.S. News* topmost tier, the dean had herself hired most of the Poets and Quants, and had labored hard—indeed, was still laboring—to fire every last one of the Bog Dwellers.

In jeans, t-shirts and sweaters, the Poets—the Law School professors who taught not law, but history, literature, legal philosophy, political science, sociology and (Heidi Hoehnemann-Mueller's field) anthropology—were in the corner of the living room closest to Jimmy, trading animated riffs on worthy thinkers, some of whose names Jimmy recognized (Weber, Heidegger, Wittgenstein, Habermas) and some (Horkheimer, Husserl and Fichte) that sounded to Jimmy like nothing so much as a succession of painful after-dinner throat-clearings. Occasionally, to celebratory oohing and aahing, a Frenchman—Foucault, Derrida—was allowed to penetrate to the front line of the Poets' assault on "legal elites."

As usual, the Poets were playing a version of what Jimmy called MeScrabble, a game that the Poets passed off as normal conversation, but was in fact a violent competition with a dense, if unwritten, rule book. In MeScrabble one Poet talks about himself while the others follow intently, waiting to grasp not the thread of the idea, but the single word or phrase—"I was coming out of the drugstore"—that will enable the quickest of the listeners to hijack the conversation—"I was in that same drugstore last week"—and to continue on with his own story until another in the group does the same to him. At this moment in Jimmy's living room, the Poet then speaking about Wittgenstein's "Sprachspeil" or "language game," paused for a fatal breath, allowing a rival leap to pounce with his own intersecting favorite, Habermas's "communicative rationality."

The Quants—the dean called them that for their pathological need to quantify and calibrate every imaginable human phenomenon—had gathered in the opposite corner, close by the fireplace. All were men and they taught, or in most cases co-taught, seminars of no more than three or four students investigating such topics as the possibility that Quant Prasad Subramaniam's latest unwritten paper, *Modelling Bayesian Inference, Ramsey Pricing and the Gladbach Conjecture to Reduce Court Congestion,* could decimate the ranks of trial lawyers and turn courthouses around the world into empty mausoleums.

Attired in chinos and business shirts cufflinked but open at the neck, the Quants in Jimmy's living room were right now estimating the financial worth, discounted to present value, of a happy marriage over an unhappy one. The dean had handpicked these men from among the survivors of the Wall Street wreck of 2008 who had not already been hired away by the business schools at Harvard, Stanford and Chicago. In College Station, the Quants deftly designed grandiose schemes for corporate governance and tax and prison reform using the same brain-scorching mathematical models that, only a decade ago, they wielded on behalf of banking clients in schemes that brought the world economy to its knees. Today they paid for their children's private schools and their second homes on the Cape with six-figure fees from the bankruptcy, securities fraud and Foreign Corrupt Practices Act trials in which they regularly testified as expert witnesses.

Jimmy had few quarrels with the dean, but he did anguish over her poor treatment of the Bog Dwellers. If they were . . . well, somewhat backward—the women in knee-length skirts and heels, the men in sport coats and ties—they were also a source of stability and order in the Law School, for they neither refashioned the law around the latest algorithm nor blew up the law's foundations with radical ideas from the Frankfurt School, but rather nibbled delicately at the edges of legal doctrine, much as they now pecked at the frozen canapés that Millicent had taken from the oven ten minutes too soon. The smallest group at the party by far, with the parlor fireplace all to themselves, the Bog Dwellers had mostly been hired by the dean's predecessor, Horace Rorabach, and taught old-fashioned courses like Contracts, Torts and Criminal Procedure. One of them, Kenny Nordstrom, the author most recently of *Is the Doctrine of Contract Consideration Dead? Can It Be Revived?*, failed last spring to get the votes he needed to win tenure at State and had since accepted a tenured offer from the University of Iowa, to which he would move in January. He had come to the party only as a personal favor to Jimmy.

Although Kenny was one of those eighty-sixed by the dean's yellow Magic Marker, he was making his sixth or seventh trip to the bar. Indeed, Jimmy noticed that the bartender, Wendell Ward—the Law School's mailroom clerk had volunteered his services for the evening—was serving other yellow-lined faculty more than their limit, too. (Wendell knew about the party because he not only sorted the faculty's mail, but opened and read it, too.) When, a year ago, Jimmy had interviewed Wendell for the mailroom job and asked him why he wanted the position, the youth said that his grandfather told him that all successful CEOs had started their careers in the mailroom. Jimmy, who had no children of his own and felt a father's protective instinct for the naïve young man, lacked the heart to tell Wendell that, however things worked out at William Morris or CAA, this was not the path to advancement in a university. From over a brimming goblet of merlot that he was pouring for Professor Hoehnemann-Mueller, Wendell gave Jimmy a wink and a small wave.

The dean had instructed Jimmy to personally keep track of the chancellor's drinks. "No more than three bourbons for Old Silver Zipper. Two, if he's growing timber." When Jimmy was a law student at State, the chancellor, a florid, imposing scholar of romance languages, had just been appointed president of the university, and even today, almost 30 years later, Jimmy could picture the cerulean robe and scarlet hood that graced the then-president's shoulders at commencement. He had retired years ago, taking on the mostly ceremonial post of chancellor, for which his only current duty was to lend his beaming, pink-faced countenance, along with his wife's, to events such as these when the president was not available. Jimmy didn't know what "growing timber" meant, any more than he did the other peculiar phrases that occasionally salted the dean's pronouncements. Whatever it meant, the chancellor appeared to be in robust health, his handshake hearty, when Jimmy greeted him at the door.

The chancellor had gone directly from the doorway to a position in front of the living room fireplace and not moved from there, relying on his wife, a pink powder puff of a figure, to shuttle drinks to him. Leaning to one side to listen to the diminutive woman, the chancellor's glass tipped in the opposite direction, splashing bourbon on the golden floorboards, forcing Jimmy to suppress the impulse to grab a napkin and mop up the puddle. The former president was as tall as Jimmy, but decades of bending to his wife had left him with a permanent stoop.

When the dean finished delivering her instructions to Jimmy last week, she had folded the list to a knife's edge and handed it to him. "I imagine Alex Coyle is going to hear about the party." She fixed Jimmy with a hard, knowing look that touched an anxious nerve. If he crashes the party, as he probably will, don't make a scene. Let him in, but don't let that snake go anywhere near my two little sylphs. I invited them to entertain the committee, not him."

The dean's "little sylphs" always arrived at her parties in pairs, and at least a dozen of them had come and gone since she first introduced them to the Law School's night life. They were young, slender and pretty, but not beautiful, except as youth has a beauty all its own. Nonetheless, a hint of some special provenance glowed like a halo above each golden head. Jimmy didn't know where Elspeth found these creatures, with their short black cocktail dresses cut just low enough to reveal the tops of creamy bosoms, or whether they were on the Law School payroll or paid as freelancers, but two or four or sometimes six inevitably appeared at each of the dean's quarterly fundraising receptions. Before the evening was done, each could be found attached like a succubus to the arm of one of the school's more generous donors. When Jimmy asked the dean about the propriety of these arrangements, she shot him an annoyed look and explained that if the Law School was going to ascend to the *U.S. News* Top Five, it was not going to be on the wings of angels, but on the backs of her little sylphs.

There were no donors to be entertained tonight, only accreditation committee members, and the two current girls were chatting with Wendell at his makeshift bar while he poured Cokes for them. Not for the first time, it occurred to Jimmy that the girls were terribly young indeed.

Alles in Ordnung. Jimmy had shepherded two previous ABA accreditation committees through the school, and even with the last-minute defection of this year's committee chairman, a Chicago trial lawyer, thanks to Jimmy's quick thinking, no visit had got off to a smoother start. To Jimmy's delight, Herschel Fairweather, the portly Feckles Professor of Legal Philosophy at Columbia, had instantly attached himself to the Poets and was now trading Tugendhats, Stumps and Schmidts with them in a lively spray of spittle. After a quick survey of the room that took in the conservatively dressed Bog Dwellers, the Columbia professor had shed his jacket and tie and handed them to the dean's slender blondes, whispering something into the little pink, well-shaped ear of each as he did.

Warren Bioff, the librarian member of the accreditation committee, was head to head in deep conversation with Lee Brown, the Law School's own librarian. The dean had warned Jimmy that Bioff was a hornet's nest of resentments, but Jimmy, who had studied books on body language and its clues to interpersonal strain, could discern no evidence in Bioff's posture or gestures of any ill feeling toward Brown or the Law School over his rejection for the position that Brown now occupied. Mother hen that she was, the dean had worried for no good reason.

Of the three committee members, it was Howard Littlefield, Jimmy's candidate as the last-minute replacement for the Chicago trial lawyer, whose presence gave the associate dean the thrilling sense that a larger governing order pervaded not only his home, but his universe. Who would have imagined that Jimmy, the first in his family to attend college, much less law school, would today be entertaining in his home not only the former president, and now chancellor, of a major university but also a lawyer who was chairman of the region's largest law firm, and the current president of the state bar association.

Littlefield appeared to be in deep conversation with the chancellor and his wife. As much as Jimmy admired the chancellor, he knew that the well from which he and his wife drew for thoughtful-sounding talk was in fact little more than a puddle, and that after five minutes, ten at most, their chat with Littlefield would turn to weedier paths—most probably, if precedent held, to the antics of the couple's twin parakeets. Jimmy knew that he had to rescue the chairman, but lifted by the pat on his back from past generations of Fleenors, he allowed himself one last private moment to savor the fullness of this gathering under his roof, the friendly din of learned conversation and easy collegial laughter.

There was little that Jimmy would not do for his school. But his own sacrifices on the Law School's behalf were nothing compared to those made by the dean, and for an institution that could not even claim of her an alumna's loyalty. In the 11 years that he had known her, she had not once taken a weekend off, much less a true vacation. Forgoing any genuine social intercourse that the always-watchful Jimmy could observe, she filled her days instead with endless meetings and fundraising trips in the Law School's service. From the itineraries she left for him as her second in command, Jimmy knew that in the last 12 months alone Elspeth had crisscrossed the country no fewer than 20 times, always economizing by changing planes at O'Hare to reduce her airfare, at times even subjecting herself to overnight layovers. Occasionally, and only in the tumult of sweet, late-night fantasies involving the two of them, did Jimmy speculate about the dean's sexuality. With mixed feelings, he finally accepted that Elspeth Flowers dwelled along with such other destiny-starred women as Mother Teresa, Eleanor Roosevelt and Golda Meir in that twilight universe where the air is too thin to transport the pulses of sexual desire.

When Gidron, the Chicago lawyer, called yesterday to tell Jimmy that the sudden disappearance, mid-trial, of his co-counsel would prevent him from travelling to College Station, Jimmy had picked up the baton as smoothly as an accomplished relay runner. Jimmy tried first to reach Elspeth (the mailbox on both her cell phone and her home telephone were full and there was no reply to his texts), but even as he dialed the numbers, he felt an unaccustomed stir of mastery in his soul. Aware that this was one of his life's small but decisive moments, a turning point, he next dialed Howard Littlefield's number.

Littlefield was a graduate of State, and although it was more than 20 years since he chaired the Law School's Board of Governors, Jimmy knew that he could count on the renowned admiralty lawyer to be more forgiving as the accreditation review progressed than would be a Chicago lawyer with no connection to the school. And there was no shortage of potholes around the Law School for a sympathetic eye to overlook. Littlefield also possessed the necessary gravitas to win the American Bar Association's approval as chair. In addition to his position as president of the state bar and chairman of his law firm, a post he had occupied for many years, Littlefield had twice chaired the ABA's Admiralty Law section.

So, when Jimmy called the Delaware securities lawyer in charge of appointing the accreditation committee, the speed with which the man approved the proposed substitution did not surprise him.

Jimmy started toward Littlefield and the chancellor, but a small hand grabbed his arm. "I have information for you." The voice was scratchy and high-pitched, almost a squeak.

"You're supposed to be watching the bar, Wendell."

Wendell's grip tightened. "This is important."

Jimmy looked across to the fireplace. The chancellor's wife had bunched her sharp-nailed fingers into little bird beaks and, emitting short shrieks, was thrusting them at Littlefield's eyes. The chancellor was one of those people who laughs with his whole body, and more of his drink spilled onto the floor. Littlefield looked genuinely frightened.

"Tomorrow, Wendell."

"This is *about* tomorrow."

If Wendell ever broke out of the mailroom to seek his fortune elsewhere, that voice was going to limit his career options to a racetrack announcer or lead singer in a rock band. Was it alcohol that Jimmy smelled on the boy's breath, or something sweeter? "Then, first thing in the morning," Jimmy said, and walked off.

Littlefield had escaped the darting parakeets and joined the small group of Quants that had gathered around Benjamin Hubbell by the fireplace. Hubbell was the Law School's most recent hire and, by the dean's account, her most brilliant ever. At the meeting convened to vote on his appointment, the dean told the faculty that Hubbell was going to be the intellectual bridge between the Poets and the Quants and was worth every dollar and reduction in teaching load it would require to win him in a bidding war with New York University, which had already extended an offer. The significant look with which she swept the meeting room was to remind the faculty that NYU was a persevering sixth in the *U.S. News* rankings, so that, tactically for State, hiring Hubbell was both a defensive and an offensive move. The vote was unanimous.

Hubbell tugged on the bill of his baseball cap as he lectured the Quants on how he structured his path-breaking course, Decision

Theory (and the Rule of Law), around the famous, and famously difficult, Impossibility Theorem, also known as "Arrow's Paradox" after the Harvard economist who devised it. Jimmy viewed it as part of his job as associate dean to cultivate and support the faculty's intellectual interests, and he made an effort to read the books and articles that they read. He had read Arrow's paper and found the theorem not nearly as complex as Hubbell made it out to be.

"To simplify it for the class," Hubbell said, implying that he was simplifying it for the Quants, too, "I pick three students—let's say their names are Alan, Betty and Carl—and I tell them that they can order a pizza, but they can have only one pizza between them."

"'Just one' is a pretty vague concept," a Quant said, looking at the others. "What are the metrics? The radius? Its depth? How much pizza are we talking about here?"

Hubbell ignored him. "So the three of them have to indicate their preferences. Alan tells the other two that his first choice is a pepperoni pizza, his second is sausage and his third is anchovy. Betty's first choice is anchovy, her second is pepperoni and her third is sausage. And Carl's first choice is sausage, his second is anchovy and his third is pepperoni."

"Empirically," a Quant said, "that seems highly unlikely. Out of three people, one of them's going to want mushrooms."

"Or peppers," said another. "Or not want pizza at all."

"I thought everyone loved pepperoni," someone's wife said.

Hubbell's response was a condescending glance. "So, let's follow Alan, Betty and Carl's votes. If they're choosing between pepperoni and sausage, Alan will vote for pepperoni because it's his first choice, and so will Betty, because sausage is her third choice. Only Carl, whose first choice is sausage, will vote for sausage."

The chancellor winked at Jimmy. The parakeets had stopped to listen, too. Was the simplicity of the Arrow Theorem as evident to the chancellor and his wife as it was to him?

Littlefield finger-smoothed his mustache and said, "This is what you teach law students? How to order pizza?"

If Hubbell heard the committee chairman, he gave no indication. "Now, let's say the next vote is between sausage and anchovy. Alan is going to vote for sausage because anchovy is his third choice, and of course Carl is going to vote for sausage because it's his first choice. Only Betty is going to vote for anchovy, her first choice, and that means sausage is going to win. So at this point the group prefers pepperoni over sausage and sausage over anchovy."

The chancellor's rosy cheeks moved up and down in happy agreement. "That means they also prefer pepperoni over anchovy, so when they go to the pizza place, that's what they'll order. *Una pizza de pepperoni, per favore!*"

"I expected someone would say that." Hubbell looked disappointed that it was not a Quant who had arrived at the wrong solution. "But of course that's not what's going to happen. They still have to vote between pepperoni and anchovy, and when they do . . . anchovy's going to win."

"*Eewww*, anchovy," said a wife.

Hubbell touched the bill of his cap and preened. "Alan's going to vote for pepperoni, his first choice, but Carl's going to vote for anchovy because he prefers it to pepperoni, which is his third choice, and of course Betty's going to vote for anchovy, her first choice."

"But," the unhappy chancellor wanted to know, "what are they going to order? They went to a restaurant. They're hungry. They have to order something!"

"That's the whole point of the exercise," Hubbell said, his eyes on the Quants, and not the chancellor. That's why Arrow called it a paradox."

Littlefield looked baffled, too, but whether it was by Arrow's Paradox or by the deeper paradox of why a law professor would waste a law student's time with this, even his body language gave Jimmy no clue.

The Quants were on Hubbell like mosquitoes. "What about the strength of individual preferences? How do you account for the fact that Betty may feel more strongly about anchovies than Carl feels about sausage?"

"Do you have longitudinal data? Have you run regressions? What's the chi-square?"

"The problem is your experiment isn't scalable."

The chancellor's wife tugged at his sleeve. "They should have gone someplace where they could buy pizza by the slice. That way they could all have their first choice. A nice restaurant with red-and-white checked tablecloths. Real linen, not plastic. That lovely wine that comes in straw-covered bottles."

Littlefield was shaking his head, and Jimmy, viewing his beloved colleagues for the first time through a visitor's eyes, realized how much the faculty had changed since the last ABA visit, and even more since he had been a student at the Law School.

As an undergraduate at State, majoring in mechanical engineering, Jimmy had no plans more ambitious than to join the men of his family at Fleenor & Sons, as the company had been renamed. No plans, in any event, until that day he found himself in the part of the university library commonly used by law students trolling for coeds and noticed a white paperback titled in austere blue letters, *The Bluebook*. Looking around, Jimmy picked up the book. Why would a white book be titled *The Bluebook*? But that enigma was only what drew Jimmy's initial interest. What stole his attention—and had tenaciously gripped it for the past quarter-century—was the book's subtitle: *A Uniform System of Citation*.

Like most undergraduates, Jimmy had arrived at college seeking answers to life's grander questions, questions that at home at the dinner table received only blank looks. What a glorious discovery, then, that where Thomas Aquinas's *Quinque Viae,* assigned in his freshman Humanities class, failed in its promised proof of the existence of a transcendent and unifying higher power, *The Bluebook* conveyed a surpassing vision of universal harmony, a *Uniform System of Citation* employed daily not only by every law student and law professor in America, but by every practicing lawyer as well, ensuring that each one of them cited, in precisely the same manner, every conceivable form of legal authority, be it municipal, state, or federal; case, statute, rule or regulation; a bill or a hearing; books, articles, even ephemera; a *Uniform System of Citation* that governed every one of these legal sources not only from the United States, but from any country, tribe or territory in the world, from *Burgerliches Gesetzbuch* [BGB] [Civil Code] art.13 (Ger.) to Chen Hongyi's *Fazhi Qimeng yu Xiandai Fa de Jingshen* (1998).

Even as an undergraduate, with no understanding of how to read a case or a statute, Jimmy studied the pages of his copy of *The Bluebook* as he might a volume of Greek poetry, comprehending none of the words, but finding deliverance in their typographical patterns. Forsaking mechanical engineering for law required not even a single complete thought, and when in his first year at State's Law School the words on the textbook page suddenly snapped into meaning, Jimmy first understood what it felt like to fall in love. Not once since Jimmy started teaching at State (by which time the color of the *Uniform System of Citation*'s cover had mysteriously reverted to blue) did the courses assigned to him to teach not include *The Bluebook* and *The Bluebook: Advanced Topics.* When he had to reduce his teaching load to make time for his duties as associate dean, Jimmy hadn't hesitated to instruct the registrar to drop his other two offerings, Constitutional Law I and Constitutional Law II (which the dean promptly renamed Constitutional Ideas and More Constitutional Ideas).

A wave of cold air blasted in from the foyer, and an abbreviated ponytail bobbed into the living room. Jimmy's blood froze. As the dean warned, Alex Coyle had in fact crashed the party. Slender and snake-hipped, Coyle was a notorious despoiler of faculty wives, and Jimmy had heard . . . well, rumors, no more than that. Still, it gave him a moment's relief to see that Coyle was not moving in the direction of the kitchen, where Millicent was now taking another tray of canapés prematurely from the oven. Nor, circulating among the faculty groups, did Coyle appear to have any interest in the dean's little blondes.

Littlefield turned to Jimmy from Hubbell and the Quants. What, Littlefield wanted to know, were the Quants doing on the

Law School faculty? "I'd think they'd be teaching at a business school or an economics department."

"They're not clever enough for business school."

"And an economics department?"

"Not shameless enough."

Littlefield was too experienced a lawyer to betray his disappointment or appear to prejudge the law faculty's qualifications. Still, his question left Jimmy no doubt about the visiting committee chairman's idea of the kinds of courses the Law School should offer.

"I'd be interested in knowing what kinds of—er—more traditional courses you have for your students. Admiralty, for example. Do you have a course in Admiralty?"

Jimmy's mind raced through the school's course catalogue for a class that came within hailing distance of Admiralty, the law of the seas. "There are Professor Morrill's courses on global warming. I believe he devotes a good deal of time to the melting of the polar icecap. Rising sea level. Things like that."

Even as he chattered on, Jimmy realized his mistake, for Littlefield might now ask to meet the instructor. There had been rumored sightings of Bob Morrill in and around College Station over the years, but Jimmy had only once met his phantom colleague in the flesh. To be sure, the Law School catalogue annually listed courses in Global Warming I and II, and a seminar in World Environmental Issues, all under Morrill's name, and the well-enrolled classes met regularly. But at the front of the room leading the classes was a never-ending parade of guest speakers— climatologists, government economists, oceanographers, marine biologists, anthropologists, even, one time, an Eskimo—their appearances orchestrated by maestro Morrill from afar in one foreign city or another. When Jimmy emailed Morrill to suggest that he might want to appear at the lectern just once each semester for the sake of form, the professor's email reply, three weeks later, observed that during his 38 years at State, no member of the law faculty had ever received stronger course evaluations from his students than he had. Why would the associate dean want him to return to College Station and ruin his track record?

Littlefield's expression turned almost benign. "Do you mean Lucy Morrill? She spoke to one of my wife's charity groups. My wife made me promise to say hello."

Before Jimmy could answer that, no, the global-warming expert was Lucy's former husband, the *other* Professor Morrill, Alex Coyle approached, attracted, Jimmy suspected, by Littlefield's mention of a colleague's wife. Alex's wiry ponytail was an arrogant, obscene affront and, braided or unbraided, it was the object of Jimmy's wide-awake nightmares: the image of that hank of hair bobbing above Millicent's supine form.

"I'm afraid Lucy's not here," Jimmy said to Littlefield, relieved that his voice stayed steady despite Alex's proximity. "She's with a group of our third-years in Sudan running an advocacy program."

Alex said, "She's leading a campaign against clitoral stimulation—"

"Mutilation," Jimmy said. "Clitoral mutilation." Jimmy looked past Alex's shoulder to his favorite artwork, a particularly colorful Milton Avery oil painting on the far wall. "Even with the few resources at Lucy's disposal, she's made the program a great success."

Littlefield glanced at Alex's homemade name tag. "And what do you teach, Professor Coyle?"

Jimmy's gut clenched. Busy as she was, had Elspeth remembered to extract from Alex a promise not to disclose his duties at the Law School to the members of the accreditation committee? Even if she had remembered, would Alex keep his word?

"Actually, like a lot of the people here, you couldn't call what I do teaching." Alex's prominent front teeth glistened through his smile. "But unlike them, I'm not a professor."

"What do you do, then?"

Alex held the smile and looked at Jimmy for a taunting five seconds before returning to Littlefield. "I'm the Law School's Director of Special Projects. The dean calls me her secret weapon.

I try to be of service where I can. Of course, not on the scale of saving women in Sudan or plugging my finger in the polar dike."

Jimmy half-listened to Littlefield and Coyle, monitoring the conversation only as necessary to keep the Director of Special Projects from straying onto forbidden ground. It was the dean who was at the center of his thoughts. What could be keeping her? His eyes hadn't strayed from the front door for more than a minute, but he surveyed the living room and parlor to see if she had slipped in without his seeing. The crowd had thinned, but somehow the din was louder than before. Nordstrom, the luckless Bog Dweller, had long ago staggered out, arm thrown around his wife's shoulder, and there was no sign of Fairweather or of the dean's two girls. Whatever shared interests earlier joined Bioff and Brown had been exhausted and, lacking any common ground with the others in the room—law librarians are such odd ducks!—the two remained side by side with the glum look of a long-married couple bored with each other but terrified of everyone else.

Wendell was gone, too, and at the unattended bar the remaining guests were pouring their own drinks, all, Jimmy noted with alarm, from his personal supply. The 12-year-old Bushmills. The Stolichnaya vodka. Good God, one of the Quants was dropping ice cubes into a tumbler of Jimmy's 20-year-old single malt! The fragrance of marijuana smoke mingled with the clouds of alcohol. The stooped chancellor was no longer just tilting forward, but listing sideways, and deep red roses had blossomed atop the pink cheeks. What was that curious phrase the dean had used— growing timber? "Things fall apart," Jimmy remembered from his long-ago, required undergraduate course in modern poetry. "The center cannot hold." Why had Yeats, that horrible Irishman, written that it was *mere* anarchy that was loosed upon the world? Never had Jimmy felt the dean's absence more deeply.

Coyle had drifted off, so that Littlefield needed attention again. Jimmy looked about for Judith Waxman, Elspeth's classmate at Yale and her closest friend on the faculty. If anyone knew where the dean was, it would be Waxman. She was in the parlor, talking to Max Leverkase, another Poet, her hand splayed across Jimmy's treasured Milton Avery oil of two horseback riders traversing a yellow beach separated by a diagonal scrim of surf from a white-capped ocean and an impossibly blue sky. Waxman's hand, with its sheen of *hors d'oeuvre* grease, lay flat over the image of the two riders. Someone had once tried to explain to Jimmy how the hammer and sickle tattooed high on Waxman's left arm and the bulldog tattooed in the same location on her right arm were connected to her specialty, Intellectual Property Law, but the explanation was confused and Jimmy hadn't made the effort to sort it out. Jimmy led Littlefield into the parlor and introduced him to Waxman and Leverkase. With his head, he gestured for the Intellectual Property professor to follow him away.

At the least, Jimmy could count on Leverkase to entertain Littlefield. Leverkase still ate free—though increasingly fewer—dinners on the celebrity of his now 15-year-old master work, *Carry a Big Stick: Penis Size in American Foreign Policy, 1823–1929*. The book, which had been short-listed for both the Bancroft Prize and the Pulitzer Prize, took as its central thesis that an inverse correlation exists between the aggressiveness, indeed bellicosity, of an American president's foreign policy and the size of the president's penis. Our fifth president, the sword-rattling author of the Monroe Doctrine, Leverkase would tell you (indeed, he would soon be telling Littlefield) was a pencil-dick. Woodrow Wilson, on the other hand, was hung like a camel. And Calvin Coolidge . . . well!

Although Leverkase was a Poet—the Quants rejected his every desperate effort to join their crowd—he had proved his bold thesis through the use of extensive mathematical manipulations, extrapolations and regression analyses of data drawn from the reports and diaries of presidential physicians, mistresses and masseuses. Also, as he would explain to a dinner partner, penis size is genetically determined on the mother's side, so that if direct evidence was unavailable, data on maternal grandfathers and great uncles worked almost as well.

Jimmy steered Waxman to a corner, noticing over his shoulder that she had left a greasy handprint on the Avery oil. "I'm worried about Ellie," he said. "I think maybe she's been in an accident."

"Where'd you find that little fellow with the mustache? Your committee chair? Elspeth's going to be very disappointed, you know."

Jimmy looked into the kitchen, where Millicent was now head to head with Alex, closer even than Bioff to Brown. They appeared to be tracing each other's words with their lips.

Waxman persisted. "What happened to the trial lawyer from Chicago? Gidron."

"There was an emergency. He had to cancel."

"Well, you're going to have your own emergency when Elspeth finds out he's not here. She was counting on him."

So the dean knew him. That explained her knowledge that Gidron was a teetotaler. "I didn't realize they were acquainted."

"Acquainted?" Waxman's laugh was harsh. "Elspeth's only been banging him for the last year and a half. Do you think all those trips to Chicago were because she's a Cubs fan? Of course she knows him."

Jimmy's heart raced, then dropped. His album of dreams dissolved, as if in acid. He wanted to cry. His mind's eye filled with the image of his home disintegrating in one of those cartoon implosions: first, the structure corseting inward, clapboard cleaving, shutters dropping, and then, after a moment's equipoise, a giant *whoosh* and an ungirdling outward, as everything—roof, beams, walls—collapsed around him in a hurricane rush of air.

A chill gust swept through the room to where Jimmy stood. It could only mean that someone had just now opened the front door.

THREE

Nothing so exasperated the dean as failed expectations. And when the expectations were for empowering crescendoes of serial orgasm, the result was a cauterizing despair. How could Dan have abandoned her when she so needed him? His dereliction blazed through her consciousness like a blowtorch, for the briefest instant purging the accumulated sludge that for these past two weeks had made it impossible for her to form a single coherent thought. Dan's desertion had not only sapped what little remained of her powers; bestowing a bleak clarity of mind, it also doubled Elspeth's torment. She exerted what strength remained to stand firm when Jimmy delivered the news.

"Why didn't he call me?" They were in the living room, but away from the crowd where they could talk.

"He said he tried, but your mailbox was full. There was an Out of Office message on your email."

Scraps of crud still fluttered about like rags on a clothesline, making it hard for Elspeth to concentrate. "I never heard of a judge refusing to suspend a trial where counsel disappeared."

"He was your *friend's* co-counsel. He was going to cover for your *friend* for the three days he was here."

The edge of complaint in Jimmy's tone was unexpected. Elspeth had never told Jimmy about her relationship with Dan, but why would it matter to him? Her concern about Jimmy disappeared behind a sad thought: that her couplings with her Chicago trial lawyer weren't one-tenth as important to Dan as they were to her. For Dan they were an hour's pleasure, or two or three, while for Elspeth they were that, but they were her future, too. She said to Jimmy, "He only had to get the trial delayed for three days."

"I don't think the judge was in the mood to do him any favors." The dean waited.

"Your friend's co-counsel ran off with the bailiff."

Why couldn't Dan do that? Just sweep her away. Elspeth knew the answer all too well: because, even if he tried, she wouldn't let him; because, as much as she needed men to sustain her powers, it was *men* Elspeth needed, not Dan Gidron in particular.

An odd vacuuming sensation sucked through the dean's inner ear, followed by an even more dazzling clarity and focus. She said, "I was counting on Dan to keep Fairweather and Bioff in line."

"Why would they need to be kept in line?"

"You're the associate dean, Jimmy. Try to think strategically for a change. Fairweather's from Columbia. What does that mean for us? If—when—we move into the *U.S. News* inner circle, what institution are we most likely to evict?"

"You don't really think Columbia would—"

A cutting look from the dean stopped him. The dean didn't know Fairweather. Nor, it appeared, did anyone else beyond Columbia's Morningside Heights campus, and the people at Columbia weren't talking. That's what was so disturbing. Law professors are a talkative, self-promoting breed, and for a chaired professor—the Feckles Professor—not to have trumpeted word of his accomplishments outside of Columbia's few square blocks had to mean that Fairweather was an inside operative, the Columbia Law School dean's secret weapon. Columbia ranked fourth in *U.S. News*, and State's rise to the top tier would have a high probability of shoving Columbia off its already unsteady perch. Fairweather's covert mission as a member of the ABA visiting committee was, Elspeth feared, to discredit State, this bumptious usurper.

"And Bioff?"

The dean realized that Jimmy didn't know the details of her encounter with Bioff three years ago, when she was recruiting a new law librarian. A young reference specialist, Bioff had been third in his class at Northwestern Law School and first in the famed Masters in Library Science program at the University of Washington. In the intimate world of law librarians, Bioff's reference skills were fabled and, momentarily stunned by the librarian's brilliance and immense energy, the dean suspended her usual criteria for hiring subordinates—How craven is the candidate? How many diversity hiring credits will the candidate win for me from the university's Human Resources Office?—and gave Bioff every cause to believe that the job was his, for the simple reason that, in those unguarded minutes, she believed so herself. They talked about the best places to dine in College Station, the possibilities for entertainment in the nearby capital, and a reasonable budget for redecorating in *deco moderne* the librarian's office on the library's top floor.

Two days later, the dean met the last candidate on her list, Lee Brown, a law librarian more sheeplike than any of the ones she had met so far, who was also willing to accept 20 percent less than the posted salary and no redecoration of the librarian's office. Also, Brown's gender was indeterminate. Though disconcerting, the dean thought this might count for something with the diversity people in H.R. She offered Brown the job on the spot and entirely forgot about Bioff until two weeks later, when the *wunderkind* arrived in her office anteroom to introduce his widowed mother who lived nearby in Beaver Falls. "Mother's the main reason I'm taking the job," Bioff told the dean. "I've always wanted to come back here and live with her."

Would the dean have acted differently if Bioff had told her this at their first meeting? Probably not. With a few carefully tended exceptions, the dean had no sensitivity to the needs or wants of others. But Elspeth would never forget the widow Bioff's stricken look when she delivered the news to the old lady and her son that someone else had filled the librarian's position.

Before answering Jimmy's innocent question about Bioff, the dean drew herself up erect. "He's peculiar, even for a law librarian," she said. "I don't know why, but he has a resentment against us." She lifted her chest, aware of its effect on her associate dean who, she knew, fantasized about her night and day. "Dan Gidron's good with men." Dan's good with everyone, she thought. Everyone but me. "Dan could have jollied Bioff along, made sure he understood our aspirations. Kept him on the right page." She looked around the room just for something to do; no man at this party could possibly substitute for Dan. And, even if one could, Elspeth had set a rule for herself 11 years ago when she joined the law faculty: Don't sleep where you eat.

Jimmy said, "I'm sure the replacement I arranged for your friend will have no trouble keeping Bioff in his place. Fairweather, too. His name is Howard Littlefield. He's an alum, a member of the State family."

The dean followed Jimmy's look to a short figure in a shapeless suit tailored not only to hide the fact that there was a body underneath, but also to discourage any interest in finding one. The suit was gray, as was the new chairman's thinning hair and toothbrush mustache. The man was gray. He was *little*. He was listening to Max Leverkase.

Jimmy said, "He's chairman of the Barnes, Major firm in the capital."

"I suppose I should introduce myself and make sure he understands how much *alma mater* loves him and is depending on him."

"You should also say hello to the chancellor."

Old Silver Zipper. Her fellow voluptuary. A man whose adventures with female staff in the campus shrubbery while he was president were legend. Old Silver's stoop appeared to be stable, but even in the short time since the dean arrived, his rightward tilt had grown more pronounced. "How much has he had to drink?"

"I honestly don't know, Ellie."

"Is he growing timber?"

Jimmy gave her a hopeless look. "I'm sure he's fine."

"Well, I'm not sure, but let's start with your Mr. Littlefield."

This was one of the many challenges at which the dean excelled, putting on a glittering institutional front in the face of complete personal disaster. Stepping back to look into the foyer mirror, she was pleased with what she saw. Jet black hair to a quarter-way down her back—yes, she had it touched up, but so what?—a still high bosom and slender hips. You didn't have to read *Archie,* Elspeth's favorite comic book as a girl, to know that men—all men—fantasize about women who look like Veronica but put out like Betty. She looked down at her feet. How many law school deans wore peep-toe pumps revealing cherry-red nail polish? Only one that she knew of, and he was a cross-dresser from Butte.

Elspeth didn't know a single woman, no matter how comely, who didn't believe that one part of her appearance was a hideous failure: fly-away hair; a crepey neck; plump fingers; thick ankles. Even her friend Bianca Barrimore, the most perfectly beautiful woman she knew, complained that her hips were too wide. But Elspeth possessed not a single feature that she disliked. She lifted her bosom another notch, and started into the living room.

She had taken no more than a step when she felt a small commotion inside her still clear head, and was aware of tiny voices stirring awake. As she walked, she imagined them as small figures, precious little goblins following her crablike, on all fours, as if to avoid low-hanging branches. Jimmy followed, too, whispering Littlefield's crucial biographical facts. "State Law grad, '66. Chair of Board of Governors. Still pays alumni association dues, but no longer active. President of the State Bar. Chair of the ABA Section on Admiralty." The dean only half-listened, for the tiny voices of her rag-tag army of sprites fought for her attention. The sludge tide of the last two weeks had sealed them off in their damp, dark cellars, but now they had come up into the light. Like silk against silk, the voices cheered Elspeth on. Screw Dan Gidron, they cried. You go, Elspeth, eyes on the prize!

From the opposite corner of the room, Judith Waxman was also advancing on Littlefield. Judith had removed her chambray work shirt, and the khaki wife-beater revealed the tattoos on both arms. The rumor around the Law School was that the hammer and sickle were to symbolize the intellectual property professor's philosophy that all property, including intellectual property, is theft, and that the bulldog high on the other toned bicep was to emblemize her tenacity in suing anyone so foolhardy as to copy even a single page from her online newsletter, *I.P. Weekly*. In fact, the dean, who had befriended Judith during their first year at Yale, knew that the hammer and sickle was to celebrate the tenth anniversary of the collapse of the Berlin Wall, and the bulldog, which appeared the following year, was none other than the Yale mascot.

The dean told herself that surely someone as unfortunate as she was in choosing male companions was entitled to better luck with female confidantes. She dispatched Jimmy to head off their colleague.

"Mr. Littlefield!" The dean extended her hand and inserted herself between the lawyer and Leverkase. Sparks of static electricity flashed when her hand touched the lawyer's. The dean reminded herself that she loathed the unimpressive little man not for who he was, but for who he wasn't: Dan Gidron. "I'm so delighted that we were able to convince you to step in on such short notice!"

"Well, yes . . . I'm . . . I'm glad that there was space in my schedule for me to do this."

Littlefield hadn't drawn back physically, but the stutter and the faintest shadow of dismay that fell over his face told the dean that he did not like to be overwhelmed. She instructed the sprites to keep their voices down. "I'm pleased that you've had the opportunity to meet my colleagues." Without turning from Littlefield, she said out of the side of her mouth to Leverkase, "Make sure to see me before you leave, Max. There's something we need to discuss." To Littlefield she said, "When I asked Jimmy to invite you to chair the accreditation committee, I wasn't sure that you would accept. You've been such a stranger to your *alma mater*. But I can see how a man as busy as you wouldn't have the time to get involved with our alumni association."

"As a matter of fact, I was once very involved with the alumni association. I served two terms as president."

"But now, running a major law firm, serving as president of the State Bar, I suppose you just don't have room in your schedule."

"No," Littlefield said, "I have plenty of time. Two associates and another partner at the firm cover most of my practice for me. The firm and the State Bar pretty much run themselves. The only reason I haven't been involved in the Law School is that I don't know that I have anything to contribute to it. My old profs are gone. Horace Rorabach, too. He was a fine dean. Also a good friend."

Elspeth wondered if Rorabach had told Littlefield about their terminal encounter. Six years ago, when Elspeth's former professors in New Haven offered her a permanent position at Yale, she surprised the starchy group by turning them down in order to return to State, but only after first having a conversation with Rorabach, a courtly but not very bright contracts scholar, who had counted on spending the remaining years of his career in the dean's post.

When she came into Rorabach's office that day, his arms were already open in welcome. "It's wonderful to see you, Ellie. What is it going to take to keep you from going to New Haven permanently?"

"Your office," Elspeth said, her eyes on the portrait of the United States Supreme Court Justice for whom Rorabach had clerked.

"You want to move into my office and me to move into yours?"

"Not the office, Horace. I don't care where you move. It's your job I want."

"You mean you want to be dean?" Rorabach's hands gripped his desk, as if to keep it from the movers.

"Starting next academic year. Six months from now."

"But—"

"When was the last time the U.S. News Number One law school tried to recruit a faculty member away from State?"

"Well, I'm not sure—"

"Me. Yale's trying to recruit me."

"Ah, well—"

"Getting me to stay here instead of going to Yale will be a triumph for you, Horace. You're going to go out acclaimed as a hero."

"But—"

"But if word gets out that you let Yale steal me away just so you could hold onto your job, you're going to lose the deanship anyway. You wouldn't last a month. The faculty won't have you. Rawleigh, either."

Rorabach submitted his resignation to the president that same day.

Littlefield looked around the Fleenor living room. "I'm afraid I don't understand what these new professors of yours are doing. Your annual report is very colorful, but the articles about your faculty's research could just as well be in Sanskrit."

Alumni received the Law School's annual report but—Littlefield wouldn't know this—they were not its target audience. Three years ago the Law School started mailing thousands of copies of the glossy four-color publication to lawyers, judges and law teachers across the country, none of whom had any connection to State, but all of whom belonged to the demographic of the law graduates whose votes determined the rankings for *U.S. News*. Lawyers, judges and law professors who believed that research of the sort described in the annual report represented the very apogee of contemporary legal scholarship.

It was for this audience, and not Howard Littlefield and his fellow alums, that the current issue contained a feature on Benjamin Hubbell describing the recent hire's work at the intersection of small-group sociology, game theory and mathematical economics; capsule summaries of faculty conferences and colloquia on even headier topics; and a six-page spread filled with architect's renderings of the new Law School building, including detailed schematics and drawings of the state-of-the-art audiovisual system, the wireless layout for laptops and the building's centerpiece, a yoga, meditation and workout facility for the faculty. The dean had examined the first copy of the current number of the alumni magazine two weeks ago, and approved the issue for mailing so that it would reach its recipients in time for the new building's groundbreaking, five days away, and—even more important— just as the annual *U.S. News* polling began.

The dean said, "I'm sure some of our faculty's interests look different from when you were a student here. But you know, Howard—may I call you Howard?—when you're working at the cutting edge, as we are, it's important to stay ahead of the blade." She looked over to where Jimmy was talking to Judith, caught his eye, and with thumb and forefinger signaled for him to bring her a glass of wine. "But now that you've had the opportunity to talk with some of my colleagues, why don't you tell me what you think."

"I'm even more baffled than when I tried to make sense of your alumni magazine." Littlefield had raised his voice to be heard over the din, but there was no rancor in it. There was no humor or understanding in it, either. The statement was a flat recitation of fact. "I made a point of getting here on time"—now the dean heard a mild reprimand—"in order to talk with as many members of your faculty as I could, but so far I haven't found one who seems to have the slightest interest in preparing your students for the practice of law."

The dean debated introducing Littlefield to the Bog Dwellers. Their work would unquestionably reassure him, but their grievances and dwindling number would not. "You mean Professor Leverkase."

"Yes, him, but the others, too. Why would a practicing lawyer need to know about something called queer theory? Or econometrics? Or what is it that fellow called it—structuralism? Social biology? Post-Marxist thought? The Bible and contemporary culture? Pizza toppings?"

Hubbell. The dean looked around the room and found her young genius, gesturing briskly with both hands as he explained yet another potent theorem to Heidi Hoehnemann-Mueller and Mr. Mueller. Elspeth hadn't noticed Hubbell's physical vigor before, and Heidi, who taught Alternative Dispute Resolution and was the country's leading expert on Nordic blood feuds, seemed entranced.

"As I said, Howard, this is the law's cutting edge." She touched the back of his hand with a finger, producing another spark. "These are the tools that lawyers in the twenty-first century need to equip themselves." Like a presidential candidate's stump speech, the words were mindless boilerplate, and the chattering sprites in her head reminded her that the man to whom she was making this claim himself ran a large twenty-first-century law firm and might actually know something about what tools his partners and associates needed to compete in the legal market-place. "The real test of our relevance," the dean said, "is how well our graduates do when they get into practice. Surely State grads have excelled at your firm."

Littlefield cocked his head, as if judging her. "I talked to the head of our recruitment committee before I came here. He told me we used to take ten or fifteen of your 2Ls into our summer program and make permanent offers to half of them. Pretty much our aver-age with other schools. But for the last five years, we've not hired more than one or two. All of them had excellent *Bluebook* skills, the best of any of our summer clerks, but there's only so far that cite-checking can take a lawyer. He needs to know how to read a case and extract its holding, parse a statute, separate the few rel-evant facts from all of the irrelevant ones. It also helps if he knows some law. That's why we didn't interview here in September. We're doing most of our hiring from NYU, Fordham, even Quinnipiac and Suffolk. Their boys and girls are well-trained, and I can tell you that in this job market they're hungry for work."

Jimmy slipped a wine glass into the dean's hand and exchanged Littlefield's Scotch for a fresh one. At a nod from Elspeth, he stayed with them. The dean sipped at the Chardonnay and con-sulted the voices in her head. She had already exhausted half the conversational topics that she usually relied on to engage alums, and made a quick decision to steer clear of the standard conversa-tion filler, the alum's memories of favorite teachers, for every one of Littlefield's old profs would in his mind doubtless overshadow the current crop. Starting with a 6 a.m. wake-up call in Washing-ton this morning, it had been a long day, and the dean was ready to give up, but the nattering sprites persisted. "Have you been following State football this season?"

"No, I'm not really a football fan."

Just as well, the dean thought. For the first time in years State had recorded more wins than losses, but that was the sum of her knowledge of the team.

"Sailing's my sport," Littlefield said. "Unfortunately, State has never sailed in competition."

Or, 120 miles from the Atlantic, out of competition either. The dean said, "Do you sail yourself?"

"I have a small sloop I dock down at Pengilley Harbor."

For the first time, the dean sensed a dollop of warmth in Littlefield's voice, and she saw a possibility glimmer. "And that explains your interest in admiralty law."

"I've always loved the sea," Littlefield said.

"Salvage and treasure," the dean tipped her glass toward him in a toast. "Hijacking. Pirates. All very romantic, I imagine."

"I wouldn't call admiralty law romantic. Mostly lost and damaged cargo, maritime liens and mortgages, claims by seamen, collisions. But, yes, I suppose it has a charm of its own."

The sprites had started a peat fire to warm themselves against the autumn night, and a glimmering possibility in the corner of the dean's mind suddenly burst into flame, one that could anneal the conversation's false starts and turn the evening into a brilliant triumph. She looked over at Jimmy. "When I asked Jimmy to call you, I told him that it would be wonderful to take advantage of your visit here to try to interest you in teaching a course on Admiralty. It's been years since we've had Admiralty in our curriculum."

"Actually," Jimmy said, "State has never offered Admiralty."

"Then Mr. Littlefield can be our Christopher Columbus," the dean said.

"I hardly think an ABA accreditation visit is the occasion to be recruiting me to teach—"

"Nonsense," the dean said. "I can think of no better time to ask a loyal alum to help refresh our curriculum. Jimmy, does any Top Five school teach Admiralty? Yale? Harvard? Stanford? Columbia? Chicago?" She was certain that if any of them once offered the course, none did so now.

Jimmy shook his head. "I don't believe so."

"Then that's what we'll do. And Howard will lead the way."

"I'm flattered," Littlefield said, "but it's not possible –"

"Of course it's possible! And while you're deciding what text-book to use, Jimmy will get the paperwork started with our cur-riculum and personnel committees so that we can announce your appointment before the end of the week." When the first round of responses for the *U.S. News* rankings would be under way. "In the meantime, Howard, not a word of this to anyone. I don't want the competition to know." Quit now, the chorus of sprites warned. Quit while you're on top. She pressed Littlefield's hand warmly. "I'll leave you and Jimmy to talk about this. If there's anything I can do to make your stay more comfortable or produc-tive, just let Jimmy know." She looked around. "Where are your other committee members? I'd like to welcome them."

Jimmy leaned into her, but the dean had to strain to hear him over the noise in the room. "I think you should see how the chan-cellor is doing."

Old Silver, his face a darker, more dangerous crimson than earlier, had partially righted himself by propping one arm on the fireplace mantle and, with the other, resting his drink on his wife's shoulder. Several others in the room were also struggling to keep themselves upright, with varying degrees of success, and the dean observed with dismay that every one of them had been yellow-lined on the list she gave Jimmy. Heidi Hoehnemann-Mueller was at the bar splashing Stoli into a tall glass.

The dean turned to Jimmy. "Where's the bartender?"

"Wendell? I don't know."

"Wendell Ward? Your hired our mailroom boy to tend bar? For God's sake, Jimmy, what were you thinking? He's a born blackmailer. Do you have any idea what he can do with the infor-mation he picks up here?" The dean had no objection to black-mail, or to extortion when properly managed, but she did object to the youth's horning in on her preserve.

"I'm sure everyone is behaving themselves."

What was it about Jimmy's background that so blinded him to chaos? Even in his own home. In the short time since the dean arrived, the party had turned hilarious, and now it was actually coming apart. People barked at each other to be heard over the cranked-up Vivaldi on the stereo and the general din. The canapés had disappeared long ago, but someone had removed a pineapple-clad ham from the Fleenor refrigerator and, lacking knives or forks, guests were now shredding it with their fingernails. Alcohol and marijuana fumes had depleted the oxygen to the point at which some in the room were gasping as much as talking.

When the dean spoke again, Jimmy pointed to his ear to indicate that he couldn't hear.

"Where are my little sylphs?" The dean was now herself a decibel short of shouting. The panicky, out-of-control feeling had subsided once she figured out that all it would take to bring Littlefield over to her side would be to make him an Admiralty instructor, but now it stirred inside her once again.

"The girls? I don't know."

"Are they with Fairweather?"

Jimmy shrugged his shoulders.

If the little sylphs had gone off with Fairweather that would be fine. Better than fine. But if they were with Wendell . . . . "Where's the librarian? Bioff?"

"In the parlor with Brown."

"Well, shut down the bar, tell Millicent to make coffee, and stay close to Littlefield. Keep after him about teaching that course. I'll handle the librarian."

What is it that law librarians do? This had been a puzzle to Elspeth, even when she was a law student studying in the Yale library, and after becoming a faculty member at State and then its dean, the mystery had only deepened. Although Lee Brown was formally a member of the law faculty, the androgynous librarian did no teaching, spent no time on fundraising or committee work or holding the hands of students, as the Associate Deans for Students and Alumni Affairs did. Brown had an ample staff to acquire books and periodicals for the library, catalogue them, lend them out and recall them from tardy borrowers, and a cadre of four reference librarians to answer questions from students, faculty and the occasional lawyer who wandered in. If Brown disappeared tomorrow, would a single ripple appear on the surface of life at the Law School, or even at the law library?

Bioff and Brown were side by side on the loveseat, one elfin, the other bulky and oafish, looking about the room as if they were in a foreign country where they didn't know the language. The dean nodded to Brown and, for Bioff, turned on her brightest smile, the one she usually reserved for the school's more generous donors. "Mr. Bioff! How wonderful to see you. How are you? How is your lovely mother?"

"Mother died," Bioff said. "Three years ago."

"Oh, I'm so sorry." It had been just three years since the episode in the dean's anteroom, and Elspeth pictured the delicate, silver-haired woman falling into precipitous decline over the mortification of the meeting.

"Mother was struck by a Google Express van crossing Wooster Street."

"Oh, good. . . ." the dean said. "I mean, good heavens! What a horrible thing to happen! You have my every sympathy—" She turned to the tap on her shoulder.

Leverkase, his coat draped over an arm, was ready to leave. "You said there was something you wanted to talk about. I'm late for another engagement."

Leverkase had no other engagement. The flowering of his celebrity following the publication of *Carry a Big Stick* had been brilliant but brief. His follow-up volume, *Mama Mia! Bosom Size Among Female Foreign Ministers and Secretaries of State*, a cynical contrivance to win praise from the feminists who had pilloried the first book, failed miserably both in the professional reviews and in the bookstores. His last book, *The Tell-Tale Dick*, about nineteenth-century American poets, he had self-published. Poor Max. With his measuring tape, all he ever wanted was to be a Quant. But the Quants wouldn't have him, for where he thought the world's reality was captured in numbers, like inches and yards, they used only symbols, a means of abstraction that he had never succeeded in mastering.

"Give me just a minute, Max."

Elspeth turned back to the librarians. If she was to have any hope of winning over Bioff, she had to bring Brown to her side. Yet, even apart from the fundamental puzzle of law librarians, there remained the enigma of Lee Brown, for the dean still had no idea whether the person she'd hired was a man or a woman. Brown's regular outfit—dark-colored jacket and slacks, button down shirt, no tie, and flat-heeled black oxfords—offered no more clues to be had than the librarian's hair—worn longer than some women's, shorter than that some men's—or voice—a reedy tenor. A roll of flesh at Brown's neck obscured the possible Adam's apple, and another around the chest, a possible bosom. Since Brown had re-assigned all of the library's bathrooms as unisex, there were no clues to be had there, either.

What the two librarians needed was a change of scene. "Lee, why don't you take Mr. Bioff on a tour of the campus. Show him how beautiful it is by moonlight." If romance was in the cards, it would more likely blossom out among the pines and spruce than here. "Be sure to show him the site of our new building. I'm certain Mr. Bioff will want to see where the new library will be."

When the librarians had gone, the dean walked Leverkase to an unoccupied corner of the room. "Where's my book, Max? I was expecting a manuscript on my desk last month."

"It's not really a book, Ellie. More like—"

"Well, a monograph, then."

"More like a longish article."

"When?"

"Wednesday morning. Maybe even Tuesday. I just need to check some data. Run the final regressions."

"This book is going to make your reputation, Max. It's going to be even bigger than *Stick*." Pride lit the historian's face, and for a brief moment Elspeth felt a kinship with this horrible little man. "I promise you, Max, this will be front-page *New York Times*.

All the law blogs. *Above the Law.* Brian Leiter's *Law School Reports.* Adam Liptak. Dahlia Lithwick."

"I'll leave it with your secretary."

"Make sure it has a plain cover. No title page." The dean put a finger to her lips. "Not a word to anyone. Our secret."

Leverkase slipped away, invisible wings gently flapping at his ankles.

On her way to the kitchen, the dean passed by the leaning chancellor, and heard his wife ask, "How many pills did you take, darling? Is this going to be like what happened with His Holiness?" The chancellor's angles of incline, forward and sideways, had grown five or ten degrees more acute since the dean last looked.

Jimmy was a fool. Of course the chancellor was growing timber.

Alex Coyle slipped out the kitchen's swinging door, avoiding the dean's look. "Don't go far," she called after him.

In the kitchen, Millicent Fleenor was tucking the tails of her blouse into her denim skirt. For an instant the dean wondered what Alex could possibly see in this angular, flat-chested woman, then remembered that his sexual arrows had always been aimed less at sensual pleasure than at undermining what he said were the Law School's illegitimate hierarchies.

"Where's the coffee, Millicent?"

"All it's going to get you is a house full of wide-awake drunks."

A devout practitioner of serial polygamy, Elspeth had never been married herself. She well knew the hard shell of resentment that faculty spouses—wives and husbands both—wore like a second skin, but she could only rarely discern if, like an oyster's pearl, the shell had formed from irritation at their partners for earning a salary that was smaller than their skill and efforts deserved, or larger.

"Just serve the coffee, Millicent." The words snapped more whiplike than the dean intended. "They're no worse drunk than sober. I just need for them to be awake."

Alex was waiting when the dean came back into the parlor. The pony-tailed Director of Special Projects had the perennially unfocused gaze that men acquire with their first set of contact lenses. "You know you're not supposed to be here. And you know why."

"Millicent insisted that I come."

"You have to stop poking the faculty wives, Alex. It's hurting faculty morale."

"You surprise me, Dean Flowers,"—it was uncanny how Elspeth could hear Alex's soft voice above the noise—"I would have thought your idea of morale was broader than that."

The dean pulled him deeper into the corner, away from the three remaining Bog Dwellers in the parlor. "That was a sad mistake, that will never be repeated."

"You should be thinking about my morale," Alex said, the unfocused yellow eyes gazing at a spot somewhere above the dean's shoulder. "I don't want any more than what everyone else already has. I just want my people to walk in the sunlight and breathe the fresh air like everyone else on this faculty."

Ask any president or chancellor or dean or department chair at a large university or a small college; public or private; in the North, South, East, or West or anywhere in the middle; ask them what their single greatest challenge is, and every one of them will reflexively utter a single syllable: *space*—parking space always, but usually office space as well. "I already told you, Alex. I'm doing everything I can. As soon as the new building is up—"

"We can't wait that long. We're suffocating."

"You haven't talked to anyone, have you?"

"You mean the ABA committee? They're here for three days, right? Sooner or later, one of them's going to want to know what the Director of Special Projects does at State. The old guy, Littlefield, already asked. By Wednesday noon, I want—"

"Oh my God!" Jimmy's voice boomed over the din.

Voices instantly went silent, leaving the long-forgotten Vivaldi to fill the room.

"The chancellor!"

Heads turned, the dean's in time to watch the chancellor go down. The large shoulders angled off the wall, and glass, ice and liquor flew from his grasp. It was like the collapse of a skyscraper in slow motion, and the crash, when it came, shook the house.

The Poets, who were closest, crowded around the prone figure. "He's fractured something," a woman's voice said. "It's horrible!"

"It looks like his thigh bone. No, a rib," a man said. "Oh, my God, it's a rib sticking out." One of the taller Quants looked down, over their heads. "Where's Leverkase?"

The dean pushed her way in. The chancellor's face was white and glossy as wax, giving a ghastly aspect to the fine red capillaries around his nostrils. The Quant was right about this being Leverkase's department, for it was no broken rib or femur that was tent-poling the chancellor's trousers, but an erection the size of an infant's arm. Elspeth had warned Jimmy to watch for this. It had happened once before, when His Holiness the Dalai Lama had come to campus, and the chancellor, a great but visibly tumescent admirer, had passed out in his seat at the banquet table between the spiritual leader and the British consul.

As on the occasion of the visit from His Holiness, Old Silver Zipper had this evening apparently dosed himself with Viagra before leaving for Jimmy's party, and as one of his extremities filled with alcohol and the other with sildenafil citrate, the chancellor's blood, forced to decide which of the two extremities to occupy, had made the least wise but most common choice and rushed downward, throwing the old man into circulatory shock.

The chancellor lifted his head, whispered a word or two into his wife's ear, then fell back. While the Poets fretted, the dean called over two of the sturdier Quants to carry him upstairs to the Fleenors' guest room. The dean took the hand of the chancellor's wife and encouraged her to follow. "I'm sure he'll want you to be there when he snaps out of this."

"Of course he will," the tiny woman said. "He always has."

The dean was curious. "A moment ago, when he lifted his head, what was it the chancellor whispered to you?"

"Why, 'Wendell,'" the chancellor's wife answered. "He asked for Wendell."

Wendell again. It was as if some transcendent dramatist or director had cast the maddening youth to play a role in the dean's rapidly foreshortening destiny. Assert control, the sprites' voices whispered, so Elspeth turned to face her faculty, lifting her arms as if in benediction. Someone switched off the Vivaldi, and when the few remaining Bog Dwellers had made their way into the living room, Elspeth lowered her arms, letting one hand rest casually on Littlefield's shoulder. "The chancellor will be fine," she said to the 20 or so faculty and spouses still present. "He is upstairs resting, but he'll be up and about in no time." The thought of Old Silver Zipper, his ass high in the air above his supine wife, depressed her.

She turned to Littlefield. "For those of you who haven't yet had the opportunity to meet him, I want to introduce the chair of our visiting committee, Mr. Howard Littlefield—or should I say Professor Littlefield—"

"Really," Littlefield said, "this is not going to happen—"

Heidi Hoehnemann-Mueller weaved her way to the front, and the dean put up a hand to stop her progress.

"Well, be that as it may—"

"Pipe Admiral Hornblower aboard, Elspeth!" A hard glance from the dean failed to silence the anthropologist. "Did you feed the Admiral your line about State being the last hope of the working class? That our mission is to open our doors to the impoverished, the uneducated, the downtrodden—to any lumpen proletariat foolish enough to go a hundred and fifty thousand dollars into debt for an education that will never earn her enough to repay the loan in her lifetime?"

Ignoring Heidi, the dean addressed the others. "I am sure that Mr. Littlefield and his fellow committee members"—she looked around to confirm that neither Fairweather nor Bioff had returned—"I am sure that they will want to speak with you over the next three days, and I am confident that you will all make time available to share your thoughts with them."

The words rattled on, meaningless, anodyne, for if the dean was thinking about the visiting committee, it was not about its mission, but its diverging possibilities: Bioff and Brown getting more closely acquainted in the moonlight; Fairweather engaged in a threesome with her two little sylphs; the chancellor stirring in the guest room above her. She did not wish these various conjugants less, only wished herself more. Her gaze fell on Alex Coyle and she thought of the single occasion on which she had breached her iron rule. It was a small solace that Alex would never know how profoundly it disturbed her, a woman who loved nothing better than to be romanced by brawny former football players like Dan Gidron that, in their single encounter, a spineless reptile like Alex had lifted her to unprecedented heights. She would never break her rule again.

FOUR

MEMORANDUM
(Dictated but not read)

TO: File
FROM: H.L.
RE: ABA Vis. Comm.
DATE: Oct. 30

Sunday evening at Associate Dean J. Fleenor's home; committee members, H. Fairweather (legal philosopher), W. Bioff (librarian), also present.

Fairweather strange bird, chattered about German philosophers, "Frankfurt School." H.L. asked, what's wrong with Americans? O.W. Holmes, Jr., B. Cardozo, J. Chipman Gray, all of them smart cookies. Fairweather departed early with two pretty girls. Fleenor's daughters?

Bioff odd duck, too. Silent; anger boiling under a tight lid. Huddled with State librarian Brown, strange, too, but H.L. can't pinpoint how. Birds of feather. Plotting? Stopped talking if H.L. looked their way.

Marijuana in air. Alcohol. Chancellor present. H.L. remembers when he was president. Big man, but first one down; giant boner, just like lunch with Dalai Lama.

Director of Special Projects, A. Coyle, shuttled about; friend only to Mrs. F. Law School no Garden of Eden, but Coyle is serpent. Squamous. Ponytail. Secretive. Must find out, what are "Special Projects"?

Three factions. Warring. Profs have egos the size of Macy's Day balloons; every sentence begins with "I." Faculty spouses sullen, drunk or both.

M. Leverkase measures penises for a living. (Like being shoe salesman, H.L. supposes.) Has secret project for dean; another mystery for H.L. to solve.

W. Ward, bartender; mailroom clerk; a rogue, even at a glance; knows where Law School skeletons buried. Disappeared with Fairweather, F's spirited daughters in tow.

Fleenor's eyes didn't leave door until dean arrived; swooned on her arrival. F. smart, but hides it; good value, though. Only loyal man there, except for downed chancellor. Faculty wouldn't lift finger if Law School burned. The unhappy Mrs. F. wants desperately to admire her husband.

Dean arrived late, sparks flying. Force of nature; on sexual rampage. Horniest creature H.L. ever saw, land or sea; same "blood-shot blinded eye" as Ahab chasing whale; "eternal sap" runs in those bones. Tried to bribe H.L. with teaching offer. Admiralty Law!

Note to Etta: remind H.L. to call H.L. Jr. Dean sure to please him; him, her.

Returning to Faculty House, H.L. thinks about dog that didn't bark: students. No one spoke of students—dissecting knotty cases; the charged rivalries of moot court; the fine camaraderie of Friday afternoon faculty-student beers at "Rat." Is Law School for students, or just for profs?

Dark woods beyond Faculty House alive with comings and goings, whispers and woodsmoke. What ABA dunce scheduled committee visit for Halloween week? Know tonight is Witches' Sabbath? Witches dance, sing and dine in Devil's honor; copulate foully with demon lovers. Legend, perhaps, but stories believed in these parts; thought to produce worst kind of havoc.

MONDAY

FIVE

The moment she awoke this morning, Elspeth knew that the boggy tide of the last two weeks had returned and that last night's brilliant clarity of mind had vanished under a suffocating wave of sludge. She did the best she could to put herself together, but hazard crowded every corner of the day ahead. When she arrived in the anteroom to her office the dark look from her normally imperturbable secretary, Eve, confirmed the dean's worst expectations. Eve's fingers trembled as she handed Elspeth a message slip. "The senator called. He wants you to call back ASAP. Jimmy, Beverly and Joyce are in your office. I think Joyce is out of sorts because you didn't buy her brownies for your party last night. Jimmy's sulking, too, but who knows why?"

The dean took a place on a corner of Eve's desk, turned the telephone around and punched in the Senator's number. His receptionist put her through at once.

"Ellie?"

Elspeth exempted only three men from her no-Ellie rule: her now-deceased father; Senator Albie Troxell; and Randy Barrimore, the billionaire Oklahoma investor who was not only the senator's most vocal and generous supporter, but had also promised $55 million to construct the new Albie and Renata Troxell Law Building. Over the course of negotiating the capital gift, Elspeth and Randy had become close friends. The reasons Elspeth forgave these three men, though complicated, were connected to the fact that she truly loved two of them; had led one of them to believe that he could in time seduce her; and understood that each in his own way held the key to her future. "Good morning, Senator."

"Did you have a good flight back from Washington yesterday?"

"Good, but late."

If he heard the implicit reprimand, the senator didn't acknowledge it. "I called to give you a heads-up. The SEC is going to court this afternoon to file a civil lawsuit against our friend Randy. Foreign Corrupt Practices Act. Something to do with bribing government officials in East Timor. Bhutan."

Just when you think your life can't get worse, it does. Even for Randy, $55 million was more than petty cash, and the lawsuit could tie up his assets for years. Groundbreaking on the Albie and Renata Troxell Building was scheduled for the end of the week, but construction couldn't start without a check from Randy, and if construction didn't start . . . even a brain as crud-clogged as Elspeth's could complete the chain of "ifs."

"My staff tried to reach Randy," the senator said, "but he's gone underground. They don't know where he is."

Hardly a minute had passed and the dean was already finding the senator tiresome. "Well you know what they say, Senator. Everyone has to be somewhere."

Background voices rose at the other end of the line, followed by silence, as if the senator had placed a hand over the receiver. His tone when he came back on was preoccupied. "How is your ABA visit coming along, Ellie? Howard Littlefield called this morning."

"I didn't know you knew him." The senator's awareness of the accreditation visit was also a surprise.

"Of course I know Howard. He's a Republican, and very much behind the scenes, but there's no one in the Capital who won't take his call. The governor. Committee chairs. Howard's a straight shooter, but as long as your house is in order, you shouldn't have anything to worry about."

"Certainly everything's in order. Do you think I would accept anything less? Really, Senator." Let him figure out for himself if she was calling him that, rather than "Albie," because he was annoying her, or simply to hide their relationship from whoever might one day listen to the tape he undoubtedly was making of the call.

"It would be quite a story," the senator said, "if in the same year my alma mater makes the *U.S. News* Top Five, it loses its ABA accreditation." There was laughter in the senator's voice, but something else, too. "You *are* going to make the Top Five, aren't you?"

"Of course we are. I'm going into a staff meeting right now to review this year's numbers. And, if you remember, we're counting on the Albie and Renata Troxell Law Building to put us over the top in the voting."

"*If* there's a building." The background voices erupted again, but this time the senator did nothing to mute them. "In light of my relationship with Randy, you'll understand that I can't intercede with the SEC on his behalf. I have to keep arm's-length."

"*Semper fidelis.*"

"And I don't mean to sound harsh, Ellie, or . . . ungrateful, but I hope you also understand that if State doesn't make it to the Top Five, your nomination isn't going anywhere."

The nomination. Why else had she led the senator on? Why had she invested the university's resources and all of her powers in bringing the Law School into the Top Five?

The senator said, "Every academic who's made it to the Court, every one of them came from a Top Five school—Ginsburg, Breyer, Scalia, Kagan." The senator's tone had become pedantic. "As fine a mind as you have, Ellie, the President's not going to make an exception for you, and neither is my committee."

"I fully understand, Senator." Now Elspeth didn't care if he knew that he was pissing her off. Still, she wondered if it had been a mistake to reject Yale's offer of a professorship in order to take the deanship at State. No, she had made the right move. Being on the faculty at a Top Five school like Yale was no longer enough to win an appointment to the Court. Nor did being a woman count for much anymore. She needed to stand out. The dean who carried a state law school into the Top Five would stand out.

"You know, there's an opening on the First Circuit," the senator said. "Your own home state. Up in Portland. I'm sure I can get it for you right now, Top Five or not."

The dean had worked too hard, and too successfully, on the senator's campaign trail and off, to settle for anything less than the Supreme Court. Hadn't she coined the slogan for his last, unusually hard-fought campaign in a state torn between voters who believed in a woman's right to choose and those who believed in an unborn infant's right to life? For a slogan that said nothing, no political flack could possibly have improved on *Protect Your Rights and Your Children's—Vote Troxell.* "Thank you, Senator, but my heart is set on moving south, not north. You take care of the nomination and I'll take care of *U.S. News.* Will I see you and the missus at the groundbreaking?"

"Not unless Randy comes out of hiding. No Randy, no funds. And no funds, no groundbreaking."

"And, no groundbreaking, no Top Five. And no Top Five. . . . I'm confident Randy will be there. I look forward to seeing you, too. Remember, it's your building."

"And Mrs. Troxell's." The senator was letting Elspeth know that he, too, put limits on their relationship.

Eve took the receiver from the dean's outstretched hand. "Remember, when you go in there, Joyce is unhappy. Jimmy, too."

Every Monday morning that she was in College Station, the dean met with her top administrators—not only Jimmy, but her associate deans for Admissions and Student Affairs as well as the directors of Placement, Facilities and Special Projects to review the week ahead and assign tasks. Today, however, she had pared the group down to three—Jimmy, Admissions Dean Beverly de la Torre, and Director of Placement Joyce Savarino—for the single matter on the table was the *U.S. News* rankings, and the discussion would be strictly need-to-know.

The tension in the room bound the three staff members so tightly that Elspeth could feel it the instant she entered. Beverly, in pencil-thin jeans and French T, a silk scarf knotted casually to the side, straddled a straight-backed chair pulled from the conference table to face the dean's desk. Joyce, a gawky former center on State's women's basketball team, had made her usual misjudgment and taken the low, cushiony couch next to the desk; when the meeting was over, it would require a full minute's struggle for her to separate herself from it. Jimmy, his back to the others, had positioned himself to gaze across the campus toward the twin spires poking out above the knoll that otherwise obscured the Metropolitan State Hospital for the Criminally Insane. It was as if he knew of the dean's secret dread of the State Hospital and was taunting her to look that way. Arms crossed, each hand gripping an elbow, he didn't respond to the dean's greeting.

On her first day as Dean, Elspeth had herself moved the massive desk so that it faced away from Metropolitan State. The gothic pile of gray stone and reddish-brown brick had been erected shortly after the Civil War, at the same time as the agricultural college that later evolved into the university. Indeed, the institutions shared the former dairy farm until the Wiscassett Parkway, bisecting the 1,600-acre parcel, was laid a century later. The same architect had designed both sets of buildings, and he had perfectly matched the twin spires that rose from the asylum's pavilions to those of the college library and adjoining administration building a half-mile away. Today, inmates occupied no more than a third of the rooms, but it wasn't their presence that caused the dean to position her desk as she had. It was the hospital's vast empty spaces that invaded her darkest dreams, the shadowed corridors and empty lock-down wards, floor after floor of them. Driving past it on her way home, her reflex was to jam her eyes shut.

The three administrators could have been numbers on a clock or strangers on a ferry, peering at some distant point rather than at each other, or at the list numbered 1–12 in black felt pen on the white board that Eve had retrieved from the storeroom and positioned on an easel in front of the dean's desk. The list wasn't there for the dean's benefit; the factors that *U.S. News* weighed in its annual ranking of American law schools had long ago burned themselves into her memory. They were there to remind, and to rally, her staff. The dean knew—because Wendell had told her—that the faculty called it the dean's 12-step program.

Elspeth picked up a wooden pointer from the easel and, skipping over the first two items on the list—Reputation Among Lawyers and Judges; Reputation Among Academics—touched the pointer to the third. The nervous silence that followed was like one that might descend at the start of a grade school quiz. "Tell us about this year's GPAs, Beverly." Undergraduate grade-point averages of admitted applicants counted 10 percent in the *U.S. News* rankings, and the dean had transformed the magazine's simple numerical calculation into an edict to be followed by her admissions dean and the recruiters Beverly dispatched to colleges across the country: recruit and admit only students with the highest GPAs. Start with 4.0, and accept lower grades on pain of having your Christmas bonus reduced. *U.S. News* wouldn't complete its final tally until March, and the magazine would look at this year's admission numbers as well as last year's.

"It's only October," Beverly said—there was an edge to her voice and a spark of annoyance glinted in the unsettling blue eyes—"but I think we can fill next year's class without dropping below 3.8."

The dean understood why Joyce was sulking—it was about the brownies, and she would fix that—but Jimmy, and now Beverly, were a mystery. "That's where we were this time last year, Beverly." Her tone was gentle. She couldn't afford to lose her admissions dean to any of the several department heads at State who were jostling for the opportunity to hire her away from the Law School. Not only was Beverly a woman, she was African-American and Spanish-surnamed—the dean's trifecta in State's diversity hiring sweepstakes. And, no matter that the dean had already exceeded the Law School's diversity quota with last year's faculty hire of the bisexual, ex-con, ex-drug addict Luis Morales, if ever Beverly came out as a lesbian or transgender, or—God forbid!—suffered an accident that left her with a partial but permanent disability, it would propel the dean's diversity record so far past those of the university's other deans and department chairs that they could never hope to catch up with her. "Just do your best, Beverly, but please try to get the numbers up."

"I can beat 3.8," Beverly said, "but Jimmy's not going to like what it does to the composition of the entering class."

Jimmy turned at his name. "Even at 3.8," he said, "we've lost any chance to recruit from the Ivies."

From deep in the couch, Joyce said, "Why would that be a problem?" It heartened the dean to see her director of placement join the conversation.

Jimmy said, "Princeton doesn't hand out 3.8 GPAs the way a local state college does. A Princeton senior with a 3.8 and a half-decent LSAT is going to Harvard or Yale. Why would he come here?"

"Jimmy's right," Beverly said, "I can fill up a class with 3.9s but none of them will be from a top school."

"I don't want 3.9s," the dean said. "I want 4.0s. And I don't need Ivies."

"Did you hear that, Beverly?" Jimmy's voice was harsh. "Forget the Ivies. Send your recruiters south. Check out the grading curves at the bible schools. And why aren't we recruiting at the for-profits? I bet Kaplan hands out tons of A's. Bryant & Stratton. University of Phoenix. Call the online schools. See if you can get them to email our admissions application with their college diplomas."

Among the State faculty, for whom the practice of irony was not next to godliness but above it, Jimmy was the rare exception: the perfect straight man, with an allergy even to nuance. Team player that he was, the dean was willing to believe that her associate dean might actually have made the suggestion in good faith. Still, her uncomfortable feeling about Jimmy persisted. She pointed at the fourth entry on the white board. "What about LSATs?"

"We're ahead of last year," Beverly said. "We can admit a class that's 168 and higher. They'll be bubble brains, but that's ten points better than last year."

Bubble brains weren't airheads, the dean knew, but Beverly's shorthand for the idiots savant who learned nothing in their four years of college, or at least nothing worth knowing, but could pencil in the correct answer in the bubbles on standardized exams with the uncanny perfection of a professional basketball player taking shots from the foul line. The essential stupidity of these applicants was not her concern. She said, "Remember, I don't want you to go too high."

"But—"

"You can admit a class of 170s, Beverly, but you won't enroll them. It's like admitting Ivies. Don't forget what happened two years ago. Everyone we accepted with 170 or better also got into Stanford, Yale and Harvard, so they rejected us. We have to reject applicants before they reject us." The dean turned to Joyce to keep her in the conversation, and pointed at number five on the whiteboard list. "Yield ratio. The number-one killer. Here's where *U.S. News* has us by the short hairs. Of the students we admit, how many actually come here? If there's any chance an applicant's LSAT is high enough to get her admitted to the competition, we have to reject her." It felt good to call Yale, Stanford and Harvard the competition.

"So, Beverly's supposed to go after applicants whose LSATs and GPAs are high, but not too high." The paradox appeared to baffle Joyce. "If they're too high, she has to reject them."

"Exactly," the dean said. "It's like dating in high school. We have to reject them before they reject us."

Joyce didn't appear to be reassured. "It's not really that hard," the dean said. "We only worry about high GPAs if they're from a halfway decent college. Our sweet spot is high, but low-quality GPAs."

Jimmy made a space for himself to sit on the edge of the dean's conference table, pushing aside the scale model of the Albie and Renata Troxell Law Building that occupied a full half of the surface. The maquette looked like a wedge from a giant six-layer wedding cake. Hidden bulbs lit the glass-walled structure from within, silhouetting clusters of miniature figures in the halls and at long U.N.-styled desks curved to follow the line of the building. The dean had overseen every detail of the fractious design process. No clash in the year-long struggle had been fiercer than the Battle of the East-Facing Wall, which had required a last-minute assist from Randy Barrimore to force the building's arrogant New York architects to clad an entire side of the wedge, the one facing the twin spires across the hill, not with glass like the rest of the building, but with stone. The dean, with Randy on the conference call, refused to let even a single window breach the shield of granite block.

Jimmy said, "I hope you're not planning to improve yield the way you did last year."

"You mean," the dean said, "not releasing our admission standards to pre-law advisors?" The mini-spotlights that had crisscrossed over the building model highlighted what Jimmy was too artless to hide. Bitterness consumed his features, from the averted eyes to the unaccustomed frown. Elspeth wondered what she had done to so injure her associate dean. "I don't see anything wrong with giving undergraduate advisors benchmarks instead of specific numbers."

"What's wrong, Ellie, is there was no bench to go with the marks. We low-balled them. We got college seniors to apply who didn't have a snowball's chance of getting in here. Kids with 2.4 GPAs and 130s on their LSATs. And why? Just so you could increase our rejection rate."

As an awkward, all-knees-and-elbows girl growing up, Elspeth had been sensitive to the mildest slights, the most subtle barbs in language, and she caught Jimmy's transition from the team-minded "we" to the accusatory "you." She also caught Beverly's exchange of uneasy looks with Joyce. Jimmy and the two women had been talking about her low-balling strategy while she was on the phone with the senator. "We give these students hope," she said. "What's wrong with that? And for the hands-down losers, the 2.4s and 130s, we returned their application fees."

"I'm not talking about application fees. I'm talking about kids whose expectations we raised for no good reason."

It's wonderful to have your second-in-command infatuated with you, Elspeth thought. Until he isn't. She didn't know how to fix Jimmy's attitude, but she knew that at some point she would find a way. Just not now, with cubic yards of crud threatening to overflow the banks of her consciousness. A thought occurred to her, and she abruptly turned from Jimmy to Beverly. "I've decided to scrap last year's free tuition program."

"You can't be serious! It's the only way we got our Harvard and Yale admits to come here."

The dean had borrowed the idea to give admittees a free ride from the University of California's newest law school, whose dean had shrewdly jump-started his institution by offering free tuition to lure away students who had been admitted to top-ranked schools. His fast-rising school was now as much her competition as NYU or Columbia, and this year she was going to do the California dean one better. "We're going to charge everyone full freight, even the in-state residents. And not just the old State tuition. We're going to charge them $58,000 a year, just like Yale."

"You can't do that," Jimmy said, "we're a state school—"

The dean beamed. Even with the encroaching sludge, her mind was working. "And every single applicant who gets into State and registers here is going to get a full $58,000 scholarship."

"Seventh step," Beverly said, delighted, clapping like a child. "Amount spent per student. Every dollar we give our students in financial aid is money in the bank with U.S. News. And if we give them full tuition scholarships, it's the same as free."

The turn in Beverly's mood warmed Elspeth. Eagerness to please is more important in an admissions dean than cleverness. When the dean calls her admissions officer, as she did some weeks ago with a request to admit the son of a corporate general counsel whose numbers were far below the Law School cutoff, she wants no questions, only a promptly mailed acceptance letter. Beverly's cleverness was a windfall, and Elspeth considered how she might take her admissions dean with her when she left the deanship.

"It's just a bookkeeping trick," Jimmy said.

"But," Joyce leaned into the conversation, "A very cool one."

So, she had won over her placement director, too. Now, she had just one question for Joyce, and it had to do with the *U.S. News*'s tenth factor. "Are all of last year's graduates still gainfully employed?"

"Every one of them," Joyce said, "even the woebegones."

The dean's woebegones were the roughly 20 percent of the school's graduates who could find jobs neither in private practice nor in public service and, with three years invested in their legal education, had too large a residue of pride to settle for jobs like real estate sales, data processing or cooking fries at Wendy's that didn't require a law degree. With the dean's help, Joyce found positions for these unemployables around the Law School—as file clerks, grounds-keepers, messengers—posts for which the job listing required a law degree as a qualification, no matter how menial the work. The result was that 100 percent of State's law students were employed at graduation, all in jobs requiring a law degree, ensuring a perfect score on the *U.S. News*'s tenth factor. And, since employment at the Law School was as much in the public interest as a job with the Public Defender or Legal Aid, for those graduates who remained in these positions at least three years, the school paid off their student debt under its public interest loan forgiveness program.

The dean said, "I'm thinking about giving them more prestigious work this year." A law school in Florida had solved its *U.S. News* employment problem by paying local law firms to hire its graduates, actually picking up their salaries. But Elspeth knew she could do even better. "Instead of giving them odd jobs around the Law School, we're going to hire every unemployed graduate as a research and writing instructor for next year's first-year students."

"Wonderful!" Beverly said, clapping her hands again. "We have to give the first-years something extra if we're going to charge them $58,000 tuition."

"Great," Jimmy said. "Our 1Ls will get their first exposure to a lawyer's most critical skill, *Bluebook* citation form, from the pea brains who graduated at the bottom of their class."

The dean ignored him. "Overnight, we'll double the size of the teaching staff without increasing the size of the student body."

"Ninth factor," Beverly said. "Faculty-student ratio."

The dean high-fived Joyce, who was closest, then gave the gangly ex-basketball player her hand to extricate her from the couch and to signal that the meeting was over. To Beverly she said, "You need to start planning for admit weekend." From her friendship with State's football coach, Elspeth had learned some of his more effective techniques for recruiting high school players. As adapted by the dean for pre-law college seniors, they included a long weekend of round-the-clock access to videogames, beer kegs, modest amounts of recreational drugs, and large quantities of sweets. "Make sure you order a few dozen of Joyce's special brownies." She smiled at Joyce who was still struggling to rise from the couch. "The admits will love them."

Even with all of the good news and anticipatory celebration, the tension in the office persisted, and although none of the three staffers was going to raise the issue on their own, none seemed willing to leave before it was raised. Because she had forbidden the topic, the dean was the only one who could broach it.

"The applicant pool," the dean said. "Is it filling up?"

"Right now"—Beverly's fine voice cracked—"we're 30 percent behind where we were at this time last year."

"Even with the bible schools?"

"We weren't the first law school to discover the fine colleges of the South, Elspeth."

"College seniors aren't fools," Jimmy said. "Give them all the scholarships you want. There still won't be any real jobs for them when they graduate."

Beverly, her voice still uneven, said, "Some schools are shrinking class size to keep their standards up."

"The legislature will never let us do that." Also, the dean thought, if the school shriveled into a dry, empty husk, so would she. She would disappear into one of those vast spaces under the twin spires of the nuthouse across the way. "I need you to be creative, Beverly. I need you to find people that our competition isn't chasing after, people who yearn to be lawyers."

The challenge was of course unanswerable, and the three understood that the dean was dismissing them. As one, they headed to the door.

"Jimmy—a minute of your time?"

After the two women left, the dean closed the door and went directly up to Jimmy so that they were face to face. She would not let him look away. "What was that about just now? Your job is to support me. To support the Law School."

"Not if it means lying to applicants." Anger burned behind his eyes. "Piling one deceit on top of another."

Elspeth piled stone and mortar on the levee against the rising tide of sludge. She moved closer to her associate dean. "How do you think Harvard and the others built their reputations? With mud and straw? Good deeds? They may put on genteel airs, but their claws are out like everyone else's. Do you really think the University of Chicago Law School is going to sit still at fifth place? They got a rich alum to give them ten million dollars, and do you know for what? Sixty full-tuition scholarships. And don't kid yourself that they're for students who need the money. They're for applicants with the highest LSATs and GPAs in the country. The ones who, without that money, would go to Harvard, Yale, Stanford or Columbia."

"Still, Ellie—"

"Still, nothing!" The dean grabbed the pointer and with it rapped the first entry on the white board. *Reputation among lawyers and judges.* "Do you have any idea what we're up against? How do you think judges know what to answer when *U.S. News* sends them their survey? They ask their law clerks. If they let their clerks write their judicial opinions for them, don't you think they're going to listen to what their clerks have to say about which schools are the best in the country? And what law schools do judges hire their clerks from? Yale, Stanford, Harvard, Columbia and Chicago. The Top Five. And what schools do you think these recent graduates of Yale, Stanford, Harvard, Columbia and Chicago tell their judges are the best?

"And lawyers," the dean said. "Do you think lawyers know anything more about law schools than judges? They know less. All they know is what they read in the newspaper. *The New York Times. The Wall Street Journal.* But where do the *Times* and the *Journal* go for information about law schools? *U.S. News.* So these lawyers read in the paper that Yale is number one and Stanford is number two and Harvard is number three . . . and guess what they write down when they get a survey asking them which are the best law schools in the country? Are you beginning to see the problem we face?"

The dean didn't wait for an answer, but dropped the pointer to the next line. *Reputation among academics.* "Law professors! They actually survey law professors! They—" She started to say that *U.S. News* had turned the asylum over to the inmates, but the thought of the spires across the hill flashed across her mind like a warning light. "Did they ever call you, Jimmy? What schools do you think the largest number of law professors graduated from? Do you want me to give you those five names again? Some of them may vote for the school where they managed to land a job, but you can be sure every one of them gives their top vote to alma mater. How many State graduates do we have in teaching? Other than you, Jimmy, what, maybe two or three? That's it. Yale has hundreds."

"Have you ever stopped to ask yourself, Ellie, why it's so important that we get into the Top Five?" The tremble in his voice betrayed his understanding that this was heresy. "So important that we cheat and lie to get there?"

Elspeth realized that she had lost her hold on Jimmy. "Do you think your Ivy Leaguers will ever come to State if we're not in the Top Five? That their parents will let them turn down Harvard and Yale and Stanford to study the *Bluebook* under the great Professor Fleenor?"

"So what if they don't come? So what if they go somewhere else? The world isn't going to be any worse off. Things will be like they were before. Everything in order. And no cheating by us."

"Do you have any idea what it's like in the second tier? Beverly was being gentle when I asked her about the Bible schools. It's open warfare down in the second tier, every one of them fighting to get students in their doors. It's Syria. Iraq. Somalia. The social order beneath us is disintegrating."

"I'm sure we'll do fine."

The dean shifted from front foot to back. "Pride, Jimmy. Don't you want to feel pride for your law school the way you do for your home? This *is* your home. We're building something here. That's why we have to do better than we did last year." When Jimmy didn't respond, she said, "Last night's party was a great success. You and Millicent have the school's thanks. Since you're the one faculty member who has extensive experience with ABA visits, I've decided to butt out of this one and let you take complete charge. Would that work for you?"

"Sure," Jimmy said, but with no enthusiasm.

"Drop everything else and give it your full attention. It would be quite a story if in the same year we make the *U.S. News* Top Five we lose our ABA accreditation." The line didn't come out sounding as witty as when the senator said it.

"Even more of a story if we lost our accreditation and *didn't* make your Top Five."

"Well, you let me take care of *U.S. News*. I want you to attend to Mr. Littlefield and the others. Where are they now?"

"Littlefield and Fairweather are in classes. I think Bioff is with Brown."

"I don't want them wandering around on their own. Looking into places they don't need to see. Have you talked up the new building?" Elspeth had conceived of the building as an essential beachhead in her assault on the *U.S. News* Top Five, but it now occurred to her that the model could do double service in distracting the ABA visiting committee from the many deficiencies of the present building. "Make sure they see the model. If I'm not here, I'll leave the lights on." The dean passed her hand over the crenellated balsa wood roof of the maquette, as if she could summon the actual building like a genie from a lamp. "Also, I want you to get the committee members copies of the faculty bibliographies. They need to see how productive our colleagues are."

"What about Alex?"

Is this what was bothering Jimmy? That Alex Coyle was cuck-olding him? "What about him?"

"If the Committee sees his 'special project' in the flesh, there's no way we'll get re-accredited."

"Then make sure they don't see it," the dean said. "Isolate Alex. Threaten him. Anything you have to do."

"Also, Wendell told me—"

There was a knock at the door, and Eve stuck her head in. "President Bartles is on line three."

"Wendell seems to think—"

"I have to take this, Jimmy." The dean crossed to her desk. "Since when is Wendell running the Law School? He's the mail-room boy, for God's sake." She lifted the receiver, but covered the mouthpiece with her hand—"To be continued"—and nodded for Jimmy to leave.

The dean left the mouthpiece muffled. It was good discipline for Rawleigh to wait, and she deserved this private moment to exult over her earlier conversation with the senator. The 113th Justice of the Supreme Court of the United States! She let the phrase trickle over her brain like honey. Thirteen had always been her lucky num-ber. At age 37 this would, at least until she subsequently rose to the position of Chief Justice, be the crowning achievement of her legal career, a prize that made almost forgettable all of those dreary meetings and the delayed flights from Washington. If the senator kept his word—and the dean had the videotapes to ensure that he did—she would within a year ascend to the institution around which, whether they will admit it or not, every American lawyer's professional fantasies orbit, the supreme arbiter that, in a nation that separates church, individual and state, exercises the power to decide between them. And, with a male-female ratio of 2:1, there was, outside of Alaska, no better place for a woman to work than the Supreme Court of the United States.

Elspeth pictured herself up on the Court's magisterial bench, the marble pillars and dark ceremonial drapes framing her every actorly gesture; the other eight justices in their black robes no more than an indistinct collage; herself in the awe-inducing foreground. She would apply makeup to underline her natural pallor: powder for her cheeks and her still firm jaw line; blood-red lipstick and matching nail polish for fingers and toes. She was a woman who looked good in black. And under that black robe Associate Justice Elspeth Flowers would be buck naked. No bra, no pantyhose. Not even panties. Spring-loaded and ready for action.

SIX

MEMORANDUM
(Dictated but not read)

TO: File
FROM: H.L.
RE: ABA Vis. Comm.
DATE: Oct. 31

H.L. arrived early for Prof. H. Hoehnemann-Mueller's Civ. Pro.
class. Anthropologist, not lawyer. H.L. asked, why teach in Law
School, not Anthro. Department? H-M laughed. Law school pays
triple what Anthro. pays; also paid to testify in securities fraud
and Foreign Corrupt Practice trials.

   H-M played hour-long video of beehive for class. Says beehive
is epitome of civil procedure; queen resolves disputes between
worker bees and drones; issues certiorari in disputes with other
queens; but no lawyers, no judges, only bees. H.L.'s torts prof.
Geo. Cruikshank called Civ. Pro. "Handmaiden of Justice," glory
of American legal system: fairness, efficiency, due process. Cruikshank know about beehive class? H.L. surveyed class from back
of room: laptops open to videogames, email, shopping, movies.

   After class, H.L. stopped boy, girl on way out. Boy said beehive class "valorizes" "standards," "norms," "path dependence."
No due process, only honey. H.L. asked boy: H-M teach how to
draft complaint? Motion to dismiss? Boy shakes head, but knows
honey. Boy says H-M is proponent of "legal realism"; law is what
judges do; what judge ate for breakfast more important than what

76

law books say; law follows judge's digestion. Boy spent summer observing judges eat breakfast; will "correlate" observations with judges' decisions. Leverkase is boy's hero; boy helped L. with new book for dean; top secret. H.L. asked boy, what do when graduate? Teach. Teach whom? Other people who want to teach.

Girl asked what H.L. does at law firm; what is law practice like? With girl, H.L. studied portraits on Wall of Heroes: *Tuttle on Contracts. Gardner on Evidence. Peabody on Crimes. Tompkins on Mortgages. Cruikshank on Torts.* Girl asked how heroes prepared H.L. for practice. H.L. asked how girl spent summer. Only 2L, but took bar prep to learn legal rules; watched old movies to see how law practiced: *The Verdict, Witness for the Prosecution, L.A. Law.* Said due process sounded important. No law firm prospects when she graduates, but $120,000 debt. Asked H.L., why didn't someone tell me there are no jobs?

Alone, H.L. again studied Wall of Heroes. Legal giants. Terrors in the classroom. Brutal verbal attacks. Heroes or sadists? How well *did* Heroes prepare H.L. for practice? Better than Beehive Prof.? (Real questions; not rhetorical.)

SEVEN

His discovery made it impossible for Jimmy to stand still. He paced the sidewalk as far as Sidell Hall, the Law School dormitory, executed a military turn, and retraced the distance past the Law School to the Branscombe Geology Building, then turned again. Wendell was at his heels and a khaki-uniformed sergeant from campus security followed a few steps behind. In one hand, Jimmy clutched his cell phone—he had left a message for the dean—and in the other was the list of demands that he had persuaded security to let him photocopy after the officer slipped the original into a plastic sleeve to be dusted for fingerprints. Something more than just the hijacking lay behind Jimmy's restlessness; a feeling of disequilibrium. All was not in order. It was as if the earth's center of gravity had shifted since the meeting in the dean's office this morning.

Jimmy's phone chimed a perfect note-for-note replica of the tower bells in the Administration Building. Flipping it open, he knew from the absence of any salutation who it was.

"What do you mean, the students took over our building? That was fifty years ago. Students don't occupy buildings anymore."

"They didn't take *over* the building. They took the building."

"The *building*?"

"The model." Jimmy unfolded the sheet of copy paper. "They left a list of demands."

Wendell craned to see the list, his elbow brushing Jimmy's arm, but Jimmy turned away. Wendell, being Wendell, was going to find out anyway, but Jimmy wasn't going to be the source.

"How could you let them take the model? Make demands? Who do they think they are?"

"They know very well who they are, Ellie. They are the former college seniors you turned into princes and princesses by recruiting them like football players. Flying them here for admit weekend. Feeding them Joyce's special brownies. Buying them laptops for their videogames. Guaranteeing them jobs. It would be a wonder if they *didn't* think they owned the place."

There was a long silence before the dean said, "I'm on my way. Does the visiting committee know the model is gone?"

"I didn't know myself until I brought them to your office to see it." When he discovered that the model was missing, Jimmy sent the committee to an early lunch at Faculty House, reminding them to return at 1:30—twenty minutes from now—for their first formal meeting with the dean. "Littlefield was curious, but I told him it was being cleaned in preparation for the groundbreaking."

"I'm outside the president's office. I'll be there in five minutes."

If architecture can be revered, Jimmy worshipped the trim Georgian structures that defined State's campus, the sturdy redbrick façades and white-framed windows with their neat mullions and black shutters, the trim dormers peeking out from under slate roofs as plain and sturdy as New England itself. The towering cupola on the Administration Building lifted Jimmy's heart, as did the twin Gothic spires that architecturally had no proper place among the ground-hugging bricks and mortar but, mirroring the towers of the Gothic asylum across the parkway, had their own logical place in the landscape. This is architecture, he believed, that bespoke not only external order but orderly conditions within; the life of the mind, but with hospital corners. *Alles in Ordnung.*

Jimmy's first, private reaction when he discovered that the architect's model was missing was not outrage, nor even concern, but relief. The very thought of that curved glass monstrosity, that assault on the dignity and elegance of academic space by a cabal of New York architects, the very thought of that . . . *thing* being dropped like a giant turd into the backyard of his intellectual

home infuriated Jimmy, who now entertained the brief fantasy
that, like darts in a voodoo doll, the model's disappearance por-
tended defeat for the building itself. Waiting on the sidewalk for
the dean, his fantasy turned to a prayer that the students who
kidnapped the model—the list of demands left no doubt that students were responsible—would somehow contrive to blow up the
building itself.

The dean's red Mercedes pulled up to where Jimmy, Wendell
and the campus security sergeant waited at the curb. The car had
barely come to a stop when Wendell, quick as a sprite, was at the
driver's side, opening the door. The dean handed him the keys
and, when he had driven off, nodded her greeting to the sergeant.
She asked Jimmy, "What was Wendell doing here?"

"He knew they were going to steal the model. He tried to warn
me about it last night. I thought that, with what he knows, he
might be able to help us get it back."

"I still can't believe you let this happen." The dean's frown
dismissed any thought that Wendell could possibly help with the
recovery. When she turned to the sergeant, the midday sun so
struck her hair from behind that the black tresses appeared for a
moment to be on fire. "What can you tell me about this?"

State's campus security rarely finds itself summoned to inci-
dents more challenging than a forgetful faculty member locking
himself out of his office or a depressed one locking himself in, so
a kidnapping, even of an inanimate object, was the kind of drama
that commanded the department's full resources. Regularly consulting his notes, the sergeant intoned a recitation of facts starting
with the duty officer's receipt of a call from the dean's secretary,
then the dispatch of an enforcement officer and police dog, followed by an evidence team, and continuing with the details of the
floor-to-ceiling search of the dean's office and anteroom while at
the same time "securing the premises."

The dean cut him short. "Let me see the demands," she said,
taking them from Jimmy's hand.

"The students may have written the list," Jimmy said, "but
Alex is behind this."

The dean skimmed the list rapidly. "Why do you say that?"

Because Alex is humping Millicent, Jimmy thought. Because Alex has turned my wife against me. "Isn't it obvious? Alex is trying to get leverage for his *special project*. And he's going to use the accreditation committee to do it."

"I don't think so," the dean said. "The students cooked this up on their own." Jimmy saw the wheels turning in the dean's head, polishing her sound bite in the event the press learned of the theft. "It's just a hard-bitten fringe. A few disaffected souls who want the old courses back." She handed the list back to Jimmy, "I want you to stay on top of this. And of course," she said to the sergeant, dismissing him, "your team, too." She turned back to Jimmy. "When's our meeting with the committee?"

Looking up from his watch, Jimmy saw Littlefield, Fairweather and Bioff coming toward them from the direction of Faculty House. "Right now."

"Put the list in your pocket. Not a word to anyone."

As the three committee members approached, the dean put on a determined face, unbuttoned the sleeves of her jacket, and then the sleeves of her silk blouse, and briskly rolled them up each arm. "Well, gentlemen," she said when they were before her, "if you come with me, I've had my conference table cleared so we can get down to business."

They followed the dean into the Law Building, all but Jimmy—who was long-legged and accustomed to the dean's pace—struggling to keep up with her as she took the stairs up to her office two at a time. Lee Brown was waiting in the anteroom, and the dean gestured for the librarian to join them in her office around the empty conference table.

"We all have full schedules," the dean said, "so why don't we get down to business. What do you gentlemen think of our school so far? Professor Fairweather?"

Why, Jimmy wondered, had she started with Fairweather and not Littlefield, the chairman? Jimmy glanced out the window, his thoughts wandering back to the argument with Millicent this morning. He had been frantic to get to the office before the dean, but Millicent, still in bed, pressed her latest complaint. "Do you have any idea how ridiculous it is? You're supposed to be a grown man. A law professor. A dean!"

"Associate dean. I need to go, Millicent. I have a full day."

"It's a little boy's name. A kid sucking a lollipop. *Jimmy*!"

Some men breaching middle age buy a sports car, others have affairs; a handful have gender adjustments. Last year, Jimmy's impassioned lunge at the final significant chapter of his life, his bespoke act of rebellion, was to change his name. After three generations of Jameses, James Fleenor IV would exist no more. Austere, saintly and even kingly, "James" was a name to set him apart from humankind, not thrust him into its bosom. He wanted the human touch. He wanted people, even strangers, to take him into their lives. "Jimmy" was at once amiable and approachable, the very man he wished to be: Jimmy Dean, the down-home country singer and sausage maker, not James Dean, the smashed-up, brooding actor.

"Do you think I would have married you with that name?" Millicent pulled the comforter over her chin. "It's *her*," Millicent said. The dean was always "her" to his wife. "She's infantilized you."

Alex had put her up to this, Jimmy decided. Still, a part of Millicent's complaint would not release him; and within its grip lay the possibility that she was right and that he had made the mistake of a middle-aged man. A sudden flash of insight stunned him: as much as he admired the dean, it was his wife he loved.

Fairweather was still clearing his throat and adjusting his tie when Jimmy picked up his pen. Jimmy was here to listen and compile a punch list of holes to be plugged and cracks to be plastered before the visiting committee members got down to the work of writing their report to the ABA. Jimmy estimated that Columbia's Feckles Professor was about his own age, in his late forties, but fleshy and with a double chin. There wasn't a sign of gray in his slicked-back dark hair. "To be honest, Dean—"

"That's what we want, Herschel—may I call you Herschel?— your complete honesty."

The dean has something cooking, Jimmy thought, some reason for putting Fairweather on edge from the start, as well as for putting him first.

"Well, then, to be honest, I was somewhat surprised by the absence of instructors from the classrooms I visited." The philosopher consulted the legal pad resting on a plump crossed thigh. "I attended three classes this morning. 'Climate Change.' 'Law and Autonomy in the Novels of Saul Bellow.' 'Job's View of Justice.' The instructor was present only for the Bellow class."

Fairweather's tone, Jimmy judged, was more Harvard than Columbia, every sentence a pronouncement, every throat-clearing an alarum. He was a man with aspirations. Was this the card the dean was playing?

"Surely," the dean said, "the students in the other two classes had their laptops open, did they not? I am sure the instructor was on every screen."

"The instructor was on the computer screen, yes, but decidedly not in the classroom." The Feckles Professor of Legal Philosophy stopped, presumably to consider the semantic and deontological implications of that statement. He continued. "One of the instructors, a woman, was chained to a tree somewhere."

"The Amazon rain forest. Marcy Cundiff. One of our most inspiring teachers. She's committed her life to saving the trees. How could you possibly expect her to come to class?"

"Well, the other one was lecturing from a *chaise longue* on what looked like the deck of a yacht on the Caribbean—"

"The Mediterranean," the dean said. "Our faculty work hard, and they take their pleasure where they can. But you know about that, don't you?" Her look took in Littlefield and Bioff as well, and their blank expressions didn't appear to faze her. She's baiting Fairweather, Jimmy thought, but for what?

The legal philosophy professor put up a hand to forestall another interruption. "This is unusual, to say the least. When the ABA asks us to review teaching quality, their baseline expectation is that the teacher we are evaluating will be in the same room as the students. But if they're not even—"

"But they *were* in the same classroom," the dean said. "Just not in person. The ability to transmit images in real time over Skype and FaceTime is absolutely transformational. It's revolutionized legal education."

"But it's not flesh and blood. Face to face." Fairweather's manner was even, his voice steady; he was not a man accustomed to being cut off.

"What authoritative research can you cite that says face-to-face teaching is required for effective education? Superb teaching comes in many forms. Just look at those ads in the *Times Book Review* for great teachers on tape. That company's cleaning up."

Littlefield said, "You're not saying, are you, Dean, that tapes can substitute for live classes with their opportunity for give-and-take? It's been a long time since I was a student here, but that was the essence of our education—"

"But this *is* live, Howard. There's as much give and take as the students could possibly want or need." She turned back to Fairweather. "You're a classroom teacher," she said. "Is teaching such an intimate activity for you that it needs to be flesh and blood? Face to face?"

"Of course it is."

Suddenly, Jimmy saw where this was going. The private investigator hired by the dean had discovered something in Fairweather's past.

"So, you're saying that teaching is no different than a professional wrestling match or . . . a sexual romp in some cheap motel. It has to be face to face to be worth anyone's time. Skype, or even a videotape, is no substitute for the joys of action on the mat or on the mattress. No matter how carefully the camera is positioned and how precise its focus."

The exchange puzzled Littlefield and Bioff but, as understanding crept into his eyes, Fairweather turned pale. The Feckles Professor was no dolt, and Jimmy saw what the dean and her conspiring little sylphs had accomplished. A honey trap. Fairweather had let the two girls lure him away from the party, evidently to a local motel. The girls had this morning briefed the dean and, unless the dean was bluffing, they had given her tapes of the encounter. Part of Jimmy wanted nothing so much as to push the dean out her third-floor window for committing a criminal entrapment like this, but another part of him yearned to embrace her for her outrageous loyalty to the Law School.

"Well, that's true," Fairweather said, recovering and turning to Littlefield, "neither of those two classes was taped."

"That's right," the dean said. "Not taped at all. Our classes never are. They're always live."

"Actually," Fairweather said, "if you think about it, this is a very effective . . . creative way to teach. Real time, right from where the teacher is, on site. In the bush—"

"Very apt," the dean said. "In the bush—"

"—in a rain forest. How better to give students a taste for the real world."

"We're the first school to do this, you know." The dean looked around the table. "It's a huge advance on the state of the art. Much better than tapes. In fact, if anyone has tapes, we burn them." Her gaze returned to Fairweather and, with a beautifully manicured fingernail, she tugged gently at the flesh beneath her eye. "We burn all of them."

"Exactly." Fairweather's color had returned. "This is a brilliant advance in distance learning. You won't mind, I hope, if I report on this to my colleagues at Columbia."

"Better that you report to them than I," the dean said, her smile a crocodile's.

"Live or taped." Bioff had been waiting his turn impatiently. "Here or there. It's of no consequence to me." The small librarian pulled his chair up to the conference table. "It is books that are the heart . . . ."

Jimmy turned off Bioff's voice and returned to his morning confrontation with Millicent. Just as a part of him wanted to embrace the dean for her felonious behavior with Fairweather, so a part of him accepted that maybe Millicent was right after all. *James.* He rolled the name around on his tongue like a grape. Smooth, even elegant. Not choppy like *Jimmy*, which felt like chewing peanuts. For Pete's sake, weren't Jimmies those brown pellets like mouse droppings that they sprinkled on ice cream cones over in Boston? Had his bold decision to become Jimmy been nothing more than a coward's surrender to contemporary fashion? Just look at the U.S. Senate. A nursery of Johnnies, Rons, Pats, Jeffs, Herbs, Als, Chucks, Mikes, Debbies! Even his own state's senior senator, Albie Troxell. Who had started this absurd flight to diminutives? Why, of course, Jimmy Carter. A peanut farmer, a man who probably relished chewing peanuts!

"Whatever the ABA lets you get away with in the classroom," Bioff was saying, "you are surely aware that re-accreditation requires you to have the prescribed number of books—law books—on your shelves."

Littlefield said, "This morning a student told me that law in books is old-fashioned."

"Absolutely," Fairweather said, with a revivalist's fervor. "Rain forests. Skype. FaceTime. The Mediterranean. Yachts. That's the future."

"But," Bioff was turning red, "this re-accreditation review is in the present."

Unless Bioff had uncovered the Law School's second greatest secret, he seemed far more aggrieved than Jimmy thought the occasion warranted, and he wondered if the librarian's resentment was in fact deeper than the dean had represented. Had Bioff discovered the secret? He couldn't have. Brown had camouflaged it too well. Jimmy looked over at the dean, who didn't appear at all ruffled.

The dean said, "How did you find our library, Warren?"

"How did I *find* it? An appropriate question, indeed. I managed to find it only by climbing through piles of bird poop. It's a miracle I found it at all."

"Ah," the dean laughed. "Our birds. The students call it the 'Alfred Hitchcock Law Library.' There are holes under the eaves. The birds nest there. We've adopted them into the State family. And we have all the books that the ABA requires."

"Do you have any idea how injurious bird poop is to books? I promise you, when I start counting volumes, I'm not going to count any with bird doody on them."

"This is an old building," the dean said. "The birds are part of its charm."

"Charm? You have a third-world law library here, Dean Flowers. Harvard's library is older but there's not a single bird in their stacks. My own institution is older, too. Perhaps not as distinguished as yours, but no birds."

State's own librarian, Brown, rarely spoke, and then only in a whisper, as if some great librarian in the sky was eternally shushing the earthly librarian with a finger to her lips. Now Brown said, "I've shown Warren the measures we've taken to protect our books."

"A noble gesture, I'm sure," Bioff said. "Paying the homeless minimum wage to wipe bindings clean."

"Hold on just a second, Mister." The dean's color was up, and she leaned forward to aim her magnificent bosom at Bioff. "Those aren't the homeless, and we're paying them a lot better than minimum wage. Every one of those people you saw mopping up is a graduate of this Law School."

Jimmy had opposed the dean's program to hit her *U.S. News* target by hiring unemployed graduates, but Fairweather looked impressed. Littlefield, however, was shocked. Jimmy's thoughts returned to this morning's encounter with Millicent and the feminine wisdom he had rejected. How many revolutionaries in waiting would have manned up and signed a Declaration of Independence authored by Tommy Jefferson? Agreed to a constitution written by Jimmy Madison? Would Chuck de Gaulle have had the gravitas to rally the Free French?

The dean turned to Littlefield. "How about you, Howard?"

Howard. Would Littlefield's law partners have elected him chairman of their firm if he went by "Howie"?

"I sat in on Professor Hoehnemann-Mueller's Civil Procedure class—"

"I'm so glad," the dean said. "Alternative dispute resolution is the only sensible answer to court congestion. To obscene litigation costs. But a beehive holds the answer only if we look at it closely enough. We're hoping that next year Heidi will be able to teach her course directly from one of the Manuka honey farms in New Zealand."

"A brilliant idea!" Fairweather adjusted his tie yet again.

"Well, yes," Littlefield said. "I also spent an hour studying your course catalogue." He slid out a copy of the catalogue from the briefcase on the floor next to him. "As I told you last night, Dean, I'm still puzzled about the relationship between your curriculum and the training of students for the practice of law. 'Critical Feminist Theory.' 'Political Theology.' 'The Good Life and Living Well.' 'Law and Culture in American Fiction—'"

"That's a typographical error," the dean said. "It's 'Law and Culture in American Film.'"

"A great improvement, I'm sure. But what do any of these have to do with training lawyers?"

Bioff leaned into the exchange. "ABA Standard 302(a)(1) requires each student to receive, and I quote, 'substantial instruction in the substantive law generally regarded as necessary to effective and responsible participation in the legal profession.'"

"Well . . . you could . . . say . . ."

Remarkably, Bioff's interruption had knocked the dean off-balance and, to Jimmy's amazement, he heard his own voice take over from her faltering one. "You're right, Howard. These courses have absolutely nothing to do with what a lawyer needs to know. Indeed, they have as little relevance to the practice of law as the courses you took as a student here."

"But those courses—"

"Think about it, Howard, what did you learn in your Contracts class that has been of any use to you in the practice of law? Vocabulary, and nothing more. Just vocabulary." The thrill of taking charge was in Jimmy's blood now. "What about Civil Procedure? Torts? Criminal Law? Corporations? All of them—

vocabulary! Words, nothing more! We can go down the list if you like. Students as smart as ours can learn all the vocabulary they need in eight weeks. That's the length of the bar review course."

Jimmy glanced for an instant at the dean. Against the pallor of her complexion, her lips looked redder than usual. She seemed, somehow, *clogged*. He had never seen her like this, but he knew that if she were able to speak her words would be much the same. The difference was that, where the dean's motive for reforming the curriculum was to boost State's prospects for entering the *U.S. News* top tier, Jimmy believed that the new courses in fact made better graduates. To be sure, apart from his courses on *The Bluebook*, few State courses bore any relevance to the skills of lawyering. But if the new courses didn't make State graduates better *lawyers*, they did make them better-rounded *people*, and that alone was sufficient reason to install them in the curriculum.

"But what about the Socratic method?" Littlefield wanted to know. "Teaching students to think like a lawyer? Honing keen analytical minds?"

"Standard 302(a)(2)," Bioff said.

Jimmy was astonished that someone still clung to this old belief. "Do you mean *The Paper Chase*? Professor Kingsfield? No law teacher in his right mind has used the Socratic method for decades. If anyone did try to use it, he'd be laughed out of the classroom. The Socratic method is the greatest hoax there ever was. Socrates would have swallowed the hemlock all on his own if he ever saw what law teachers call the Socratic method. There's only one way for us to graduate students who think like lawyers, and that's to admit students who already think like lawyers and then make sure we do as little as possible to ruin them. And we do that by admitting the smartest students we can with the highest LSATs we can."

"When I was a student here—"

"Don't kid yourself, Howard. When you were here, ninetenths of your class were one-tenth as smart as our students today. The reason you've done so well in practice is that you, yourself, are one very smart fellow. I checked. You were first in your class every year. The professors who taught you did their best to turn you into a numbskull, but it's a tribute to your integrity and intellect that they didn't succeed. We've gotten very good here at not polluting our students' minds with all of the hokum that the old men on the Wall of Heroes shoveled at you. That's why we teach what we teach today. It does no harm, and it's a lot more interesting."

The dean's color had returned. She said, "The other reason you've been so successful, Howard, is that you have excellent judgment. You know when to tell a client to move ahead and when to step back. When to file a lawsuit and when to settle. But you didn't learn that here. You learned that by keeping your eyes and ears open as you went about your practice. It may also have something to do with how your parents raised you. But, like Jimmy, I can guarantee you that it's not anything that anyone taught you in a classroom."

"Surely," Littlefield said, "it wouldn't hurt to teach your students some law. Say, how to draft a complaint and answer. I met a girl this morning, a 2L, who gets her law by watching television shows."

The dean had now fully recovered. "If it's law they want, they're free to go to Brooklyn or St. Johns. There are plenty of third-tier law schools that will gladly take their money."

"Third tier?"

"*U.S. News & World Report*," the dean said. "You're talking about schools that take students by the hand and show them where the courthouse door is. You want a trade school. No first-tier law school does that."

"Do you mean to tell me that you let a news magazine dictate your curriculum?"

"Well, . . . no . . . of course not." Again the dean's composure stumbled. "There are just certain academic realities . . . goals. . . ." The words came out in gasps, as if she were struggling for air.

This time Jimmy couldn't rescue her. Nor, he realized, did he want to. To his mind, for a school to make it into the Top Five was not only an irrelevant goal, but a deadly one. Once there, there was no way for an institution to exit without terrible injury.

"Then how do you grade these courses of yours? Or do you think posting grades is also going to ruin your students' aptitudes for law?"

"Of course not, Howard." The dean looked over at Jimmy. "We have a deep and unshakable commitment to grades."

In his years as associate dean, Jimmy had shepherded the last two revisions of the grading system and knew the complete history of grading reform before that. "When you were a student here," he said to Littlefield, "we had the same grading system we had in 1953, when the Law School was founded: grades ran from 4.8 to 2.0, top to bottom, carried to five decimal places so that we could tell you exactly where you stood in your class. Your own GPA, if you remember, was 4.73564, close to the school record. But the Vietnam protests and student takeovers changed everything. Students complained that the system was too hierarchical—"

"I thought that's what grades are supposed to be. Hierarchical."

"I said, '*too* hierarchical.' So a couple of years after you graduated, we moved to letter grades. A+, A, A−, down to D and F. That lasted a few years until the students protested that pluses and minuses are hegemonic and had to go. Of course they were right."

"So you went to A, B, C, D, F. But that also was too hierarchical," Littlefield said, catching the logic, but none of the spirit, of the progression.

"Well, yes," Jimmy said, so we moved to Eagles, Bluejays, Sparrows, Crows and Grackles, but the Audubon people objected. So we went to Honors, Pass and Fail."

Littlefield was bemused. "And since by now you were admitting only the very smartest people to State, none of whom had ever failed a course in his life, you handed out only Hs and Ps."

"Exactly," Jimmy said. "To do otherwise would have invalidated them as individuals. But that created a new problem." Out of the corner of an eye, Jimmy was aware that the dean was nodding her head vigorously, cheering him on.

"Your students were also too smart for Ps, so you handed out only Hs."

"No," Jimmy said, "if we handed out nothing but Hs, there'd be no grading system left. We believe too deeply in grading to do that. What happened was, students were getting Ps on exam papers that were just a hair's width away from getting an H. Maybe the student got an equation wrong or the date some philosopher's master work was published, but on his transcript that P would look no different than a P for a student who never went to class or cracked a book."

"You mean, a student who would have received an F if you handed them out," Littlefield said.

"So, in our last grading reform we gave in to student demand and returned to the system that was in place when you were here—4.8 down to 2.0."

Littlefield allowed himself a smile. "Well, at least that's some good news—"

"But with one small difference," Bioff said, glaring at the dean, and then turning to the others at the table. "According to my research, your students now do the grading. They grade their classmates' exams and papers."

"We used to do that," Jimmy said, "but your research is out of date. We found that the students were far too harsh on each other."

"And?" The challenge to the librarian's research skills had fired his resentment to a boil.

"We decided it would be fairer to have the students grade their own papers and exams. But of course, to ensure precision, they are still required to grade to five decimal places."

"Is that really so?" Littlefield's moustache wrinkled. "You let your students grade themselves?"

The dean waved the question away. "Who knows a student's performance better than the student herself? The system's worked beautifully. For the first time, we've had no complaints."

"I'm sure," Littlefield said.

"Another brilliant innovation," Fairweather said.

Bioff just glowered at the dean.

Littlefield slid the course catalogue back into his briefcase. "To be continued," he said.

"Of course. To be continued." The dean drew back, erect in her chair. "But this has been a productive first meeting. We've learned a good deal about your interests, as you have about our program. Jimmy has been taking careful notes as, I am sure, has Lee."

Brown had neither pen nor pad that Jimmy could see.

The dean rose and, starting to the door, said to Littlefield, "How would you like to attend one of Professor Cruikshank's classes? Compare how we do things now with the way we did them forty-five years ago?"

"George Cruikshank? Is he still teaching?"

"Very much so. He was a young man when you were here, probably no more than ten years older than you. He's in his mid-seventies now."

"Why, that would be very special," Littlefield said.

The dean opened the door for her guests to leave. "I'm sure it will be." Her smile, which took in the whole group, was beatific. "Jimmy will let you know when and where."

When all but Jimmy had gone, the dean said, "You were wonderful with Littlefield just now. You made it sound like you actually believed it."

"I do."

She gave him a curious look. "Well, I think that seeing Cruikshank may help us with Littlefield. But Bioff's a problem and Brown's not the solution." When Jimmy didn't respond, the dean said, "Is there something you're not telling me? You seemed out of sorts last night. In our meeting this morning."

Of course he was out of sorts. Wouldn't any husband be who suffered the unremitting presence in his bedroom of Alex Coyle? Jimmy caught himself. If it were not for Millicent's midlife adventure with Alex, would she have challenged his own midlife decision to change his name from James to Jimmy? His thoughts leapt. If he had let Millicent down by changing his name to Jimmy, had he let the dean down by calling her Ellie? If names create expectations, what would people's expectations have been if Mother Teresa had gone by "Terry?" Golda Meir by "Goldie?" Queen Elizabeth by "Lizzy?" What a profound mistake he had made. He was "James," not "Jimmy," and his dean was no more "Ellie" than was Eleanor Roosevelt.

Still, there were offenses for which Jimmy could not forgive Elspeth. "Were those girls last night underage?"

At first the dean didn't understand. "Oh, you mean my little sylphs. Of course not! Sara's 21 and Hyacinth is 22. They just look like teenagers. Really, Jimmy. I always check my girls' driver's license. There aren't any tapes, either. Or sex for that matter. There was just the two of them romping around on a motel bed in bra and panties with the Feckles Professor of Legal Philosophy. Their job is to stoke the fantasies of our middle-aged donors. But no sex."

"Then why did Fairweather let you threaten him?"

"Because he didn't know that the girls aren't underage and that there isn't a tape."

"And you knew it would work because—"

"Because, among Fairweather's other delicts, the report from the private investigator I hired includes two reprimands for sexual harassment of his students at Columbia. I think that even a legal philosopher understands the concept of three strikes and you're out."

Against Jimmy's will, an idiot's smile formed on his face. He didn't know whether to feel humbled or proud to be working for this woman. "You know, El . . ." The diminutive caught on his tongue. "You know, Elspeth, what you did was blackmail."

The "Elspeth" jarred the dean, and she returned Jimmy's smile with a more modest one. "Blackmail only works if the victim's done something wrong. If it gets the job done, that's enough for me. But I don't want anyone accusing me of running an escort service."

"Never," Jimmy said. "Except you did try to fix Bioff up with Brown."

"Unfortunately, it looks like that didn't take. Keep an eye on them. Make sure Brown keeps him away from the basement."

"The sub-basement, too. What about Littlefield?"

"I wish I knew what he was thinking. Don't kid yourself that anything you or I said convinced him about the curriculum. When's Cruikshank's next class?"

"Wednesday morning. Torts. Do you want me to let him know that Littlefield is coming?"

"No," the dean said. "Just let him be his usual self. Have you talked to Judith about getting Curriculum Committee approval for an Admiralty course?"

"She hasn't answered my email yet."

"Tell her I want this done by Wednesday noon. The Personnel Committee, too. I want to be able to hand Littlefield the key to the lecturers' office before his committee has its last meeting. Are we all set for the closing banquet?"

"Faculty House. Cocktails at 6:00. Dinner at 7:30."

"And then we'll be done with this misery. We can get back to what's really important."

"What about the building model? How do you want to deal with the student demands?"

"We can't let this get out. If the press gets hold of it, they're not going to stop until they have the whole story. And that will be the end of our run at the Top Five."

An idea lit the dean's face. "Find out from Wendell which students are behind this, then sit them down and make them understand that what's at stake is nothing less than their future. If State makes the Top Five when *U.S. News* publishes its list in March, every large corporate firm from New York to Los Angeles is going to line up to interview them. The judges interviewing for clerkships will be right behind. But tell them that if they talk about this to anyone, they can kiss the Top Five goodbye. They'll be lucky to get a job typing and filing for a one-man collections shop. On the other hand, if they keep this quiet and get the model back in my office by nine o'clock tomorrow morning, I can promise them that they'll graduate from a Top Five law school."

"Anything else?"

The dean seemed to be thinking, but said nothing. Then, after a long moment, she bared a look of pain and hunger so fierce that Jimmy saw before him not his admired leader, but an injured and famished beast blundering through deep jungle. It occurred to him that Elspeth's adversary was not the students, nor even Fairweather, Bioff and Littlefield, but some larger, more implacable force.

EIGHT

Wendell took a deep hit off the fatty, held his breath and exhaled deliberately as he considered the shipping boxes stacked in the back of the rented van. This was only the second of his life's great crossroads, and it was going to be far trickier to negotiate than last year's decision to drop out of college. Although his grandfather, whom he venerated, had warned that he would forever regret his decision to leave school, the tedium of a university education—textbooks without pictures, instructors who failed to entertain—had in fact made the choice a no-brainer. Who, other than grandpa, would spend his days in such a dreary place and think it better than a holiday?

In the Big Y parking lot, with the van's windows closed against the evening chill, inhaling and exhaling weed were pretty much the same. Today's decision was one that his college philosophy professor would have called *existential,* involving as it did a choice between (a) the comfortable life of an information manager (the dean called him a blackmailer, but Wendell preferred to think of himself as a knowledge worker) and seller of soft drugs to faculty and students, and (b) taking a giant leap into the unknown, grasping for a business opportunity that would not only push the envelope but shred it. Nor was this opportunity, which alternately beckoned and frightened Wendell, merely about money or power and what they could secure—hotter chicks, a better grade of drugs. It was about growing up—becoming a man who could touch and improve the lives of others. There was still time for him to turn around and go back to his apartment. Wendell glanced into the rearview mirror and asked the boxes in the back, "Where's the Chinaman?"

Kids in costumes—there were many sheeted ghosts in these hard economic times—trailed parents pushing shopping carts filled with Halloween candy and last-minute pumpkins. From his grandfather, Wendell had learned that it is wise to arrive early for meetings, particularly first meetings. That way, when your appointment arrives, you will have established the meeting ground as your territory, not his; you will be the host, he your guest. But maybe Lionel Teng's grandfather had dispensed the same advice as Wendell's, and perhaps the China-based financier had in fact arrived in the supermarket lot before him. The number of Asian faces around him surprised Wendell, and he realized that he had no idea what Lionel Teng looked like. He had checked out QingXing University Law School online only to find that its website was still under construction. There were pictures neither of the school's faculty nor, as Teng signed himself in his emails to Wendell, of its "proprietor."

Wendell opened the window a crack and, like smelling salts, the ammoniac air in the parking lot snapped him alert. He wondered, does working on a university campus actually make people dumber? Wendell's practice when he encountered an unfamiliar group was to look hard at each face and quickly assess whether the person was dumber or smarter than him. Past each countenance he'd proceed: *dumber, dumber, dumber, smarter, dumber.* The dean was smarter than him; but Fairweather, the Feckles Professor of Legal Philosophy, was dumber. How bright could he be to have fallen into the dean's baited trap? A single calm appraisal would have told anyone with a brain north of his zipper that Sara and Hyacinth didn't put out for the middle-aged goats the dean set them up with. Wendell wondered about Teng. From his emails, the Chinaman sometimes seemed smarter, sometimes dumber than him. It would be necessary, he told the stacked boxes, to look the man square in the eye and size him up.

Wendell's correspondence with Teng had started not with an email, but with a letter, one of the few to appear in the Law

School mailroom since the Internet had turned Wendell's domain into a desert. Apart from the occasional bill, bank statement, demand for child support or pornographic DVD, most of the envelopes that arrived for faculty contained glossy brochures and alumni magazines from other law schools, touting their programs and implicitly seeking votes for *U.S. News*'s annual ranking of law schools. To any faculty member who asked him why, with so little paper mail, the Law School needed a mailroom, much less a mailroom clerk, it took no more than a feint and a wink from Wendell to remind the inquirer that this mailroom clerk knew at least one mortifying secret about every member of the faculty, including the dean and the inquirer himself.

It was the postage stamp on Teng's letter to the dean that first caught Wendell's attention: the depiction of the sad-eyed, electric-red bull reminded him of a favorite children's book that his grandfather read and reread to him as a child. The envelope was thin as tissue, but no harder to steam open than the others that Wendell regularly investigated. Teng's letter, following several obsequious flourishes, finally got to the point: he sought the dean's collaboration in establishing the QingXing University Law School as a sister institution to her own, universally esteemed State University School of Law.

It didn't surprise Wendell that, when he intercepted it, the dean's answer to Teng's letter was a polite "No," because, in her truncated view of the world, partnership with a Chinese law school would advance neither of the two items at the top of her personal agenda: getting State into the *U.S. News* Top Five and herself onto the U.S. Supreme Court. So, the dean was smarter than he was, except when she let her own plans blind her to reality. Unlike the dean—and thanks to the side career in ganja sales that brought him into regular contact with the currents of international trade—Wendell understood that the future of world commerce lay not in America, but in China. And where commerce flows, lawyers follow.

Wendell substituted for the dean's return letter to Teng a message of his own, and not on the dean's stationery, of which he had an ample supply, but rather by email, for speed. This is a splendid idea, he wrote to Teng on the dean's behalf, a wonderful opportunity for our two world-leading institutions to work together for the greater social and economic good. I will ask my associate, Wendell O. Ward, who has my full authority to pursue this glorious relationship with you, to be in touch—would a Chinaman understand "in touch"?—in order to arrange for the next steps in moving our joint venture toward a successful completion.

The vehicle that pulled into the parking space next to Wendell's van was the last that he would have expected a sophisticated Chinese financier to drive. (It was also the last vehicle to which Wendell would have expected to see the honored name of Dr. Ing. h.c. F. Porsche affixed—a clunky SUV designed for dentists' wives, not quick-reflexed race-car drivers—although the executives in Zuffenhausen did drop a hint that the SUV was a cosmic German prank when they chose to name it after a chili pepper.) Wendell had left his own Porsche in the driveway of his apartment building and walked the half-mile to the U-Haul depot to rent the van. In transactions like the one about to be concluded, even in the vast Big Y parking lot on the edge of College Station, a Speed Yellow Carrera 4S with the vanity plate, WOWWOW, was no way to preserve Wendell's anonymity.

"Are you the dean's emissary?" Teng said when Wendell came out of the van to meet him. "I was expecting, oh, dear . . . In any event, you are Wen-dall, I suppose. I am most grateful to you for meeting me here."

At once, Wendell felt naked, foreign and dumb. Naked, because his t-shirt and jeans—what was he thinking?—were no match for Teng's impeccably cut, pin-striped navy suit, snow-white shirt and patterned burgundy foulard. Foreign, because, although Wendell was born and raised in College Station and had arrived in the parking lot first, Teng's presence and his elegant British accent had instantly and definitively made the territory his own. And dumb because, well, despite his choice of vehicles, Teng was undoubtedly very much smarter than he was. For the first time in his life, Wendell found himself questioning his grandfather's omniscience. Still, Wendell silently implored his grandfather to instruct him what to do next.

Teng said, "Have you brought the literature about which we corresponded? It would help if I could examine a copy so that I may be certain that it suits our purposes."

It struck Wendell that he had not met anyone like Teng before. Their email correspondence had prepared him for the Chinaman's formality, but not for the fierce energy that lay behind it. No handshakes, no small talk, no opening for Wendell to offer him a joint as he'd planned. Wendell pulled the van's side door open and, with a slender hand, Teng waved away the flood of fumes that escaped.

Wendell pulled out a box from the nearest stack, slit through the paper tape with a car key and handed a copy of the glossy-covered publication to Teng. It was the Law School's annual alumni magazine. Produced on heavy coated stock, the amply illustrated magazine had been ready to mail two weeks ago, shortly after Wendell's correspondence with Teng began.

Wendell must have mentioned the report in one of his emails to Teng, for the next communication from the Chinese law school proprietor expressed a keen desire to see if the magazine might be appropriate to send to Chinese university students and their parents interested in the law school that he was establishing in QingXing. If the magazine was suitable, Teng was prepared to pay Wendell a price per copy comparable to the American newsstand price of GQ magazine. The two thousand copies addressed to alumni Wendell had mailed at once, lest an avid alumnus complain to the dean that his copy hadn't arrived. But the remainder, now in the rented van, boxed and ready for shipping to the dean's U.S. News voting pool of thousands of lawyers, judges and law professors across the country, Wendell had agreed by return email to embargo awaiting Teng's inspection.

While Wendell stamped his feet and rubbed his arms for warmth, Teng leafed methodically through the pages of the magazine, nodding his head in approval, oblivious, it appeared, to the cold. "This is most attractive, Wen-dall. Excellent presentation. Fine four-color reproduction." He smiled at something he saw on the inside back cover and held it out for Wendell to examine. In fine print at the bottom was the legend, *Printed in the People's Republic of China.* "I am certain that the workers of the People's Republic were honored to invest their labors on behalf of such a great law school as yours."

The symmetry of the alumni magazine's roundtrip appealed to Wendell: the publication had been planned, designed, written and edited in the United States; a single master had been shipped to China for printing; copies were then shipped back to the United States where mailing labels were applied; and now they would travel back to China for removal of the labels and replacement with others that would dispatch the magazine into every corner of that vast country, contributing either to a revolution in Chinese legal education or to a landfill-sized collection of super-calendared stock.

Teng reached into an inside jacket pocket. Instead of the wallet that Wendell expected, the entrepreneur withdrew a scarlet ribbon that fluttered in the parking lot breeze as Teng secured it around the copy of the magazine. Gold-printed Chinese characters danced across the ribbon as Teng tied off a neat bow. Teng held the ribbon-bound magazine against his chest. "Do you read Chinese, Wen-dall?"

Wendell shook his head.

"The ceremonial sash has the name of your fine institution in large type and, underneath it, 'First Catalogue of Sister Institution QingXing Law School, L. Teng, Prop.' What do you think?"

"I think that this is a most auspicious beginning to the partnership between our two institutions," Wendell said, trying not to be too obvious in his imitation of Teng's formal locution. "But how many law school applicants in China know English? How will they be able to read the report?"

"Why should anyone want to read it?" Teng flipped through the pages again, this time rapidly. "A few people may look at the pictures. I hope they do, for the pictures of your new building are truly colorful, are they not? But, in truth, all that any of them will want to see is this"—he tapped the red ribbon. "This is all that they will care about. They will take its meaning into their hearts."

"But how will a ribbon—"

"Please, Wend-all, listen to someone with experience in the world. Listen and learn."

This was the voice of Wendell's grandfather, finally answering his prayer for guidance. Listen and learn.

"How many of your countrymen in America, when they purchase a polo shirt with the name of the great designer Ralph Lauren on it, how many of them will take the time to learn the conditions under which that shirt was made? How many will seek to identify the source of the fabric, the details of the needlework? Do they inquire into these matters? No. They just slip on the shirt, puff up their chest so that the polo pony grows erect, and pat themselves on the back for their admission into the international upper crust of the polo set. That label and pony declare to the world, in a voice that these purchasers could never summon on their own, that they are in with the in crowd."

"And you're saying the shirt is a counterfeit. It's made in China. It's not a real Ralph Lauren shirt."

"No, Wen-dall, I am saying that *all* of these shirts are counterfeits, whether they are made with Mr. Ralph Lauren's approval or not, whether they are sold in a Ralph Lauren store or by some urchin on a street corner. After all, in the world of commerce, what is a counterfeit, and what is an original? Did you know that these Ralph Lauren shirts that you call originals and the ones you call counterfeits both come from the very same factory in Qingdao? One is no less a counterfeit than the other."

Wendell shivered in the evening air. He wondered if it would offend Teng if he lit up.

"What I am trying to explain to you, dear Wen-dall, is that, unless the great Ralph Lauren sat down at a work bench in Qingdao and cut and sewed that shirt himself, the resulting product will be a counterfeit."

"Because, if he didn't sew it himself, and it was sewn by some Chinaman, it's just the same as any other shirt sewn by that Chinaman."

Teng frowned at the word, "Chinaman," but said, "Exactly, Wend-all. You are a quick study."

"And by putting that red ribbon on the report—"

"—we are linking our school to your great institution, with a name, just like the name Ralph Lauren, that is recognized and admired around the world." Teng's teeth when he smiled were movie-star white.

In addition to being impressed by the teeth, it struck Wendell that Teng was, in his choice of designers, showing off his very un-Chinese mastery of "Rs" and "Ls." It also occurred to him that, before he got around to writing to the dean, Teng's proposal had been turned down by Harvard, Yale, Stanford, and every other law school higher up than State in the *U.S. News* rankings.

Teng said, "Americans are both foolish and terribly insecure, not only in their purchase of clothes, but of any item to which a designer, a movie actor or even some hip-hop celebrity attaches his name—bed linens, house paint, perfume—also dog food and salad dressing, I am told. In their purchase of a legal education, too, for how different are your *U.S. News* rankings from these labels? This behavior of Americans is even more insane than pushing quarters into a slot machine, for with the slot machine at least there is a chance of winning a prize. But with labels, what do Americans get? A momentary rush of borrowed, but ultimately false, prestige, no more."

Teng paused to make sure that Wendell understood. "However, at long last, after all the many years that I have patiently waited—I am not as young as I may look to you—the people of China have finally grown as stupid as Americans. Even more so, because now they have all the money in the world; literally all the money—dollars, pounds and Euros as well as yuan. The Chinese people will see this magazine with your law school's name and my school's red banner and, without reading a word of this superb publication, they will queue up—no, they will trample over each other—to pay for admission to QingXing University Law School."

Teng untied the red ribbon and replaced it in his inside jacket pocket, at the same time removing a slender white business envelope. "You will, I hope, accept a poor Chinese educator's humble expression of his law school's appreciation."

The envelope, when Wendell took it, felt too insubstantial to contain the amount of money that he had calculated as his due, and for a scary moment it occurred to him that Teng was paying him in Chinese currency. But when Wendell lifted the flap and looked inside, he understood that even a slender stack of thousand dollar bills quickly added up to six thousand copies of *GQ* magazine and several months of payments on the Carrera.

"I like you, Wen-dall. You have a fine instinct for turning ideas into cash. Perhaps you should enroll in law school. Maybe even come to QingXing. You can make a good deal of money as a lawyer, you know."

"Not as much as I can taking lawyers' money away from them. Doing what you do."

Teng beamed at his alert student and turned to the page in the report with the photographs of the new Albie and Renata Troxell Law Building. "QingXing must erect for itself a fine building like this one. Perhaps a building exactly like this one."

"You don't have a building?"

"Not yet. No building, no faculty, no students. But you will, I hope, agree to help me change all that."

This was an existential moment, after all, and Wendell realized that, in sliding open the door of the rented van, he had opened up a whole new chapter of his life. Brief as it was, his exchange with the Chinaman had rocketed him to a new and unimagined realm where the decision he was about to make was the most fitting one he could imagine. It could have been the ganja weed, but Wendell suspected not, for the flutter in his heart felt like the real thing. He was falling in love.

Wendell gestured at the pictures. "That's just the model." And if, as he anticipated, the government seized Randy Barrimore's assets, that's all it ever would be.

"A model, yes, I see. Your dean must have retained a first-rate firm of architects to design it. Do you agree with me that it would achieve a new ideal if we at QingXing could have a building identical to this fine structure of yours?"

"Have you ever been to Hong Kong?"

Teng smiled. "I was born and raised there."

"I read in GQ that a man can bring a suit to a Hong Kong tailor, a suit made by a first-class designer—Armani, Brioni, Zegna, even Ralph Lauren—and the tailor will make a perfect copy of the suit for him. Is that right?" Grandpa's voice was telling Wendell that the best way to make people like Teng, and thus yourself, happy is to keep them on the hook. And the way you did that was by promising them more.

"As I told you earlier, Wen-dall, everything today is a counterfeit. And, of course, China is the leading producer of counterfeits, even though we are beginning to outsource the work to places like Thailand and Vietnam. But"—a wink, another flash of those teeth and a finely manicured index finger pointing at a photo of the building model—"are you telling me that you can bring me an Armani suit? A Brioni? A Ralph Lauren? Something in three dimensions that we can copy from?"

Wendell fingered the envelope and shot a parting glance at the pictures of the new law building. "Let's say, for triple the payment that QingXing has made for this shipment of alumni magazines?"

"Double," Teng said.

Wendell took a moment to create the appearance that he was deliberating. "Double would be fine."

"That would be perfect," Teng said. "When?"

"Tomorrow," Wendell said. "Here. At the same time."

"I hope your Dean realizes how fortunate she is to have a representative as . . . skillful as you. Have you ever eaten authentic Chinese food, Wen-dall? Been to New York's Chinatown? Baxter Street? If you follow me in your van to the offices of my freight forwarder, we can drop off these boxes, and then I will treat you to a true Hong Kong banquet. Bird's nest soup. Roast suckling pig. The works. A feast that you will never forget. How does that sound to you?"

How had Teng guessed that he was experiencing a serious case of the munchies? "That sounds just fine," Wendell said.

NINE

MEMORANDUM
(Dictated but not read)

TO: File
FROM: H.L.
RE: Trick or Treat?
DATE: Oct. 31, evening

Dean says H.L.'s education worthless; Cruikshank, others, charla-
tans; bar cram course all students need. If so, who needs Law School?

Assoc. Dean Fleenor fabricated story about missing model;
shares Dean's views on curriculum. (In Dean's thrall?) Sad; too
good a man to lie. Dean has the goods on Fairweather; blackmail
bright as day. Bioff still bitter; reported to H.L. (confidentially)
mysterious nocturnal doings at Law School cargo dock. A. Coyle
nowhere to be seen; what are "special projects?"

Scotch in hand on Faculty House balcony, H.L. awaits Fairweather, Bioff, dinner. Candlelit jack o' lanterns bob about in
woods below. Children jabber. H.L. dressed up as pirate in youth;
later as sailor; once as girl in wig. Never as Admiralty lawyer. Nip
in breeze; fine fragrance of leaves turning. H.L. senses change like
sparkles in the air about him; nostalgia, no more, but yearns to
connect with boy he was 50 years ago.

Dean still horny as a sea lion in heat; barks, ruts on rocks. All
about her is riggish, fecund scent of low tide.

(Etta: Please ask H.L. Jr. to take H.L.'s place at closing dinner,
Faculty House, Wednesday eve.)

TEN

Driving home, the dean weighed the day's successes and failures. The scorecard was woefully lopsided. On the positive side, Fairweather had surrendered even more easily than she expected. But Bioff gave no sign of forgiving the humiliating encounter with his mother, and Littlefield, for all of his mild manner and courtly nods, was asking questions too hard for the dean to finesse with silt and crud now oozing into every crevice of her consciousness. If Jimmy was right, and Alex had engineered the students' hijacking of the building model, their loyalty to her Director of Special Projects, abetted by their youthful irrationality, may be too strong for her to win them over with the promise of job offers. Press reports of the hijacking would cut short the Law School's climb to the Top Five, and if that happened—hadn't the senator said so himself?—the chances for Elspeth's Supreme Court appointment would collapse.

Then there was the mystery of Jimmy Fleenor. On which side of the balance sheet was he? Although Jimmy rallied to her aid in their afternoon meeting, he had never before opposed her as he had today. Elspeth didn't resent him for this; indeed, a part of her cheered that this ill-starred cuckold was at last taking charge of one corner of his life. But, on the seesaw that balanced power in the Law School, Jimmy's ascent necessarily implied her own decline and ebbing powers. And why, after all these years, had he now decided to call her Elspeth?

Yet another debit: If the SEC proceeding made it impossible for Randy to write his promised $55 million check, or his bank to cash it, Rawleigh would return the university's celebratory silver shovels to the storage vault. The SEC's hubris infuriated her. Randy was no briber of foreign officials. Her billionaire friend had only one defect of character: his fireman's grip on the vow of fidelity he made when he married Bianca, his sweetheart since their days at the University of Oklahoma where for two years he was the Sooners' starting quarterback and she, for three, its loveliest and most exuberant cheerleader. Randy was the only man in Elspeth's 14 years on the prowl whom she had failed to seduce.

Her houseguest must have been watching and seen her pull into the condominium's underground garage, because he was standing in the open doorway when Elspeth emerged from the elevator.

"It's good to see you, Ellie."

Did he know that he was one of only three men who could call her that without incurring displeasure? "Same here, Randy."

He moved aside to let her in. "Thanks for leaving me the key."

When she came into the foyer, Randy took her briefcase and set it down next to the closet door. Soft brown eyes studied her for a long, thrilling minute before he threw his strong arms around her shoulders for a hug, turning only at the last moment so that it was her side, not her breasts, that pressed into him, the same respectful dancer's move that her father employed so many years ago. Elspeth would gladly have lost herself in that embrace.

"You look all worn out," Randy said when they separated. "Can I get you a drink?"

If any other man told Elspeth that she looked worn out, he would be on his knees by now, begging forgiveness, but coming from Randy, the words had the effect of lifting a sodden cloak from her shoulders. "You know, I've always wanted a house husband."

"What would you like?"

"How many fingers is the Boy Scout salute?"

Randy looked down and counted. They'd played this game before. He held them up to show her.

"Good. Bushmills, then. Three fingers."

On a corner of the dining room table, three of the four cell phones were ringing in their chargers and, as he passed on his way to the kitchen, Randy stopped to mute them. "I threw the old phones in the Rhine River. I leased these a couple of days ago in Liechtenstein and put them under the names of companies the government's never heard of. No one's going to trace me here. Make yourself comfortable, and I'll bring us both a drink."

Elspeth went into the living room where Randy had already lit a fire and set a bowl of her favorite smoked almonds on the coffee table. She took the sofa that looked out past the sliding doors and balcony into the woods, kicked off her shoes and put her feet up on the coffee table. The woods stretched all the way to campus, ending a mile beyond Faculty House, but Elspeth thought of them as her private forest, dark and guarded by spirits, an impermeable domain from which no rolling hills or Gothic spires were visible. Under a gibbous moon, jack-o'-lantern lights zig-zagged like fireflies in a bottle.

Randy switched on the lights, but Elspeth said, "Let's leave them off for now. Just the fire." He handed Elspeth her drink and they clinked glasses. "How's Bianca handling this? The SEC?" Bianca, like Randy, was born and raised in the Oklahoma Panhandle. Elspeth had met her once, at a banquet for Senator Troxell in Washington, and—unusual for Elspeth, who from birth got on better with men than women—they were like loving sisters from the start, with not a splinter of jealousy between them, staying up late in Elspeth's suite, talking about men, clothes, places they'd been, with no ambition greater than to talk and to listen to each other. Alone, later that night, Elspeth wondered what it would have been like to have a sister, and decided that it wouldn't have been anything like it was with Bianca.

"Bianca's grateful to you for putting me up. So am I. She sends her love."

Elspeth nodded in the direction of the dining room table. "Were those your lawyers on the phone?"

"P.R. people, too. They didn't want me to drop out of sight. They think I should take the high road and explain my foreign activities to the public. They prepared a two-pronged strategy."

"Only two?"

"They want to paint me as a champion of the little guy, a business leader who spreads his wealth among world's most desperate, most forgotten countries."

"And desperate leaders," Elspeth said. "Like tribal chiefs in the sub-Sahara. I hope the other prong is better."

"They want to get the message out that, despite its moral shortcomings, bribery is environmentally sound, one hundred percent green. My carbon footprint is no bigger than a baby's bootie."

"With advice like that, I'm not surprised you decided to disappear. Who are your lawyers?"

"I've got Curtis, Bradley in New York, Rachman & Summers in D.C. and Ames, Hightower back home in Oklahoma City. They all think they're going to make this year's budget on Randy Barrimore's back. But you know, Ellie, I'd fire every one of them in a bull rider's second if you'd agree to represent me."

Like so many entrepreneurs possessed of unerring business judgment, Randy's instincts for legal representation were irretrievably askew. "You don't want me as your lawyer, Randy. Trust me. But I may have someone for you. Start by telling me what the SEC thinks you did wrong."

"You need to know right off, I didn't bribe anyone."

"I know you didn't."

"How do you know that?"

"Because I know you. I know that, to my lasting regret, you are a completely moral man. Ever since they arrested Madoff and the financial press exposed them for the limp dicks they are, the SEC's been like a hamster on a wheel, chasing any target they can find. Goldman, Sachs. The Wyly brothers. Now you. They're not going to take any of these cases to trial because they know they can't win any of them. Not yours, either. All they want is a settlement big enough to get them a front-page headline. So tell me what they're saying you did."

As Randy described it, the government's civil enforcement proceeding against him for violating the Foreign Corrupt Practices Act was proof of the maxim that no good deed goes unpunished. Three years ago, shortly after they first met, Elspeth had introduced Randy to Marcy Cundiff. Although Marcy was on her way back to the Amazon rain forest to re-chain herself to a favorite tree there, she counselled Randy that if he wanted to apply his wealth and entrepreneurial skills to their highest and best use, he should bring electric power to the smallest villages of sub-Saharan Africa. "Do you realize, these people have to walk for a whole day to get to a place where they can recharge their cell phones? Can you imagine how much improved their lives would be if they had electric power where they lived?"

"But they have the sun," Randy said. "What about solar energy?"

"Exactly," Marcy said. "What you need to do is install solar panels in every small village in Africa."

Within a month, Randy had established the Guinea-Bissau Energy Corporation, with plans to spearhead the installation of solar panels, first throughout that nation, and from there to Guinea, Benin and Burkina Faso. Local government officials were willing to cooperate, but for a price. "We wish to be paid for your use of our sun."

"But the sun's up there," an astonished Randy said. "No one owns the sun."

"But the people are down here," came the reply, through a grinning translator, "and you are on sovereign territory."

Randy acquiesced, but the deal was quickly nixed by his lawyers back in Oklahoma City on the ground that payments to government officials for use of the sun would be viewed as a bribe in violation of the Foreign Corrupt Practices Act, exposing Randy to both civil enforcement by the SEC and criminal enforcement by the Justice Department. Just a year earlier, Siemens had paid a $450 million fine for violating the FCPA. If he could find a way to get construction permits without giving the tribal chieftains "money or anything of value," only then could he proceed. Otherwise, his lawyers counseled, the risk of prosecution was too great.

That was when, in a moment the dean now profoundly regretted, she introduced Randy to the Bucholz twins, Garry and Larry, Quants she had recruited out of the still-smoking ruins of the

Lehman Brothers bankruptcy. In no time the two Quants had devised a complex, leveraged financial cocktail in which, instead of cash, Randy would pay the local officials with debentures composed of several tiers of other instruments, including global short positions, domestic short-shorts, and a mix of long-shorts, with a convertible feature that entitled the bearer to exchange the debentures at any time for a sum specified in millions of Greek drachmas. Greece had, of course, abandoned the drachma a decade ago, when it adopted the euro, so that, for all of its appearance of value, the Bucholz twins' instrument was essentially worthless— at least for purposes of the FCPA—or so the twins attested in a formal opinion letter to Randy's lawyers.

Then, of course, the Greek government began defaulting on its obligations, talk grew serious that the country was about to leave the Eurozone, and banks—initially second-tier Swiss investment banks, and subsequently first-tier megabanks—began buying up the drachma against the possibility that it would once again become Greek legal tender. The worthless instruments devised by the Bucholz twins suddenly had value and became true bribes, and the twins disappeared from College Station. (Because they didn't teach regular classes, but only met irregularly with advisees, weeks passed before anyone noticed that the two were gone.) Rumors surfaced of their sighting, first in East Timor and then in Bhutan.

Randy studied the quietly burning fire for what felt like a long time, then turned back to Elspeth. "You don't have to worry about the money for your building, Ellie. There's $55 million cash in an account in Vaduz with the Law School's name on it. It's yours whenever you need it. That's what I was doing in Liechtenstein."

Elspeth didn't know what advice Randy's lawyers were giving him, but she hadn't the heart to tell him that, if it hadn't done so already, the SEC would in a day or two freeze all of his assets worldwide. "Are you sure you want me to know this?"

"You're as close as family, Ellie. Of course I want you to know. It's your building."

In the fireplace, a log popped, sending up a spray of sparks.

Elspeth said, "There's a lawyer I want you to talk to. Billy Rubin."

"The B.P. lawyer?"

"B.P. Barclays. The Hunts. Madoff, behind the scenes." The one time, Elspeth thought, that Billy kept his profile low. Ask any trial lawyer what the most dangerous place in the entire American criminal justice system is and he'll tell you it's the space between Billy Rubin and a television camera. "Billy's the Law School's next hire. We're making the announcement at the end of the week." Like the groundbreaking for Randy's building, just in time for the beginning of the *U.S. News* polling.

"Where'd you find him?"

"Boston College. Harvard was courting him, but we nabbed him."

"How'd you manage that?"

"Not how you think." Randy didn't have to be Elspeth's lover to know about her sexual appetite. "I reminded Billy that Harvard already has more celebrity litigators on its faculty than any other law school in the country. They don't need him any more than North Korea needs another nuclear warhead. He'd be lost in the crowd. And we beat Harvard on salary." By a significant margin. Still, it was only half what the football coach got, and Billy had more wins last year. An ample slice of the 15 percent budget increase Elspeth extracted from President Bartles yesterday was going to pay for Billy and his support staff of research assistants, investigators, paralegals and secretaries. She was subsidizing a small law firm for him. "I gave him a reduced teaching load to sweeten the offer." In fact, Elspeth had deferred Billy's teaching obligations for a year, and after that he would teach one course every other year, a seminar on white-collar crime.

Randy rose to stretch. In the darkness, silhouetted against the fire, he could have been her father 30 years ago, rising to carry his little daughter to bed.

"Do you want some dinner?" For a self-made billionaire from the Oklahoma panhandle, Randy had a remarkably gentle voice. "I defrosted a couple of steaks. I can cook them up in no time."

"Does Bianca know how lucky she is?" Elspeth didn't wait for an answer. "Of course she does."

"Do you ever think about getting married?"

"Not once. I live on feminism's last frontier."

Randy waited.

"I'm single and I won't settle. A smart, talented woman will marry the dumbest, most arrogant oaf, and she'll tell you it's for money or love, but the truth is she's settling. A man can be wide awake and still be only half as smart as the woman sleeping next to him."

"I read in *Parade* that married people live longer than single people."

"Married people don't live longer," Elspeth said, "it just feels that way."

"Ellie Flowers, Superwoman."

She made a mock groan. "There's a couple of bags of groceries in the car you can bring up when you get a chance. I figured you didn't want to be seen out and about."

"So, steaks for dinner? I think you have the makings for a salad."

"No, we can call out for pizza. But later. Right now, let's just sit here a little longer."

Randy took the couch and stretched out his long legs, again setting his boots on the coffee table. An easy silence settled between them. From their collaboration on the new law building, Randy regularly exasperating the New York architects with his insistence that they trim the structure down to its bare, functional bones, Elspeth had grown accustomed to the Oklahoman's long silences when they regrouped after a rebuff from the New Yorkers. She felt no impulse to break the silence, or to fix whatever she thought the problem to be. Randy's quiet calmed rather than stirred her. Outside, evening had descended and the jack-o'-lanterns disappeared. The forest, still teeming with spirits, was a dark band of shadow against the sky.

Finally, Randy spoke. "I'm sure this fellow Rubin is a crackerjack, and if you set up a meeting, I'll talk to him. But I have to tell you, Ellie, I'd rather have you at my side. You're the smartest lawyer I know. Hell, you're the smartest *person* I know."

"Whatever I know about the Foreign Corrupt Practices Act you can put on the back stoop and watch it blow away. My legal expertise begins and ends with Real Property Law."

"A field that qualifies you brilliantly for the Supreme Court."

"How did you know that?"

"About your nomination? The senator told me. And I'm sure you're going to be a damn fine Justice, Ellie."

Had she told the senator her reasons for specializing in Real Property, or had Randy figured that one out his own? At the start of her teaching career, when she was picking a field in which to specialize, Elspeth had summarily rejected Constitutional Law, not because the field was already crowded with swelled heads— Elspeth was confident that she could out-talk and out-argue the best of them—but because, for a nominee being grilled by the Senate Judiciary Committee, there is no more dangerous field of expertise than Constitutional Law, none that required more slippery evasion by the nominee. And Elspeth would never equivocate in public or private. Dean Flowers, What is your opinion of the Doctrine of Worthier Title? Arbitrary! Abolish it! And the Rule against Perpetuities? Outdated! Too complex! Get rid of it! And second-trimester abortion? I'm sorry, Senator, but that question lies outside my field of specialization.

"When did this girl from a small town in Maine—"

"Skowhegan."

"When did this little girl set her sights on the United States Supreme Court?"

"Long before law school."

"It was your Daddy's dream for you."

This was new territory. They had not talked about family before. "Did the senator tell you that, too?"

"No, but if Bianca and I were blessed with a child—I always dreamed of having a girl—and she wanted to be a lawyer, my hope would be for her to sit on the Supreme Court."

"My father said that what he wanted for me was that I devote my life to something larger than myself. That I should always aim to make the lives of other people at least as good as mine. When I said I wanted to be a Supreme Court Justice, he said that would be just fine."

"Is your Daddy still alive?"

"No, he was killed by a bowling ball when I was still in law school. He was driving in his pickup to deliver a meal to a sick neighbor and a bowling ball flew down from an overpass, bounced once on the pavement and went right through the windshield. The coroner told me that falling coconuts kill 150 people a year."

"No coconuts in Maine," Randy said.

"Only bowling balls."

"What did your Daddy do up there in Skowhegan?"

"He was a fireman, but that was just his job. He was always on the school board or the Board of Selectmen or the Heritage Council. I didn't have any brothers or sisters, but he was a troop leader in the Boy Scouts for years. Deacon in the church." Elspeth felt her eyes fill. It was a long time since she'd thought of her father. Not since five minutes ago, watching Randy in front of the fireplace.

"And your Mama? Is she alive?"

"She was as devoted to her husband as a woman can be. When he died, she couldn't stop crying. I went back to Skowhegan to be with her and help bury my father. She was crying when she picked me up at the airport and a week later, when I left, she was still crying. She even cried in her sleep.

"After that, neighbors told me, she just drifted off. She would show up at the fire station and ask where my father was. She'd walk up and down the main shopping street, talking to my father as if he was on her arm. She went for days without eating. She stopped taking care of herself. In the middle of a Maine winter she would wander about downtown with nothing more on than a house dress. The woman from social services wanted to put her in the county mental hospital in Augusta, but I said no. I was still a law student and had loans to pay off, but I used the money from my father's pension and from selling our house to put her in a private residential facility up there. I still send them a check every month."

Outside, beyond the sliding door, nightfall obliterated the already darkened woods. The inferno in the fireplace sparked and crackled, and the fire's reflection off the sliding glass doors gave it the appearance of springing from the center of the forest. "That residential facility is the finest in the state," Elspeth said. "There are clean linens daily, good food, plenty of activities and doctors and nurses night and day."

"But still," Randy said, "every time you drive by the state mental hospital down here, you think it's your Mama you're going to see at one of those dark windows."

Maybe that's what she loved most about Randy, this easy-going, good ol' boy billionaire who, just when you forget how wicked smart he is, demolishes you with a zinger.

"You're a good daughter," Randy said.

Randy's presence for the time being suspended all of Elspeth's worries. So what if the law building didn't get built? So what if Littlefield and Bioff blocked State from making it into the Top Five, and so what if she didn't make it to the Supreme Court? In that moment, Elspeth's unmet yearnings to be heard, nurtured, loved and laid flew away from her like soaring doves. "Would it stretch your marriage vows to put your arm around me again? Hold me?"

"Of course not. If Bianca were here, she'd hold you herself."

A heavy, muscular arm encircled Elspeth's shoulder and gave it a gentle squeeze.

"You'll do just fine," she said.

TUESDAY

ELEVEN

No leader has greater mastery than her secretary thinks she has, and the dean strained to radiate vigor and self-confidence as she strode past Eve's desk to her office. But Elspeth had tossed and twisted most of the night, kept up by the thunder-claps of Randy's snoring from the guest room and by unrelent-ing anguish over the future. How many years remained before the breasts that sailed like the prows of two great ships into the 11-year-old imaginations of her admiring boy-men collapsed into a bargelike mono-bosom? When would the sexily perched derriere slide to the back of her knees in a porridgy mess? One morning, blinking her eyes awake, she would understand with the certainty of mortality itself that her chances of ever getting laid again were about as good as the chances of State actually displac-ing Yale from the *U.S. News* number-one spot.

But as soon as she saw the object on the conference table, Elspeth let out a cry of joy. For there, where formerly had been the now-purloined model of the Albie and Renata Troxell Law Build-ing, was a pile of typescript one inch thick. The dean's dreams took flight. Bosom and butt each rose a fraction, impelled upward and outward to a realm where the party would never end.

As Elspeth requested, Max had left the cover page blank. All men may be little boys, but women, too, have been known to carry youthful preoccupations into adulthood. In Elspeth's case it was secrets. Big ones, small ones, size didn't matter. So long as it was secret, she throbbed with an almost sensual pleasure. Other than Max Leverkase and herself, no one, not even Eve, knew what lay beneath that blank page, for if word got out of the manuscript's contents, Elspeth's confirmation hearings would turn into a nightmare and the president would at once withdraw her nomination. At some point she would have to explain to Max why the product of his prodigious researches must forever remain unpublished; why, indeed, no more than a single copy—hers— could ever exist.

The dean took a deep breath and turned over the blank page. In crisp 12-point Times Roman was the title that she had only guessed at since the day she dipped into her discretionary fund to commission Max to write the book: *Hanging High: Peckers of the Supreme Court Justices*. "Peckers" was a bit twee, Elspeth thought, but then perhaps Max had already guessed that no one but he and she would ever see the book.

Even as a girl, Elspeth ate the vegetables on her plate before the roast beef, and she opened the manuscript to Max's introductory essay instead of skipping, as she truly wanted, to the, *er,* meat. The introduction consisted mainly of Max wringing his hands over the difficulties he had encountered in data collection. Supreme Court Justices, it seemed, were far more discreet about whom they exposed themselves to than were presidents of the United States, and the Mafia code of *omerta* was a child's crossed-heart promise compared to the vow of silence taken by Supreme Court clerks. There had been no depositions of Beltway lap dancers for Max to draw on, no emails to pubescent campaign aides, no photos on Instagram, no diaries of White House interns.

The introduction also whined that, unlike Max's landmark research into the presidency, his comparison of Supreme Court judicial opinions to their author's size revealed the Justices to possess more nuanced and complex leanings. Extrapolating from his findings on the relationship between presidential size and foreign policy, Max had taken as his starting hypothesis that the more staunch a believer in private property and individual liberty a Justice was, the smaller would be his endowment; or, as Max reduced his hypothesis even further in a footnote, Justices appointed by Democratic presidents would be hung, while those appointed by Republicans ... well, would not. But, try as he might, Max could discern no pattern among the Justices that factually fit the one-to-one relationship between anatomy and ideology that he had found among the presidents. Max was a Quant wannabe to the core, and the abundant pages of graphs and neatly columned charts, the numbing, fine-print footnotes, regressions and equations, extensively documented these failed attempts. As much as the depleted hypothesis crushed Max, it counted little for the dean, whose mind was on inches, not equations, logs, not logarithms.

At last Elspeth turned to the profiles of the Justices. The entries were chronological and, again putting discipline first, she started with the early Chief Justices. Her hero, John Marshall, the fourth and doubtless greatest Chief of all, supporter of a broad role for the federal government in the nation's economic life—well, no surprises there, even for Max. Roger Taney, the fifth Chief Justice and author of the much-lamented *Dred Scott* decision—well, no surprise there either. As she came to the twentieth century, Elspeth slowed, studying the data on the Associate Justices as well. McReynolds, Butler, Van Devanter and Sutherland, the Four Horsemen who opposed Franklin Roosevelt's economic programs, and all of whom would have been shrimp dicks if Max's hypothesis about Justices favoring private property had been correct, were, it turned out, horsemen, indeed. Throughout, Max's exposition, like Max himself, was humorless. Felix Frankfurter, a Justice whose name alone should have invited a sly wink or jest, received only the driest recitation of fact.

Eve's voice over the intercom startled the dean out of her reverie.

"The president's on the phone, Elspeth."

"The president?" *The president!* Elspeth blindly flipped through the pages as if cramming for an exam. She hadn't in her most urgent dreams expected the call to come this soon. The senator should have warned her. The president! But she wasn't prepared to talk. "Tell him I'm in a meeting. I can't get away. I'll call him right back. No, in ten minutes. Get a number."

Moments later, Eve was back on the intercom. "He says it can't wait. It's about the budget."

"The budget?"

"That's what he said."

Oh, Elspeth realized. *That* president.

"Hello, Rawleigh, what can I do for you?" Hopefully, the brusqueness in her tone would warn him to keep it short. She hadn't yet reached the Justices of the twenty-first century and was impatient to get back to her reading.

"How is the visit with your accreditation committee proceeding?"

"Very well, Rawleigh. Not a cloud in the sky."

"Hmmm. From what I hear, two of your committee members have had some difficulty staying focused on their task."

Elspeth's heart thudded. "What do you mean?"

"If you can't keep them academically engaged, isn't there something you can do to keep them out of trouble? Entertain them? A dinner party? Cocktails with faculty—"

"We did that Sunday night." This is ridiculous, the dean told herself. He told Eve he wanted to talk about the budget. She wanted to get back to her Justices. What did the president know that she didn't? "What's the problem, Rawleigh?"

"The College Station police picked up this fellow from Columbia, Fairweather, in a sting operation last night. Downtown. Apparently, he propositioned a decoy police officer."

She should have anticipated this. Elspeth understood as well as anyone—better!—the extremes to which sexual desperation can drive a normally sane person, and it had been a mistake to let her two little sylphs tease the Feckles Professor of Legal Philosophy. But hadn't she instructed Jimmy to mind the Law School's visitors? "Where is Fairweather now?"

"Wendell got him out on bail an hour ago."

"Wendell?" If anyone belonged in jail, it was the mailroom blackmailer.

"Apparently Wendell and this Fairweather struck up a friendship. Your other committee member got himself into some mischief, too."

"Bioff or Littlefield?"

"The librarian. Fortunately, the police weren't involved, just campus security. They caught him climbing over the fence you put up by your loading dock. I can't imagine why you think you need a fence there, especially one topped with concertina wire. It looks like a prisoner of war camp. But you certainly caught yourself a fish, if that's what you were looking for."

A minnow, but a worrisome one, if the president had any idea of why she'd had the fence installed. "Did he tell security what he was doing there?"

"I don't know if they got a statement. You'll have to ask them. Your librarian, Brown, showed up and vouched for him, so they let him go."

Bioff's detention concerned the dean more than Fairweather's, and this time she blamed herself as well as Jimmy. She shouldn't have encouraged the two librarians to tour the campus by moonlight. During their stroll, Bioff must have seen something suspicious enough for him to return last night. But what had he seen? She put a hand over the receiver and, on the intercom, asked Eve to call Jimmy and have him come to her office at once.

"At least," the president said, "I have no worries about Howard Littlefield."

"Do you know him?"

"We've met once or twice in the capital. He seems to be well known there. Well respected, too. He's taken a particular interest in the legislature's Higher Education Committee."

"Well, I'm sure I'm grateful to you for keeping tabs on my committee, Rawleigh." The dean's fingers drummed the cover page of Max's manuscript. "You said something to my secretary about the budget—"

"Do you have any idea how deeply it would humiliate State to have the ABA withdraw your accreditation?"

Where had that come from? Why would Fairweather's arrest or Bioff's detention have any bearing on the Law School's reaccreditation? "There won't be any problem with accreditation."

"Have you cancelled your Friday groundbreaking?"

Where were these questions coming from? And Elspeth didn't like the president's repeated *your.* "Of course not. We already requisitioned the hard hats and silver shovels from storage." Randy.

The president was going to ask her to cancel because of Randy's troubles, and she had to head him off. "We mailed the invitations weeks ago. We ordered a full bar from Dining, and a couple of bartenders." No more amateur catering like the party at Jimmy's.

"Do you know if your donor is planning to attend?"

Again, that *your*. "I don't know anything about Randy's plans." It was the truth. Randy was still hiding out in the condominium, but he had said nothing about Friday.

"Well, if he has any plans to be there, I'm sure you will want to see that he cancels them. Indeed, I—"

"I have no reason to call off the groundbreaking."

"Come now, Ellie. Your Mr. Barrimore is in a state of public disgrace."

"The SEC is only investigating him. I'd tell you that he's innocent until proved guilty, except that this isn't even a criminal proceeding. It's a civil action."

"Ellie, when the time comes that you are charged with the stewardship of a major public institution"—the president's tone admitted no possibility that Elspeth would ever be so charged— "you will understand that we live in a fishbowl. Everyone is watching us. Caesar's wife, and all that. Criminal, civil—it makes no difference in the public mind."

"The SEC investigation will be history by the end of the week."

"How could you possibly know that?"

The dean hated sharing her secrets, but she couldn't risk cancellation of the groundbreaking. "Randy is meeting with Billy Rubin tonight. The trial lawyer. By tomorrow, Billy will have the SEC lawyers begging Randy to forgive them for even suggesting that he did something wrong. Which, by the way, he did not."

"This Rubin is the fellow you just hired at twice the salary we're paying heart surgeons?"

"How much help is a heart surgeon when the SEC is coming after you?"

"That's quite a snappy comeback, Ellie. I wish I'd thought of it when the chairman of the General Assembly's Education Committee asked me why we were paying Rubin so much." The president sounded genuinely aggrieved. "I also wish you spent more time cultivating the members of that committee. Lavishing your considerable charm on them. It could help you out in a tight spot. Help me, too."

Elspeth, who rarely took advice from anyone, balked at taking instruction from a man whose doctoral dissertation had explored the difference in composition between sandy clay loam and silty clay loam. "I'll be sure to go to the capital as soon as we finish with the groundbreaking."

"I'm afraid that until this SEC business is resolved, the ceremony is off."

"You can't do that!"

"It may be your building, Ellie, but it's my ground that you're breaking. And I don't think the senator wants it either."

The dean hadn't anticipated the president's resistance, or its implications for her Supreme Court nomination. It wasn't like Rawleigh to succeed in stymieing her at every corner. Rapidly she reviewed the conversation, looking for a weak point. Finally she said, "Without that building, we'll never make it to the Top Five."

"You told me you already had that locked up."

"People are voting now. If they hear the building is—"

"Then don't let them hear it," the president said. "All they have to see are those fine photographs in your annual report and they'll think it's already built."

"They're just pictures of a model." Why was she letting herself be cowed like this?

"Why would anyone know the difference? You still have it, don't you? The model."

Did the president also know that the model had been stolen? "Why wouldn't I?" The empty space on the conference table now gaped like a hole at the very pit of her being.

"Good," the president said. "You can take it with you to the Supreme Court as a souvenir of your achievements here."

He knew that, too! Elspeth felt violated. If the president knew about the missing model and about her plans for the Supreme Court, what remained of her privacy? "You surprise me, Rawleigh. I never thought you particularly cared about the mundane details of life at the Law School."

"Information, Ellie. Ask the president of any major university what business he's in and he'll tell you: parking lots and information. That's how I spend ninety percent of my time. And with the Law School now making its way to the Top Five, I think it's incumbent on me to learn everything I can about your institution. Prepare myself for press inquiries."

"And the budget?"

"What about the budget?"

"You told my secretary you had something urgent to discuss with me about the budget."

"Oh," the president laughed, "that was just to tear you away from the trash you were reading when I called. You really surprise me, Ellie, spending time on Max Leverkase's nonsense. Actually subsidizing him out of your discretionary fund. As I said, going forward, I'll be watching the Law School a good deal more closely. You're the jewel in the university's crown."

"We blush to have you think of us that way, Rawleigh."

As the dean hung up, Jimmy, who had been waiting at the doorway, came in. "What do you want, Elspeth? I'm late for a meeting with Littlefield."

That *Elspeth* again. And there was the continuing puzzle of Jimmy's crankiness. She said, "What's the story with Bioff?"

"Campus security picked him up—"

"I know. Rawleigh told me. Have you talked to Bioff?"

"He called this morning. He wants to know where to submit an expense voucher for a new pair of pants. His were torn when security pulled him down from the barbed wire."

"Did he tell you what he was doing there?"

"He says he'll only talk to you." The president, Jimmy, and now Bioff. What did these unhappy men want?

"Call campus security. See if he gave them a statement."

"I already checked. He didn't." Jimmy glanced at his watch.

"There's only one reason he could have been poking around in the middle of the night." Through the muck and crud that clogged her consciousness, Elspeth could make out the faint voice of a lone sprite. The voice was warning her that Bioff's discovery was the beginning of the end to the dean's aspirations. "The books. He knows about the books."

Jimmy said, "Why don't we wait until you can talk with him. I scheduled a meeting for 1:30. Eve said you were free."

"It's only a few shelves, after all."

"A few shelves? For Pete's sake, Elspeth, it's two entire floors of books. Virtually the entire library!"

"Consider what a tragedy it would be," the dean said, "if, after all of our hard work bringing the Law School to the brink of greatness, all of this turns to crap over a handful of books."

"Well, we'll find out at 1:30. I have to go. Littlefield's waiting."

"What about Fairweather? Rawleigh told me the police picked him up for soliciting."

"He's out of jail. Wendell found a bail bondsman and put up the collateral himself."

"What kind of collateral could Wendell possibly have?"

"His Porsche."

"Where would Wendell get the money for a Porsche?" As soon as the words were out, Elspeth knew. Wendell was churning his blackmail operation for money as well as power. "Why would Wendell want to do a favor for Fairweather?"

"I don't think it was a favor. It was a commercial transaction. Wendell's not letting him out of his sight. Someone said handcuffs are involved."

"Why do I have to wait for a telephone call from the president of the university to find out what's happening in my own school?" And why was Jimmy, a subordinate, looking at his damn watch again? "I know you have your meeting, but this is important. Why is it that no one tells me anything?"

"If you have to know, Elspeth, it's because people don't find you very . . . inviting."

"Not inviting?" The dean tensed to lift her bosom, then remembered that it was just Jimmy, and relaxed. "What is that supposed to mean?"

"Maybe I used the wrong word. You don't impress your colleagues as being very welcoming. People don't see you as someone with a soft smile and an open heart."

"Soft smile? I'm not some Raggedy Ann doll. I'm the dean of the State Law School! I run this place. How am I supposed to have an open heart?"

"You have secrets, Elspeth. All of these side deals you make. All of these little compartments."

"I don't know what you're talking about."

"Well," Jimmy nodded in the direction of the conference table where the manuscript of *Hanging High* lay open. "There's the money you gave Leverkase to write that book. That was a secret. You surround yourself with secrets."

Not as many as I thought, Elspeth decided. Did Jimmy know about the Supreme Court, too? Would that explain this change in his attitude toward her? "Maybe I wouldn't need to make these private arrangements if people around here could be trusted to do their jobs. Maybe I wouldn't need to know about the criminal activities of my accreditation committee if the colleague who is supposed to be in charge of overseeing their visit saw to it that they behaved themselves."

"You're blaming a librarian because he's interested in a collection of books? A horny philosopher because the teases you set him up with may have stoked his middle-aged fantasies a bit too much?" Jimmy blushed, as if he'd just had an outburst of Tourette's.

For Elspeth, a day momentarily brightened by Max's manuscript had again grown dark, impacted and bone-numbing. "All I want is for everything to run smoothly. No surprises."

"*Alles in Ordnung*," Jimmy said.

"What?"

"Everything in order. The family motto. I'm doing my best, Elspeth. If that's not good enough for you—"

"That's not what I'm saying."

"Then what are you saying?"

This time the dean did lift her splendid bosom, not for Jimmy, but for the sake of her own pride and to put the law of gravity on notice that it would have to wait its turn. "I am saying that if I wanted to waste my life bickering, I'd be married. All of this back and forth is my idea of hell." Just saying the words, telling the truth like that, lifted a weight from her. "Tell me how you did with the students who stole our building."

"They rejected your offer. They said it would be great if the Law School made it into the Top Five and they were flooded with job offers. But getting them jobs isn't going to be enough."

"What do they want?"

"They want to be able to do their jobs once they get them. Keep their jobs. Clients aren't paying $300 an hour for a first-year associate to explain Wittgenstein to them. The students want to know something useful by the time they graduate."

"And what do they expect us to do about that?"

"They understand it's a radical concept, Elspeth, but they were hoping that the Law School could teach them some law. And not just the Bog Dwellers. They're willing to start small."

"And if we meet them partway, they'll return the building? At once?"

"I can ask," Jimmy said.

"We need it in time for the groundbreaking."

"Are you sure you can deliver on this? Actually bring more law courses into the curriculum?"

"All we need is window dressing," the dean said. "Admiralty's a law course. You saw how eager Littlefield was to teach it. And there's Cruikshank. I'm sure we can come up with two or three others. We are a law school, after all. Now hurry along to your meeting with Littlefield."

Jimmy turned to go, but the dean, having basked for a moment in this pale ray of sunshine, wanted to prolong the glow. Of course she would succeed in her campaign to lift the Law School into the Top Five, the first state law school ever to occupy those heights. *State.* Never again would anyone confuse *her* State with the menacing twin-spired pile that slumbered across the parkway. "I gather everything's well with Littlefield? No arrests? No convictions?"

"Everything's fine. He just got out of Luis Morales's class."

"Morales?" A cloud drifted across the sun. "You let Littlefield go to one of Luis's classes?"

"What's wrong with Luis?"

"Luis? Our out-of-the-closet ex-con, ex-junkie Latino? There's no problem with Luis. He's as fine a diversity hire as I ever made. Right up there with Beverly."

"I know," Jimmy said. "I did the paperwork. So what's the issue?"

The problem isn't Luis. It's Littlefield."

"What's the problem with Littlefield?"

"The same problem that apparently afflicts our students. They somehow have it in their heads that it's our job to teach them law. As you know, what Luis teaches isn't always the law."

"Maybe today will be one of the days it is. I'm sorry if—"

"Don't be sorry, Jimmy. Just fix it. Put everything back in order."

TWELVE

It took Jimmy 20 minutes to find Littlefield in the university's Rathskeller, a vast subterranean maze of secret rooms, murky corridors and private alcoves. Jimmy had spent little time in the "Rat" during his undergraduate days, and none at all when he was a law student, for the place was the very embodiment of disorder. The search for Littlefield took him from one dark room to another in what seemed like a meandering chain, but left Jimmy with the feeling that he had all the time been circling through the same five rooms. When at last he found the committee chairman at a table in an otherwise empty nook, Littlefield was dictating into a handheld unit. It wasn't yet noon, but a glass of beer was on the table next to half a sandwich.

Littlefield switched off the device. "I hope you don't mind that I started without you. I've been up since five and I was famished. But please, join me. This sandwich is marvelous. Can you believe, the fellow at the counter told me he made the sopresata himself. Baked the roll, too. In this day and age, in this marvelous place, someone actually prepares food from scratch!"

There was something peculiar about the lawyer's upbeat manner, the glitter in his eyes, that couldn't have come from the artisanal sandwich or barely sampled glass of beer, and certainly not from the Rat's dismal, even mildewed, ambience. Had Jimmy misjudged the sober, judicious lawyer? Was he actually finding joy in recording the Law School's various shortcomings in his report? Jimmy pulled out a chair from a table scarred with decades of penknife engravings, and nodded at the dictation device. "Preparing your report?"

"Without my committee to consult, there's not much I can report, is there? Fairweather's gone missing, and Bioff might as well be. He has some notion about books disappearing, but he won't talk about it to anyone but the dean."

Jimmy knew what Bioff had discovered, and if the visiting librarian wanted to keep it between the dean and himself, that was fine with him. "What about the classes you visited?"

"You already know my thoughts on that." Littlefield's tone was mild, a poker player's.

Jimmy glanced a second time at the paper plate in front of Littlefield. To avoid yet another confrontation with Millicent, he had left home without breakfast, and the sandwich looked inviting. "I'm confident that we have as fine a curriculum as any law school in the country. There's always room for improvement, of course—"

"Like the Admiralty course your dean thinks I'm going to teach?"

"You're having second thoughts?"

"I never had first thoughts. If you must know, after 44 years of practice, the very thought of *demurrage* and *despatch* makes me break out in hives."

The news was not going to please Elspeth.

Littlefield sipped at the beer. "If you really want to know what's wrong with your curriculum, I was just in Professor Morales's class—"

"How did you enjoy it?" Jimmy's tongue swelled around the words, and the question came out more like the bark of a circus seal.

"Enjoy? I don't think that's quite the word I would use. How in the world did State manage to hire that fellow?"

Jimmy had an answer to that, an honest one, and it had to do with the Diversity Office's displeasure at the Law School's hiring three years ago of Mira Comerford, whose résumé had identified her as one-eighth Cherokee, when in fact her great-grandfather, a physician who had won the hearts of tribe members for his gentle and always generous care, had been no more than an honorary member of the tribe. Luis, an authentic *puertorriqueño*, was the school's hastily-made amends. But to tell this to Littlefield would so diminish the Law School that Jimmy decided this would be a good time for lunch, after all. When he excused himself, Littlefield waved him away agreeably. "I have plenty of work to occupy myself here."

It took Jimmy 15 minutes to find the food counter, and while he waited for his order he reflected on the conversation that he had overheard on his way to the Rat. The faces of the three law students, a woman and two men, walking in front of him had been familiar but he didn't know their names. To the men on either side of her, the woman had said, "You're telling me you stole the model from the dean's office, but then you lost it?"

"I don't know what happened," one of the men said. "We had it stashed in the copy editor's office at Law Review—"

"—and locked the door," the other man said.

The woman wanted to know why they themselves had stolen the model.

"The relevant question," the first man said, "is why would anyone want to steal it from us?"

As the woman turned from one companion to the other, she noticed Jimmy a few steps behind them. Turning an attractive shade of crimson, she poked each of the men with an elbow. "Hi, Dean Fleenor. We were just talking about Randy Barrimore. Do you think the SEC investigation is going to affect the new building?"

"I'm sure it won't," Jimmy said. "The dean has it all under control. But I'm sure she'll be grateful for your concern." He wanted to ask the men about the theft, but he was already late for his meeting with Littlefield, so he walked around them, giving a brisk wave as he widened his stride toward the Rat.

Heading back to Littlefield's table with his sandwich and coffee on a tray, Jimmy considered the dean's belief that Billy Rubin's name alone would intimidate the SEC lawyers into abandoning the lawsuit against Barrimore. Rubin might be eloquent and quick on his feet, but did he have the all-important skills required to write a winning brief? In his job interview at State, the trial lawyer couldn't hit even the easiest softballs Jimmy tossed him about proper *Bluebook* form for citing state law decisions in federal court.

The sight of the committee chairman reminded Jimmy that his worries about the missing model, and now Rubin, were just distractions to avoid coming up with an answer to Littlefield's question about Morales. Littlefield was, even now, dictating a memo to the American Bar Association that, Jimmy was certain, would deplore—no, condemn—the quality of teaching at State. What more harm could it do to tell him the truth about why the Law School hired Morales?

"Diversity," Jimmy said. "It's an important consideration these days. Diversity—"

"Diversity!" Littlefield said. "That's it! That's it exactly. Luis Morales is as different from the rest of your faculty as an apple from an orange. He is by miles the best teacher I've encountered here . . . no offense intended to you or the dean."

"None taken," Jimmy said, his heart lifting. Offend me as much as you want. The dean, too. Just don't change your mind. How was it possible that Littlefield could approve of Morales? Jimmy bit into his sandwich. Littlefield was right. It was at once crispy and succulent: just the right proportion between the hard-crusted roll and the layers of sopressata; the salumi itself a succulent balance of spicy pork and unctuous fat; the lettuce, tomato and olive oil astonishing in their minimalism. How, in an instant, had the Rat transformed from a hellhole into paradise? How had abject disaster turned into unsullied grace?

"Was there anything in particular that impressed you about Luis's class?" Tell me what you liked, Jimmy thought, and I'll get more just like him, wherever I have to go to find them.

"In particular? It's hard to say. The man's presence. His eloquence and erudition. His selfless attention to the students, of course. But above all, his ideas. My next stop is the library to look up his publications on this approach he's developed. *Mind-ful Narrative*."

"Don't waste your time," Jimmy said. "You won't find any-thing. Not on *Mindful Narrative*, or anything else." There were any number of reasons why Littlefield's trip to the library would be futile, and Jimmy selected the one that he thought would be least damaging to State's chances for re-accreditation. "Morales has no publications."

Littlefield's features fell. "This is because he's a diversity hire?"

"No, in fact it's because, as strenuously as we can, we discour-age our faculty from publishing. We give them summer stipends to find other things to occupy their time. Travel to conferences. Reading. Hiking. Yoga. Meditation. Expanding their horizons. Deepening their knowledge. Anything but writing and publish-ing. Did you meet Nordstrom at my house on Sunday? Poor fellow refused to hear the message. That's not why we denied him ten-ure, of course, but his publications didn't help. We have a saying at State: publish and perish. Fortunately, Luis Morales under-stands our mission."

"But certainly you have tenured colleagues who publish. What about Professor Leverkase? He told me he's written three books."

"Of course, there are exceptions. I have my two-volume trea-tise on the *Bluebook* that I update semiannually, and you are probably aware of the dean's landmark study of the Rule against Perpetuities. But we paid a price for that. You can find others, particularly among the older faculty. But, as I said, we do nothing to encourage publication."

"Why wouldn't you want your people to publish? I would think that, along with teaching, scholarship is the lifeblood of the academy."

"Plagiarism." Jimmy leaned confidentially over the table, the way he remembered Paul Henreid doing in *Casablanca*. "Inevita-bly, sooner or later, if you write and you publish, you plagiarize. Did you know that in one year alone three senior, tenured fac-ulty members at Harvard Law School were accused of plagiariz-ing other scholars' works in their books? Of course, this was

Harvard—the H-bomb—so naturally they didn't fall out of the *U.S. News* Top Three. But it's also the reason Harvard will never be Number One."

"Surely the professors had an explanation."

"Of course they did. They said they hadn't plagiarized. It was their student assistants who had cribbed their sources and handed the research in to their professors as their own work."

"But the professors copied verbatim what their students gave them."

"That's why they were charged with plagiarism," Jimmy said.

"You're missing my point," Littlefield said. "What if the student assistant hadn't plagiarized? Say he actually wrote every word of the research memo himself. If the professor copied that memo verbatim, he would still be committing plagiarism by putting his name on another person's written product. The student's."

Littlefield was so unprepossessing that it was easy for Jimmy to forget that he had graduated first in his class. Everyone knows that professors have for generations put their name on the work of their research assistants. But who would have the moral courage to label the practice as precisely as Littlefield had: plagiarism. The thought made Jimmy reckless. "I suppose you could say the same about judges who let their clerks write opinions for them."

"Or," Littlefield said with a rueful smile, "lawyers who let associates write their briefs for them. I suppose none of us is innocent."

"So then you understand, the danger of plagiarism is everywhere you turn. Which is why the only safe course is not to publish at all." Even as he went back and forth with Littlefield, Jimmy realized that he was engaging in plagiarism himself, for the words weren't his, but the dean's. He believed deeply in the value of scholarship—how else to push back the veils of ignorance that surround the law like a forest?—and if plagiarism was a worry, then colleagues could simply do as he did with the volumes of his treatise on the *Bluebook*: write every word themselves.

"What about the faculty bibliographies you gave me yesterday? I don't think there was one that didn't have at least a half-dozen books on it. Some must have had fifteen or twenty. Leverkase's list was the shortest of the lot."

"Blurbs," Jimmy said. "Quotes. The one-line reviews that publishers put in an advertisement or on the jacket of a book to get people to buy it. Blurbs are a highly specialized field, and we like to think that at State we've perfected the genre. That's what those bibliographies are: books that our faculty members have blurbed."

"And that's their scholarly output?"

"Don't dismiss blurbs," Jimmy said. "That one- or two-line quote will often be the most important thing about a book. Sometimes it will be more significant than anything inside the covers. It's how a scholar gains eminence in his field, becomes a high priest. When you see Judith Waxman's name next to a blurb that says *Pink Pirates* or some other tract on feminist legal theory is magisterial, the most trenchant critique of false consciousness since a book by some French philosopher thirty years ago, whose name do you remember? The author's? No, you remember Judith's name, the professor who wrote the blurb. After all, if she weren't one of the leading authorities in the field, why would the publisher have asked her for a blurb? So, Judith wins three times over: the author whose book she praised will for the rest of her career tout Judith as the field's leading expert, thus enhancing the author's own credentials; Judith gets invited to all the important conferences by professors who want her to blurb their books; and the publisher continues to ply her with free books and, so, more opportunities to enlarge her reputation."

Again, the words were the dean's, not his; Jimmy thought blurbs were a trick and a deceit. But good citizen that he was, Jimmy plodded on. "Blurbs also get good press for the Law School. A reporter wants a quote on a new Supreme Court case? He may try to reach the author of the latest book about the Court, but it's just as likely that he'll call the professor who blurbed the book. Usually one of ours. Still, even with blurbs, you have to be vigilant. A publisher will sometimes send one of our colleagues some 'suggested' language for a quote. Of course, we have strict rules against that. Every blurb has to be original with the person who attaches his name to it."

"Otherwise he'd be a plagiarist."

"Exactly."

"But if law professors don't publish, what will become of all the law reviews?"

"You mean, ideally?" Jimmy smiled. Finally, here was a topic he could expound on truthfully. "They'd disappear."

"Why would anyone want that? Law reviews are . . . are . . ."

"—are run by law students," Jimmy said. "Do you think that if law reviews actually mattered, law faculties would let students run them? Students! Top to bottom, from the editor-in-chief to the lowliest copy editor, law students still run the law reviews. *Harvard Law Review. Yale Law Journal.* All of them. Can you imagine if *The Journal of the American Medical Association* were edited by a second-year medical student? *The New England Journal of Medicine*? Someone barely out of college deciding what research makes it to the front lines of medical practice and what doesn't? If you told a physician or a biochemist, or an historian or sociologist, that the most prestigious journals in your field are edited by students rather than by the recognized leaders in the profession, they'd tell you you're crazy."

"As a matter of fact," Littlefield said, "I was editor-in-chief of our law review when I was a student here."

Jimmy hadn't known this, but Littlefield had been such a standout at the Law School, it wasn't a surprise. "Then maybe you can explain to me how a student editor who hasn't even taken a course in Legislation is in a position to decide that an article on 'States as Laboratories of Statutory Interpretation: Methodological Consensus and the New Modified Textualism' is worthy of publication in his law review and not just an incoherent pile of nonsense. How does he go about editing the article, this student who doesn't even know the difference between law and equity?"

"Our professors taught us how to read cases and pick apart a weak argument," Littlefield said. An undercurrent of displeasure had erased his earlier cheer. "That was enough for us to separate the articles that were worthy of publication from those that were not. But I gather from your dean that you no longer teach those skills here."

"When was the last law review article published that had any real consequence, either in the world of commerce or the world of ideas?"

Littlefield took a hurried swallow of beer.

"Take a look at the most recent issue of State's law review." Jimmy had lobbied hard for the law review's elimination, but the students who ran it pushed back, believing that editorships would help their career prospects, and the dean had caved in to the student pressure. "What earth-shattering contributions do we have in the State law review this month? 'Tying, Bundled Discounts, and the Death of the Single Monopoly Profit Theory.' 'Mobile Capital, Local Economic Regulation, and the Democratic City.' Real pathbreakers, wouldn't you say?"

Earnest faces of State football teams of the 1940s looked down from framed black-and-white photographs on a wall layered with decades of cooking oil and cigarette smoke. Jimmy said, "I bet there were mornings when you were editor-in-chief that you jumped out of bed and rubbed your hands at the thought of telling some poobah professor at Yale or Columbia Law School that their article wasn't suitable for publication. Sending a note to one of your own professors, maybe even George Cruikshank, saying that he would have to rewrite his article on proximate cause. A bit grandiose for a third-year law student, wouldn't you say?"

The observation must have sparked a memory, because the lively twinkle returned to Littlefield's expression. "So, no books. No law review articles. Just these blurbs of yours. And that's it? That's the scholarly life at the Law School? Reading books and writing one-line book reports?"

"Actually, the more experienced faculty find that they can often write a blurb without reading the whole book. A few pages, maybe even just the introduction, is all they need. Sometimes, the title and knowing the author's reputation is enough."

"And you grant your people tenure on the basis of these one- or two-line quotes."

"Of course not," Jimmy said. "We also weigh their contributions to the intellectual life of the Law School. We take great pride in State's being a lively home to the oral tradition."

"Ah, small seminars. Students learning at the feet of brilliant faculty."

"Well, yes, but without the students—"

The light in Littlefield's eyes went off again, alerting Jimmy to his mistake. "Of course, there's no question that we appreciate an engaging classroom lecturer like Luis Morales. But, as compared to teaching, what really counts at tenure time is how well the candidate participates in our lively faculty discussions over coffee or at the lunch table." Jimmy made a quick decision not to explain MeScrabble to his guest.

Littlefield's eyebrows went up the same distance as his chin dropped. "I thought that universities established tenure to preserve academic freedom so that a faculty member can publish his views, however unpopular, without fear of being fired. But now you tell me that, other than these little blurbs, your tenured colleagues don't publish a thing. They just talk. And not in public, but to each other. So they really don't need lifetime tenure, do they?"

Jimmy had from time to time pondered the puzzle of tenure— permanent lifetime employment; *you can't be fired!*—and the closest he had come to an answer was that he and his colleagues had been magically transported to an enchanted island far from the hard-bitten mainland where workers get fired because their sales, or their division's sales, or their company's sales are down; or the corporation has been sold to a larger one or has acquired a smaller one, or has moved its activities offshore; where partners in law firms—*partners*—are fired because their billables have dipped, their field of expertise has lost its luster, or a key client has moved its business to another firm.

Jimmy said, "I can promise you that Luis Morales will not have a problem with tenure. He lives and breathes the oral tradition."

"Like the great poet Homer," Littlefield said. "*Mindful Narrative.*"

"Exactly," Jimmy said, still not knowing what *Mindful Narrative* was, and hoping that it was nothing like the chancellor's "growing timber," but pleased to see Littlefield's features brighten once more.

THIRTEEN

MEMORANDUM
(Dictated but not read)

TO: File
FROM: H.L.
RE: *Mindful Narrative*
DATE: November 1

Make yourself comfortable, dear Etta, as this memo will extend well beyond my customary few words. To answer your question, why, I can tell you only that less than an hour ago I had an encounter that I believe will irrevocably alter the final chapters of my life. Even now, within the calming embrace of my beloved "Rat," a place that preserves memories of my seven years at State the way amber embalms an insect, these once-familiar rooms appear as alien to me as might the landscape of Mars. Of course, it is I and not the rooms that have changed, and were I to gaze into the washroom mirror, I believe that my own face would be that of a stranger.

What has produced this transformation? Who would believe that a law school lecture could be responsible? I will describe the class presently, but first I must record the business of my re-accreditation committee for, be assured—and you may reassure my partners as it becomes necessary—however dramatically the events of the past hour have reset the bearings of H.L.'s compass, his grip on the more mundane obligations of his professional life has slipped not a degree.

And this matter of our re-accreditation report is, it saddens me to say, a dismal business, indeed. While I have in all of my dealings with the people here in College Station maintained the reserve and probity of a judge, our accreditation report will reveal shortcomings in the Law School's academic program that, I believe, place the school's re-accreditation in great jeopardy. Teachers here literally "phone their classes in" from distant parts, using a computer telephone service called Skype. The curriculum is dominated by classes such as "Political Theology" and "The Good Life and Living Well" that have no observable connection to the professional life of practicing lawyers—and no abundance of glib observations on "relevance" by the dean or her associate dean can alter that fact. I say "our" accreditation report, although that, too, is now in question as Fairweather has disappeared and Bioff seems intent on pursuing his own agenda (or perhaps I should say "vendetta," for he certainly seems to have placed the dean in his crosshairs).

Ah, Associate Dean Fleenor approaches, and even from this distance he looks harried. He is intelligent enough, but I must revise my earlier estimate of his worthiness, so besotted is he with his dean, who appears to have cast some sort of spell over him, much as she did over poor Fairweather. But here he is now. I will pick up my narrative shortly. . . .

Poor, impressionable Fleenor, who has just now gone off to find sustenance. He appeared shocked to find me with a sandwich and glass of beer at 11:30 in the morning, and not at all upset about his being almost an hour late for our meeting. (The beer is an unaccustomed expedient, taken not so much to lift my spirits as to subdue them after my experience in Professor Morales's class.) I fear that I did little to resolve the associate dean's puzzlement over my condition, for I am at a loss to explain to anyone— even to you, Dear Etta, my closest confidante of these past 28 years—the profound personal significance of *Mindful Narrative* as expounded by Professor Morales. But I must make the effort, and there is probably no better way to do so than to record what transpired in Professor Morales's class. By tracking the grooves of the young professor's own *Mindful Narrative*, perhaps I may begin to acquire its method for myself.

Certainly the title of Professor Morales's course—"Real Estate Transactions"—offered no greater hint of what was to come than the title "Civil Procedure" did for Prof. Hoehnemann-Mueller's class on beehives. When I arrived and took a seat five minutes before the class was scheduled to start, the students, perhaps 30 in all, were already in their chairs, hands clasped and resting on the desks in front of them. There was no chatter, but the silence was easy. Indeed, I would call the atmosphere meditative. No laptops were in view; not even old-fashioned notebooks. Here and there I saw a pencil and a small pad or note card. The lights may have been dimmer than in other classes, but that may have been my imagination; no incense burned, but there was an ineffable sweetness in the air.

The figure and demeanor of Professor Morales when he entered Room 217 precisely on the hour was the first definitive sign that this class would differ from those that I have observed so far during this visit, and favorably so. A slender young man, clean-shaven but with a mop of curly, coal-black hair, Morales had on a narrow black suit and, under it, a dark plaid shirt and slender black tie of the type that movie cowboys wear when they dress up for town. He moved slowly, but with a natural grace, approaching the podium as a dancer might, and spoke in a matter-of-fact tone that was somehow at once grave and rounded. This will sound odd, I know, but the only comparison I can draw to Professor Morales's serenity is that of the Dalai Lama, with whom I was privileged to attend a leisurely banquet lunch some years ago at Faculty House, where His Holiness's tranquil dominion over the event transcended even the calamitous fainting episode of our banquet's host, the chancellor. Although it anticipates the development of my narrative—but you may accept this, Etta, as evidence of a beginner's *mindfulness*—I can say here that I left Professor Morales's class with the same glad spirit and lightness of step that I experienced when I left that lunch with the Dalai Lama.

Luis (he addressed the class in the most familiar terms, and I will adopt that voice for myself, as well) was born and raised, an only child, in a public housing project in a notoriously high-crime neighborhood in eastern Brooklyn. Until the death of his father from traumatic brain injury suffered from a falling coconut during a visit to relatives in Puerto Rico when Luis was 11, and his mother's subsequent descent into drug abuse, Luis's family was loving and intact. But then everything changed. Luis, who until that time had excelled as a student, dropped out of school, his sorrow and lack of self-esteem drawing him to a life on the streets and a career that at first involved him in petty theft and small burglaries to support himself. Later, to support a drug habit that ultimately evolved into a costly addiction to crack cocaine, he turned gay tricks for money and, as he reached adulthood, Luis committed crimes of violence as well. His only time away from the street was his periodic confinement in jail or prison.

It was during one such incarceration, his last, that Luis experienced the personal revelation that ultimately transformed his life. As a public school student in New York, Luis had enjoyed a free subscription to *The New York Times*, and in the ensuing years, whether on the streets or in prison, he never once surrendered his daily habit of reading that newspaper—he joked to the rapt classroom that his *Times* habit was no less addictive than crack cocaine. It was in a prison reading room on Rikers Island that Luis came upon the *Times* article that altered the direction of his life. The story was of a Sioux girl on the Devil's Lake Reservation in North Dakota who, at age 11, one day started speaking and writing in a language that none of her teachers, nor her parents, nor the girl herself, recognized; even specialists called in from the university failed in their efforts to identify it. Not until the husband of one of the girl's teachers sent samples of her writings to a linguist at MIT in Cambridge was it discovered that the girl had been communicating with perfect fluency in Myene, a Bantu language associated with Gabon in West Central Africa, a country with which the young Sioux had never had contact, not even through a pen pal.

No one in Luis Morales's classroom even breathed, so absorbed were the students by his story as he explained that, perhaps it was the girl's age—recall, the same 11 years as Luis when his father died—but he sensed that her story was intertwined with his own. The article touched a chord inside him, like a cellist's bow across the instrument's strings, and what Luis heard was akin to music, an internal voice as tonally different from the one he had known his entire life, as Myene was from the Sioux girl's native tongue. However, unlike the Sioux girl's experience, the language in Luis's inner ear was no different than the language of his daily life; it was the very English that he had learned in school. But the voice, the tone, the choice and direction of the words were literally a revelation to Luis, guiding his footsteps, pulling him, even when he resisted, in a previously unimagined direction.

Why did he resist? Luis told the class that he battled this unrelenting pull because it—and its mysterious, beclouded terminus—were completely alien to his every understanding of himself. Repeatedly, he willed himself to leap outside the path laid down by this inner voice and ease himself back into his more familiar, and thus comfortable, life of crime and drugs, but the pain of departing the new path proved too excruciating. For nights on end he found it impossible to sleep. So finally Luis gave himself up to instruction by this newfound voice. And all the while he wrote about the progress of his life down this path—what he called *Mindful Narrative*—as if his pen were a wise and experienced guide taking him safely through a strange city until he arrived at the place where the narrative ended; his new home. By writing, the voice told him, he would find his way.

And where did this path of *Mindful Narrative* lead Luis? Neither to a prison cell nor back to the streets of East New York, but to the very opposite: a three-bedroom pre-War on Fifth Avenue in Manhattan with two working fireplaces and a view over Central Park. Nor was his new life a hell of crack addiction, larceny and gay tricks, but one of practicing real estate law as a partner in the midtown offices of a large Manhattan law firm with branches around the world, and having as his clients all of the great families of New York real estate—the Dursts, the Rudins, the Tishmans and the LeFraks. Of course, Luis did not step from Rikers Island directly into a plush corner office on the 42nd floor of a midtown office tower. High school equivalency, college at City University and Brooklyn Law School at night came first. But that office and that lustrous career, so different from where Luis had started and where he thought his life was destined to end, lay at the terminus of the path dictated to him so compellingly by his inner voice. Luis listened to the voice; "mindfully narrated" his progress; and, as he told the class, when he and his narrative reached the path's end, he "connected the dots" and embraced the extraordinary life to which the path had led him.

By now, dear Etta, the class was on its feet, offering Luis a magnificent ovation. To this day, he told them once the applause died down, on his once-weekly chauffeured commute from his home on Fifth Avenue to his Real Estate Transactions class at State, he still picks up *The New York Times* before he does *The Wall Street Journal* or the *Financial Times*, or *Shopping Center World*, the single artifact of his previous life that he hasn't abandoned.

Luis, having done with his *Mindful Narrative*, and having exhorted his class to *Connect the Dots*, turned to the whiteboard and quickly sketched for them the interlocking legal and financial relationships that lie at the heart of a new shopping center in Dubai, in which Luis is representing the Dutch developer—a dense and dazzling skein of ground leases, first- and second-lien leasehold mortgages, fee mortgages and offshore tax shelters far more complex than anything the real estate boys do in our firm. From out of nowhere, laptops and notebooks appeared on desks, and students took notes as avidly as they had listened tranquilly just moments before. The transition was barely noticeable. But, to be honest, Etta, I was so transfixed by Luis's earlier narrative that I was unable to concentrate on the words and concepts that flew from the front of the room, apparently engaging the students as completely as had the story of Luis's life.

I say that I was transfixed, but I will now make a confession. I was also—and, indeed, still am—deeply disturbed, for Luis's tale not only moved me, but touched a chord in me, just as the Sioux girl's story touched a chord in Luis. It wasn't a cellist's bow, but notes of a deeper, darker timbre, perhaps an echo of whatever the impulse was that I felt last night on the balcony at Faculty House—a tremor in the autumn air portending profound personal change. Last night I thought that it was just a ripple from Witches' Sabbath—always an unsettling passage in these parts—but it occurs to me now that it was something deeper. And, like Luis, I shrink from following this new path—not because I am unsure of where it will lead me, but because I believe that I already know. Indeed, I have every reason to resist the path more vigorously than Luis did, for when Luis first heard his inner voice he lay at the very bottom reaches of human existence; any change in his life could only be an improvement. But, for me, who is now at the top of his career, with neither material nor professional want, what will it mean to take the path of *Mindful Narrative* and ultimately to *Connect the Dots?*

But Fleenor has arrived, laden with food and drink, and he will doubtless want to tax me with more of the Law School's madness about law teachers who teach no law. . . .

Fleenor is gone, off to attend Bioff's showdown with the dean. I declined to join them, using as an excuse my scheduled visit to George Cruikshank's class—now, there was a professor who, like Morales, could hold a classroom in his grasp—but in truth I am already more than sated with the dean's facile spins and deceits. The latest lunacy that she has inflicted on the poor, brainwashed associate dean is that it is a bad thing for legal scholars to write and to publish legal scholarship! But where would the life of the law be today without such great scholarly treatises as *Williston on Contracts* and its dueling foe, *Corbin on Contracts? Wigmore on Evidence? Cruikshank on Torts?*

How bittersweet it is that I must report to the ABA on this latest depressing fact about the Law School's academic practices at the very moment when, in my personal life, I am about to embark on this noble, though inevitably perilous, voyage.

Did Howard Jr. get back to you about taking my place at tomorrow's Faculty House reception? Please tell him the dean will be there and that she is on the prowl for a Hail Mary quarterback. He will understand.

FOURTEEN

The dean weighed the possible reasons for Senator Troxell to be calling against the hard fact that the visiting committee was arriving in less than five minutes. In what she guessed was Bioff's present mood, she didn't want to keep him waiting. But if Randy Barrimore was the senator's most important patron, right now the senator was hers.

"Good afternoon, Senator."

"We just got a call from one of the Justice's clerks, Ellie." There was an echo to the senator's voice, as if he was calling from a long, empty corridor. "The Justice has decided to put off her retirement until next year. Apparently there are some cases coming to the Court she wants to leave her mark on."

"That can't be!"

"I thought you'd be pleased. This gives you another year to make it into the Top Five."

"We're going to make it this year."

"Then you'll have money in the bank when your nomination goes forward next year."

Apart from the fact that Elspeth's plan was to join the Supreme Court in months, not years, a Justice who changed her mind once could do so again. On the present fading evidence of her powers, Elspeth didn't know if she could sustain the Law School's momentum into next year's rankings. Had abstinence ever before clogged her consciousness so obstinately or for so long? It was like being in the throes of some debilitating illness, when it seems that you will never in your lifetime feel better. And nothing can be more damning than to be admitted into the *U.S. News* enchanted circle one year and evicted the next.

The senator anticipated her next thought. "Don't worry about us, Ellie. You'll always have our support—so long as you keep that pretty little nose of yours clean."

The *us* and *our* were a politician's grandiosity; the senator spoke for no more than himself. But at the word "pretty," Ellie heard a small whimper in the background, presumably from one of the senator's aides.

"You've forgotten the magic of the Internet," Elspeth said. "Just imagine if our little video went viral."

The whimper at the other end turned into a groan. "We both want the same thing, Ellie."

"Actually not, Senator. You want to be reelected, which means you don't want Mrs. Troxell to divorce you. I just want to be appointed to the Supreme Court of the United States."

"Then I'd be a bit more discreet if I were you about . . . *ahem* . . . boning up on that study you paid one of your professors to prepare for you."

First Rawleigh, and now the senator. How many other people knew about *Hanging High*? Leverkase had breached their secret. No, she quickly decided, not Leverkase; he was far too terrified of her inevitable wrath. Then who? And how dare the senator attempt to blackmail her! "What makes you think there's a study?"

"Ellie, your law school is leakier than the Clinton White House."

Wendell. It was Wendell. He saw the manuscript when he delivered the bag of taffy to her office earlier. The dean pictured her hands twisting the mailroom clerk's thin neck.

"You really ought to do something about that," the senator said.

"Be assured, Senator, I already have the matter well in hand."

A commotion erupted in the anteroom. Bioff was loudly insisting to Eve that he had an appointment to meet with the dean *right now*.

Everyone and everything were escaping Elspeth's control. The recalcitrant Justice. The senator. Bioff. Wendell. Littlefield. Jimmy. Why do people think that the opposite of control is powerlessness, when in fact it is madness?

"That was smart of you to cancel the groundbreaking, Ellie. With the trouble Randy's in, it would only be an embarrassment."

"I didn't cancel the groundbreaking."

After a silence long enough for him to consult with his aide, the senator said, "We got the word straight from President Bartles's office."

Add Rawleigh to those over whom she had lost control. "Trust me, Senator. You have no reason to be concerned about your name and Mrs. Troxell's being connected to a building paid for by Randy. I promise you, by the end of the week Randy will be completely in the clear."

"How could you possibly promise that?"

"I've arranged for Billy Rubin to represent Randy. I'm sure you know how effective Billy is in getting cases dismissed." She suspected that the SEC wouldn't have gone after Randy if he had spent less lavishly on the senator's campaigns. The more feckless it became, the farther up on its moral high horse the SEC climbed.

"I hope this doesn't mean the two of you have been in contact. If word gets out that you had intercourse with Randy while he was a fugitive from justice, the nomination hearings will blow up in your face. And ours."

"I can assure you, Senator, I've had no *intercourse* with Randy. He's meeting with Billy tonight, and you can count on the SEC dropping its case by Thursday, in plenty of time for our groundbreaking. You will have no need to explain your absence from an event at which you and Mrs. Troxell will be the unquestioned center of attention."

In the anteroom, Bioff's voice had turned still more combative, rousing two or three of the sprites who had been dozing in the bog of Elspeth's consciousness. "I look forward to seeing you turn over the first shovel of dirt, Senator. The Albie and Renata Troxell Law Building. It will be a great day for you and the missus."

"I thought Rubin was a criminal lawyer." The senator must have had another aside with his aide. "The SEC's case is civil. Why would Randy need to talk to Rubin?"

If she was to have any hope with Bioff, Elspeth had to end the call now. "A trial is a trial; it doesn't matter if it's civil or criminal."

"But you just told me there won't be a trial. That the SEC's going to drop this."

How can someone so smart about politics be so dumb about everything else? "The SEC lawyers are going to drop the case because they know that if they go to trial against Billy, they're not only going to lose, but they're going to suffer a profound humiliation in the process. An extravagantly public humiliation."

"Well, let's hope so."

Seconds after the dean put down the receiver, Eve led Bioff into her office, followed by Brown, then Jimmy. Bioff had on an oversized, blousy pair of black gabardine trousers, cinched by a length of clothesline at his waist. With its cuffs abundantly rolled, the trousers gave him the appearance of a court jester, albeit one in ill humor. The dean remembered that Bioff had torn his own pants in the course of last night's adventure and evidently had borrowed the present ones from Brown. He balanced two heavy volumes and a slender, familiar-looking one under a thin arm. In his free hand was a zippered plastic envelope. Brown had the stooped, downcast look of a troublemaker summoned to the principal's office.

"Where's Howard?" the dean asked. "Herschel?"

"Mr. Littlefield is sitting in on Professor Cruikshank's class," Jimmy said. "Professor Fairweather is . . . well . . . I don't know."

"He's with Wendell," Brown said. Always subdued in the dean's presence, Brown seemed this morning to be jittery as well. "He's been with him since Wendell got him out on bail."

The dean took the chair at the head of the conference table, directing the others to their places, making certain that Bioff was immediately to her right, her good side, and then waited while he set down the three volumes and inspected the seat of his chair, presumably for bird droppings. Earlier in the day, she had Eve telephone Bioff's assistant in Chicago to find out what the reference librarian's favorite treat was, then dispatched Wendell to locate a store that stocked Annabelle's Original Atlantic City Salt Water Taffy. When Bioff finally sat, the dean pushed a bowl filled with the wax-paper-wrapped salt water taffy toward him.

Bioff dismissed the offer with the back of his hand. "I will not be bribed."

"This is hardly a bribe," the dean said, "just some candy left over from Halloween. Trick or treat."

"I can assure you," Jimmy said with a smile, "if Dean Flowers wanted to bribe you, it would be with something far more substantial than a bowl of taffy."

Since their encounter in her office yesterday morning, the dean was uncertain of Jimmy's loyalties, and she was glad for a sign that he had returned to her camp. Brown reached across the table and with pale, sausage-like fingers scooped up a handful of candies.

"I think we need to clear the air," the dean said. "I hope, Mr. Bioff, that you weren't seriously inconvenienced by your unfortunate encounter with campus security last night."

Bioff slid a legal pad from the plastic envelope, and the dean leaned over to look. She could ordinarily read handwriting upside down as well as backwards, but Bioff's script was so tiny, each letter barely larger than a grain of sand, that she could make out only that each line was numbered.

"My first observation," Bioff said, "concerns the physical condition of your library. The pigeons—"

"We've already been over this," the dean said. "Yesterday."

"Of course we have been over it." Bioff's smile, small and tight, bore a remarkable resemblance to a cat's anus. "But if I am to make a comprehensive report to the American Bar Association, it must be . . . well, comprehensive. ABA Standard 703, 'Research and Study Space,' requires a law school to provide, and I quote, 'sufficient quiet study and research seating for its students and faculty.'"

"I can assure you that an airtight and one hundred percent bird-proof library will be the central feature of our new building. We break ground on Friday."

"No doubt," Bioff said, placing a check mark next to the first line on his legal pad.

The dean didn't know if the mark meant that he accepted her explanation or was merely confirming the correctness of his own. Across from her, Brown unwrapped a taffy nugget from the now small pile and popped it between two plump lips.

"Next," Bioff said, "'The law library shall provide a core collection of essential materials accessible in the law library. ABA Standard 606(a).'"

This, and not the pigeons, was why Bioff was in her office. The 11-year-old boys at the ABA, who had doubtless been shushed and cowed by librarians since their school days, required not only that an accredited law school's library have books, but that it possess them in outlandishly large numbers, no matter that any source a lawyer or law student needed to consult today—*any* source—was readily available online from Westlaw, BNA, and Lexis. Not just statutes, cases and articles, but texts and treatises. And the law librarians' lobby had not stopped with the mandarins of the ABA. They had similarly intimidated the *U.S. News* staff, with the result that this idiotic number-of-volumes requirement was one of the few points at which the magazine's ranking criteria coincided with the ABA's re-accreditation rules.

The diminutive librarian said, "I'm sure that I needn't elaborate on my concerns in regard to this standard."

A half-dozen more sprites joined the first two in a solid but irregular row, hands positioned like megaphones around their lips, jeering at Bioff. "Elaborate away," the dean said. "We have plenty of time." Maybe Bioff hadn't discovered the full extent of the library's deficiencies. Brown jammed a third pink taffy nugget between thick lips.

"Sunday night, when Lee took me on a tour of your campus, I noticed a convoy of golf carts pulling little wagons across the hills over there." He pointed to the window and the twin spires beyond, but the dean didn't follow his eyes to the awful vista. "The carts passed through the gate in the fence that surrounds your loading dock, unloaded their cargo, turned around, and, then passed back through the gate in the direction of the hills." Bioff could have been describing the Allies' D-Day invasion at Normandy, so close was his tone to the cadences of a black-and-white documentary of decades ago. "Unfortunately, Lee didn't let me stay long enough to observe exactly what was happening. Indeed, Lee seemed quite anxious to steer me away. But I had the clear impression that I was witnessing a shuttle service of some sort between your law school and that institution over those hills."

Brown looked over at the dean. Had anyone with a mouthful of sweets ever looked so miserable? Another nugget disappeared into the swelling jaw.

"The Metropolitan State Hospital for the Criminally Insane," Jimmy said.

"I visited them yesterday morning." Bioff set down the legal pad. "The staff was pleasant enough, but tight-lipped. So last night I returned alone to the area of the loading dock and, sure enough, the golf carts were again shuttling back and forth. I scaled the fence—I don't want to boast, but I was a gymnast in college—and whistled an imitation of a bobolink to distract the driver closest to me." Bioff nodded at the three books piled in front of him. "I managed to retrieve these volumes from one of the carts parked outside. But I hadn't counted on the arrival of your security force and, needless to say, the weight and bulk of the books slowed my retreat when they approached. This resulted in my apprehension, but not before I secreted the volumes in the shrubbery, to be retrieved upon my release."

"All very cloak and dagger," the dean said. "But what does it amount to?"

"Come now, Dean Flowers. Even a humble reference specialist like me, not qualified to lead the library in a grand institution like yours, can see what you're up to. At some point in the past, and for reasons that the staff across the parkway will not disclose, but which I can guess were not purely philanthropic, you transferred the great bulk, if not all, of your library to that institution. When you realized I wasn't going to be a pushover, and that at some point during my inspection visit I might want to look behind the curtain and see if in fact there were any books in your library, you belatedly—very belatedly—arranged for the hospital to lend the books back to you so that you could put on a show for me. But that is all it is. A show. A hoax. A Potemkin Village."

With his index finger, Bioff poked aside the volume of *Wigmore on Evidence*. Beneath it was volume 256 of the Federal Reporter 3d and beneath that, to the dean's chagrin, was her very own slim monograph, *The Rule against Perpetuities Today and Tomorrow*. Bioff rose and gestured vigorously at the volumes as an outraged prosecutor in a not very good courtroom drama might point to the accused. "Are these not part of your 'core collection of essential materials'?"

There had been a reason for the dean to deaccession the law library's collection. In fact, there had been two reasons, both excellent. By emptying out the law building's basement and subbasement where the books were shelved, she had been able temporarily to sate Alex Coyle's ravening appetite for space. And Met. State, which had been ordered under last year's health-care legislation to provide a library for use by inmates seeking release or improvement of their conditions, had both the motive and the funds to assemble a major law library of its own. Met. State paid the dean top dollar for her library collection, funds that she used in part to buy dozens of computers so that students could access all of these "core" materials online. The rest of the money went to the expense of Billy Rubin's recruitment to the faculty.

"Like most libraries," the dean said, "perhaps even your own, our law library lends books to its patrons. In this case we lent some books to Met. State."

"Except it appears that you lent them your entire collection. And what kind of patrons?" Bioff lifted the volume of *Wigmore on Evidence*. "What is someone who's criminally insane going to do with this book?"

"I don't know," the dean said. "Look for errors in the conduct of his trial? Propose reforms to the hearsay rule? However they use *Wigmore*, it's got to be more productive than keeping it on our shelves where, Lee here will tell you, no one has checked it out for years. So we lent it to Met. State."

"Lent? When I went back there this morning, I got one of their staff members to confess that they paid for the books. How many library patrons pay to borrow books?"

"Security deposits," Jimmy said before the dean could answer. "Remember, they aren't only insane over there. They're criminals. Who knows what condition the books will be in when we get them back? *If* we get them back."

In that moment, the dean saw the reason for Jimmy's changed behavior these past two days. Poor Jimmy probably didn't know it yet himself, but inside the head of this son and grandson of German machinists the great turbines of power had started to turn. Jimmy was going to make a run at the deanship. He was going to attempt a palace coup. Well, bring it on Jimmy, the chorus of sprites cried. For, when Jimmy mounted his attack, he was going to find at the battlements a far stauncher defender than the dean encountered when she overthrew Horace Roraback. Until the White House called and she got her day in the Rose Garden, the dean wasn't going anywhere.

Bioff lifted *Wigmore*. "Is this what a borrower does to a book?" He pointed to where the gold lettering on the spine that identified the book as belonging to State's law library had been defaced, and "Met. State Library" rubber-stamped over it.

"That's what I was trying to explain to you," Jimmy said. "That kind of abuse is why we required a deposit. We knew there might be some abuse of the collection."

The sprites were shrieking now. Just thinking about Met. State, and now Jimmy's coup, was giving the dean a headache. "Anyway," she said, "if a law student needs a book, all he has to do is go across the street and borrow it."

"But," Bioff said, reading from the legal pad in front of him, "Interpretation 606-1 of ABA Standard 606(a) says 'All materials necessary to the programs of the law school shall be complete and current and in sufficient quantity or with sufficient access to meet faculty and student needs.'"

"However," the dean said, "if you look at Interpretation 606-4 of that same standard, it says, 'Off-site storage for non-essential materials does not violate the Standards so long as the materials are organized and readily accessible in a timely manner.'"

The dean watched Jimmy's eyes fill with wonderment. Did he have any idea how much a dean needs to know? Does anyone but another law school dean know how hard this job is? How extensively you have to prepare for meetings like this? Meetings with vengeful faculty, ungrateful students and unsuccessful job applicants like Bioff? The Supreme Court was going to be a vacation after her tenure here. But the Supreme Court was not going to happen if she didn't win over Bioff, for not only was the Law School's accreditation in peril, but also the school's ascension to the *U.S. News* Top Five. She said, "My construction of Interpretation 606-4, and really the only reasonable construction, is that so long as students can get *Wigmore* online in our library and a hard copy across the way, that's all the access we need."

"What about your law librarian?"

Three heads turned toward the small pile of wax paper wrappers that had collected in front of Brown. The librarian's cheeks pouched out like a chipmunk's, but seemed frozen in place.

"What about our librarian?" Jimmy said.

"Interpretation 603-1 provides that 'The director of the law library is responsible for all aspects of the management of the law library including budgeting, staff, collections, service and facilities.' I have the clear impression, Dean Flowers, that you have wrested control of the law library from a professional librarian and that you are running it yourself as your own little fiefdom."

"I'm sure that Lee can speak for . . . for . . . Lee." Why did she still not know her librarian's gender? Elspeth looked across the table a second time to check that, jaws engorged by taffy, the librarian couldn't speak at all. "I can assure you that in all matters affecting the library, Lee and I collaborate closely."

The idea flashed through the dean's brain to fire Brown and give Bioff the post that she had originally offered to him, but a second thought stopped her: It would be wrong to fire Brown for being the very coward that she had so purposively hired. She remembered what her father once told her: If you must screw up, make sure that your mistake is one of generosity, not meanness.

Another idea, a generous one, occurred to the dean. "Is your dear mother buried near College Station?"

As the dean intended, the question startled Bioff. "At Cedar Hill."

"Good. How would like you to move here? Be close to your mother's grave. Lee will tell you how great the burdens of running the law library have become"—jaws sealed shut, Brown was turning scarlet—"and now, with the move to our new building, I'm sure Lee would find it a relief to have someone trained in library science take a supervisory position over the librarian, say, an Associate Dean for Library and Services—"

"Really, Dean Flowers, I won't—"

"Then how about Vice Dean for Information Management, at three times your present salary?"

"You cannot imagine how offensive this is. As I told you, I will not be bribed. This is not a bargaining session. We had our negotiation three years ago. And since I am told that you are so skilled at the art, let me say that I am not attempting to blackmail you. No matter what you do or say, I plan to include all of these observations in my report to the ABA."

"This isn't a report, you're describing. It's an indictment."

"Really, Elspeth. I'm sure Mr. Bioff only means that—"

"No, Jimmy, Mr. Bioff is a small, vindictive man." The ragtag sprites had broken ranks and gone amok. Like frantic terriers, they pawed up tsunamis of soil. They shook twigs and branches in vigorous accord. "He solicited his appointment to the accreditation committee with only one purpose in mind: to take revenge on me for what was no more than an innocent oversight."

"The dean is completely mistaken. I am only fulfilling my obligations as the librarian member of an ABA visiting committee."

"Swear to me on your mother's grave that you didn't call that lawyer in Delaware and lobby him to be assigned to this committee."

"For Pete's sake, Elspeth, just apologize to Mr. Bioff, and let's move on."

"Apologize to this little weasel? Where's your backbone, Jimmy?" Drums. The dean heard drums. Her little army was clubbing hollow tree trunks with their twigs and branches. Her eyes spun around the room, freezing at the sight of the wretched twin spires across the parkway. That was when she heard the bagpipes. Kilted sprites on the march, chuffing bagpipes!

Bioff narrowed his eyes at Jimmy. "Since you seem to be the one sane person in this law school's administration, would you please explain to your dean that none of this is personal. It is all strictly professional, dictated by ABA rules and standards. Only a crazy person would—"

In one moment there were drums and bagpipes; in the next the dean was across the table with Bioff's thin neck between her clutching hands, throttling him, just as 20 minutes ago she had imagined doing the very same to Wendell. Even with Jimmy barking words that she couldn't decipher, tugging at her shoulders to pull her from the librarian, the feeling in Elspeth's soul was of blessed release. Jimmy's hands clutched at hers and, after a small struggle, pried them open so that Bioff fell away from her, against the table. Elspeth reached for the volume of *Wigmore on Evidence* and, hefting it firmly in both hands, brought it down with all her force on Bioff's head. The concussion loosed *Wigmore* from her grasp and sent it to the floor. The *Federal Reporter 3d*, when she grabbed it, was for some reason damp and slippery, so instead she seized her own slim volume, *The Rule against Perpetuities Today and Tomorrow*, and with it pummeled Bioff's head, face and shoulders. Astonishing quantities of blood splashed everywhere.

When the dean regained awareness of the room around her, the first thing she noticed was that Bioff's nose lay against the surface of the conference table at an angle that, outside of a boxing ring, no nose should ever lie. Next, she saw that Brown was on the floor with *Wigmore*, prone, jaws locked. The librarian's face was a shade of blue the dean had never before seen on a human being or, indeed, on any living thing. She was aware of Jimmy talking into the telephone, but his voice seemed to be coming from far away. He was requesting ambulances. Had people suffered injuries so serious as to require transport to a hospital?

When the paramedics arrived, the condition of the librarians did in fact require two stretchers—Bioff, because he had apparently suffered a concussion as well as a crushed nose, and Brown to accommodate the oxygen tank and the mask affixed to the librarian's bulging jaws. The paramedics debated between themselves over an emergency tracheotomy and intubation, but decided to leave that to the doctors in the emergency room at Misericordia Hospital, two miles away. (The University Hospital's emergency room, less than a hundred yards away, did not treat trauma victims.)

After the paramedics had gone and Jimmy was mopping up blood from the conference table with tissues from the box on the dean's desk, the dean said, "How much damage do you think we did?"

"*Damage? We?*"

"Well, I don't suppose I changed Bioff's mind about his evaluation of the library." The senator's jest yesterday morning, that State would be the first law school to make it into the Top Five after losing its accreditation, echoed, like Jimmy's voice, as if from a distance. "Stop playing with those tissues, Jimmy. I want you to do some research on whether a law school has to be accredited to be included in the Top Five."

"One man is carried out of here with a broken nose, and who knows what internal injuries. Another is breathing from an oxygen tank. You've seriously injured two people, and you're thinking about the *U.S. News*? Are you crazy?"

This time, at the word *crazy*, the dean turned her insides into steel. She thought of the Spartan boy who suffered the stolen fox hidden in his cloak to bite and tear at his viscera rather than have his theft discovered. "Those two will be fine," she said. "They will be better for the experience. Toughen them up. That's one of your problems, Jimmy. If you want to be a leader, you need to look at the world through a wide-angle lens, not focus on the minutiae of the here and now."

"But you don't have to hurt people to do that. And I don't mean just physically. You trample people's feelings, Elspeth."

Jimmy was telling her that she had somehow injured his feelings, and probably more than once. "It's kind of you to put it that way, Jimmy, but for every person who may have his feelings hurt, or his nose broken, there are dozens that I'm helping. Once we make it into the Top Five, just think how many of our students, students from a state law school, are going to have their first chance at working for a Wall Street firm. Think about your faculty colleagues being inundated with books to blurb, substantial books, and better quality than the fluff they get now." And, the dean thought, think of me escaping this madhouse with dignity and honor. She caught herself. She had never before thought of the Law School as a madhouse, even metaphorically, or thought about its possible kinship to the institution and its inhabitants across the way. She had to change the subject. "Tell me how your meeting went with Littlefield."

Jimmy averted her look. "It went fine. He loved Luis's class."

"That's wonderful. Luis must have stuck to how his students can make a fortune in real estate and spared them another rehash of his memoir."

"No, in fact Luis's autobiography was all Littlefield wanted to talk about. He loved it. But that's not going to help us with the ABA. Bioff's report is going to kill us."

"Maybe not. Littlefield is the committee chair. He controls what goes into the final report, and if he feels upbeat about the Law School, that's a good thing. Littlefield's our answer, Jimmy. He's a clever fellow and a steady helmsman. He is also"—the thought came to the dean in a flash—"the State Law School's inaugural Senator Albie and Renata Troxell Endowed Lecturer in Admiralty Law."

"That's not going to happen, Elspeth."

"Don't tell me Judith hasn't done the paperwork."

"I don't know if she's done it or not," Jimmy said. "But I know that Littlefield has no interest in teaching Admiralty Law."

"You just take care of Judith, Jimmy. I'll handle Littlefield."

FIFTEEN

The pothole was the size of a moon crater, and College Station's corrugated streets had long ago destroyed the shocks on the U-Haul. But, jouncing in the driver's seat, Wendell dove straight into the dip, straining every bolt and weld in the rented van. He was running late and, despite all his planning, Teng was going to arrive at the parking lot before him. Wendell's early-morning quest for a supply of Annabelle's Original Atlantic City Salt Water Taffy had taken him to Rye, New York, setting his schedule back by hours. Shaving, grooming and dressing—pressed trousers, a shirt with a collar (his only one), sky-blue cashmere sweater (a gift from his mother)—had consumed precious time. Then, when he saw that the rutted roads were endangering his precious cargo, he had to return to the mailroom for twine and duct tape to secure the treasure.

"Can't you go any slower?" The voice from the back of the van was plaintive, pleading. "If you didn't completely objectify me, you would understand what it's like to be back here on the floor."

If Wendell had known that his passenger was such a whiner, he would have left him at the apartment and locked him in. He switched on the inside light and glanced in the rear view mirror.

Crouched on the van's metal floor, his outstretched wrists manacled to the struts on either side of him, the Feckles Professor of Legal Philosophy glared back at Wendell. "If you can't slow down, then let me sit up there with you. My butt is killing me."

"You mean," Wendell said, "you think we should have an *Ich und Du* relationship, not *Ich und Es*."

"You know Buber? I-Thou? Why, that's splendid!"

Right, splendid, Wendell thought. "Martin Buber was one of about a hundred reasons I quit college. Kierkegaard. Feuerbach. All of your big-deal philosophers. If I wanted a headache, I could have had more fun getting wasted on Jell-O shots."

"Well, of course, philosophy can be difficult, but surely you had a mentor to guide you through the writings of the great thinkers."

"He sort of looked like you." Wendell shot a quick glance at the rearview mirror. "A fat guy, but just a graduate student. He spent half the course trying to prove to us we didn't exist. We had no reality, he said. One day after class, I went up and slammed him in the gut. Coldcocked him. I said, 'If I don't exist, who's that fat guy lying on the floor and how'd he get there?' I quit school before they could kick me out."

"But certainly you learned, even in a survey course, that an I-Thou relationship, a true dialogue with me, would be immensely more rewarding than I-It, where you view me merely as an object."

"But you *are* an object. You're the collateral for my collateral. My Porsche." Another crater shook the van, and Wendell, watching the road, heard but didn't see Fairweather's head strike metal. Wendell said, "This is the gratitude I get for doing you a favor."

"Favor? What favor?"

"I didn't see a crowd of admirers lining up at the bail bondsman's office." Wendell swerved to avoid a gully, slamming Fairweather's head against the wall. "Your wife, for instance."

"What makes you think I'm married?"

"Of course you're married. No single guy is so dumb he'd hit on a police decoy. Or so desperate to get out of jail he'd pay me forty percent vig on what I paid the bondsman. You would have given me sixty if I asked. No, you're married. I bet the last time you did this, your wife said she'd let you rot in jail if it happened again."

"This isn't fair."

"What—that I'm up here and you're back there? What's fairness got to do with it? I'm protecting my investment."

"How can you possibly believe that fairness doesn't matter!"

This time when Wendell looked in the rearview mirror, he saw the glitter of a preacher's fire in the philosopher's eyes.

"Surely," Fairweather said, "in the course of your college studies, you must have heard of John Rawls. If he were alive and sitting in this vehicle right now, Rawls would tell us that this arrangement—you in the front, me handcuffed in the back—is terribly unfair."

"Would he know you got picked up for soliciting a hooker? That you're a guy who hits on underage girls?" Wendell had dated one of the dean's blondes for a couple of weeks, and knew that the girls only looked underage. But his collateral didn't know. "What would Rawls think of that?"

The Columbia professor ignored the question. "Rawls's great contribution was to posit the 'original position' as a substitute for Hobbes's raw and savage state of nature where some people have power and others don't."

"Like me driving this van and you handcuffed in the back."

"Exactly! In the state of nature, people who are strong enjoy a natural advantage over those who are weak."

"And people who are smart have an advantage over people who are dumb." Wendell checked the mirror to see if the Feckles Professor understood which of them was smart and which one wasn't.

"Well . . . yes. But that's why Rawls came up with the original position. It's one of the most important philosophical ideas of the twentieth century. He hypothesized a situation in which people are ignorant of whether they are strong or weak, smart or dumb."

"That's a lot of ignorance," Wendell said.

"Rawls called it the 'veil of ignorance.' He argued that if people allocated power among themselves from behind this veil of ignorance, that is, not knowing whether they are themselves strong or weak, they will always reach a result in which the weak won't suffer. You ask, Why? He argued that it's because everyone is afraid that when the veil's removed, it's going to turn out that he's one of the weak ones."

More and more, Fairweather was reminding Wendell of his sucker-punched section leader. "Who was he arguing with?"

"That's just a philosopher's convention—argument." Fairweather allowed himself a condescending chuckle.

For someone who hadn't bathed or shaved for two days and was manacled to the interior of a rental van, Fairweather seemed remarkably self-confident. It occurred to Wendell that this knucklehead actually thinks he's winning an *argument*. That I'm actually going to unlock the handcuffs and let him drive. Maybe even clap the handcuffs on myself!

Fairweather twisted in his restraints. "Let's say that, right now, you and I are behind the veil of ignorance. Neither of us would know, when the veil is removed, which one of us would be in handcuffs and which of us would be driving. Only a coin toss would determine who gets to sit where. Would you want that coin toss to be between driving and captivity? Of course not! You'd be afraid that you'd wind up back here instead of me. So you think: I'd rather that the choice was between driving and sitting next to the driver, so that the worst that can happen to me is that I'm sitting next to the driver—"

Wendell smiled. This guy really thinks I'm going to change places with him.

"So, the point is, if you want to reach a just and fair result—"

"But I told you, I don't. All I want is to protect my investment. If I remove those handcuffs and you disappear, the bondsman's going to get my Porsche. And I don't think this guy's ever heard about any vale of tears."

"Ignorance. Veil of ignorance."

"Anyway," Wendell said, working to lower his voice to signal that the conversation was over, "I personally subscribe to Kantian meta-theory." He in fact knew nothing about Kantian meta-theory, or even if there were such a thing, but he'd overheard one earnest law student say precisely those words to another who seemed impressed by it, and hoped that it would be enough to silence the Feckles Professor, whose presence in the van was giving him second thoughts about the wisdom of charity and of posting bail for a stranger.

Wendell switched off the light so that Fairweather couldn't see the sadness that suddenly overtook him. The Columbia professor's mindless rant had indeed pulled back a curtain and confirmed a truth about academic life that Wendell had previously glimpsed, but only as a fleeting shadow on the wall: Academics *do* live behind a veil of ignorance. No State law professor had even the loosest grasp on the hard facts of the real world. But why did the confirmation of this truth sadden Wendell as it did? Was it that he felt diminished, taking money from these people? The phrase popped into his mind, "Like candy from a baby." He was meant for greater challenges than this.

The sadness dissolved at the sight of Lionel Teng's black Cayenne in the Big Y parking lot. The Chinese law school proprietor had arrived before him, but Wendell was surprised to discover that he felt only joy, not resentment, at seeing him here. Teng was a true mentor who, like his grandfather, could give him the inside edge on life's otherwise hard-learned lessons, a man who could lead Wendell to challenges of which he was worthy. And a man with whom Wendell could make a great deal of money. Even at his young age, Wendell understood that there is no bond between two human beings quite like the bond of making mountains of money together.

Teng had on another impeccably cut suit, this one with a subtle nailhead weave, and he looked as out of place among the dinnertime shoppers pushing carts as would a visiting royal. "Good evening, Wen-dall. You are looking very snappy."

Wendell hoped that the dark of evening masked his embarrassed flush.

"Have you brought your Ralph Lauren Purple Label suit with you so that my Hong Kong tailor may make a copy?"

There was no suit, and of course Teng meant the model of the new law building. The law school proprietor was once again showing off his mastery of R's and L's.

Wendell reached into the passenger compartment, switched on the inside light and threw back the side door of the van. Teng's eyes went immediately to the balsa wood maquette that Wendell had carefully secured to the van's interior. The model lacked the dramatic spotlighting that had illuminated it on the dean's conference table but, between the overhead light and the indirect illumination from the shopping center parking lot, it still possessed a magical glow.

A sigh escaped Teng. "This is even more magnificent than I imagined from the pictures in your magazine. This building perfectly captures the noble aspirations of the QingXing Law School."

So transfixed was Teng by the model, inspecting every corner, peering into the doll's-house corridors populated by tiny mannequins, that he appeared not to notice Fairweather, his manacled arms stretched crucifix-like against the wall of the van. The fear across the Feckles Professor's face was that of an abject supplicant. Finally, after some minutes, Teng said, "My, my, Wen-dall. One of your friends from the drug trade?"

Wendell wondered how Teng knew about the drugs until he remembered the fumes that almost overpowered his new business partner when he opened the van door yesterday. "No, he's a law professor from Columbia."

"Bogota or New York?"

"New York," Fairweather said, rattling his handcuffs.

Teng shot Wendell a shrewd look, but his voice was gay. "Does he come with the building?"

Wendell guessed that the laughter at the back of Teng's question was to let him know that he was joking, but not so much that this couldn't become the subject of further discussions. "Perhaps. But not today," he said. "Are you sure the building will fit the architectural style of your campus?" Wendell loved the new building's contrast to State's stodgy architecture, but he realized that he lacked even the flimsiest concept of Chinese architecture. Was it all steep-roofed pagodas, or was that Japan?

Teng's laughter broke open, and then he lowered his voice so that Fairweather couldn't hear. "Our campus? Dear Wen-dall, you are as close as a business partner now, so I can tell you in confidence that there is no campus to speak of, not yet. Just eighty hectares of land. The land is level, though, and there are some wooden barracks left from the old days when it was used as a political re-education camp. The prisoners built the structures themselves. I will be marketing them as artisan dwellings."

"You're going to use them as dormitories?"

"No, in fact I plan to rent them out as faculty housing. How many law schools today offer their instructors below-market rate apartments? NYU, I understand. But what others? This should be a strong selling point in faculty recruitment."

"And the students?"

"Sleeping bags. There is nothing like living in the open air, out in nature, to invigorate a lively mind. We'll sew the QingXing Law School crest onto the bags and sell them for three times what they'd bring otherwise. Just like our friend Ralph Lauren."

If Wendell thought that he had fallen in love with Teng yesterday, he was wrong. It had been infatuation at best; a crush. What he felt now was true love. "So your selling point is QingXing's natural beauty."

"Natural beauty?" Teng threw an avuncular arm around Wendell's shoulder. "QingXing, dear Wen-dall, is a shithole. It is a barren marshland, a breeding ground for scorpions. Also for mosquitos and all of the diseases that they carry. The reason there aren't more mosquitos is that the toxic waste in the water supply keeps the insect population down. The air is so thick with fumes from the surrounding chemical plants that on boiling-hot days, and there are many such days, the atmosphere actually condenses into plastic pellets, literally millions the size of hail stones, that fall like snow."

"Then why are you building there?" Wendell was sure that he knew the answer, but he wanted to test his entrepreneurial imagination against his mentor's.

"For the very best reason, Wen-dall. QingXing is in the west of China where land is cheap, and it is close to Vietnam which, per square meter, has even more money-hungry capitalists than China. Do I gather that you are pleased to learn that your sister school is so ideally situated?"

"I am. But how do you know that students will come?"

"If you look at the statistics as I have, Wen-dall, you will see that the school can't possibly fail. First, there is a phenomenal demand for law and legal education in China. In no time at all, the country will give the appearance of being governed by the rule of law. The Chinese people's innate greed to acquire and hold on to property guarantees that. And how can one prosper under an apparent rule of law without a well-trained lawyer at his side? And if, as your great American visionary Thomas Friedman tells us, the world is flat, and our businessmen are to compete on a level playing field with yours, then the lawyers advising them must be every inch as clever as yours.

"Second," Teng gestured in the direction of the maquette, "we will have the finest law school building in all of China." He reached into an inside pocket of his coat and withdrew a long white envelope, gazing as he did so at Fairweather. "And there is a third selling point that I hope you will be willing to discuss with me as well. But, before that, please satisfy my curiosity. What does a young man in America do with all this money?" He handed the envelope to Wendell.

The envelope had the same heft as yesterday's, and Wendell didn't bother to open it. He trusted his new partner, but not enough to disclose to him that the money would go to pay off an acquisition as frivolous as a Porsche. He started away from the van, where Fairweather might overhear him, and touched Teng's elbow to follow. "You could say that it's my college fund."

"How admirable! When do you plan to matriculate?'

"I already have. I spent two years at Harvard." Few people knew this, and no one at the Law School but, as with the money in the envelope, Wendell trusted Teng. "It didn't take too much research for me to figure out that Bill Gates and Steve Jobs and

Mark Zuckerberg wouldn't have made the fortunes they did if they had stayed at Harvard. So I dropped out, too."

"Reed," Teng said, surprising Wendell. "Jobs went to Reed College. You should read his biography. But you are right. He was also a dropout."

"Oh," Wendell said. What a magnificent world he was now entering, in which your pedigree is burnished not by the university from which you graduated, but by the one from which you dropped out. If only he had dropped out of Stanford, not Harvard!

"I'm giving myself another six months to accumulate some real wealth, and if I don't succeed, I'll go back to Cambridge. It's as good a place as any to make connections."

"And sometimes even to get an education," Teng said.

Wendell experienced a sudden, inexplicable burst of pride for his forsaken school. "Did you know that John Rawls was on the Harvard faculty?" Although Rawls was dead by the time Wendell enrolled, *A Theory of Justice* figured importantly in the philosophy class where he coldcocked his section leader. So did *Arrow's Impossibility Theorem* that the new guy, Hubbell, now one of his biggest ganja customers, was tripping on at the party Sunday night.

"The political philosopher? *The Veil of Ignorance*? Of course. I myself attended the other Cambridge. In England." His smile turned shy. "But, like you, I dropped out."

If only Wendell's grandfather could see him! Standing in a supermarket parking lot, talking one on one with Teng as he might with Gates or Zuckerberg. "And because you made your fortune," Wendell said, "you didn't have to go back."

Fairweather may have overheard Teng's mention of the *Veil of Ignorance*, because he called out from the van, "Could you please ask this fellow to release me from these handcuffs?"

"Why should I want to do that?" Teng winked at Wendell. "We can hear you perfectly well from where you are."

"Because," Fairweather shouted, "it's not fair for me to be locked up here. You're a Cambridge man. Surely you understand that."

"Fair or not," Teng said, "it is against my code to interfere with another businessman's collateral."

Wendell warmed at Teng's reference to him as a businessman, as his equal. And he liked the idea of a businessman's code. Grandpa had never spoken of a code.

Teng turned from Fairweather to Wendell. "To complete my answer to you about the likely success of our new law school, as I said, the building will be an important part of that. It is an absolutely superb building. But what good is a wonderful law building without an equally wonderful faculty to fill the classrooms with their wisdom?"

"You haven't hired a faculty? There must be loads of lawyers in China who can teach for you."

"Chinese lawyers, yes. But that is no selling point. You may not know this, Wen-dall, but American law schools are by far the best law schools in the world. Do you know why?"

Wendell thought he knew what his mentor was about to say and, as in the van earlier, a profound sadness instantly overtook him.

"American law schools are the best in the world," Teng said, "because American law professors are the best in the world."

No, this sorrow was different. In the van he had been depressed because American law professors are so dumb. Now the sorrow was that his new business partner didn't know this.

"Or at least," Teng said, winking again, "people in China *think* Americans are the best law professors in the world. And as long as they think that, what does it matter if in fact your professors are a bunch of . . . what would you call them?"

"Knuckleheads."

"Yes, knuckleheads like that fellow in the van."

Teng's redemption overjoyed Wendell. "And," Wendell said, "you would like me to arrange for American law teachers to join your faculty at QingXing."

"You are so quick, Wen-dall! Precisely."

"How many?"

"To start, let's say twenty. Can you manage that?"

"I'm sure I can." It would require intercepting faculty emails and initiating and rewriting some on his own, but Wendell was confident that he could deliver 20 State law professors to the barracks of QingXing. "But since American law professors are the best in the world, this is not going to be cheap."

"How much?"

Wendell quickly calculated what it would take to pay off the Porsche with enough left over to launch a modest hedge fund. "Eight times what you paid for the building model. For each professor I get for you."

"That seems perfectly reasonable," Teng said, extending his hand. "What about the one in the van?"

"For him I would need double that amount."

"Why would he be worth so much?"

"He's going to be your new dean. You'll never find anyone better qualified."

"Why do you say that?"

"Because he was born to wear handcuffs. A proprietor of a great law school like QingXing never wants to lose sleep over where his dean is. And he teaches legal philosophy. If your students ever try to shut down classes and occupy your office, he can explain to them how the problems they're complaining about don't exist."

"But why would he agree to come?"

"He has a wife in New York who I don't think he wants to see right now."

Teng again put his arm around Wendell's shoulder and walked with him to the van. "What a pleasure it is to work with you, Wendall. I will give you the highest compliment that I can pay to anyone: You think like a Chinese. Now if you will follow me in your van to New York, we can drop our new law building off at my freight forwarder and then go out for another Chinese banquet."

Wendell ripped a strip of duct tape from the building model. "No thanks. I'll just untie this and put it in the Cayenne."

"Last night's banquet was a bit too rich for you?"

"Not really," Wendell said, although he had experienced some regrets when, after finishing the bird's nest soup, Teng told him how it was prepared. "It's just that I've been around lawyers long enough to know that it's not a terrific idea to cross a state line with a handcuffed man in the back of your vehicle."

"Do you think, Wen-dall, that it is foolish for a college drop-out like me to dream that the QingXing Law School will one day be ranked in the listings of the *U.S. News and World Report* magazine? Even, indeed, among the Top Five schools?"

"Not foolish at all," Wendell said. "Just expensive."

SIXTEEN

MEMORANDUM
(Dictated but not read)

TO: File
FROM: H.L.
RE: Narrative of a Lawyer's Life
DATE: November 1

As you know, Etta, I am no complainer, but this quest for *Mindful Narrative* and to *Connect the Dots* has proved difficult. The effort requires something like a monk's meditative repose, but my recent visit to Professor Cruikshank's class has entirely unsettled me, confronting me as it has with yet another life-changing concept: *Law's Great Lie*. More on this and on Cruikshank anon, for now I am procrastinating over my *Mindful Narrative*.

Upon the deepest reflection, if I were compelled to identify a single preoccupation of my life growing up on our family farm, I would characterize it as the search for connections. Cause and effect are evident on a farm in a way that they are not in town, and my childhood investigations took me from such obvious links as how the quality of hay we fed our cows affected the taste of the milk they produced to broader, more global speculations. In high school, my biology teacher opened my eyes still wider, telling us of research demonstrating that an action as minuscule and distant as the flapping of a single butterfly's wings in faraway Argentina could, through a series of interconnected and gradually escalating atmospheric events, set off a tornado in Brooklyn. You can imagine the grip such an idea had on a young man's imagination. What if that butterfly had died in its cocoon, or been netted by a boy like myself, so that the tornado would not have occurred? What lives lost might have been saved, what unborn future scientists born?

At the suggestion of my beloved high school English teacher, Miss Purdy, I set down my thoughts about this dazzlingly interconnected world. Early in the morning, and after chores in the evening, in every spare moment that I could find, I put pen to paper, writing not just accounts of my investigations, but poems, short stories and—I am embarrassed to confess this—even the beginnings of a novel. Would you believe, dear Etta, that H.L., your faithful author of memos so brief that they could pass as haiku, once devoted the evenings of an entire summer to writing and rewriting an epic poem exploring the interdependence of life's infinite symmetries? Think Homer; think Virgil.

Law school brought this all-absorbing effort to a crashing halt. In the interests of time, I will omit the conditions that caused H.L. to enroll at State's Law School rather than its veterinary school, where he had originally been headed, and will describe instead how that first year of law school exploded every delicate link that the young H.L. had forged between worldly cause and effect, action and reaction. And explosion is the correct metaphor, for it all began with the explosion of a package of fireworks.

Consider: A man carrying a newspaper-wrapped package dashes onto a platform of the Long Island Railroad to catch a train that is already moving out of the station. Two railroad employees, one on the train and the other on the platform, come to the man's aid, one employee pulling him onboard, the other pushing. In the tumult, the package slips from the man's hands onto the rails, causing an explosion—inside the nondescript package was a bundle of fireworks—and the shock of the explosion topples a commercial scale at the other end of the platform. The falling scale strikes one Helen Palsgraf, who sues the railroad for her damages.

Is the railroad liable to Mrs. Palsgraf for her injuries? But for the clumsy efforts of the company's employees, the package surely

would not have fallen, nor the explosion occurred, nor Mrs. Palsgraf harmed, which is exactly how H.L., this young student of
interconnectedness, reading the recitation of facts at the start of
the court's opinion, viewed the case of *Palsgraf v. Long Island
Railroad Co.* Of course, H.L. concluded, the railroad should pay
for Mrs. Palsgraf's care, and perhaps some extra for her trouble.

That was not, however, how the opinion's author, Judge Benjamin Cardozo, viewed the case, nor H.L.'s brutal classroom inter-
locutor, Professor George Cruikshank. Actual cause, Cardozo
wrote, was irrelevant to legal cause, and to the marking of the
railroad's duty. "The risk reasonably to be perceived defines the
duty to be obeyed," opined Cardozo. Since it was not foreseeable
that aiding a passenger at one end of the platform would injure a
passerby at the other end, neither the employees nor the railroad
could be held liable. Legally speaking, then, there was no connection between two events that in this first-year law student's
mind were knit tighter together than a butterfly and a Brooklyn
tornado. From that day on, H.L.'s first year of law school was a
minefield, and if any threads of connection lingered in his mind,
Professor Cruikshank, that master bone-breaker, demolished
them with machine-gun efficiency.

Other professors at State similarly took delight in this frac-
turing of the natural world into tiny, meaningless shards. Is a
hunter guilty of shooting a deer out of season if he is unaware
that the object in his rifle's crosshairs is a taxidermist's stuffed
animal, and not a live deer as he imagines? It is no crime to shoot
a stuffed deer out of season, the judge said, and that was the end
of that. But, H.L. objected, what of the hunter's corrupt intention to shoot a live deer, and also what of the fact that he injured
a stuffed one? *Slam!* The professor's open hand came down on
H.L.'s desktop.

This bit of personal history will explain the apprehension that
H.L. felt, 45 years later, standing at the threshold of Professor
Cruikshank's Torts classroom, for here was the man who, above
all of his colleagues, altered the course of H.L.'s life, transformed
him from a naïve young farm boy seeking connections in the world

about him to the embryo of a skilled lawyer whose life's work has been to sever those connections wherever necessary to serve his client's wealth or convenience. I will confess, too, that another fear froze me in that doorway: the terror that, were I to enter and take a seat, Cruikshank would call on me to stand and recite as he had that first time almost a half-century ago. For, though my mind was a blank all the while that I spoke on that long-ago day, I remember the event as if it were yesterday. Forget whatever you think you know from movies about the grinding crucible of a law school classroom. No hawk ever eviscerated its prey with the deftness or sheer malice of that master-predator Cruikshank. After that class, the fellow sitting in the next chair told me that from a foot away he could feel the wild beating of my heart.

These fears detained an older H.L. some moments, but eventually he entered the classroom and took a seat in the back. Close to half a century had changed Cruikshank in some respects, but not others. There was the same three-piece suit of heavy tweed, the tartan plaid tie, tortoise shell glasses and the unruly shock of hair. However, the hair was white, the glasses were dusted with dandruff, and the tall man's posture was stooped. But the greatest change was that Cruikshank no longer commanded students to stand and subject themselves to his lacerating questions, nor did he pace the room as he once did, sneaking up behind a student and clapping an oak grip on the student's shoulder or barking into his ear.

Today, Cruikshank remained in the front of the room as if tethered to the podium. (Is it envy I feel toward today's students for getting off so easy, or is it regret for what they are missing?) In fact, this new, amended Cruikshank didn't call on students at all, but rather lectured in a distracted way about the case before them, the very *Palsgraf* decision to which I earlier alluded. If a hand went up and a student asked a question or offered an observation, no matter how harebrained, Cruikshank answered in the mildest tone, assuring the student with no detectible irony that the insight was profound and had measurably moved forward the development of the common law.

Midway through the class, I saw that Cruikshank had noticed me at the back of the classroom, and when the session ended, uncomfortable as it was to approach him, it would have been impolite for me not to do so. As soon as I introduced myself, Cruikshank's eyes acquired that glassy, *who the hell is this fellow?* look that I suppose afflicts professors the world over when students from generations past approach to tell them how fondly they remember their class and what a powerful influence the professor had on their lives. That last observation would certainly have been true for me, but by the time Cruikshank at last connected my name with my reputation in the State Bar and congratulated me on my "magnificent" career, I knew that it would be dishonest for me to thank him for his part in shaping it. For, profound as his influence on me may have been, I felt at the moment nothing but remorse for my legal education.

You see, dear Etta, standing before the great man, it came to me that my law school education had robbed me of my hopes and of my humanity. Surely, the critical, indeed brutalizing, mental habits that Cruikshank and his fellow professors drilled into me have done little to enhance my personal relations. Even the fourth Mrs. L. complains of my problems with intimacy, and what, after all, is intimacy but *connectedness*? As to my humanity, what if my pre-law school ruminations were correct, that all things in this world are connected, and that it is *Law's Great Lie* that they are not? A lie so great that it makes anything possible? If the law says that a wealthy railroad company is not liable to its guest when the reckless behavior of its employees causes an explosion that injures her, then the law will also permit a giant bank to evict a family from its home, even though it was the reckless greed of the bank's managers that caused the bank to write a mortgage loan that it never should have issued.

No wonder civility has so precipitously declined in this republic of lawyers, for to disconnect our acts from their effect on our fellows is to strip responsibility from each of us. If I am right about *Law's Great Lie*, then my entire professional life has been not just a travesty, but a sin against humankind.

These were the difficult thoughts that the professor's presence inspired in me, and as I entertained them, I noticed that Cruikshank's teeth when he smiled were perfectly even and of a size and alignment that is possible only with dentures. Cruikshank, the great barracuda, the fire-breathing dragon—Cruikshank was toothless! Surely that had not been his physical condition 45 years ago when he was my teacher, but I could not exclude the possibility that toothlessness had even then been his moral condition. Why, today, do I find this possibility so disturbing?

So, dear Etta, I have at length come to the end of my *Mindful Narrative*, no closer, I fear, to *Connecting the Dots* than I was at the start; closer only (if I must be honest as well as mindful) to an aching sense of loss.

SEVENTEEN

The sight of Randy at her dining room table, laptop open in front of him, cellphones flashing, cheered Elspeth, but not enough to lift the heavy cloak of fatigue, disappointment and accumulated worry over the indecisive justice, the faithless senator, the cranky students, the missing architectural model, the cancelled groundbreaking and Jimmy, Littlefield, Bioff and Brown.

It was as if overnight her arms had shrunk and all the objects of importance in her life now lay beyond her reach. Even when she averted her eyes driving past Met. State on the way home, the twin spires remained fixed in her mind, the vast, unmoveable presence of the place once again filling her with dread. The applicant pool will shrivel by a third this year, another third the next, and so on, the contraction ending only with the Law School's disappearance, and her with it. Elspeth thought of Jimmy's words this afternoon. Was she really that heedless of the injury she inflicted on others? Was she in fact crazy, or was it only thinking about it that made her so?

If Elspeth was going to turn her luck around, she might as well start with Randy and the new building. "Hi," she said, throwing her coat over the back of a chair. "Did you get through to Billy Rubin?" A thick paperback, her copy of *The Brothers Karamazov*, was on the edge of the table, next to Randy's laptop.

"I'm on hold." Randy turned the laptop to face her.

Videotape images moved across the computer screen: Billy Rubin racing down courthouse steps to talk to the waiting press. Billy lifting a client's arm, prizefighter style, to crow success. A courtroom artist's sketches of Billy staring down a prosecutor. Billy huddling with an instantly recognizable celebrity client at counsel's table.

"Now that everyone has Skype and FaceTime, I suppose this is what's going to replace call-holding music," Elspeth said.

"From what I've seen, Ellie, this fellow looks like a criminal lawyer. My case is civil."

First the senator, now Randy. How little even the most sophisticated non-practitioners knew about law practice. "A trial is a trial, Randy, and the other side is the enemy. The bad guys. You couldn't be in better hands."

A television clip of a much younger Billy filled the screen. He was leaving a Senate hearing room, a bulging briefcase in each hand. At a remarkably young age, Billy had been Minority Counsel to the Senate Judiciary Committee, the committee that Senator Troxell now chaired; the committee that was responsible for reviewing Supreme Court nominations. Even as Minority Counsel, Billy's had been a respected voice in committee deliberations, and he had maintained his relationships there—facts that, during Elspeth's recruitment of him to the faculty, made her pursuit of the lawyer even more intense. It was a comfort to know that as her nomination made its way through the Judiciary Committee, she could count on Billy's support from one side of the aisle, as well as the senator's on the other. Just thinking about the confirmation process brightened her thoughts. She realized that she hadn't yet decided where she would live in Washington—definitely in the District, not in Virginia—and whether to rent the College Station condo or sell it. She turned the computer back to Randy.

"Whatever happens on this call, Ellie, I'm leaving as soon as it's over. My being here can only hurt you. If Troxell's Committee finds out that you were harboring a fugitive from justice, you can say goodbye to the Supreme Court. I can't let that happen."

Randy had done this before; read her mind. "You're not a fugitive. As you said, this is a civil case. Anyway, I can take care of it." She wanted to say that she could take care of him, but even the loving Bianca wouldn't risk saying that to the self-sufficient

Randy Barrimore. "When we finish talking to Billy, you can rub two sticks together and make that steak for me. I wouldn't be surprised if Billy's already wrapped this up with the SEC lawyers."

As if summoned, Billy's voice came over the laptop, which Randy turned back toward Elspeth. The image of Billy on the screen was not of the lean-faced, animated young man of the videos, but a countenance as sullen and thuggish as a mug shot. It may have been the laptop, but the lawyer's complexion was red and beefy. His nose was oddly squashed, as if he were pressing it against the inside of the computer screen, and the image flashed through Elspeth's thoughts of the unfortunate Bioff.

"Ellie. It's good to meet you, Mr. Barrimore." The voice was hurried, intense. Billy was in New Orleans where he was dealing with the long-lasting legal repercussions of the BP oil spill. "I made a few calls to Washington. I think we have some progress."

Elspeth shot an "I told you so" look at Randy, who said, "Did you get my assets unfrozen? I promised Ellie she could cash a check by the end of the week."

"The asset freeze is going to be a problem. If there's a settlement, there are going to be fines, and the government wants to be sure you have the cash to pay them."

Randy half rose, as he would if Rubin were across the table from him. "But I made Ellie a promise—"

"And I'll make a promise to you, Mr. Barrimore. I promise that I'll do everything I can to get your assets defrosted."

"But how do you—"

Elspeth put a hand on his arm. "Don't worry about the assets. Billy will get it straightened out. If not this week, then next. The building can wait." To Billy she said, "What should we be doing here to get this resolved?"

"For starters," Billy said, "we need to round up every expert witness who could possibly testify in the case. I'll send you the names of the seven forensic accountants I want you to put under retainer. Two are at Harvard, two at Stanford, and one each at Wharton, Kellogg and Booth. Pay them whatever they ask."

"Pay them with what?" Elspeth said.

"I'm sure Mr. Barrimore is not going to disappoint us when it comes to finding some spare cash lying around to pay for expert witnesses. And to pay his lawyer. I already placed a lien on your residences, Mr. Barrimore. To secure payment of my fees. On your personal property, too. By the way, congratulations on your art collection. Jeff Koons and Richard Prince are favorites of mine. But rest assured, in today's market, I'd rather get paid in cash than have to foreclose on a client's houses, paintings and sculpture."

"Why would I need seven accountants to testify? Why wouldn't one be enough?"

Elspeth answered before Rubin could. "Forget Perry Mason cross-examining witnesses until they confess; Paul Drake pulling rabbits out of a hat. What a top trial lawyer like Billy does is orchestrate teams of expert witnesses."

"We're not actually going to put seven experts on the stand. At the end of the day, if we play this right, no one's going to have to testify because if we get these seven under retainer that means they won't be available to testify for the government. And if the government can't hire them, it's going to have to reach down into the second tier of experts for its witnesses. The minor leagues— Duke, Michigan, USC—if they can even find someone in the minors willing to go up against the top men in the field. So if we move quickly and sign all seven, none of them will have to testify because there won't be a trial. The government knows it can't win without at least one first-tier expert."

Elspeth said, "What other experts do we need?"

"There are a dozen securities law professors, all major leaguers. I'll email you the list."

Randy said, "How do you know they'll support my position?"

"Because I write their opinions for them."

"*You* write the expert opinions?"

"Actually, my assistants write them, but I review every word."

"And then these professors sign them."

"Some read them first, and a few suggest a word change or two, but sure, if they want to be paid, they all sign." He glanced at Elspeth before looking back at Randy. "This whole thing will be over by the end of next week. As a favor to Ellie, I'll settle the case on Friday afternoon so it falls out of the news cycle. Did you hear that, Ellie? Less coverage than I usually get. I'm banking favors with my new Dean."

On the screen, Billy's bloodshot eyes shifted from Randy to Elspeth. "See if you can sign up that anthropologist of yours—what's her name?"

"Heidi Hoehnemann-Mueller."

"I want her to testify on the tribal customs of investors like Mr. Barrimore here. We can use her to back up the psychiatrists' testimony on *mens rea*."

Randy didn't have to know the meaning of *mens rea* to object. "Why would you need a psychiatrist to testify in an SEC case?"

"Because even I can't put on an insanity defense without one."

"An insanity defense?" Randy said, looking at Elspeth.

"Exactly," Billy said. "We're going to take the position that you weren't in your right mind when you set up this deal."

"What Randy means is, why would we need an insanity defense in a civil case?"

Billy looked away and angrily shook his head at someone with him in the New Orleans room. When his face came back to the camera, he said, "I forgot to tell you the good news. This isn't a civil case anymore. It's going to be a criminal case."

"A criminal case?" Elspeth put a hand up to calm Randy. To Billy she said, "Did the government tell you that?"

"No," Billy said. "*I* told *them*. I guarantee you, Mr. Barrimore, it's the surest route to victory."

"No," Randy said. "It's the surest route to jail."

"Only if you lose. And we're not going to lose. Think about how much easier it's going to be for us to win a criminal case than a civil case."

"There's a reason for that," Elspeth said. "The penalties for losing are much greater."

Billy ignored her and spoke directly to Randy. "For the government to win a civil case, all they have to do is prove their facts by a preponderance of the evidence; prove that it is more probable than not that you violated the Corrupt Foreign Practices Act—"

"Foreign Corrupt Practices Act," Elspeth said.

"Right. For a prosecutor to win a criminal case, he has to prove his facts beyond any reasonable doubt, and that's a hell of a lot harder. And if we've signed up all the experts, the government won't even be able to prove beyond a reasonable doubt that your name is Ricky Barrimore."

"Randy," Elspeth said. "Randy Barrimore."

"Even if I win a criminal case," Randy said, "the civil case is still there. Nothing's changed except that I've paid you and a posse of experts six figures to create reasonable doubt in a criminal case."

"Seven figures, not six," Billy said. "Mid-seven. And do you really think the government's going to proceed with a civil action after they've lost the criminal case? They'll be ashamed to even show their face in court. The press won't let them hear the end of it."

Elspeth saw a certain loopy logic to Billy's plan.

"The *Times* is going to paint you as a victim of government harassment," Billy said. "*The Wall Street Journal* and the *Washington Post*, too. They'll call you the government's favorite punching bag. The media are going to whip up overwhelming sympathy for you."

"Like they did for Bernie Madoff."

Irony was as alien to Randy as self-pity, and Elspeth guessed that the trial lawyer was making her friend very angry. Still, she was torn between taking Randy's side and trying to convince him to go along with Billy's strategy.

"Bernie Madoff was different," Billy said.

"Why, because he really was a crook?'

"No," Billy said, "because he didn't have me as his lawyer."

"I thought—" Randy said.

"I helped the Madoff defense, but only in the background. I'm the reason he didn't get a longer sentence."

At 150 years for a 71-year-old man, Elspeth wondered what difference a longer sentence would have made.

"I value my good name almost as much as I love my wife," Randy said. "There's no way I'm going to be a defendant in a criminal case and have my name dragged through the streets."

"Randy's got a point, Billy." The Albie and Renata Troxell Building had grown wings and was taxiing down the runway, taking with it Elspeth's hopes for the *U.S. News* Top Five.

Billy's face on the screen grew redder, turning from a rare porterhouse to a raw one. "Do you have any idea how many chips I had to cash in at Justice to get them to agree to a criminal indictment?"

"You can't be serious, Billy. You're telling me this wasn't just a conversation you had with some Justice Department lawyers. You actually got the government to indict Randy?"

"Signed and sealed. My P.R. firm's already drafted the press release calling the indictment 'irresponsible and overreaching.'" A sheet of paper appeared on the screen just below Billy's eyes, and he read. "'This indictment blatantly distorts both the facts and the law in an attempt to grab headlines. Mr. Barrimore intends to defend himself vigorously against these meritless and unfounded claims.'"

"And this is what you meant when you said you made good progress in Washington today?"

"You have to trust me, Ellie. Mr. Barrimore. This is going to work. By the end of next week there won't be a criminal case against you. Or a civil case. Your assets will be unfrozen. The government will be sorry it ever caught you in its sights."

"No," Randy said. He was up and walking around the dining room. "There's no way you're going to drag my wife and me through a criminal trial."

"I told you, there won't be a trial."

"The only reason I'm talking to you, Mr. Rubin, is that Ellie here, who is the only lawyer I trust, told me you're the best there is for this kind of case."

"And I am."

Elspeth instantly saw the solution to the conflict between her loyalty to Randy and her need to appease Billy, who was no less important to her future. "Tell the government to drop the indictment," she said. "Just represent Randy in the civil case."

"I'd love to, Ellie, but I can't. My P.R. firm tells me it's impossible to get press coverage for civil cases. They won't let me take any more of them. When you called me about this, I thought Mr. Barrimore would be overjoyed to have me turn it into a criminal case. And don't ask me to change P.R. firms, because they're the best there is."

"Well, I guess I won't be retaining the best," Randy said. "Thanks just the same."

Billy said, "Don't try to make a decision now, when you're all mixed up."

Apart from her father, Randy was the least mixed-up person Elspeth knew, and he showed no sign of confusion now. She was the confused one. The small army of sprites that had gathered during her meeting with Bioff suddenly divided into two jabbering camps. Protect Randy, some cawed; he's your friend. Blow off Billy. No, the others cried, keep Billy happy, or he'll quit your faculty. He'll kill your nomination."

"Randy and I will talk about it, Billy. But in the meantime, get the government to hold off on the criminal prosecution. Give us a chance to think." She punched a button to end the connection.

Night had fallen while they were on the call, and with the laptop screen off, darkness filled the dining room. Elspeth switched on a light.

"That was quite a workout." Randy rose from the table. "How about I grill up those steaks for us?"

That's what I'll do, Elspeth thought. I'll have a nice, quiet dinner, the way normal people do, then sit with Randy by the fireplace and open up that new translation of *Anna Karenina*.

She kicked off her shoes. "I'm sorry about Billy," she said. In fact, Elspeth was sorrier about herself, and her betrayal of Randy's friendship. "Billy's a fine lawyer, but sometimes he has tunnel vision."

"I'm going to ask you one last time, Ellie. I want you to be my lawyer."

"I already told you—"

"It doesn't matter that you don't know about this Corrupt Practices Act. What matters is that you're someone who succeeds at everything you do, and with your track record you can get rid of this case."

"I succeed only because I don't try to do things that are outside my reach." Elspeth had never voiced that thought before; in fact, until coming in to the apartment less than an hour ago, she had not even entertained the thoughts that anything could lie outside her reach or that she might fail at anything. She lifted the paperback of *Brothers Karamazov* from the table. "Some light reading?"

"With my assets frozen, I have no deals to do. I needed something to keep me occupied. I thought you'd be a history reader. Biography. Politics. Current events. But all you have are novels. Dostoevsky. Tolstoy. Eliot. Trollope."

"These days, I trust fiction for the truth more than I trust nonfiction."

When Elspeth put the Dostoevsky down, Randy said, "I liked the part where Ivan lays it on the line and says, `If there is no God, then nothing is permitted.'"

"I think he says that if there is no God *everything* is permitted."

"Well, maybe the translator got it wrong."

"Or," Elspeth said, "maybe Ivan got it wrong." The last thing she wanted was to unsettle her God-fearing friend. What if Randy was right and, God or no God, she was damned for her heedless trampling of others? And if she couldn't tell Randy about her fear of going mad, who could she tell?

A cellphone rang. "Is that one of yours?"

"It's yours," Randy said. "I turned mine off when I saw your car come into the garage."

Elspeth flipped open the phone and instantly recognized the number. "What can I do for you, Jimmy?"

"It's Littlefield." Jimmy was out of breath. "He's been to the basement. After 6:00. At night."

Elspeth's next-to-worst fear about the accreditation committee's visit had just come true. "Has he been to the sub-basement?"

"He's on his way there now."

That was her worst fear. "Is Alex there?"

"Who do you think is giving Littlefield the guided tour?"

"Well," Elspeth said, "there's nothing we can do about it now. Tell Alex I want to see him in my office first thing in the morning. 8:30. You be there too."

"Anything else?"

"I don't know," she said. "What else could there possibly be?"

WEDNESDAY

EIGHTEEN

MEMORANDUM
(Dictated but not read)

TO: File
FROM: H.L.
RE: The Other Law School
DATE: Nov. 2

Early yesterday evening I took a break from this arduous business of compiling my *Mindful Narrative* and, after a fine bratwurst and red cabbage dinner at my beloved "Rat," a meal far superior to the tired fare they serve at Faculty House, I strolled back to the Law School to investigate Bioff's excited claim that the school has jettisoned its entire library collection—not just the tedious texts and monographs that I remember all too well from my three years haunting the stacks, but the case reporters, law reviews and treatises that constitute the very heart of the collection. My spirit quickened as I passed through the main floor's double entryway for, like yesterday's visit to Cruikshank's classroom, I anticipated this to be one of those fraught moments where past meets up with present and no promises are made as to which, if either, will survive. Or was it just that yesterday's earth-shaking revelation of *Law's Big Lie* had left me overly fearful?

The first evidence of the truth of Bioff's claim was the absence from what I remembered as the Dictionary Corner of the four-inch-thick *Black's Law Dictionary*, that repository of the law's countless Latin deceits. No great loss, that. But then I saw that,

where once a floor-to-ceiling rack had displayed current issues
of all the major law reviews, a carousel now offered a newsstand
array of popular magazines, *Cosmopolitan, GQ* and *Esquire* the
most dog-eared among them. Beyond the carousel, a dozen or
so students worked at computer keyboards. Looking over their
shoulders on the way to the basement, I saw that all but two were
playing what looked like video games.

The basement, which had the appearance of an abandoned
warehouse, amply confirmed Bioff's claim that in fact the library's
books were gone. Not only had the space been emptied, but the
bookshelves, too, had been removed, exposing long parallel strips
of concrete between the carpeting, the holes unfilled where formerly the shelves had been bolted to the floor. Everywhere were
olive-green desks and chairs with the battered, cheesy look of government surplus. The only books in sight—two or three hundred
volumes haphazardly stacked along one wall—were presumably
the ones Bioff witnessed being shuttled back to the library last
night. I lifted one off the top of the pile. *Powell on Real Property.*
Stamped boldly, if crookedly, on the title page was PROPERTY
OF METROPOLITAN STATE HOSPITAL FOR THE CRIM-
INALLY INSANE and, beneath that in much fainter ink, the
imprimatur of the State Law School.

When I turned, I saw people drifting into the vast space, chatting and laughing, moving tables and chairs. They came not from
the stairway that I had taken down, nor from the elevator bank,
but from some hidden entry. The human flow was uninterrupted
and, surrounded as I was by high bare walls, I felt like an intruder
at the bottom of an empty swimming pool that was rapidly filling
with water from some secret source. The newcomers were men
and women of all ages dressed warmly, if not well. Some of the
women carried infants bundled against the chill outside. Better-
heeled figures, all of them men, walked about the periphery, and
although I recognized none in particular, it was impossible to mistake the look and carriage of a prospering middle-aged lawyer.

The visitors formed zig-zagging queues at the government surplus desks, each attended by a young man or woman in business
attire who made notes on a legal pad as he or she asked ques-

tions of the first in line. This was, I concluded, a legal clinic, the young men and women were students, and the lawyers circulating among the desks were their adult supervision, there to correct any of the students' more life-threatening mistakes. This subterranean law firm opened for business at 6:00 P.M., just when firms above ground were preparing to close. As for *Law's Big Lie*, disconnecting cause from consequence when it risks exposing the rich or powerful to the claims of victims like poor Mrs. Palsgraf, these earnest students were doing what lawyers for the poor have been doing for generations everywhere the poor can be found: they were looking for loopholes through which wrongdoers can be connected to their wrongs and forced to pay for them.

How can I express the thrill of my discovery? Law students training to be lawyers! Using their skills and legal knowledge to serve humankind! (But where had they acquired this knowledge? Certainly not in the Beehive Court!) How different this was from the esoteric doings on the upper floors! How distant from the dean's mumbo-jumbo about what a law school should and should not be teaching! All—well, if not *all*, then *much*—that I had hoped to see at State when I agreed to chair the re-accreditation committee, I saw right there, albeit late in our visit and at an unusual hour, and, alas, hidden away in the Law School basement.

From behind the press of bodies, that snake-like fellow from Sunday night's party emerged and signaled for me to stay. The secretive Director of Special Projects, Coyle. What was he doing down here? I struggled to connect the dots, A to B to Coyle.

The yellowish eyes blinked as he approached. "It appears that you have discovered the Law School's dark underbelly."

If a forked tongue had darted out, it would not have surprised me. "Is this a clinic? No one told me the Law School has a clinic."

"Impressive, isn't it? We have eight clinics. We added two in September."

What had been a sneer turned into a smile of simple pride as Coyle pointed at the desks, identifying the specialty at each. "Immigration. Landlord-Tenant. Small Business. Disability and Workman's Comp. Abused Women. Child Support." This last was the one with the straggling line of mothers and infants. He pointed to two others at the far end of where the stacks once were. "Credit Card Workouts. Mortgage Foreclosure."

I guessed. "The ones you just added."

"The rotten economy's been a windfall for us. Out here in the sticks it's not as easy to scrape together a clientele like the schools in Boston and New York. Even Yale has all the clients it can handle in New Haven. We need to find our clients where we can."

"How do they know you're here? I've been practicing more than forty years, and I had no idea this existed."

"Word of mouth. The drums." He pantomimed a set of bongos. "Go to any homeless shelter in the county, or food pantry or home for abused women and ask anyone about the State Clinic. They'll give you our phone number and tell you where to find us. We don't have to make client pitches with PowerPoint presentations and coffee and Danish." The dour look returned. A prideful smile for his clinics, but a sneer for white-collar lawyers like H.L.

I looked about the bustling space. Is this what Morales meant when he spoke of *Connecting the Dots*? How could a single building encompass the lunacy that fills the classrooms above and the hard, practical legal services that were being delivered here? "This is as different from what I've seen of the Law School as—"

"Night and day?"

"Well, yes, night and day. Exactly."

"And why do you think that would be?"

A snake, I was learning, is a creature of many smiles. The present one mocked me. "That's impossible," I said. "I would have known. I'm an alumnus. I chaired the Law School's Board of Governors."

"That was, when?"

"Twenty-four years ago. When did this happen?"

"Horace Rorabach started it. The last Dean. We've been in business nine years."

"A night school," I said. I could have been speaking a foreign language, the words felt so alien on my tongue. "Who would have thought that State would have a night law school?"

"Well, not the present Dean, that's for sure."

"What problem could she possibly have with a night school? It serves people who need to work during the day to support themselves—"

"And their families."

"And it . . ." What else did it do that was good?

"It brings in more money than the day division. No scholarships. Everyone here pays for his seat with hard cash."

This was Coyle's "Special Project." He was the *de facto* dean of the night law school.

"No cream puff jobs either, cleaning up bird shit in the library."

"Then, why—"

"Come on, Howard. You really can't be that naïve."

"Well, I suppose I am. I walk down a single flight of stairs and suddenly I'm in a foreign country." A third-world country by the look of it. A place with unseen entrances and exits; hidden dangers.

"*U.S. News* is why this is secret. Have you ever seen a law school with a night division ranked in the Top Five? The Top Ten? There may be one or two in the top 25, but you would never know it by looking at their catalogues. Or their website. You won't find a word about the night program in any of the law school's publications. Night divisions are the law school world's most shameful, best-kept secret. If you're a dean and you want your school to move up the ranks, you do it on the backs of your night students. You use their tuition payments to pay for your fancy day programs. But you never let anyone know they're here, because if you did, you'd have to include their numbers—their GPAs and LSATs—in your admissions statistics, and that would kill you with *U.S. News*. Think about it, Howard: the Law School is a feudal system and we're the serfs that hold it up."

Where, I thought, did these students come from?

"You're thinking, if it's a secret, how do students know to apply here? Like our clients, they hear the word on the street. These are real people. Grown-ups. They're real estate brokers, accountants, data managers, car salesmen. People laid off from retail. Anyone who wants to get a leg up on life but keep his day job, if he still has one."

"How do you keep it a secret?"

"You were a farm boy, weren't you?" The eyes that studied first my face, then my hands turned from yellow to gold. "You didn't grow up soft, but you didn't grow up on the streets, either. Do you read Dickens?"

"A long time ago," I said. "In high school." What did Dickens or my childhood have to do with the improbable secrecy of Coyles's teeming basement operation?

"Well, reread *Oliver Twist*. The underclass, the lumpen proletariat, whatever you want to call them, live in a world of their own. No secrets among themselves, but with outsiders, their lips are tight as a sealed jar."

"And that's what you were threatening the dean with Sunday night. You're going to let the rest of the world in on the Law School's biggest secret."

Coyles's head jerked back, as if I'd slapped him. "Personally, I don't mind basements. I live in a basement apartment, so being below ground makes no difference to me. But these students don't like being shoved down and away like poor relations. The faculty, either. If you want to do the right thing for your alma mater, you'll bring us up to ground level."

"I don't think so." For a change, it felt good to have the upper hand with this fellow. "This is between you and your Dean."

"She's been promising to get us out of here from the day she took over. Her latest promise is that when the rest of the school moves into the new building, we'll get this one. But that building's not going to happen. Randy Barrimore's screwed. That's why we need you."

"I can't imagine how I could help you."

Across the room, from the same spot where I first saw Coyle, Associate Dean Fleenor was gesturing at me frantically. Where was this secret entrance that everyone appeared to use?

"All you have to do is give the school a negative report," Coyle said. "When you write up your visit for the ABA, tell them how nasty the facilities are down here. That will get the dean's attention. The president's, too. They'll do something to get us out of here."

"I'd like to help you, Mr. Coyle, but—"

"You won't be helping me. You'll be helping our students and their clients."

In fact, my impulse was to help if I could. The clinic was a good thing, and it deserved a better home than this. Chairs for the clients to sit on, not the floor. A receptionist. Private offices where an abused spouse could share confidences with her student lawyer without the woman behind her eavesdropping on every detail of last night's fracas. Still, there was only so much I could do. "It's crowded here, and I'm sure it's uncomfortable for your clients, but the heat seems to be on and the ceiling isn't falling in. These aren't conditions that are going to give the ABA second thoughts about State's accreditation."

"What if I show you conditions that will give your ABA people more than second thoughts? Conditions that will give them nightmares for the rest of their lives. Will you write that up?"

"This isn't the only place you meet?"

"Do you really think clinics are all there is to a night law school? We give our lecture classes in the sub-basement. Eight to twelve of them every weekday night."

"What kind of lecture classes?" Even as I asked, a tremor inside me whispered that this next descent would again bring me directly face to face with my now unsettling past.

"The usual. Contracts. Torts. Criminal Law. Real Property. Tax. Corporations. Evidence."

Coyles's "the usual" could have been pearls dropped by angels. Or the Devil's burning fires. "But no courses in Law in American Film? Job's View of Justice?"

"Take a look at these students." He gestured around the clinic. "Do they look like they have spare time for that crap? These people barely have time to eat and sleep." Coyle touched my elbow and steered me toward where Fleenor was waiting across the room. "So, will you tell the ABA?"

"I'd have to see what's downstairs before I can promise you anything."

Fleenor, arms folded across his chest, leaned against the wall. Then I saw how he, and presumably Coyle and the others, had entered. There was no door frame or even door handle, just a panel—a swinging door—cut into the wall and painted the same pea-soup green. "You know you can't take him downstairs, Alex. That's the agreement. You shouldn't have brought him here either."

Coyle stared at him hard, but Fleenor averted his look. A heaviness in the air suggested that there was more business between the two men than Coyle's promise not to leak word of the night law school.

"Get out of the way, Jimmy."

A dog can be a hero and save his downed master from a fire. Even a cat can dial 911. But can a snake rescue a law school? Is it possible to admire someone so physically repellent? Alex Coyle was not someone H.L. would invite to dinner, but H.L. could not fail to respect him.

"The dean will fire you for this," Fleenor said.

Coyle could have told him the truth, that I had found my own way to the basement, and that it was I who had insisted on seeing the sub-basement. Instead, he said, "You don't realize, Jimmy, I care about my night school more than you evidently care about Millicent."

"You mean you care about it more than *you* care about Millicent."

"That goes without saying."

The exchange made no sense but, from his expression, the effect on Fleenor was crushing, and the associate dean moved away from the swinging door, which hissed as it closed behind Coyle and me.

The narrow stairway was lit by a single incandescent bulb. There were no handrails and, when I reached out to steady myself, the whitewashed walls on both sides were damp; in places, rivulets of water streamed into puddles on the stairs. But it wasn't until Coyle swung open the door at the bottom to a blinding light, and my eyes adjusted to the harsh glare and shadows cast by the hanging fluorescent lamps, that I appreciated why Coyle referred to the sub-basement as a place of nightmares.

As on the stairway, the stone walls wept and there were, of course, no windows. Unlike the floor above, the ceiling was low, and although there was more than enough room for me to stand erect, I found myself stooping. The scene was like nothing so much as an emergency operating theater on the edge of some infernal battleground. Opaque muslin screens of the sort used in hospital rooms to separate patients were lined up end to end at regular intervals, and there was a low, susurrous murmur that could have been of suffering patients and consoling medics. The odor of rot and mildew hung in the damp air, and if ventilation actually reached this forsaken place, its ducts had crossed and married those of the also-subterranean Rathskeller, for the odor of rancid cooking oil poured out from the dust-feathered vents.

"Come this way," Coyle said. He directed me to the first line of hospital screens and gestured for me to look behind them. Twenty or so students were at desks that were really no more than chairs with a hinged surface at the arm to be swung up for writing, the kind of desk that I remembered from grade school and that I had supposed disappeared with my youth. Unlike the day students in blue jeans on the upper floors, the men were in coat and tie, the women in skirt and heels, and in front of them on their little fold- ing desks were old-fashioned looseleaf notebooks, not laptops. At the front of the room was a card table on which lay an open casebook and a legal pad with what must have been the instruc- tor's lecture notes. The instructor's back was to us as he drew on the portable blackboard a diagram that I instantly recognized from my law school days as an illustration of the hoary doctrine of adverse possession in real property law.

The scene in the other jury-rigged classrooms that we walked past was much the same, although in some I recognized the teacher in the front of the room. Herb McIlvaine, one of the stars of the state trial bar, was teaching Civil Procedure from what looked like the same casebook I had been assigned as a student. No Beehive Court for Herb. Silvio Scileppi, a bankruptcy lawyer from my own firm, was teaching the contracts class. How could

Silvio have kept this a secret from me, the firm's chairman? And there at the front of the next room was Nordstrom, the unfortunate fellow from Sunday night's party who had been denied tenure because he published law review articles.

Mindful Narrative, Luis Morales had enjoined, and as I reflected on my passage from basement to sub-basement, it seemed to me that I had stepped down through the stages of my life, from the bustle of counseling clients and attending to their needs on the floor above, to here in the sub-basement, the traditional case-bound classes of my law school days. Modest as those long-ago classroom furnishings were, they were more functional than these. As we approached the last of the screened dividers, I heard the booming voice, at once biting and quizzical, the questions that ended not with a question mark but with a needle-sharp dart, and knew that I had indeed returned to the place that changed my life.

Coyle pulled back a screen, and there at the front of the room, oblivious to our presence and waiting for the student who stood quaking in his shoes to answer the pending question, was George Cruikshank. But this wasn't the toothless, defeated Cruikshank I had observed upstairs fewer than five hours ago. No, this was the man whose portrait hung on the Wall of Heroes, the dazzling, exasperating, hopping-smart man who, 45 years ago, regularly gutted my classmates and me when we stood in that student's place. As in his hallway portrait, Cruikshank's cheeks were pink and his eyes bright as he dismissed the student's answers one after the other, not with an answer of his own, but with yet another unanswerable question, another hypothetical set of facts that drew the student, and the class, further and further into the very depths of tort law, that deep, bottomless pool of fear and greed whence the common law springs. *Law's Big Lie*. Finally, Cruikshank dismissed the flayed and filleted student, waving him back to his seat, and in the next beat had another student, a woman, on her feet, the questions and hypotheticals once again an unceasing barrage, the students like ducks in a shooting gallery.

I told Coyle that I could find my way out on my own, and took a seat in the back of Cruikshank's makeshift classroom. Twenty minutes later, when he had retired the last of his victims with the easy athletic shrug of an ace closer after the last strike-out of a hard-fought game, Cruikshank clapped his casebook shut to signal that class was over. As the students filed out, I walked to the front, where the professor was tossing his text and notes into a ragged briefcase that had been an antique even when I was a student. He said, "I was wondering if you would discover our night classes," and pointed to a chair for me to pull up to the card table. "You were an inquisitive young fellow, as I remember, so I'm not surprised."

"I'm still trying to put your two classes together. It's like different worlds."

"You mean, *Upstairs, Downstairs.*" Cruikshank pulled over a chair for himself. Even after teaching on his feet for an hour, the old man's back was straight, his movements vigorous. "This is all the dean's doing. She's a witch, you know. No funny hat or broomstick or wart on her nose, but she's a witch, through and through. She cast a spell on this place the day she came here, years before she became Dean. That's how she became Dean."

A spell? Cruikshank's adept performance with his students had deceived me. The old man must have lost his bearings if he truly thought the dean was a witch. In my third year at the Law School, a group of us had sat around the Law Review offices one afternoon, trading observations about our teachers and, as the stories multiplied, we realized that every one of our instructors possessed some striking eccentricity. Old Everidge, who engaged in frottage with doorway frames. Winthrop, who sniffed coeds' bicycle seats. Mann, who wore at least two watches on each wrist. Only Cruikshank had emerged as entirely normal that afternoon. "There's no such thing as witches," I said. "Spells. Except for Witches' Sabbath, they only exist in storybooks."

"Well, call it what you will. She put her spell on that old fool, Rorabach, who was Dean back then; got him to put her in charge of faculty hiring. And then she started bringing in the new crew, these Poets and Quants. She threw in a few old-fashioned types to appease the rest of us Bog Dwellers so we'd rubber-stamp her hires. Of course, a couple of years later, she'd see that they didn't get tenure while the others all did."

"And you?"

"I already had tenure, long before she arrived."

"No," I said, "I meant did you fall under her spell?"

"Well, I certainly didn't vote for the chuckleheads, these sociologists and anthropologists she was hiring, but I was so wrapped up in my teaching and my treatise that I really paid no mind to what she was doing. I suppose I could have organized an opposition. So maybe in a way I was under her spell, too. After she became Dean, it was too late. By then she had the president and the chancellor in her grip."

"Why didn't you retire, or go to another school?"

"I was 71 years old. Who was going to hire me? And, I'll never retire. Teaching these kids is my entire life. This night school is a blessing for me. The students are wonderful. They're working-class kids, the first ones in their families to finish college, much less go to professional school. That puts a responsibility on a teacher to see that he shapes them into skilled lawyers."

"Shape" seemed to me an odd word to describe the brutal mayhem I had just witnessed. "From what I saw, you're still turning your students into piles of splinters."

"Of course I am. If I didn't tear them down, what reason would they have to build themselves back up? I'm not the one who's turning them into skilled professionals. They are. They're the ones doing the real work. But without me, they wouldn't do it." His smile revealed the perfectly even false teeth. "It didn't harm your career, did it?"

Not my career, I thought. Just my life. "I suppose not."

"You're thinking," Cruikshank said, "I didn't ruin your career; just your life. But of course you're wrong."

"People around here have a way of hearing my thoughts."

Cruikshank laughed, showing those awful teeth again. "It's the spell," he said, moving his jaw and lips in an odd, clicking syncopation. I realized that he was adjusting his false teeth, or even preparing to eject them onto the card table. As a small boy, rising early one morning, I saw my grandfather's dentures, all pink and white, in a tumbler of water by the side of his bed, and I suppose I have nerve endings that have still not let go of the terror that struck me at that moment. A man's mouth in a glass on the nightstand while he snored peacefully less than a foot away!

"And," I asked, doing what I could to hide my revulsion, "you have no complaints about the conditions down here?" I now pictured not my grandfather's dentures, but a set of those wind-up novelty teeth chattering on the tabletop.

"It sounds like you've been talking to Alex Coyle." Lips and jaw paused momentarily. "A truly creepy fellow, wouldn't you say? I sometimes think he has scales rather than skin."

"So," I said, "you have no objections to the sub-basement?"

The loathsome mouth movements resumed, even more vigorously, accompanied by a wet, sucking sound. I waited, aghast, and just when I was sure that the loudly clacking dentures were going to eject, Cruikshank broke wind. Teeth back in place, he sniffed and smiled. "No, I don't have any complaints. In fact, I've never been happier."

"And your students?" A toxic cloud enveloped us.

"Do you mean, are the students happy? I know it's all the rage today, but the idea that students should be happy is just about the dumbest thing I have ever heard. I can't imagine what kind of nincompoop came up with it."

Cruikshank must have seen me glance at my watch, for he lifted his briefcase and snapped it shut. The resonant *click* of that lock could have been H.L.'s bones breaking, so completely did it affirm the law's annihilation of my youthful quest for connections. This path that Cruikshank and his colleagues paved for us may have been the right trajectory for other lawyers, but I fear that it was not the one intended for H.L. As you know, Etta, I am a sucker for the epigrammatic precision of bumper stickers, and one that I remembered from my Sunday drive to College Station pierced me in retrospect like a nail through the heart: TOO SOON OLD; TOO LATE WISE.

So, dear Etta, H.L. took leave of his early mentor, having learned what it feels like to be wiser, if not smarter, than your professor. If I could choose again between a worldview that destroys nature's connectedness at every possible turn and one that celebrates it, I would not hesitate to choose the latter. But I fear that this encounter with my old mentor has brought me no closer to my goal of *Connecting the Dots*. Or has it?

NINETEEN

It sometimes seemed to Jimmy that he had married two women: Millicent, their vows blessed by the Lutheran Church, and Elspeth, their union forged through countless faculty meetings, first-year student orientations, third-year commencements, and all the crises and triumphs in between. Elspeth's barometer, to which Jimmy was as attuned as the most diligent weatherman, had been dropping precipitously for the past three days, while at home the storm had already passed, leaving vast wreckage behind. Millicent, though she was the erring party, had exiled him to the living room, where even the consolations of Jimmy's treasured Milton Avery were marred by the impress of Judith Waxman's greasy hand. Jimmy knew that Millicent thought him incapable of poetry, and that Elspeth believed him incapable of irony, but it was poignant to him that the parallels between his two marriages should become so brutally evident at the very moment that both were falling apart. If this was his punishment for committing bigamy, it occurred to Jimmy that he might yet rescue one marriage by renouncing the other. The question was, which to save and which to consign to the crapper.

The dean pushed her coffee cup and the half-eaten sweet roll to the side of her desk and regarded Jimmy. "Where's Alex?"

"I left a message for him to be here at 8:30." Jimmy decided against adding the dutiful husband's consoling, *I'm sure he'll be here soon.*

"And Littlefield? The rest of the committee?"

"Littlefield's walking in the woods." When Jimmy called Faculty House to check on the committee chairman, the receptionist told him that, at 5:30 each morning since he checked in, Littlefield went into the forest that lay on either side of Faculty House and could be gone for as long as two or three hours.

"Bioff's still at Misericordia." Jimmy checked the dean's expression, but saw no sign of remorse for the injuries she had inflicted. His words to her yesterday, that she *hurt* people, had not made a dent. "They're releasing him this afternoon. Brown, too. No one's seen Fairweather."

"If you'd been doing your job, you wouldn't have let Alex get to Littlefield. That's one of your problems, Jimmy. You're not aggressive enough." The dean's eyes narrowed. "You know, if you had been more forceful with Millicent, Alex would never have gotten into her panties."

The cruelty of the remark, in its way as harsh a betrayal as Millicent's own, brought tears to Jimmy's eyes, followed by intense embarrassment, then rebellion. "James," Jimmy said. "My name is James." He knew that his timing was off. He had planned to introduce the change to Elspeth in a quiet, even intimate moment, and blurting it out now completely undermined the expected thrill of liberation from the mewling nursery of Billies, Randies and Bobbies.

"And that's why you've been calling me 'Elspeth'—as a way of telling me I should call you 'James'? That's the silliest thing I ever heard. 'Jimmy' isn't why no one takes you seriously. You could have a name plate on your desk that said, 'James Ludwig Fleenor III' and people still wouldn't take you seriously."

"James or Jimmy—either way, I'm not the one who buried the night program under a rock where Littlefield was sure to find it. Who sold off the library to pay for Billy Rubin. Who battered Bioff—"

There was a knock at the open door and Alex came into the dean's office. He rested a narrow haunch on the edge of the conference table.

"Am I interrupting something personal?" Each word slipped out as if it had been individually lubricated.

The dean said, "We were just talking about how Jimmy let you singlehandedly wreck the future of this law school. How you betrayed us. Somehow, six hundred night students and the fifty lawyers who teach them, even old Cruikshank, can keep their lips zippered, but you, who expressly promised not to speak to any member of the accreditation committee, decide not only to talk to its chairman, but to give him a guided tour."

"Littlefield came to the basement on his own. I found him there. What did you want me to do—throw him out?"

"You didn't have to talk to him. You didn't have to take him to the sub-basement."

"He'd already made up his mind. Even Jimmy couldn't stop him."

Jimmy straightened at this acknowledgment of his power from a foe.

If the dean heard the reply, she ignored it. "And don't think I'm unaware of your role in stirring up the students who stole the model of our new building."

Alex looked at the empty conference table, yellow eyes brightening. "I don't know what you're talking about." Either he was a good actor, or this was the first he'd heard of the model's abduction.

"It was the day students who stole it," Jimmy said to Elspeth, "not the night students." He wasn't siding with Alex, just trying to bring clarity and order into a morning mired in havoc. Even as he rejected the logic that the adversary of my adversary is my ally, he felt an uncomfortable affinity with the man who was cuckolding him.

"Of course they were day students," the dean said. "But you"— she nodded at Alex—"think that if I cave into their demands and give them the old-fashioned law classes and clinics they want, it's going to create a beachhead to bring your operations above ground."

Alex said, "The model doesn't mean anything to me. The new building, either."

"It should," the dean said. "Until that building goes up and our regular faculty moves in, there's no place your people can go."

"But there's not going to be a building. Daylight may not reach us downstairs, but we do get newspapers. Even television. We know the SEC's frozen your donor's funds."

"So then you know you're going to have to stay where you are."

Alex said, "You disappoint me, Ellie. I thought that after my tour with Littlefield, you'd realize you have to move us upstairs. We're going to be in our new offices and classrooms by the beginning of next semester."

"That's ridiculous!" The dean glanced at Jimmy, but he didn't reciprocate with his usual reassuring nod. "Do you know how close we are to the Top Five right now? *U.S. News* would drop us to the bottom tier if they found out we had a night school. That it's occupying our top floors while the school's leading scholars and teachers languish in the sub-basement."

Alex said, "And what do you think they're going to do when they hear you've lost your accreditation? Littlefield was appalled at the conditions he found downstairs. How do you think he's going to write up the Law School's facilities in his report to the ABA? No, Ellie. You're going to be the first Yale Law graduate who's dean of an unaccredited law school."

"You don't know that."

Jimmy prayed that the rattle he heard in the back of Elspeth's voice wasn't fear, for nothing breeds chaos like fear. On the carpet next to the conference table, the stain of Bioff's dried blood was the size of two hands positioned like a butterfly and reminded Jimmy of the dangers of disorder. He said, "Think about it, Elspeth. A third of the faculty is out of the country. Most of the others only come in for classes one or two days a week. We have loads of free office space. And you don't need a classroom for Skype. The students can watch in their dorm rooms."

Elspeth didn't once glance at Jimmy while he spoke. Her attention was still fastened on Coyle. "Littlefield's only one member of the committee," she said.

"I heard about Bioff." Coyle's tongue darted. "Really, Ellie, a big girl like you picking on a little fellow like him. No doubt he'll want to dissent from Littlefield's reservations. Support you to the hilt."

"Fairweather loves how we use Skype. I'm sure he'll report that. And he's the only committee member from a first-tier law school."

Coyle shook his head, "But where is he? Do you even know if he's alive?"

"You can't raise yourself up by pulling us down," the dean said.

"I don't want to pull you down, Ellie. I want us all to be lifted. And remember what my students bring to the law school. They're on the income side of the ledger. Also, my faculty work for nothing more than coffee and donuts."

"Maybe that's because that's all they're worth," Elspeth said. "Most of them are part-timers. Not a single one of them has an advanced degree. Has any publisher ever asked them to write a blurb for an important book? Your teachers would kill us with *U.S. News*. So will your students' GPAs and LSATs."

"Georgetown has a night program," Alex said, "and they're ranked fourteenth."

"That's exactly my point," the dean said. "I didn't pull State up from the bottom just so we can be ranked fourteen."

Something was very wrong, Jimmy thought. "Why is it so important to be higher than fourteen? Than fifty?" Jimmy realized that he was shouting, but finally he had Elspeth's attention. "Why is it important to be ranked at all?"

Elspeth clasped her hands and set her jaw, biting back on her impatience with him. "We've already had this conversation."

"But Alex hasn't. He needs to hear this." Again, this unfamiliar sense of allegiance to his foe unsettled him.

"For one thing," the dean said to Coyle, "it's for the applicants we admit. Applicants study these rankings the way they once studied the pecking order of fraternities and sororities. If we drop just one notch down the *U.S. News* list, the students we're trying to recruit, the smart ones, are going to sign with whatever school replaces us. That means the students who do come here are going to be less smart than the ones we have now."

"And—"

"And," the dean continued, ignoring Jimmy, "less smart means lower GPAs and LSATs, so that when *U.S. News* looks at our numbers again next year, they'll drop us another notch—if we're lucky. More likely several notches. So the following year we get students who are even less smart, with even lower numbers."

An impulse of the old loyalty toward his dean rose in Jimmy like a fluttering of wings. He said, "And with the applicant pool shrinking, the GPAs and LSATs get worse."

The dean nodded, but her eyes stayed on Alex. "Do I have to explain how a death spiral works? The only way you escape a complete collapse is to do what Chicago is doing with that $10 million gift it got: you bribe the best students in America to enroll at your school. But the legislature won't give me that kind of money."

"So what if the worst happens and we spiral down to the bottom?" Jimmy was aware that Alex was studying him, and he thought that he detected a glint of respect in the golden eyes. "That means we get to teach people who may not be blessed with brilliance, but at least have a genuine desire to become lawyers. Someone has to teach them."

"But who, Jimmy?" Elspeth leaned back in her chair as if she had won the argument. "Our present colleagues? Do you think Benjamin Hubbell wants to teach a classroom of clods? That Billy Rubin wants dunces drafting expert opinions for him and preparing his witnesses? Writing his briefs? No, our colleagues—your friends—are going to pack up and take jobs where the smart students are because they need smart students to do their work for them. And what impact do you think their leaving is going to have on our ranking?"

Alex said, "Tell him, Ellie. Tell Jimmy the real reason it's so important for State to make it into the Top Five."

Jimmy heard in Alex's voice the same occluded menace that he'd heard in Judith Waxman's at Sunday night's party when she

asked him why he thought Elspeth travelled so frequently to Chicago. He was afraid to hear Elspeth's answer.

"Why do people climb Everest?" the dean said.

Alex said, "I can't believe it, Jimmy. I can't believe that you're
the only person in the Law School who doesn't know that Ellie's
headed for the Supreme Court. The Top Five is her ticket to the
Court."

Jimmy's heart shrunk. "That can't be true," he said, even as
he understood that it was. It was the only fact that could possibly
make sense of this whole Top Five madness. As much as it hurt
him to do so, Jimmy looked directly at Elspeth. "You wouldn't
do this, would you?"

"It's well off in the future, Jimmy. The Justice isn't going to
retire this term. She's—"

"I thought that we were building something here. An intellectual home."

"A school, Jimmy, not a home. One of your virtues as associate dean is that you've never drawn a line between your work and
your life. But this is a workplace. Not a home."

There was a tenderness behind her words that Jimmy hadn't
heard before, but the ring of a warning bell, too.

"Just think, once I go on the Court, you can be the school's
next dean."

"Right," Alex said. "You can be the dean of an unaccredited
law school."

"Of an unaccredited Top Five law school," the dean said.

A profound chill gripped Jimmy; his forehead grew damp.
Everything around him was crumbling. The dean's warning rang
louder. Not only was the Law School at risk, but his home, too.
He remembered Sunday's nightmare vision of his house imploding.
"You're moving into my house," he said to Alex. "You're going to
evict me from my home!"

"Bravo, Jimmy," the dean said. "Now you'll know to be more
careful in choosing your allies."

"As a matter of fact," Alex said, "Millicent and I have talked
about my moving out of my apartment and into your house. We're

thinking about right after Thanksgiving. You can still have the living room if you like."

To Jimmy's surprise, there was no malice in Alex's voice. And the news itself shouldn't have surprised him. He had, as Elspeth said, always put work over home, and for too long, it now appeared, for Millicent's loyalty to last. Already he missed her terribly. How was it possible for a woman to betray her husband with another man, yet still make dinner for him—albeit take-out, as often as not—and wash his laundry and fold his underwear?

Alex cast a significant look at the dean. "Millicent is the first woman who understands me. She also says that I'm the first man who truly understands her. Understands her needs."

"Nobody's moving into your house, Jimmy," the dean said. "I also promise you that no one is moving Alex's night school above ground."

Alex said, "I know how important order is to you, Jimmy. Trust me or not, it's important to me, too."

Jimmy believed him. Alex may be cuckolding him, but he never tried to hide it. He never betrayed and deceived him as Elspeth had. Would Elspeth wash and fold his laundry? He thought not.

"There's a difference between disorder and change," Alex said. "Particularly when change leads to a new order. That's where we are now, in the midst of a transition to a new order. And people who are smart about change can always do better for themselves in the new order than in the old. Are you going to be smart, Jimmy?"

Jimmy couldn't believe that this was happening, and so swiftly. In less than a month, he was going to lose his marriage, his home and his beloved school. He glanced at Elspeth for support, but she was looking out the window toward the twin spires across the parkway, something he had never seen her do before.

Jimmy's first, scary thought was that he was on his own. His second thought was that he was not alone at all, for the blood of generations of German engineers and precision machinists, the ethos of *Fleenor und Söhne*, coursed through his veins. The chill departed, his brow cleared, and Jimmy apprehended the layers of meaning beneath the family motto. *Alles in Ordnung* meant not only that everything is as it should be, but also that there is an underlying and universal order to events and consequences, one step preceding another; gains to be sacrificed if necessary to avoid still greater losses. Surrender is not surrender if it leads to victory. Or something like that. A rapid but precise calculation removed any doubt that the first step was for Jimmy and his colleagues in the day program to surrender the upper floors and move to the basement, and even the sub-basement, if that was what it took to save the accreditation of his school. As to the steps required to restore him to his rightful place in his beloved home and in Millicent's heart, that would come next. First things first.

"You have to give Alex what he wants, Elspeth."

The dean, who had been riveted to the sight of the twin spires, turned back to the two men, her face ashen. "That is simply not possible. I won't let it happen."

"It's for the greater good of the school," Jimmy said.

"Don't you tell me what's for the good of this institution!" Ash instantly turned to crimson. "Who has been slaving since she came here to make something of this place, to bring a measure of distinction to this school's name? Tell me one thing Alex has done, or, for that matter, you have done, Jimmy, to bring this school into public esteem."

Jimmy said, "You have no choice, Elspeth. You have to move Alex's people upstairs and our people down."

Amusement flickered into life across the dean's face. "You want to replace me, don't you? That's what this is all about. You want my job."

"No one could possibly replace you, Elspeth." He meant the words as he spoke them but, having spoken them, he wondered if he was right.

"Well, I'm sorry, Jimmy, but until the president of the United States calls, I'm staying right here. And the president is not going to call if I exile my highly paid and highly talented faculty to the basement."

"Then I have no choice but to resign as associate dean," Jimmy said.

"To do what?" Elspeth arched an eyebrow. "Teach? No offense, Jimmy, but you've never been particularly strong in the classroom. That's why I made you associate dean."

"I know that," Jimmy said. "But, if you don't go along with the plan I've described, I'm leaving the school."

"To do what? You're 53 years old, you've never practiced law, and your only area of expertise is *The Bluebook*. Does anyone other than law review editors even use *The Bluebook* anymore? No, Jimmy, I think you're going to stay right here."

How pathetic had he become that, in the barrage of the dean's insults, it still mattered to Jimmy that she remembered his age. But he was not going to back down.

The dean's secretary, Eve, appeared at the door. "The president's on the line. He says it's urgent."

Alex looked at Jimmy and winked. Whatever Elspeth's fantasies were, the two men knew that the call was not from the Oval Office.

Jimmy reflected. Elspeth. Millicent. Which marriage should he save? Which one abandon?

TWENTY

Apart from the occasional rattle of chains, or the whimper when a swerve threw him against the side of the van, Fairweather was as quiet this afternoon as he was talkative last night. Was this the end of philosophy, Wendell wondered—or the beginning? Had the Feckles Professor learned from Epictetus that a man's worth is to be measured not by what he says, but by what he does and that, so far as *doing* goes, the most virtuous behavior is that which aligns itself with the fates? Walk that path and you will be immune to all misfortune. Hadn't Wendell's section leader at Harvard said precisely that on the very day that Wendell coldcocked him?

Wendell himself was jittery and not feeling at all aligned with the fates. His last two transfers of contraband to Teng had been at night, but today the law school proprietor had insisted on 3:00 in the afternoon, and the exchange was going to be a good deal more overt and consequential than handing off a dime bag of ganja to a law student. His drug dealer's second sense warned Wendell that this could be a setup. Yet there is no lure like commerce, so here he was under a cold but brilliant autumn sky, turning into the Big Y parking lot where anyone, including an off-duty cop helping the missus with her shopping, could see him.

Teng had beat him to the parking lot. This time he was standing next to a Cadillac Escalade, its ebony paint so jewel-like that the SUV could have just come off the showroom floor. "American, Wen-dall!" Teng cried as Wendell approached. "Now I drive a fine American car!" He rapped the door panel with a knuckle.

Today's suit was a three-piece charcoal and ecru glen plaid that Wendell was certain he had seen in *GQ*. The pocket handkerchief was of the same color and pattern as Teng's perfectly knotted polka-dot tie.

Wendell slid open the van's side door so that Teng could look in. "May I assume, Wen-dall, that the professor is not here just to keep you company? That this is in fact a delivery?"

"As promised," Wendell said. "But that makes him a bond jumper, so you have to cover the bail."

Teng paused for an instant's calculation before saying, "Agreed."

Wendell had given up trying to match the elegance of Teng's dress and today wore only a t-shirt and jeans. He shivered against the cold, anxious to complete the exchange and get away. He didn't know what the rules were in China, but did Teng understand that in the United States it is against the law to trade in humans?

Teng climbed into the van and proceeded to examine the legal philosophy professor with the same care that he had inspected the building model last night, peering into his ears, resting a palm on his chest, checking his pulse, striking him just below each knee with the edge of his hand to test his reflexes. Fairweather didn't utter a word of complaint.

"I promise you," Wendell said, "he is in perfect health. All of the faculty will be. State has the best employee health insurance of any university in New England, and I'm sure Columbia will stand behind Professor Fairweather. If any problems come up, just send him back and I'll give you your money back or replace him with someone equally suitable. Even another legal philosopher, if you want."

"He smells," Teng said. "Haven't you bathed him?"

"I'm sure that as soon as you get him to QingXing he'll clean up just fine."

"Unfortunately," Teng said, "as of yet we have no running water in QingXing. It is on the drawing board, of course. After we erect our new law building." He reached out a hand. "The handcuffs?"

With the key Wendell handed him, Teng unshackled Fairweather from the van and led him to the Escalade. Fairweather
rubbed one wrist, then the other, but otherwise maintained his
stoic silence.

"Cat got his tongue?" Teng's look was meaningful.

Wendell opened the back door of the Escalade, but Teng leaned
in and slammed it shut with one hand, while pinching his nose
with the other. "Hertz will charge me for the stink." He pointed
to the roof of the SUV. "Help me get him up here."

"You can't drive with him on the roof." Ever since Mitt Rom-
ney strapped the family dog to the roof of his station wagon,
the state police had been on the alert for this form of transport.
"They'll have questions you won't want to answer."

"Well, just for now, then. We'll take him down when I leave."

Each man took one side of their captive and, with a good deal
of grunting and time-outs, but with no resistance—or help—from
Fairweather, Wendell managed to situate him on the roof of the
Escalade, face upward. He secured the philosopher's right wrist
to one end of the chrome-plated luggage rack and used the other
set of handcuffs to secure his left ankle to the other end.

Teng was out of breath from the effort, and spoke in gasps.
"Where are the others? You promised me twenty. Our founding
faculty."

Surely Teng hadn't expected him to pack 20 more faculty
into the van like forced laborers. Wendell went to the vehicle and
returned with a fat manila folder. The deal was almost done. Just
the exchange of money and he could be on his way. This was the
moment in the movies when the police descended from everywhere, revolvers drawn. Still, as much as he wanted the transaction to be finished, Wendell felt regret, too, for he had grown as
fond of Teng as he might of a spiritual master. He handed the
folder to Teng. "They're all in there."

Wendell was proud of the folder's contents. It had required an
all-nighter in front of the computer downing endless cans of Red
Bull, but he had assembled a complete package for each of the 20
members of State's law faculty who would spend the next aca-

demic year in QingXing. There was a résumé for each, of course, and a bibliography listing their dozens of blurbs. But most of the paper in the bulging file was copies of emails that Wendell had intercepted and emails that he had sent; travel arrangements cancelled and rerouted; visiting professorships declined; sabbaticals and leaves of absence applied for. He hadn't yet had a moment to sign up any one of the professors, but with a deft wielding of the carrot and the stick—the faculty's absorbing penchant for foreign travel and its susceptibility to Wendell's blackmail—he had no doubt that he would have commitments from them all by the end of the week, maybe even by the close of tonight's reception for the visiting committee at Faculty House.

The bill of sale that Wendell was delivering to Teng included State's very best: Heidi Hoehnemann-Mueller (from a map that Wendell consulted on the Internet, QingXing appeared to be in the middle of a desert, but surely Heidi would find a beehive somewhere); Max Leverkase (a whole new field of research for his measuring tape beckoned); Bob Morrill and his former wife, Lucy, had in nearly thirty years never been in the same hemisphere at the same time. (Wendell felt like cupid, bringing them together.) There were no Bog Dwellers in the file, for if Teng was serious about aiming for the U.S. News Top Five, he surely didn't want anyone who taught traditional subjects, and Wendell had decided against Alex Coyle on the theory that he could earn a premium for the Director of Special Projects the next time the Chinese celebrated the Year of the Snake. As it was, this shipment would seriously diminish State's law faculty, but at least half of these people would be away from the campus anyway, and there was always Skype, of which the dean was so fond, to connect the twenty with their students in College Station. Skype did work in China, didn't it?

When at last Teng finished paging through the file, he said, "Where is this fellow I see all the time on television? The criminal lawyer. Mr. Billy Rubin. If we are to achieve international prominence, I must have a star of his magnitude on my faculty."

"Our deal was for twenty, and that's what I bought you. And in less than twenty-four hours."

"Of course, Wen-dall, and you have done brilliantly. Apart from Mr. Billy Rubin, this is the faculty of my dreams. A fantasy faculty! You have brought me the *U.S. News* first team."

The entrepreneur removed a folded, thick brown envelope from an inside pocket, and Wendell marveled at how he could have lodged so bulky an object in his suit jacket without ruining its elegant line. This man still has much to teach me. Wendell said, "What about the building? Will it be ready for classes?"

"Such a thoughtful young man," Teng said, "to be concerned about the working conditions of your faculty. Yes, of course it will be ready. I immediately FedExed the model to QingXing, and tomorrow morning a team of laborers will start laying the foundation. Twenty-four hours a day they will work, in shifts of course. In no more than three months, the building will be completed, and every last desk and doorknob will be in place. This is China, Wen-dall."

Wendell looked into the envelope. Bundles of $500 bills, stacked three thick, filled it to the top. There was enough here to cover Fairweather's bond and pay off the Porsche, with more than enough left over to start up his hedge fund. No more drugs or blackmail or any business that required so much of his own labor. The only way to accumulate real wealth is to leverage the labor of others or, even better, their greed. He glanced up at Fairweather, shackled to the roof of the Escalade, prone and entirely still. True stoics have many virtues, among them silence, but sometimes you can't tell if they're alive or dead.

A breeze wafted through the parking lot, stirring in Wendell's mind the image of his grandfather. Why was the old man shaking his head? Was grandpa disapproving of this transaction? No. The transaction was fine. Grandpa disapproved only of his taking the envelope. Was it too little money, or too much? No, it wasn't about the money, either. Something was missing. Or overlooked. An opportunity. Wendell heard himself say, "Am I right that you are planning to make money from your law school?"

Teng laughed. "Why of course, Wend-all. A great deal of money. Why else would I want to own a law school?"

"How will you do that? My grandfather told me that a university loses money on every student it enrolls. No matter how much tuition it charges, it loses money."

"Do you really believe that?" Teng's smile turned instantly to a frown. "I do not wish to question the wisdom of a grandfather, but please don't tell me that I misjudged your intelligence."

"Well—"

"Tell me, Wen-dall, how much does an American law school charge its students for tuition?"

As a reader of the *U.S. News* rankings, Teng surely knew the answer, and Wendell understood that the entrepreneur was testing him. "Around $48,000," he said. "But that's the private schools. State schools charge less."

"Rest assured," Teng said, "there is no question but that Qing-Xing will be a private law school. The Chinese want the very best. They want to pay top dollar for everything. How many students are there in an American law school?"

"A big one like State or Harvard, 1,600. The smaller ones like Yale—"

"No. Big. The Chinese want the biggest as well as the best."

"What does this have to do with making a profit?"

"Multiply $48,000 times 1,600, and what do you get?"

The economics of Wendell's commerce in marijuana never reached beyond five or six hundred dollars, and Wendell was mentally still moving zeroes around when Teng said, "$76,800,000. And you understand, of course, there is really no limit on how much a school can charge. Law school tuition is like your housing prices here before the bubble burst. When no one pays cash and everyone finances, the sticker price is the last thing anyone looks at. QingXing could easily earn revenues of $100 million or even double that. But, never mind. Let's use your number."

"The $76,800,000 isn't profit," Wendell said. "A law school has expenses."

"Very good, Wen-dall. And tell me, what is a law school's biggest expense?"

Wendell's position in the mailroom gave him access to every professor's paycheck as well as the school's annual budget. "Faculty salaries."

"Which are how much?"

Wendell had no idea where this was going. "Maybe $200,000 a year on average."

"Yes, but who makes this average? Surely a man like Mr. Billy Rubin makes three times that, almost as much as your football coach. And Harvard faculty, I believe, *average* $300,000 or more. But to be conservative, let's use your number, $200,000. How many people does a large law school have on its full-time faculty?"

Wendell was certain that Teng knew the answer, and was still testing him. "Maybe 100 or 120."

"And how many hours a week do they teach?"

"The ones who teach the most hours? Six hours a week."

"How many weeks a year?"

"Each semester is fourteen weeks, so they teach twenty-eight weeks a year."

On the roof of the Escalade, a ray of sunlight bounced off the luggage rack. The Feckles Professor, haggard and unshaven, had turned on the rack and was intently following the conversation.

"Do these faculty spend any time writing? Preparing books or articles for publication?"

"Not at State."

"And it's the State faculty I'm hiring," Teng said. "How much time do they spend grading exams and papers?"

"At State? None. The students do all the grading."

"Excellent," Teng said. "So let's see where we are. We have a faculty member earning, conservatively, $200,000 a year for 168 hours of work. What does that come to per hour?"

Wendell didn't even try.

"It comes, dear Wen-dall, to just over $1,190 an hour. Or, if you multiply that over a forty-hour week and a fifty-week year— it is fair and reasonable, isn't it, for people to take a two-week vacation?—that means that, for the work that they do, every

member of your faculty is being paid, on average, at a rate of
$2,380,000 a year."

Speechless, Wendell could do no more than nod.

"And they all have tenure, don't they? That means"—Teng
seemed astonished, as if he had just discovered this—"that means
that for this amount of income, a Wall Street banker's income,
they don't even face the risk of being fired or going to prison the
way an investment banker does!"

Wendell had never heard of a banker being fired, but he
nodded.

"Just think, Wen-dall, these faculty make the equivalent of
$2,380,000 a year without taking any of the risks that a busi-
nessman like me takes every day. The risk of losing everything!"

Lionel Teng was a genius. Wasn't that the mark of genius—
to see truths that no one else saw? Wendell could talk with Bill
Gates, or even Mark Zuckerberg, for hours and still not receive
one-tenth of the wisdom that Lionel Teng was dispensing in mere
minutes.

"Do you understand the meaning of this, Wen-dall?"

As in the minutes before his first meeting with Teng, Wendell
sensed that he was at a pivotal moment in his life, on the cusp of
a great change, and the thrill of it surged through him. On the
Escalade roof, even Fairweather twisted at his restraints to listen.
Nothing in Wendell's life would ever be the same.

"So, now you can see why American law schools look like they
lose money," Teng said. "At the equivalent of $2,380,000 a year,
the professors have sucked all the profit out of the system. Right
here, on your capitalist American soil, your law faculty has perfected socialism to a degree that would bring tears to the eyes of
Karl Marx and Vladimir Lenin. Even Mao Zedong would weep
in admiration. These professors of yours are no mere wage earn-
ers. No, these running dogs have appropriated to themselves all of
their institution's profit, and then some, for if these schools operate
at a loss, as your grandfather says, that can only be because the
professors are further fattening their incomes with donations from

the law school's alumni. We in China, with our socialist market economy with Chinese characteristics, can only look with bitter envy at what your American law professors have accomplished."

A sudden fear overtook Wendell, the fear that if he moved from this spot, if he even breathed, Teng's revolutionary insights would evaporate, the golden tablet would dissolve into a cloud, and with it any chance for Wendell's likeness to be carved onto a mountainside next to those of Gates, Jobs and Zuckerberg. But something was missing in Teng's formula.

"You are wondering, aren't you, Wen-dall, how I will change this at QingXing." Teng beamed. "Capitalism, dear boy, pure capitalism." Teng's smile actually wrapped around his face. "I will restore profits to where they belong, to capital—to me—and pay only wages to my faculty. What is the minimum wage in America?"

"Here, in College Station?" Wendell told him. He knew the figure because it was what State paid him to work in the mailroom. The rest, from drug sales and blackmail, was gravy.

"I am a generous employer." Teng tapped the manila folder. "I will pay these faculty U.S. minimum wage, although even that is higher than a professor's wage in China. The faculty can live like kings on that."

"Not if they teach only 168 hours a year."

"Good for you, Wen-dall. I admire your concern for the worker class. Of course you are right. This is not enough money to survive on, even in QingXing. So we will find other courses for them to teach, enough so that they are working forty hours a week, fifty weeks a year."

"There aren't that many law courses," Wendell said. He knew there would be a problem like this. His face fell—in his mind's eye, literally—off the mountainside.

"This is not a problem! We will find other work to fill their forty-hour week. On the outskirts of QingXing I own a small factory. Tire recapping. We make retreads. The automobile business in China today is enormous. Everyone in China owns a car, or soon will. Everyone needs retreads."

It occurred to Wendell that, even as clueless as they were, no
State professor would travel to China for minimum wage. Even if,
in the excitement to sign on, no one asked him about the financial
arrangements, the fever would subside once they arrived in Qing-
Xing. When word got out of what Teng was paying, it would be
impossible for Wendell to recruit the next twenty, and the twenty
after that. A responsible entrepreneur must consider the long term.
This was the most perplexing dilemma Wendell had confronted in
his brief start-up career, but for some reason he was confident that
he would think of how to fix the problem, and soon.

Wendell's expression must have betrayed his worry because
Teng said, "You should have no concern. My factory will be the
perfect place for your professors. You can't imagine how hard it
is to find Chinese laborers today. Every Chinese wants to start his
own business. But that is the great virtue of professors. They have
no talent for business, so I can be confident that they will never
leave the factory floor."

"Except," Wendell said, "to teach their classes. Six hours a
week." On the Escalade roof, Fairweather looked stricken.

Teng put an arm around Wendell's shoulder. "I can speak to
you man-to-man, Wen-dall? Businessman to businessman?"

The arm could have been his grandfather's for the warmth that
suffused Wendell's entire being. "With our faculty at work in my
retread factory, do you realize we will not have the costly sexual
harassment suits that so distract your universities in America?
Senior professors making goo-goo eyes at new faculty members.
Teachers chasing after their young and pliant students. I expect
this is how our friend up there—" he shot an eyebrow in Fairweather's direction "—got into trouble. He couldn't keep his fly
zipped. But after eight hours a day recapping tires—I am told
that this is brutal, killing work—I promise you they will be too
exhausted even to think about hanky-panky with our students."

What did Teng mean by *our*? Was he referring to his corporate
self, or to his partners in China, or did the arm around Wendell's
shoulder mean that Teng was prepared to include him as a partner?
Throughout the conversation, a single number—$76,800,000,

Teng's nimble multiplication of student population by annual student tuition—remained lodged like a splinter in Wendell's mind. Year in, year out: $76,800,000. But, still, the thought nagged at him that something was wrong about this arrangement. The parking lot breeze carried an urgent plea from Wendell's grandfather, but what was it? After a long, mindful moment, Wendell handed the fat, money-stuffed envelope back to Teng. "I'm sorry. I can't take this."

"What?" Teng looked truly surprised. "Please don't disappoint me, Wen-dall. I understand that you may feel some scruples, some sympathy for these professors, but remember that they are the most mercenary sort of people, not the kind of professionals who drive industry. As I said, they are dogs, and deserve no sympathy at all."

"Fifty percent," Wendell said.

"What's that?"

"Fifty percent. In return for delivering the faculty for our law school, I want fifty percent of the school's revenues." He didn't know if he would regret this later, but he added, "You can keep whatever you make on the retread business."

Teng laughed. "No, that is impossible. You are a fine young man, Wen-dall, and I have great admiration for you. But you are . . . *young*. Merely a novice. And," Teng tried to hand the envelope back to Wendell, "this was our agreement."

"Then, you don't care about the *U.S. News* ranking."

"What does *U.S. News* have to do with this?"

"One of the most important numbers that *U.S. News* weighs is faculty–student ratio. Twenty faculty and a dean may be a start, but at $48,000 a year tuition, I'm sure you are going to want to add a great many more students, and if you want to keep up with Harvard, you're going to have to add a great many more professors. American law professors. As you said, the best in the world. The gold standard. *U.S. News* will accept no less. And if I'm going to assemble that faculty for you, provide the engine that drives the school's profits, I figure I should get a share of those profits. Fifty percent."

"Oh, Wen-dall, I truly love how you think. And it will be good to have a junior partner. A young man to carry on my work someday. So, let us say five percent."

Wendell smiled to himself, for he had Teng now; he had got him to buy into the principle of partnership. Now he just had to raise the share to the fifty percent he deserved. What a joy commerce is! "How would you like to have Billy Rubin as the twenty-first member of your founding faculty?"

"You are an intriguing young man, Wen-dall!"

From the emails that he intercepted, Wendell knew that Rubin was a smart and tough negotiator, but if Teng was any indication of the moral qualities of China's new entrepreneurial class, this would be an opportunity for Rubin to get in on the ground floor of a massive white-collar crime spree. Wendell said, "If we keep his legal fees for ourselves, he'll be a better investment than all the others put together."

"Alright, then," Teng said. "Twenty-five percent."

A croak came from the roof of the Escalade where, eyes bulging, the Feckles Professor had pulled as far from his restraints as was humanly possible. "I want five percent. I'm going to be your Dean. That makes me management, not labor. Just five percent."

Fascinating, Wendell thought. The answer to the riddle of how many figures it takes to turn a stoic into a Wall Street banker is eight. He followed Teng's example and ignored the legal philosopher. "You know, Lionel"—it felt good to call his partner by his Christian name—"the way an up-and-coming law school like QingXing gets attention for itself isn't with its regular faculty. They're just the laboring engine. No, if you're an upstart and you need instant prestige, you have to rent it, like a tuxedo. You have to hire celebrity lecturers. We call it the 'halo effect.' It's why so many American law schools in the *U.S. News* bottom tiers turn somersaults to get a U.S. Supreme Court Justice to spend a day or two on campus, giving a speech or conducting a phony seminar."

"And you can get us an American Supreme Court Justice?"

"I can get you much better than a Supreme Court Justice. But for this I want to be an equal partner in the business."

"Who?"

"Fifty-fifty."

"Who? Tell me!"

"The Dalai Lama would make quite a splash, wouldn't he?"

"A *splash*? Do you read the newspaper, Wen-dall? Watch the television news? The Dalai Lama would never travel to China."

"He owes me a favor, Lionel." It felt wonderful to be able to say to a man as worldly and accomplished as Teng that the Dalai Lama owed him a favor.

"A favor?"

"My grandfather is a big fan of the Dalai Lama. That's how I met him. Do you know the way he arranges his robes so that his bare arms hang out, like he's showing off how buffed and toned he is? Well, the Dalai Lama *is* buffed. So I asked him what his work-out program was. He told me, free weights. He seemed to like the yin and yang in that, "free" and "weight." I suggested that he look into the Universal weights system. He'd have less risk of injuring himself. You can still get Universals on the secondhand market. A month later, I got a note from him saying how Universal equipment changed his life, and if there was ever anything he could do for me, all I had to do was let him know. If anyone is going to keep his word, it's got to be the Dalai Lama."

"I'd think that if he gave you one request, you would ask that, when he reincarnates, you would be the next Dalai Lama."

Wendell grinned at his new mentor. "Is that something you would settle for?"

After a moment's reflection Teng shook his head. "I suppose not. The only thing that beats making money is making more money."

"And the only thing that beats that is for two people to make money together."

"Wen-dall, you are a joy."

"Fifty-fifty?"

"Fifty-fifty." Teng extended his hand. "You will find that I, too, am a man of my word."

No sooner did Teng's fingers touch his than Wendell's thoughts raced ahead. Profitable as this new venture would be, especially once the school's student body scaled up to match the country's size, the QingXing Law School was just a beginning. If people in fact believed that American law schools and law teachers were the best in the world, then the opportunities for franchising State were tremendous, not only through Asia, but throughout the developing world, and maybe even into Europe. Wendell considered whether his likeness on the mountainside should be perhaps just a few feet higher than those of Gates, Jobs and Zuckerberg. Whoever made these decisions, he'd have to have a word with him.

Questions tumbled over each other. Should he include Teng as a partner in his rapidly expanding law school chain? Better to have him as a partner than as a competitor, Wendell decided. Also, there was still so much he could learn from his remarkable mentor. Like how, without fail, he manages to work that perfect dimple into the knot of his polka-dot tie.

TWENTY-ONE

I f Rawleigh Bartles's office looked like Hollywood's idea of a university president's domain, that's because it once was. Rebuffed
in their quest to use an Ivy League president's office for scenes
in the campus comedy, *Dude, Who Moved My Bong?*, the film's
makers turned to State, which instantly agreed. As it turned out,
the president's office couldn't accommodate the full complement
of cameras, lights, sound equipment and crew, so the filmmak-
ers made do instead with a nearby staff lunch room, decorating
the space with mullioned windows, dark mahogany wainscot-
ing, faded Persian rugs, a huge, carved oaken desk, tufted leather
chairs and a grand *faux* marble fireplace. The then-president (now
chancellor) found the transformation so successful that, after paying the film company a larcenous sum for the furnishings, he took
possession of the former lunchroom himself. The damp aromas
of Yankee pot roast, stewed vegetables and Salisbury steak still
clung to the walls.

Although Elspeth couldn't imagine why it would be necessary
for the chancellor to participate in the meeting, Rawleigh had
gone down the hall to collect his predecessor, who now occupied
the original presidential office. While Jimmy, Alex and Littlefield
inspected the elaborately sculpted *papier maché* fireplace, the
dean affected to study the framed objects on the walls. (According to the brass plate set into each heavy, gold-filigreed frame,
the works, which on earlier, more hurried visits to the office she
had thought were dark, expressionist oil paintings, were in fact
soil samples collected by the president from regions across the

state. She found herself wondering what would be on the walls
if Sheldon Lustig, the Nobel short-listed podiatrist, had beat out
Rawleigh in the competition to be president.) But in the main,
Elspeth's thoughts were elsewhere, for she knew that unless she
locked down her worries and ratcheted her intentions this meeting
was going to be a catastrophe.

"Well, here we are then!" The president came into the office,
followed by the erect and ruddy-faced chancellor, completely—
even pleasurably—recovered, it appeared, from his Sunday night
collapse. When the president directed the chancellor to one of
the two chairs by the side of his desk, and then indicated to the
others the chair that each should take, Elspeth realized that he
had planned the seating as carefully as if this were still a movie
set. The chancellor and Littlefield were on the president's right,
Jimmy and Alex on his left. Elspeth was in the chair in the middle, directly across from the president. Now she understood why
Rawleigh had brought the chancellor and the others to his office.
This was going to be more than a knuckle-rapping for the incident with Bioff, and the president wanted behind him not only
the moral authority of the chancellor and Littlefield, but also the
operational strength of Jimmy and Alex.

The president glanced at the others to harvest their support,
then lowered his brow at Elspeth. "This is very difficult for me,
Ellie, but for a law school dean—for anyone—to do what you did
to this librarian Bioff is completely unacceptable. I understand
that you just snapped. That you turned into a wild woman. Such
behavior is totally unforgivable. Indeed, after consulting with
university counsel, there is no doubt in my mind that it was a
criminal act."

No, Elspeth thought, what was criminal was for the president
to order her here and reprimand her in the presence not only of
the chancellor and Littlefield, but two of her subordinates. Who
could have informed on her? Only Jimmy, Brown and Bioff himself knew what had happened, and, according to the nurse she'd
spoken to at the hospital less than an hour ago, Bioff was in no

condition to communicate with anyone. Also, the nurse told her, Brown's jaw was still sealed shut by yesterday's massive wad of salt water taffy, and the dean thought it unlikely that this timid soul would have committed the incident to writing.

That left one person.

The president looked at his allies a second time before speaking. "It pains me to do this, Ellie, but I am going to have to ask you to request a medical leave."

Elspeth had expected Rawleigh to ask her to resign, but this was even worse, for though she knew that his lips formed the words, "medical leave," what her brain heard the president say was "psychiatric leave." Fear sliced through her thoughts: crazed former law deans, even ones as smart and charismatic as Elspeth Flowers, simply do not get appointed to the Supreme Court of the United States. It occurred to her that Rawleigh's earlier use of the word "criminal" had also been premeditated. In the view of the president and the others in the room, the attack on Bioff had been the criminal act of a lunatic, the very sort of behavior that, if she resisted their entreaties today, could get her committed to the institution for the criminally insane across the parkway. Jimmy, her loyal lieutenant, had known from the beginning that this was the president's plan, but had said nothing.

"Associate Dean Fleenor has already agreed to fill in for you during your absence."

Of course he has. Why else would he inform on her? This also confirmed Elspeth's guess about the recent change in Jimmy's behavior. He was indeed making a run at her office. Jimmy, her amiable dunce, had stage-managed her exit. Bravo, Jimmy!

"As a precaution," the president said, "I have instructed Facilities to change the lock to your office suite at four o'clock today. That will give you sufficient time to return to your office, collect your personal effects and say goodbye to your staff."

"I'd like the dean to stay for the rest of our meeting," Jimmy said. "She may have some suggestions about how to get us out of this accreditation mess."

How different this meeting was going to be from the one that she and Jimmy had planned only weeks ago! With the experience of two previous ABA visits behind him, Jimmy had explained to her that the report to the university president that concludes these visits is not the candid assessment that it appears to be, but is in fact a scripted collaboration between the dean and the visiting committee—the regulated and the regulator—to extort the president. Before the presidential meeting, the dean itemizes for the visiting committee chairman those corners of the law school's operations—scholarships, say, or salaries—that need more funds, and the chairman, in his report to the president, explains that unless the law school receives the additional support, its re-accreditation will be in jeopardy, surely a black mark for the university over which he presides. But today's meeting was going to follow a very different script. What had gone wrong?

Rawleigh made a pretense of looking about. "Where is your other committee member, Ellie? This fellow from Columbia. You haven't killed and dismembered him, have you?"

Before the dean could answer, the chancellor said, "I believe he's with Wendell. The boy has arranged some kind of administrative post for him at a new law school in China."

"China? Wendell has connections in China?" The president's mood lightened at the news. "I don't know when I've met such an entrepreneurial young man."

Only if you count blackmail as entrepreneurship, the dean thought.

The chancellor returned the president's smile. "I like to think, Rawleigh, that the boy has benefitted from my advice over the years."

This is some kind of private joke, Elspeth thought. "You advise our mailroom clerk? Wendell Ward?"

"He's my daughter's boy. The only one of my seven grandchildren who has ever shown a willingness to listen to me."

Maybe it was the president's demand that she take a medical leave that had put her off-balance, but Elspeth heard herself say the dumbest thing she could imagine anyone saying: "Wendell is your grandson?" She looked over at Jimmy and Alex to see if they knew, but their expressions were blank.

The chancellor beamed. "When I told Wendell that all great American careers started in the mailroom, I meant it only as a metaphor, that they all started at the bottom. I didn't expect him to take me literally. But he's certainly done well for himself, wouldn't you say? Sadly, no matter how strongly I encourage him, he refuses to return to Harvard. I do believe he's dropped out for good."

This time Elspeth restrained herself from asking whether Wendell was a Harvard dropout.

"You really didn't know about Wendell?" the president said. "That just shows how out of touch with your own institution you are, Ellie. Where do you think I get my news of developments at the Law School? About what's happening in your office? I'm certainly not going to find out from you. Wendell tells the chancellor and the chancellor tells me."

So this was how the president learned about the Supreme Court nomination. About Max Leverkase's secret manuscript.

"Well," the president said, turning to Littlefield, "perhaps you can advise us on what we need to do to clean up this little mess, as Jimmy calls it. But please bear in mind that, despite the dean's free-spending ways, we are under severe budget constraints. My cash drawer is far from full."

Did Rawleigh actually think that throwing a few dollars around would resolve the committee's problems? Could the intelligence that Wendell passed on to him be that faulty? Or had the president and Littlefield scripted their own Passion Play in which Rawleigh would act out the part of the straight man?

Littlefield turned his chair a degree to include the dean and her two associate deans. "Actually, President Bartles, the role of an ABA visiting committee is only to identify broad areas that have fallen below standard, not to prescribe specific remedies. Those are for the dean and—" here he looked at Jimmy—"his or her faculty colleagues to address."

"And you're saying that there are such . . . substandard areas at the Law School?"

"Only three, really. The curriculum, the teaching facilities and, as Mr. Bioff would tell you if he were here, the library collection."

Inside Elspeth's head, the few sprites who had gathered for the meeting cheered at the chairman's omission of Skype from his list of miscreancies. Perhaps Elspeth had convinced him of the technology's merits, and even without the threat of blackmail that she had employed with Fairweather.

"The ABA requires approved schools to offer extensive instruction in substantive law, and I'm afraid that the great majority of the Law School's courses don't even come close."

"That's not true," Elspeth said. "Just look at the first-year curriculum. We have all the basic first-year courses. Torts, Contracts, Property, Civil Procedure—"

"Yes, those are the names on the courses, but do you have any idea how your first-year instructors in fact spend their time in the classroom? I don't think the ABA considers the rules of advocacy inside a beehive to be Civil Procedure."

"What about Admiralty? The course you're going to teach next semester."

"Those are your plans, Dean Flowers, not mine. I have absolutely no interest in teaching Admiralty."

"But you're the state's leading practitioner—"

"You know, Dean Flowers, you have a way of making up your mind about what people will do without even consulting them. If you had only asked, I would have told you about my lack of interest just as I told Dean Fleenor here."

The president coughed to clear his throat. "And the library collection?"

"You don't have one," Littlefield said. "It no longer exists. At least not on the Law School's premises. The dean has apparently sold the collection to the institution for the criminally insane across the parkway."

"Well," the president said, "then we'll just have to get it back."

"That's going to take more than snapping our fingers," Jimmy said. "They paid cash for the books, and the librarian there told me that the inmates actually line up to borrow them."

Elspeth thought, for all his ambition, Jimmy is going to have to learn that it's not enough for a dean to point out problems. He is going to have to identify solutions, too, if he wants to survive in this job.

The president leaned back in his chair, a portrait in fatigue. "And the teaching facilities? What's our problem there?"

Alex said, "Mr. Littlefield has visited the basement and the sub-basement. Where the library used to be. Where we now run the night school."

"And?"

"And," Alex said, "the conditions down there wouldn't pass the Geneva Convention's standards for the minimally humane treatment of prisoners of war."

"That's only because your faculty are spoiled children," the dean said. "I haven't heard any of the old-timers complain." She looked at Littlefield. "George Cruikshank loves teaching down there."

Alex's tongue darted dangerously. "That's only because, at his age, he's glad to have a place to teach."

"What you need," Jimmy said to the president, "is for the Law School to get everything back in order."

"Exactly," the president said, glancing over at Littlefield. "Whatever it will take for the Law School to be re-accredited."

Littlefield gave no sign that he had heard. In fact, for the past several minutes he had entirely abstracted himself from the conversation, and his gaze, though directed at the fireplace, was unfocused.

"It's very simple," Alex said to the president. "Jimmy's first action as Acting Dean will be to move the clinic and night classes upstairs."

So. Her two associate deans, the cuckolder and the cuckoldee, had conspired. Elspeth said to Alex, "I've been telling you for a year now that as soon as we move into the new building, you and your crew can have the upstairs."

"Except," the president said, "there isn't going to be a new building. Even if Randy Barrimore gets access to his funds, I got a call from the senator that he's had second thoughts about putting his name on the building. If you remember, Ellie, the senator is the only reason there was going to be a building in the first place."

Silence fell on the room. Since running the gauntlet of architects and contractors together, Elspeth had come to think of the building as Randy's tribute to the intensity of the friendship that had developed between them. The silence persisted. Whole minutes passed and the atmosphere grew dense with expectation, as if the room itself was daring one of the six to say something worthy of breaking the quiet.

At last, Littlefield pressed his hands on his lap and rose. "Just connect the dots."

"Do what?" the president said.

Everyone waited.

"All things are connected," Littlefield said. "Some are just more obviously connected than others. One problem with people today is that they don't think. They let clichés do their thinking for them. 'No-brainers' are just that: brainless. People say, 'As different as night and day,' but in truth how great is that difference? A mere millisecond separates midnight from morning, darkness from dawn. There need be no greater separation between the night law school and the day law school than there is between night and day. Just connect the dots."

"But where would the classes meet?" Jimmy asked. "And there's still the problem of the library—"

"Apparently you didn't hear me," Littlefield said. "Follow the example of your colleague, Luis Morales: trace where you have been; look at the future possibilities all around you; pick the one possibility that will save your life; and connect the dots. If a man is drowning, you throw him a life ring. If an institution is failing, you throw it a line."

"But what's at the other end of that line?" the president said.

Frustration edged Littlefield's voice. "As Mr. Coyle has proposed, it's very simple. You just move the clinics and night classes upstairs, and you move the day faculty—"

"Where?" The president was still baffled. "Mr. Coyle has just told us that the sub-basement is unfit for human occupation."

Mentally quicker than the others, and desperately more fearful, the dean knew exactly where.

Littlefield gave the others a sympathetic look. "Why, to the nut house across the way, of course."

All jaws in the room dropped but Elspeth's.

Littlefield didn't appear to notice. "Since the legislature expanded the insanity defense four years ago, they have plenty of vacant space over there. Empty rooms. Wards the size of lecture halls. And your library books, or most of them, are already on site. I couldn't imagine a more straightforward solution to where to hold your day classes or to keep your library."

"This would take money," the president said. "Money we don't have."

"I don't see why it should cost anyone a dime," Littlefield said. "Met. State provides the space and the books—they already have both—and you provide the people. The day faculty just have to take the footbridge over the parkway to occupy their offices and teach their classes."

Elspeth's heart froze. The prospect of confronting those twin spires daily, of actually walking through the empty, cavernous halls, was too large and incomprehensible for her to absorb with an emotion as small as terror. Finally, she said, "But what about the inmates?"

"Why," Littlefield said, "I suppose they could audit your faculty's classes, maybe even register and take them for credit. If they're as engaged as their librarian says they are with reading law books, I'm sure they'll be fascinated by Professor Hoehnemann-Mueller's Beehive Court. Professor Hubbell's instruction on how to order pizza."

"But these people are crazy!"

"Who do you mean?"

"The inmates!"

"Ah, yes," Littlefield said. "The inmates. This will be a whole new life for them. Think of all the good you will be doing. Opening up new vistas for them. The Amazon rain forest. The Arctic. Ideas even their fevered minds could never dream of."

Elspeth looked at the president, who had been nodding approval of Littlefield's plan. "What about our regular students? Why don't you move the night school over there instead?"

"Because the night students have no reason to go," Alex said. "Your day students won't go either. As Howard said, we're going to merge night and day. They're all going to stay in the old building, enroll in my clinics and take classes from my faculty."

"Why in heaven would they do that?"

"For the same reason they hijacked the model of your new building, Ellie. That's always been your blind spot. They were demanding that the Law School teach them law. All of them are going to stay on this side of the parkway and take the traditional law classes they want and need."

"And I'm supposed to send my faculty over there? To teach lunatics?"

"I wouldn't worry about it," the chancellor said. "Wendell tells me that a good number of your faculty are going to be in China next year. Teaching in some small town there. It sounds very pleasant."

The dean had to find out what Wendell was up to. But first she had to extinguish this fire. "What do you expect my Poets to do at Met. State? My Quants?"

"The same as they do on this side of the parkway," Alex said. "Not meet their classes. Not publish books or articles. Not teach law. Basically, not do anything law teachers are supposed to do. And it will be fine, because none of their students over there is ever going to graduate. We don't have to worry that they are going to be set loose on unsuspecting clients."

When Elspeth turned back to the president, he had swivelled his chair toward Littlefield and the chancellor for a whispered conference. On the other side of the desk, Jimmy was exchanging *sotto voces* with Alex. She felt like a guest at a dinner party, abandoned by her table partners, able only to capture snatches of their conversations. From the whispers that she caught, it seemed that the president, Littlefield and the chancellor were reviewing the political hurdles to effecting a merger. All agreed that the chairman of the legislature's Higher Education Committee would need to be consulted, but they differed on which committee would have jurisdiction over the merger—the Public Health Committee, Human Services or the Judiciary Committee, which, the chancellor insisted, had jurisdiction over prisons and, therefore, over Met. State. Would it be necessary to get clearance from the governor's office? The president would call Senator Troxell to encourage him to intercede. "I wish," the president said, "that she had spent some time making friends on the Higher Education Committee," leaving no doubt among the two others, or Elspeth herself, about who he meant.

The words between Jimmy and Alex were even more intense. "This is going to happen with your support or not," Alex said. "Maybe," Jimmy said, "but the transition will take a lot longer without me smoothing the way. You already said so. How important is this to you?" "There is nothing more important," Alex said. Jimmy said, "Millicent? My home?" The question stopped Alex for no more than a few tense seconds. "She's a terrific lay," Alex said, "and I like your house. The rugs, the pictures, the fireplaces. But moving my people upstairs is more important."

"Then we have a deal?" Alex nodded and Jimmy said, "This is where we're supposed to shake hands, but you'll understand if I don't."

Elspeth had not felt so alone or unprotected since the afternoon in New Haven when she had been called out of class to take the telephone call informing her that, 300 miles away in Skowhegan, her father had been felled by a bowling ball. She felt powerless against this conspiracy of 11-year-old boys that was forcing her to choose between the ignominy of a medical leave and the horror of exile to the snakepit across the parkway. Drawing on her every last shred of will, and in a voice resonant enough to cut through the tumid cloud descending over the gabbling heads, she said, "I hope that you gentlemen have ironed out your personal disagreements and legislative maneuvers, because none of your plans can move forward without my say-so."

The president was first. "You have no power, Ellie. I—"

"You're going to say that you can fire me? I suppose you can. But do you want me to explain to these men why you won't?"

The president shifted uneasily in his chair.

Littlefield said, "I'd like to hear. The Law School is too important to me for its future to be sacrificed because of some personal history between the two of you."

The president looked at Littlefield. "I really don't think, Howard—"

"You can hear it now," the dean said, "or you can watch it Friday on the six o'clock news. The story of the lawsuit I will file to enjoin the president from firing me. The story of how this president has sought at every turn to put hurdles in the way of innovations introduced by the Law School's first woman dean, innovations that brought the Law School to the very brink of admission into the *U.S. News* Top Five—the first state law school even to come within mooing distance of that distinction—hurdles that the dean surmounted, and innovations that she accomplished, only by outsmarting a not very bright university president. There will be a photograph with the story. It will show me in a low-cut evening gown and Rawleigh with his arm thrown around my shoulder, and it won't take much for a viewer to imagine the expression on Rawleigh's face as a leer. I'm sure the reporter will add that the picture sits in its own special place in Rawleigh's private den, on a bookshelf, like a *Playboy* centerfold. A sex toy. And don't even think about shredding that picture, Rawleigh, because, if you do, the first question I will ask at your deposition is why you destroyed evidence in a lawsuit."

The dean rose as if to leave. "Consider—Howard, Rawleigh, all of you—consider the misery that such a lawsuit is going to bring down on this place."

"This is blackmail!"

"Actually, Rawleigh, it's extortion. You can ask the very expensive lawyers you're going to have to hire to defend this lawsuit to explain the difference to you between blackmail and extortion. And as to this crazy idea to merge the Law School into the loony bin across the parkway, I can tell you right now—"

"No, not right now," Littlefield said. "Please, Dean Flowers, give the plan the benefit of calm reflection. Tonight will be ample time for you to make your decision. Say, by midnight. Unfortunately, I won't be able to join you at your banquet, but I'm sure the others will be prepared to hear what you have decided."

Rawleigh Bartles had called the meeting, but Howard Littlefield had taken command of it from the moment he rose from his chair, and there were no dissenters.

"That will be fine," Elspeth said. "Tonight will be fine."

TWENTY-TWO

MEMORANDUM
(Dictated but not read)

To: File
FROM: H.L.
RE: Only Connect
DATE: November 2

How wrong I was, dear Etta, to think it necessary to travel a great distance in order to *Connect the Dots*. Who would have thought that, geographically so close but with such diverging missions, the Law School and the Metropolitan State Hospital for the Criminally Insane would be such logical candidates for a merger? But, then, insanity is no stranger to the Law School. What but madness can explain the decision to hire law graduates to chase pigeons from the library? To double tuition only in order to double scholarships? To discourage applicants whose grades are higher than needed for admission, while encouraging those who fall below the admissions cutoff? Only lunacy can explain why law is more of a stranger to the Law School than it is to Met. State, where I am told the inmates get in line to read case reporters and treatises. How easy it is to connect the dots if we just put away our preconceptions!

Nor in the end was it necessary to trudge miles of forest in order to connect the dots of my own life. Just as the taste of that tea-soaked madeleine opened the floodgates of memory for poor Proust, so for me the cafeteria aromas in the president's office swept memory back a half-century to those long afternoons in the "Rat," writing epic poems for the literary magazine by day, exposés for the college newspaper at night, and light verse for the local shopping paper in between. The surge of memory reconnected me to the bursting joy that writing once held for me, the rapture that spurred my youthful pen to connect the quality of yesterday's hay to the flavor of this morning's milk, butterflies to tornadoes, before that sad and fateful day when law school shattered my vision of a vastly interconnected world.

So, dear Etta, as you may yourself have connected the dots by now, I have resolved to embark on a writer's life or, more precisely, to embark on a writer's life *again*. Yes, this will require me to abandon my law practice—you alone know how weary I have grown of admiralty law!—but be assured this will not be the occasion for us, you and me, to separate. I have invested a great deal of my life in this law firm (too much of my life, three former wives would testify, and a subject on which wife number four will invoke the Fifth), and I am confident of persuading the Executive Committee to provide me not only with an office, but also with the continued services of you, my muse.

Since you thought so well (thank you for expressing the compliment!) of H.L.'s small narrative tracing his journey through the Law School's basement and sub-basement (I have come to think of it as my own *Notes from the Underground*), I have decided as my first writing project to expand on my visit to the Law School, starting with Sunday evening's party at Dean Fleenor's home. Every word of my account will of course be true, but is it bold to think that a commercial publisher might take on such a piece of writing by a novice like me? Even in college, as I was writing my epic verses, it was my dream that someday a publisher would bring my efforts to an audience larger than family and schoolmates.

Modest though it will be, I suppose that the details of my work in progress may touch certain sensitivities, and prudence would dictate the use of a pen name—for credibility's sake, perhaps the name of an already published law professor-novelist who would be familiar with the nature, if not the particulars, of this academic *mis en scene*. Could you, dear Etta, inquire after someone who might agree to lend his (or her) name to this little enterprise? Yale of course overflows with law professor-novelists, but I don't believe anyone in New Haven would consent to have his (or her) name associated with so humble an effort. Maybe you can find someone at one of the West Coast law schools—a novelist, to be sure, but not a particularly famous one.

Oh, Etta, I have not felt such bliss since I was a young scribbler haunting the swampy corners of the "Rat"! The prospect of compiling this account draws me back to the great works of my undergraduate days at State, not only *Notes from the Underground* and *Remembrance of Things Past*, but Waugh, Huxley, Orwell and Forster, back to the shock of recognition when, opening *Howard's End*, that epigraph—"Only connect"—leapt off the page, capturing in two words my consuming youthful passion to connect the many fragments of existence, all of them. "Only connect the prose and the passion, and both will be exalted, and human love will be seen at its height. Live in fragments no longer." What nobler, more thrilling object could I possibly pursue? I tell you, Etta, these old bones fairly vibrate with the excitement of an 18-year-old boy!

Finally, thank you for confirming that Howard Jr. will attend tonight's banquet at Faculty House in my place. Please inform the members of the firm's Executive Committee that I will be unable to join them for our monthly dinner meeting as planned, as I must be elsewhere. More anon.

TWENTY-THREE

Because she was in a rush to get home and dress for the banquet, the dean took Wiscassett Parkway, even though that meant driving past the Metropolitan State Hospital for the Criminally Insane. Curiously, she didn't think about this until miles later, at which point she considered whether it was a good or a bad sign not to have reacted to the institution's proximity. A good sign, she decided, for unless she took the medical leave that Rawleigh ordered, Met. State was about to become a permanent feature of her daily life.

She removed the ringing cell phone from her purse.

"Is this Dean Flowers? This is Melinda Hines from *U.S. News.* You know, *U.S. News & World Report.*"

Do I know? The dean's heart raced, but she kept her voice cool. The reporter sounded young. "Yes, Melinda. How can I help you?"

"I'm working on a story about the decision to expand your law school."

What decision? She had left the meeting in the president's office with the understanding that no decision on the merger would be reached until tonight, and then only after consultation with her. Someone—Jimmy; it had to be Jimmy—had leaked a false report in order to make the merger a *fait accompli.* Acting dean for less than a day, and already Jimmy had grown shrewd. From long experience with the press, the dean knew that she needed to be careful with the reporter. She should say something that sounded concrete but wasn't, and at the same time she should probe for information. "Well, you could certainly say we're sailing into uncharted waters. How did you learn about this?"

"We *are* a news magazine," the reporter said. "Maybe we're not on newsstands anymore. But you can find us on the Web."

"Of course you're a news magazine." Even as she heard the defensiveness in the reporter's voice, the dean realized that she had indeed forgotten that *U.S. News* was a news magazine. "And one of our finest ones, too. Miles ahead of *Time* and *People*. Right up there with *The Economist*. What I meant to ask was, how did you find out so soon?"

"Off the Bloomberg wire. We don't have a bureau in Beijing, but they do."

"Beijing?"

"I'm sure it was Beijing, but maybe it was Shanghai. Does it matter?"

"Of course, you're right, it doesn't matter at all." Why would Jimmy use this roundabout route to leak news about the merger with Met. State? "It's amazing, isn't it," the dean said, "the way the Chinese are moving ahead on so many fronts."

"Well, isn't that the reason you're opening a campus there? To be the first American law school to catch the Chinese wave? Everyone here is saying it's a brilliant move. Visionary." The reporter paused. "I'm not sure I'm pronouncing it right. Is it 'QingXing'?"

"Your pronunciation is perfect," the dean said to what sounded like loose change falling on a hardwood floor. She thought, if you're a news magazine, not a television or radio station, why would it matter if your pronunciation was correct? She strained to focus on the meaning of the reporter's words. What was happening in this place called QingXing? Wendell, she remembered. In the president's office, the chancellor had said something about Wendell, his little entrepreneur, arranging a position for Fairweather in China. She had to handle this carefully. For all she knew, the reporter had a direct line to the people at *U.S. News* who were responsible for the annual rankings. "I don't know how Bloomberg found out, and none of this is authorized for public release, Melinda, but I'm glad to help a reporter whenever I can.

Why don't you tell me what you know, and I'll tell you, strictly off the record, whether it's true or just a rumor."

"My information is that you are actually building an American law school from the ground up."

"That's correct," the dean said. "I can confirm that." Where did Wendell get the idea to do this? Where did he get the money?

"We know of course that there's already a law school in Shenzhen—am I pronouncing that right?"

"Perfect," the dean said.

"And that it's run by the former dean of the University of Michigan Law School—"

Michigan was number nine in the *U.S. News* rankings. Not bad company, the dean thought, but she was about to do a lot better.

"—but we also understand that this other school is part of Peking University, not a stand-alone law school like yours. Also, their American teachers are just part-timers. We've been told that your faculty will be full-time."

Other than Fairweather, where had Wendell found American law professors do this? "As full-time as academic work can be," the dean said, fighting to keep the mounting excitement out of her voice.

"Are you going to seek accreditation? The American dean at Shenzhen has been trying to get the ABA to accredit his school so its graduates can practice in the United States."

You're asking this, the dean thought, of someone who can't even get accreditation for a law school on American soil. "Really, we haven't yet opened our doors, so any talk of accreditation would be premature. But even without accreditation, we have thousands more applicants than we can possibly admit."

"I understand that the building in QingXing is going to be a copy of the one you're building in College Station."

Not a copy, now that Randy's funds were frozen, but an original; the only one. But the dean was not ready to spread that bad news. "Yes," she said, "you could call it a Chinese copy." The students had stolen the model from her, and evidently Wendell had stolen it from them. She felt a warmth toward her mailroom boy that she would not have thought possible. He was the little brother she never had—or wanted.

"According to Bloomberg, the school's going to be a subsidiary of People's Tire & Rubber Company of QingXing. Is that to avoid resentments among Chinese toward American businesses?"

"The Chinese are a splendid people." The dean rounded the corner onto her street. She couldn't wait to share the news with Randy. She wanted the interview to be over. "They are marvelous hosts. They have been extremely generous to us in every way. But we are guests in their country and we want to fit in as best we can."

"What can you tell me about the curriculum?"

"You're much too clever for me, Melinda. You've taken me well beyond confirming or denying a Bloomberg wire report, which is all, really, that I should be doing. But, I'm curious, what does *U.S. News* think of our plans?"

"Like I said, everyone here thinks it's brilliant. And that's not just me. The whole newsroom thinks so. My editor says it's the most foresighted step taken by an American law school since Langdell introduced the case method at Harvard over a century ago."

If the former dean at Michigan could run a law school in Shenzhen, why couldn't Elspeth Flowers run one in QingXing? She instantly dismissed the thought. Her future was on the Supreme Court bench, and if she managed the news of the Chinese campus carefully, that future could now be secure.

The dean turned, one-handed, into the driveway and coasted down to the condominium's garage. She spoke into the cell phone. "Is anyone in your newsroom . . . er . . . speculating on the impact that our new campus might have on State's ranking next year?"

"Well," the young reporter said, breathlessness rising in her voice, "everyone knows that, on the numbers, you're a shoo-in for the Top Five. But, on reputation—and you know this is the time of the year when the voting starts—"

I know, the dean thought. I know. This is the cycle of my life.

"—and, when news of your Chinese branch gets out—"

"Not a branch," the dean said. "An identical replica."

"—well, when the news gets out, there's no predicting where in the Top Five you'll wind up. My editor, who is never wrong about anything, thinks you may actually knock Yale off its perch. And Yale has never *not* been in first place. Amazing isn't it?"

The dean didn't know if the reporter meant it was amazing that Yale had been number one forever or that State was going to displace it. It didn't matter. She was in her parking space, her free hand in a fist and pounding on the steering wheel. It required all of the willpower she possessed, but in a completely collected voice she said, "I hope you will keep me up to date on any developments in the rankings."

"Of course. I'd be glad to. But I hope you'll let me know about any further developments with your China campus. I don't need an exclusive, but I do want to be the first reporter you talk to."

"Agreed," the dean said. "You'll be the first to know." Indeed, she thought, unless I get control of this story, you'll know before I do.

Randy Barrimore was a man whose presence filled any space he occupied, but Elspeth's apartment when she entered felt like a void. No logs burned in the fireplace, no cell phones lay charging on the dining room table. There was only a legal pad borrowed from her study. Elspeth could guess at the content of the childishly scrawled message, but she picked up the pad anyway.

Dear Ellie,

As my grandma would say, I flew the coop! You told me it would be no problem to stay in your home, and I know that, loyal friend that you are, you would say that all over again if you were standing here right now. But since Mr. Rubin has arranged for me to face criminal as well as civil charges, my staying would only get you into deeper trouble. If we were face to face right now, I know you would use your lawyerly powers to get me to stay. That's why I am taking the coward's way out and leaving now.

As you must know by now, Ellie, the government has seized all my assets, including the funds that I set aside for your new building. You had pinned your hopes on that building lifting your school into the top rank of American law schools, and I apologize for letting you down.

Your kind hospitality has given me the chance to think, and not only about my situation (and, of course, Bianca's) but also about you and the things we talked about Monday night in front of the fire. I hope you will pardon me if I correct you on a couple of counts. (Since Mr. Rubin has kindly arranged for me to face 15 counts, this lets you off easy!)

Do you remember when I said that what frightened you about that building across the parkway from your office was that one day you would look up and see your mama looking out of a window there? Well, Ellie, I was wrong, and I hope you will forgive me for saying that the person you are truly afraid to find looking back at you from one of those empty windows is yourself.

But I hope you will listen to your friend Randy and have no fear. You are not only the smartest gal I know, but also one of sanest. (Although, to be honest, the only people I spend my time with these days are New York bankers and Washington lawyers!) You were just a girl when you lost your daddy, a man whose love never failed to make you feel powerful. Of course his passing knocked your compass needle off a degree or two. But I know your daddy brought you up right and, trust me Ellie, you have the strength inside you to set that needle true.

When your daddy told you to dedicate your life to something larger than yourself, I don't think he meant that you should set out to be a Justice on the U.S. Supreme Court (although if that should come to pass, and my case comes before you, I hope you will put in a good word for me with the other Justices). I don't think your daddy would have set his sights so low for little Ellie. Why not Chief Justice? Or President of the United States? No, what I believe your daddy meant (and I say this because, from what you told me, he sounds a lot like my own daddy) is that you should devote your life to the service of some cause larger than just yourself. Mother Teresa did more good for humankind than all the Justices of the Supreme Court put together.

What should you do? Well, I don't know anything about this whole law business, but there is something very wrong when a government lawyer decides if he's going to sue me based on how the story will play on the evening news. (No, Randy hasn't done the perp walk, and never will. Not ever!) Your daddy told you to work for something larger than yourself—not to be larger than yourself. Be right-sized, Ellie. Be a teacher and instruct your students for jobs in society that are sturdy and just. You can't do that up there with the Justices, juggling cases like they were apples and oranges, with no regard for the little people down below.

I hope you will forgive the scribblings of a former college football player who majored in Classics, not English, in order to make his way through school, and I hope you know how much Bianca and I both love you and pray for your happiness.

Yours always,
Randy

Elspeth still had the legal pad in her hands when the phone rang. Her first thought was that it was Randy, calling from the airport to tell her that he had changed his mind and was coming back to the apartment. Her second thought was that it was the reporter from *U.S. News* with the promised update on next year's rankings. It was the long-distance operator, asking if she would accept a collect call from a "Mr. Smith."

"What can I do for you, Senator?" If the senator was calling collect, that meant he was at a pay phone somewhere—did pay phones still exist?—without aides or FBI wiretappers listening in.

"I just got off the phone with Rawleigh Bartles. He told me about your accreditation problem. Howard Littlefield was on the call, too."

"Why would they need to bother a United States senator with something as trivial as the re-accreditation of a state law school?" The fatigue that Elspeth heard in her own voice startled her. The ceaseless work and responsibility had exacted a toll. If she worked every Saturday and Sunday all year long, no wonder she was exhausted by Wednesday. She longed to join the sprites in their boggy slumber.

"You mean," the senator said, "why would they think I'd be concerned that, thanks to your boneheaded moves—burying the night school, selling off the law library—one of my great state's greatest jewels, my alma mater, is going into the toilet?"

"My boneheaded moves didn't seem to bother you when they got Randy Barrimore to build us a new law building with your name on it."

"What Bartles and Littlefield described to me is preposterous. You're a fine little sales gal, Ellie, but I don't know how you sold them on the idea of merging State and Met. State."

"It wasn't my idea, Senator. It was Littlefield's."

"More likely, you let him think it was his idea. The legislature will never support a merger."

The idea of a merger had so shaken Elspeth when Littlefield proposed it that she hadn't considered either the difficulty of exe-cuting it or the consequences for her assault on the Top Five if the execution failed. Or, for that matter, succeeded.

The senator's breathing was heavy, as if he'd just climbed a flight of stairs. "Do you have any notion how strong the mental health lobby is in this state? I had one of my aides drop a quick dipstick into a few of the key do-gooder groups, and he told me they are absolutely appalled at the prospect of letting a bunch of your law professors loose on these inmates. You should spend some time in the state capital. See how much love these folks have for the Law School. Some of the smarter heads in the legislature are beginning to wonder why, with applications dropping the way they are, the state even needs a law school."

"Come now, Senator, the Law School is a source of—"

"—of twice as many graduates as there are jobs for lawyers. And that's before you count the graduates coming into the state from schools in the rest of the country."

Elspeth caught herself. It was Littlefield and the president who wanted the merger, not her. "Well, if you can't—"

"I didn't say I can't. I'm just saying that I'm going to have to dig deep into the honeypot to get this done for you."

Elspeth decided not to correct the senator a second time on the origin of the merger proposal. She still hadn't sorted the proposal's pros from its cons.

Dump the merger! It was a sprite, gasping for air as it surfaced through the muck.

No merger, no accreditation, another thin voice cried.

In her imagination, Elspeth twisted a volume knob to turn down the voices.

"What do you want, Ellie?" The senator's breathing had accelerated dangerously.

"What have we been talking about for the last ten minutes? I need you to get me nominated and confirmed for the Supreme Court. That means I also need you to get the legislature to approve the Law School's merger with Met. State."

"Maybe I can manage one of those," the senator said, "but there's no way I can do both."

Did you hear that, Elspeth? The senator still sees you on the Court!

Forget the Court. You're dead anyway without the merger!

The dean imagined an algae-covered pond with thousands of croaking frogs. "Why do I have to choose? They're completely separate. One's the U.S. Senate and the other's the state legislature."

"But they're both politics. You're never going to make it as a Justice, Ellie, if you don't understand that politics is a seamless

web: federal-state, legislatures-courts—they're all part of the
same package, and you need to know how to play one off against
the other."

*Go for the Top Five! No one will know you lost your accredi-
tation until after the voting's over.*

*No! The Justice changed her mind. Your nomination's not
until next year. You'll be off the Top Five by then!*

*Melinda at U.S. News says you have it made. They'll love the
merger, too!*

Elspeth tried to estimate the chances of making it into the Top
Five if the merger failed and the Law School lost its accreditation.
Melinda's editor at *U.S. News* may have been excited about the
Chinese campus, but would QingXing be enough to outweigh a
disaster like that?

"I can give you the Supreme Court," the senator said, "or I can
give you the merger. But you have to choose."

"I suppose I could make the selfless choice and go for the
merger. But if I am not for myself, who will be for me?"

"Ah, you've been reading Newt Gingrich."

"No, that's Rabbi Hillel, and he also said, 'If I am only for
myself what am I?'"

"Well, you tell me, Ellie. What are you?"

"I want the Supreme Court and the merger."

"You're not listening, Ellie. What's it to be?"

What will U.S. News say?

What about Littlefield?

"I need to think about this."

"From what Rawleigh Bartles told me, you don't have much
time. Tonight, I believe he said."

The Court!

The merger!

"Shut up!"

There was a silence at the other end of the line before a strained
voice said, "Excuse me?"

"Not you, Senator. Some people here."

"I didn't know you had anyone listening in. Really, Ellie—"

"No one's listening." Just jabbering, she thought; not listening.

"If you want my advice—"

"Nothing personal, Senator, but I think I'll do this one on my own."

"Will you let me know what you decide?"

"You're on the top of my list," the dean said.

TWENTY-FOUR

It was only the first week of November, but State's interior decorator, moonlighting from his regular job at the WalMart in the Big Y Shopping Center, had spider-webbed the ceiling of the Faculty House dining room with string upon string of tiny Christmas lights so that the candlesticks, cutlery and white linen cloths on the two dozen tables below glowed like a scene from a holiday catalogue. Rumors had leaked of the afternoon summit in the president's office, and word had traveled through the Law School community that the evening's events were likely to be momentous, more consequential than just a send-off of the accreditation committee. The stir among the drinking and chatting crowd was electric, and the bracing fragrance of spruce, even if it was from an aerosol can, slowed the dean as she strode into the room, instantly transporting her to the wooded depths of her native Maine.

The dean had never before seen a crowd this large at a law faculty affair and, scanning the room, she realized that her itinerant faculty had somehow heard about the event and come back to College Station to hear the news firsthand. Marcy Cundiff had unshackled herself from the Amazon rain forest and, yes, even Bob Morrill, tanned and gleaming in a cream flannel suit, had flown in from Huilo-Huilo. But who were all these other people?

After what felt like hours of to and fro with the sprites chattering in her head, the dean had reached her decision only as the car door slammed shut behind her in the Faculty House parking lot. Randy was right: he *didn't* know the first thing about this "law business." It might look like the Supreme Court did little but juggle cases, but in fact there was no more important legal body in America or, for that matter, in the world—deciding where people will live, work and go to school; the quality of their home and work lives and what they learn in school; whether criminals live or die, remain incarcerated or go free, or whether they are criminals at all; even who the American president will be. This was not only important work, but work for which Elspeth's training and experience had prepared her. Of course she would go to the Court. Why, then, if the logic behind her decision was so compelling, did it feel like a hole a mile wide gaped inside her?

A small band was playing at the front of the room and, except for the couples dancing, most of the 200 or so guests had gathered around the drink and food tables, the men in jacket and tie, the women—even Judith Waxman—in skirts and heels. Each cluster of talking heads fell silent as the dean walked by, only to start up again after she had passed. Bioff, still wearing Brown's oversized trousers, was at a table in the front, plaster bandages obscuring his small features. Brown was next to him, jaw wired shut by a device that looked like a catcher's mask. Under his baseball cap, Benjamin Hubbell was in earnest conversation with Heidi Hoehnemann-Mueller, who, in the short time that the dean looked their way, had twice emptied and filled her punch glass. Jimmy was at an *hors d'oeuvres* station, his back to the dean, as was Millicent's, but Elspeth noticed that their elbows touched, a heartening sign for her luckless associate dean. On the other side of the room, the chancellor was already listing, his left arm around his wife's shoulder for support, his right ear tilted down to an effervescent Max Leverkase. Alex Coyle, an isolated figure, surveyed the crowd.

George Cruikshank was at the center of at least a half-dozen beaming acolytes. Former students? Yes, it occurred to the dean, but there were other vaguely familiar faces, too. Lawyers, some from around College Station, but others from as far away as the capital. She realized with a start that these were the lawyers who taught the night classes and supervised the basement clinics. Which of her associate deans, Jimmy or Alex, had possessed the temerity to invite them to a faculty event? Jimmy, she concluded.

Elspeth also wondered where Jimmy had found the budget to pay for the remarkably polished band now playing Rolling Stones songs. Then, as she came closer, she saw that the lead guitarist on the makeshift stage, fingers working frantically over his electric guitar, was none other than Wendell, her mailroom *wunderkind*, in a suit so tight that he might have worn it at his confirmation, and around his neck—the neck that just hours ago she had so wanted to throttle—a gorgeous, impeccably knotted polka-dot tie that matched the silk handkerchief in his breast pocket. Another youth was on guitar and one each on saxophone and bass. Elspeth recognized the three as law students. Behind the towering, ruby-red drum set, arms flailing, head thrashing—could it really be?—was Billy Rubin, who had apparently escaped for the evening from his labors in New Orleans. At either end of the stage were the dean's two little sylphs, their eyes riveted to Wendell, blonde tresses circling as they threw themselves into the music. When Elspeth drew still closer, she realized that none of Wendell's fingers actually touched the guitar strings, and that the gravel-throated voice wasn't his, but Mick Jagger's. Wendell was lip-syncing his way through "It's Only Rock'n' Roll." The drumsticks in Billy Rubin's slashing hands came no closer to the skins of the drums in front of him than Wendell's fingers did to his guitar.

In front of the small stage, among the dancing couples—their presence even less probable than everyone else's—were Garry and Larry, the Bucholz twins, the designers of Randy Barrimore's ill-fated solar energy investment vehicle, each with his chin on the other's shoulder. Why would the twins leave their legal refuge in East Timor and risk arrest here? Why were they dancing so close? That was when the dean realized that the two weren't twins at all, nor even brothers, but simply Garry and Larry; husband and . . . er . . . husband. Narcissist and narcissist. How many times, glancing at the gay marriage announcements in the Sunday *Times* Style section had it struck the dean that the betrothed could have been fraternal, if not identical, twins, they looked so much alike?

What a special thrill it must be to look across the pillow in the morning and see your own image looking back!

The dean stepped onto the stage, and Wendell took that as a signal to switch off the amplifier. The room turned still. Public speaking was as natural for Elspeth as breathing, so she was startled by the tornado of butterflies that spun around her heart. She knew that she had to open with upbeat news. That put out of bounds the accreditation committee findings, or at least a strictly accurate version of them, along with her own, personal decision for the future. But what good news was there to report? Of course. It had been handed to her hardly more than an hour ago!

The dean dismissed the microphone that Wendell offered. "Dear, dear colleagues," her voice boomed over the crowd, "what a pleasure it is to welcome you here this evening to celebrate not only the completion of our accreditation committee's visit—a visit not without its own successes—but also to celebrate some thrilling news that I received just this afternoon." In crowds, if not one-on-one, the dean had a sensitive ear for her audience, but she heard no intake of breath in the room, no evidence at all of anticipation. Fine, she thought, see if this doesn't knock their socks off. "I have learned today, strictly in confidence, but from the most unimpeachable source at the magazine itself, that our Law School, yours and mine, will this year breach the citadel of the *U.S. News* Top Five!"

There was a resonant, *Hear! Hear!* from the chancellor, but he was at that advanced age at which the ear registers tones more than words; oldsters, like dogs, will bark agreeably at whatever the speaker says, so long as the tone is buoyant. A few hands clapped, but without passion, followed by a hollow silence. What had gone wrong? Had she been flogging this beast too long? Or was it possible that, though the unprecedented achievement meant everything to Elspeth—a state law school in the Top Five!—it meant nothing to her colleagues. Should she report that she had learned from the same impeccable source that the Law School might actually topple Yale from first place when the results were released in March? No, Elspeth decided. The Top Five was apparently no more than a dean's prize, and of little concern to the faculty. The mile-wide hole inside her grew wider.

Then the galvanizing thought struck her—tell them *why* the *U.S. News* reporter had called her. *China.* What American academic's pulse didn't quicken at the mere mention of that vast, roiling, exotic country? She looked over at Wendell, who held out the microphone to her a second time, then turned back to her audience. "I have a second announcement, but first I'd like to see a show of hands. How many of you have visited the People's Republic of China?"

To Elspeth's surprise, no more than a half-dozen hands went up from her well-traveled faculty, but the sharp catch of breath from the crowd, the sense of anticipation that she had expected earlier, now filled the room. "Well, how many of you here would like to go to China? How many of you would like to teach there, all expenses paid?"

There was a sudden release and in unison scores of hands followed Elspeth's example and flew into the air. "Well, that is just wonderful," the dean said, "because for those of you who don't regularly follow the Bloomberg wire, I can report the truly exciting news that we have today formally established, in the ancient city of QingXing, the very first full-fledged American law school in China. Indeed, State can today proudly claim to be the first American law school anywhere outside the borders of the United States!"

A succession of rim shots from Billy Rubin underlined the announcement, muting Wendell's cry—"It's Lionel Teng's school! It's not ours!"—from all but Elspeth. The dean raised her arms to the rising murmur in the room. Done right, there is no better way to get credit for an achievement not your own than to award credit to the individual actually responsible. "No, please don't applaud me. This remarkable achievement was not my doing at all, but rather was the result of hard spade work by our distinguished ambassador to foreign parts, our part-time mail specialist and full-time blackmailer"—she turned to Wendell and shot him a dramatic "only-kidding" wink—"Wendell Ward! Of course, my hand was always there in the background to guide him, but it was

Wendell who negotiated the establishment of our new campus in QingXing, China." The dean realized that with these few words she had exhausted everything she knew about the Chinese campus. "I would like to invite Wendell to share with you our unique vision for QingXing."

Wendell lifted the microphone, and a voice that was more like an amplifier's squeal echoed through the room. "Well, everyone, as the dean said, we're opening in QingXing next year, and we've already selected twenty of you to teach with us in this vibrant, much-visited city."

Twenty? How had Wendell rounded up that many in so short a time? With leaves and sabbaticals, who would be left to teach classes here in College Station? And who was this "we" and "us" responsible for issuing these invitations? There was something in the youth's manner that seemed to exclude the Law School from the party. And where had Wendell acquired such polish? Harvard, the dean remembered. The chancellor's grandson was a Harvard dropout.

Wendell took a clipboard from off the top of a nearby amplifier, but the dean grabbed it from him and quickly skimmed the list for her name before he could deliver it into the outstretched hands at the foot of the stage. Her name was not there. She thought to ask someone for a pen before she remembered that at this time next year, when twenty of her colleagues were off in QingXing, she would be in Washington, D.C., in the midst of her confirmation hearings or, if the Justice moved up her resignation, already sitting on the Court. She returned the clipboard to Wendell, and he immediately handed it into the jostling crowd.

"For those of you who are on the list," Wendell said, the microphone just under his lower lip in the manner of the old-time crooners, "if you want to teach at QingXing next year, just put your initials next to your name, and we'll get you your visa and travel information inside of a couple weeks. If you're not on the list but you want to go, just put your name on the waiting list on the second page, and if there's an opening we'll get back to you in the order in which you sign up."

As the clipboard shot from colleague to colleague, Elspeth found herself thinking about lists. Not just the *U.S. News* top law schools. The World's 10 Best Cities. *Vanity Fair's* 10 Best Dressed. Some English snob's 10 Worst Dressed. Why are Americans so addicted to lists? The 20 Best Restaurants in New York. In Cincinnati. The 15 Best Fast-Food Burgers. Listmania was more than a craze; it was the way a country with no aristocracy kept score. No wonder a failed news magazine like *U.S. News* could make a business out of academic rankings.

"What's QingXing like, Wendell?" It was Judith Waxman, whose name was not on the list.

"For those of you who aren't familiar with QingXing," Wendell said, "we have chosen it for its natural beauty, fine food and abundance of cultural activities, and even some of the drugs that you like so much." He cocked his head and winked at the dean. "Only kidding. Our website isn't up yet, but when it is, just go to *Recaps & Retreads. cn.* and check out the campus. The provincial capital of Kunming is close by and, like QingXing, it offers a wealth of Asian cultural and dining possibilities.

"And as ancient a city as QingXing is, our Chinese hosts have promised us only the most modern accommodations and workplace facilities. Also, as I'm sure you will want to know, you won't suffer any loss in pay. Of course, Chinese law professors don't get paid like American law professors, so you will be paid only a nominal salary by QingXing itself, no more than minimum wage here. But as long as you Skype your classes back to College Station, the dean has agreed that you will continue to receive your regular State salary."

Wendell's brazenness in taking control like this angered the dean for no longer than an instant. As the *U.S. News* reporter said, the China campus was her guaranteed ticket to the Top Five, and wasn't she already paying full salary to Bob Morrill and the others who rarely made more than a video appearance in College Station? Also, if State was providing the salaries, that meant that Wendell's "we" and "us" did in fact include the Law School.

Even before Wendell finished announcing the financial arrangements, pens were out and faculty members who were on the list
were initialing their names, while others were adding theirs to the
waiting list. "And none of you have to worry about changing the
way you teach your courses," Wendell said. "The motto for our
campus is: 'Consistency, not Excellence.'"

"*Constantia virtutis non*," the chancellor cried out.

Squinting, Wendell looked out at the audience and waved.
"Hi, Grandpa!"

What a brilliant correction it had been to let Wendell and China
be the opening act for her own, more sobering announcement. The
dean returned to the front of the stage and, as if they were a pair
of victorious politicians—why did the schoolbook image of Nixon
and Agnew at the 1968 Republican Convention flash through her
mind?—she lifted Wendell's hand in hers. "So let's show our appreciation to Wendell for literally putting State on the world map."

Behind the happy hoots and applause, Elspeth whispered to the
mailroom clerk that now that he was moving on to bigger things,
he would no longer need his trove of incriminating emails, at least
those that pertained to her. Their eyes locked and an understanding
of offer and acceptance, consideration given and received, traveled
like electricity between them. After gesturing for quiet, the dean
said, "In recognition of Wendell's continuing support for all of us
here and abroad, I am pleased to announce that President Bartles
has concurred in my decision to promote Wendell from his position in the mailroom to the new post of Assistant Dean for Foreign
Campuses."

"Global Marketing," Wendell said into the microphone.
"*Associate* Dean for Global Marketing."

At the back of the room, the president looked over at the chancellor, and a moment later nodded his approval. *Hear! Hear*! cried
the chancellor, whose sideways list had grown more acute.

"Of course," the dean said, "Associate Dean for Global Marketing." Wendell's news had brought the room to a level of such
good cheer that Elspeth was certain that there could be no better

time for her own personal news. "I have another announcement for you, one that is not quite as earthshaking as Wendell's, but—"

A tall figure raced through the crowd, scarcely more than a blur, and in seconds Jimmy was on the stage behind her, instructing Wendell to turn the music back on. The opening chords of "Sympathy for the Devil" blasted from the loudspeakers, Wendell lip-synching and beating his guitar mightily and Billy Rubin pounding—almost—on the drums.

"You're going to sell us out, aren't you?" Jimmy had come up beside her, so close that his words tickled Elspeth's ear. "Wendell's Chinese campus was a distraction. You're going to kill the merger so the senator will support you for the Supreme Court."

The senator would not have called Jimmy to tell him about the choice he had given her. Her associate dean must have figured out her decision for himself. Elspeth said, "What would you have me do—stay here in College Station? Dying would be a better career move."

"Better than holding the school together? Moving it forward?"

This was a Jimmy—James—Fleenor that the dean had only begun to recognize over the last two days.

Millicent, looking chic in a black sheath dress, her hair swept up into a French knot, came onto the stage and linked her arm through Jimmy's. If Elspeth had at one time intimidated her, Mrs. Fleenor gave no indication of that tonight.

"And, if I leave," the dean said, "and the merger falls through, and the school loses its accreditation, what will you do? This morning you told me you'd quit if I didn't give Alex what he wanted."

"That was this morning. If you sabotage the merger, I'll stay here to help hold the school together. Bring it back to where it was."

Elspeth wondered if he meant bring the school back to where it was before the re-accreditation fiasco, or to where it was before she arrived at State.

"And how would you do that?" The dean was genuinely interested. "What's your plan?"

"I'd start by giving Alex the upstairs floors."

Millicent gazed up at her husband with the kind of dreamy look that Elspeth didn't think existed outside of romance novels. "Where would that leave the Poets and Quants? The historians, anthropologists and philosophers you care so much about? If there's no merger, there's no place for them to go."

"I'd find space somewhere. Rawleigh told me they're closing the Veterinary School. I'm sure there'll be an empty barn or two."

Millicent, in awe of her newly commanding husband, was everything that Elspeth had spent her career opposing: the adoring, submissive housewife whose husband, lord and master could do no wrong. A chill ran through Elspeth at the memory of what Randy had written on the legal pad: that she had averted her eyes from the asylum's windows not for fear of seeing her mother there, but of seeing herself, and she wondered if what she now saw in Millicent was what most frightened her about herself.

"Do really think they're worth saving, Jimmy? Courses in Decision Theory? Law and Culture in American Film?"

"Really, Elspeth, after all you've done to bring State's faculty and curriculum into the twenty-first century, you can't possibly ask that!"

"You know as well as I do, Jimmy, those courses are just window dressing for *U.S. News*. We put them in the curriculum only so that we can write about them in the Annual Report, and we do that only so that when lawyers, judges and law professors across America read the annual report, they will see that we are as far out on the law's cutting edge as any school in the top tier. It's the Bog Dwellers who drive the law's development, just as it's the clinicians who drive its practice."

Jimmy drew closer. "But what good is law if it has no roots in how people live? If it has no regard for their worries and aspirations? Law by itself is no more than an empty box. A geometry of rules and hard edges. By itself, law does nothing more than define the lowest acceptable standard of human conduct."

"I thought that's what you lived for. What is it—*Alles in Ordnung*? Your *Bluebook* rules."

"No civilized society can exist without rules. But an empty box is . . . well, an empty box. Law wants to be filled with history and literature, philosophy and economics if it's to have any meaning, if it's to bring any joy to those who practice it. Why do you think lawyers burn out after fifteen, twenty years in practice? Why do you think women leave altogether? It's not to have children, like everyone says. It's because women are smarter than men and they know that life is short and that practice is a dead end. Lawyers—men and women—look at their practices and all they see are rules and tricks for getting around rules. We can do better than that for our students. We owe it to our graduates to teach them how to fill their lives with a meaning that will outlast the next real estate closing or summary judgment motion."

Jimmy's little speech had made Millicent's worshipful eyes grow dewier, if that were possible. If all men are 11-year-old boys, all women are their older sisters. Curiously, Jimmy's words had moved Elspeth, too. If the dean needed proof that her once-transcendent powers had abandoned her, this afternoon's exchange in the president's office with Rawleigh, Alex, Jimmy and Littlefield were Exhibits A, B, C and D. With the force of Jimmy's plea still reverberating around her, Elspeth's knowledge that her powers were gone for good left her feeling, if not entirely adrift, then *different*.

Different, but not dumb. If she could not fit the world to her will, she would have to conform her will to the world's. But what was that will? And why, of all people, was she looking at Jimmy for an answer? Elspeth said, "What do you think I should do?"

"About staying or leaving? You have no choice. You must stay in College Station. You can't abandon the people who have entrusted their future to you." Jimmy's gaze was stern. "But about how you live your life, you do have a choice. You have to decide which is more important, the world's opinion of you or your opinion of yourself. I used to worry about what people thought of me. Most of all, I worried about what *you* thought of me. But thanks to you, I learned something very surprising."

Elspeth's *What?* could have been a schoolgirl's.

"I learned that the people who I worried were thinking poorly of me weren't. In fact, they—*you*—weren't thinking of me at all. They were too occupied thinking about themselves."

Elspeth gestured for Wendell to turn off the music. She drew Jimmy, and with him Millicent, to her side as she moved to the front of the stage. This wasn't the decision that she had brought with her to Faculty House, but it was the one with which she was going to leave.

"Dear colleagues, this is a night not just for one thrilling announcement about the future of our law school, but several." Even without the microphone, her voice filled the great room. "First, I am delighted to inform you that our night law program—both the clinics and our night-time classes—will at long last, and deservedly, move from the basement and the sub-basement of the Law Building to the floors upstairs. They will, as it is said in the Good Book, 'Come up into the light.'" Elspeth didn't know if the line was in the Old Testament or the New, but it had a nice biblical tone to it, and must have appeared in some good book somewhere. A cheer erupted from the lawyers gathered around Cruikshank and a "Hip, hip, hooray" from Cruikshank himself. There was a "Hear! Hear!" from the chancellor, but no more than a curt nod from Alex.

Soon enough, the steel-trap minds of the Poets and Quants would grasp the fact that if the night school was moving up, that meant they were moving either down or out. So, without dropping a beat, the dean continued: "And just as we have, with Wendell, celebrated our expansion to a foreign campus on the other side of the world, we can also salute the imminent move of our day faculty to a campus much closer by—indeed, to a campus just across the parkway."

An anxious buzz swept the room, and the dean realized that, while most knew about the afternoon's presidential summit, none apart from Jimmy and Alex knew of Littlefield's proposal that the Law School merge with Met. State. "Yes, dear colleagues, as soon as we receive the necessary approvals from the appropriate legislative committees for this farsighted and notably humane adjustment, approvals that I am assured will occur in the ordinary course of legislative business, and in no event later than the beginning of next semester, the classes now taught on the upper floors of the Law Building will be taught across the way at our sister institution, the Metropolitan State Hospital for the Criminally Insane. Of course"—here the dean resisted the impulse to lower her voice to an unheard whisper—"the day faculty offices will move there as well."

Jimmy leaned down to whisper to Millicent, no doubt as surprised as was the dean herself at the decision implicit in what she had just said: she was forfeiting the senator's support for her Supreme Court nomination in favor of the merger.

It took a full minute for the implications of the announcement to penetrate the room, and the dean waited for the shock to dissipate. What would it be like for the Poets and the Quants when, next semester, they entered classrooms fashioned from the dim empty wards across the parkway, only to discover that their usual students had stayed behind in the Law Building to work in the clinics and take the old-fashioned law courses formerly taught in the sub-basement? What would they do when it dawned on them that their only students were the certifiably criminally insane?

That was when the dean realized that the merger was the answer to all her problems: not just to the precipitous fall-off in Law School applications, but also to the unyielding need in the face of this downward spiral to boost her applicants' LSATs and GPAs still higher. The merger was nothing less than a blessing, for now she didn't need 6,000 applicants, or 600, or 60. All she needed were one or two dozen applicants with scores high enough to get them into Yale, Stanford or Harvard. Because U.S. News looked only at the average scores of the admitted class and not class size, she could reject all the others. If it truly came down to this, she need admit only a single student, ideally one with a perfect GPA and a perfect LSAT, to stay on top of the U.S. News list now that she had vaulted there! And she could attract these well-credentialed applicants if, instead of spreading hundreds of modest scholarships among the needy, she concentrated a handful of obscenely generous stipends on the talented, bribable few.

But then who would fill the classrooms? The inmates, of course. Who would pay their auditing fees? The state, of course, and, with more health-care funds than it knows how to spend, gladly so.

The Poets and Quants far outnumbered the others in the banquet room, and though the candles burned brightly and the Christmas lights glittered, the mood in the room turned dark as they peered into their future. The dean looked about for a friendly face, but found none until her eyes reached the table on the other side of the bandstand that had been reserved for her and the accreditation committee members. Sitting alongside Bioff and Brown, his long legs casually crossed, was a thick-chested man who, for one exhilarating moment, the dean thought was Dan Gidron, his Chicago trial over at last. But the face that smiled back at her was not Dan's; it was a stranger's. A very handsome stranger.

Before anger or even violence could erupt in the darkness around her, the dean raised a calming hand and said, "In order to provide the bold leadership required to advance and sustain this transformative event in the life of the Law School, I am proud to announce the promotion of Director of Special Projects Alex Coyle to the position of Dean of the Law School"—she paused—"Night Division."

Cheers rose from the clinicians and lawyers, but not from the others, as she beckoned for Alex to join her on the stage. Even across the room, the festive lights threw an enigmatic glint into the yellow eyes.

While Alex eased his liquid way through the crowd, the dean threw up both hands as a cheerleader might. "And, I am even more pleased to announce the promotion of our beloved and most loyal colleague, Associate Dean James Fleenor, to the position of Dean of the Law School, Day Division. In that position, his domain will encompass the study and teaching not only of law and legal rules, but of legal philosophy, literature, history, economics, and all of the arts and sciences that give meaning and content to the law. I cannot overstate the importance of these disciplines in enlarging not only the study of law but its practice, for, without them, what is law but an empty box? And who better to oversee this great enterprise than our own . . . James?"

In a quick, balletic move, Elspeth inserted herself between Jimmy and Millicent, threw an arm around their shoulders and waited for the ovation that she anticipated Jimmy's loyalty, earnestness and humility would inspire, and that would at last lift the darkness from the room. The response, when it came after a few astonished moments, was a roar that rattled the Christmas lights and guttered the candles.

Millicent stepped back and out from under the dean's arm at the same moment that Alex stepped onto the stage, giving the appearance that a cord connected the two and that Millicent was pulling on it. The dean lifted Alex's arm with one hand and Jimmy's with the other, this time announcing two victors. "No more upstairs, downstairs," she cried to the assembly, "just night and day." "Dean of Darkness." She pumped Alex's hand. "And Dean of Light." She pumped Jimmy's.

"Dean Dark! Dean Light!" Judith Waxman chanted. "Dean of Day! Dean of Night!" On the drums, Billy Rubin picked up the beat and the sing-song spread quickly across the room, gathering voices in its repetition. *Dean Dark! Dean Light! Dean of Day! Dean of Night!* The saxophone looped and wailed around the words. *Dean Dark! Dean Light! Dean of Day! Dean of Night*!

With a gentle prod from the dean, Alex, followed by Jimmy and Millicent, left the stage, and Elspeth raised her hands to quiet the room. Beehives of conversation replaced the chanting. If Jimmy was to be Day Dean and Alex the Night Dean, what was the dean herself to be? Elspeth's mind spun to grasp what the next step in her own life would entail. She had closed the door to the Supreme Court, for the present at least, and with less overwhelming regret than she would have expected an hour ago. The Court might be waiting for Elspeth Flowers, but if a simpleton like Jimmy Fleenor could outmaneuver her as he had, could she possibly be ready to confront the wily brilliance of the Justices? Alito alone could squash her with a pinky. But if not the Supreme Court, toward which her entire life since childhood had aimed, then what?

Elspeth leaned over the edge of the stage and swept a champagne flute from the tray of a passing waiter. She lifted the glass and waited for complete silence. "I propose a toast to the next, glorious phase in the life of our pioneering institution, and to the robust health and good spirits of its new leaders: Deans James Fleenor, Alex Coyle and, ah . . . Wendell Ward. As for myself . . . ." Yes, and what was her next move to be? She felt the intoxicating chill that a trapeze artist must feel, having let one bar go and waiting for the next to swing into her hands; hanging in air, holding onto nothing more than a faith that her powers had not completely deserted her.

The answer came not in Jimmy's solemn tones, nor in the high-pitched buzz of the sprites, but in a voice that she hadn't heard in many years: her own. And it came not as an intellectual formulation, nor even as an emotional impulse, but as a thrumming sexual response. The air fairly sparkled around her as she submitted to the wracking joy of it.

"As for myself"—Elspeth played with the void, the silence of the room and the tantalizing space between the trapeze bars, as she would with a lover, teasing, bringing the instant to its unbearable brink—"as for myself, I have decided to step down as Dean and return to full-time teaching." She knew that this is what fired deans always say, just as dismissed corporate executives invariably claim that they're resigning to spend more time with their family, even though neither eager students nor loving wives and children ever get to see any more of either than they did in the past. However, Elspeth had every intention not only to teach, but to carry a full load.

But what to teach? To return to her specialty, Real Property, was out of the question. Just the thought of delivering one more lecture on the Rule against Perpetuities made her feel like she was chewing dry paper. She remembered Littlefield's odd credo that created this mess. *Connect the Dots.* So, if she would not teach the law of land, then she could teach the law of . . . the sea.

Elspeth could almost smell the heady, fecund spume of an ocean current, could imagine a crew of burly merchant seamen on their first night ashore after a lengthy voyage. *Hello, sailor!*

"My first teaching commitment," she told her colleagues, "will be to offer the Admiralty Law class that the curriculum committee has scheduled for next semester, and that we had hoped Howard Littlefield would teach, but for which, it turns out, he will not be available." She glanced over at her table. Where *was* Littlefield?

Elspeth knew nothing about Admiralty Law; indeed, less than nothing, to judge by Littlefield's response to her description of the specialty at Sunday night's party. But how hard could it be to master the field? The most laughable part of law is how quickly and easily, once you have learned its language, even an average intelligence can absorb all of its rules and doctrines. At least among law teachers, this was law school's great inside joke, and also its greatest threat: that students would at some point during their three years of classes discover this banal truth. It was why the old white men on the Wall of Heroes spent their classroom hours playing hide-the-ball with cases and doctrine: they were hiding not the ball, but the fact of how incredibly simple law is, and how correspondingly useless they were. If in the eight weeks of a bar review course State's graduates could learn all of American jurisprudence, from Agency to Workers' Compensation, with twenty or twenty-two other fields in between, then Elspeth could pick up all that she needed to know about Admiralty Law in one relaxed weekend. And, she reminded herself with glee, now that for all practical purposes she was no longer dean, every one of her weekends would be relaxed.

"To fill out my teaching load," she continued, "I plan next year to establish an Admiralty Law Clinic under the auspices of Dean Coyle, and to offer an entirely new course, 'Law, Literature and the High Seas,' at Dean Fleenor's campus across the way." It would take some time to get comfortable teaching in the madhouse of Met. State, but Elspeth could feel Randy's hand on her shoulder, and hear his voice telling her that she could do it. "And, if Associate Dean Ward is willing to have me, I also plan to offer a course on the Pirates of the South China Sea at our new campus in QingXing."

Rising waves of applause greeted each announcement, but something was still missing. Elspeth felt a lightness in her being, but it was *too* light. She felt a closeness to her colleagues, but it was *too* close. Then it presented itself, the missing jewel for the center of her now-diminished crown. "In returning to the class-room, I have agreed to accept President Bartles's generous offer to follow in the . . . er, footsteps of the Nobel-shortlisted podiatrist, Sheldon Lustig, and become State's second Distinguished University Professor, a position that, as described in the university's charter, grants me the privilege to teach any course I wish in any department of the university that I choose." The dean had no intention to offer a course in meat science or grain management. No, all she really wanted was the title—to continue to be *of* these people, but *above* them, too. If she couldn't have power, then prestige would have to do. Denied the Chief Justiceship, John Marshall would have done the same.

To Elspeth's relief and pleasure, the applause and cheers grew louder. Rawleigh had not offered her the Distinguished University Professorship, but he would. For, as the ovation—an ovation all her own!—confirmed, the unparalleled sacrifice that she had made to preserve the Law School's accreditation could not go unrewarded. What other law school dean did the president know who had turned down a position as Associate Justice of the Supreme Court of the United States in order to serve her school and her university? This reminded her that she had a few more words to say.

Elspeth lifted her hands for quiet. "I know that there have been rumors of a vacancy opening on the Supreme Court this spring; of my nomination to fill that vacancy; and of my decision to accept that nomination when it comes. And, yes, I will confess that from time to time, in idle moments, I have thought in the abstract about this possibility. But so that there remains no doubt, let me dispel these rumors now: if nominated as an Associate Justice, I will not seek confirmation; if confirmed, I will not serve.

My future lies here in College Station, with you, my treasured colleagues."

The long-awaited trapeze bar swung neatly into Elspeth's grip, and this time the ovation blew off the Faculty House roof.

The dean stepped down from the stage and Wendell took that as his cue to switch on the Stones' rendition of "Ruby Tuesday." As she walked to her table, couples moving to the dance floor congratulated her. The handsome stranger at her table rose and reached out his hand. "I'm Howard Littlefield, Jr.," he said. "My father asked me to come in his place."

His grip was at once firm and gentle, and for the first time in a long time, Elspeth felt the full meaning of the word *swoon*. "You look nothing like your father."

"I take after my mother's side of the family. The Majors." Howard pulled out a chair for her at the table. "Pop asked me to apologize for him. He's in New York. I don't know what happened during his visit here, but he's enrolled in a creative writing class at the New School."

"How thoughtful of him to ask you to come in his place."

Howard took his own chair. "He said to tell you that he was sure you were going to make the right decision."

When he leaned in to speak over the noise, Elspeth was aware of an autumnal fragrance of turning leaves and wood smoke. It was as if Howard Jr. had brought the outdoors in with him. He said, "Is that what you did up there—announce the right decision?"

"I suppose we'll see." The dean prayed that he wasn't a lawyer; that he did something more agreeable for a living. No trials, no co-counsel, no word games.

Howard looked up at the ceiling and then around the room. "When I was a student at State, I always wondered what went on in this building. 'Faculty House' has a mystery about it."

"What did you study at State?"

Howard smiled to give the answer meaning. "Animal husbandry."

"I understand there used to be a lot of that when this was just an Ag School."

"If you grow up on a farm," Howard said, "there's not much about animal life that surprises you."

"Where do you live now?" Elspeth found herself praying again. She was tired of air travel and of snowbound nights at the O'Hare Hilton.

"The farm's less than fifty miles from here. We have almost a thousand head of dairy cows now."

"And you run the farm"—one last prayer—"together with Mrs. Littlefield?"

"Mrs. Littlefield's my Mom. Pop's first wife. She lives in Florida now. I don't know if anyone uses the word 'bachelor' any more, but that's what I am. A bachelor farmer."

"The farm," Elspeth said, "what do you love most about it?"

Howard thought before he answered. "There's lots of things I like about farming, but none that I love."

"Then tell me what you do love." This was moving fast, like a roller coaster, and Elspeth exulted.

"I love beautiful, brilliant women."

"And what do you love for them to do?"

Howard looked around the table—Bioff was whispering to Brown from beneath his bandages; the other chairs were empty—before shooting Elspeth a look that blistered. "It's complicated, so let's just say it involves a roll of waxed paper, a bottle of extra virgin olive oil and the rubber-bound edition of *Mastering the Art of French Cooking*."

"Did you play sports when you were a student here?"

"Baseball."

"Not football? You have the hands of a quarterback."

"I didn't start at quarterback until my junior year."

Elspeth let her hand rest on his. "It's true what they say, isn't it, that if a man has big fingers it means that—"

"—he wears big gloves." Howard's smile wrinkled the corners of his eyes.

The dean fought for air, and to calm herself she observed the ebb and flow of colleagues on the dance floor and at its periphery. The chancellor's left arm rested more heavily than before on his wife's shoulder as he leaned in to hear whatever Max Leverkase was telling him. It was impossible to be certain from this distance, but Elspeth was sure that the white ribbon in Max's hand was a measuring tape. At her own table, Bioff appeared to have slipped his hand into Brown's which, she realized, still told her nothing about her librarian's gender. On the other side of the room, Alex was in earnest dialogue with President Bartles, his hand clutching the soils scientist's elbow. Power can reform as well as corrupt, and something about Alex's posture told the dean that in his case it would do the former.

Up on the stage, Wendell had set down his guitar to dance with the dean's two lithe little sylphs. None of the three touched, but Elspeth suspected that Wendell would find space in his Porsche to take them both home tonight. Like his priapic grandfather on Sunday night, she didn't wish him any less, only wished herself more. Judith Waxman's jacket was off, and her glittery sleeveless top displayed a particularly fierce-looking Yale bulldog this evening (did the poor beast know that he was about to be defeated by State?) and high on the other arm a noticeably fading hammer and sickle, as she led young Hubbell around the floor. Jimmy glided by, Millicent's body pressed into his, as close as a woman can be to a man fully clothed, her eyes not once leaving her husband's.

At the table, Elspeth's hand still rested on Howard's. He grasped it, rose and led her to the dance floor. Once there, he held her with the same embracing strength as Randy had two nights ago in front of the fire, with the difference that for Elspeth this was about two people, not one.

"I can't very well call you 'Dean,'" Howard said. "What would you like me to call you?"

"Ellie," the dean said. "You can call me Ellie."

ACKNOWLEDGMENTS

I am deeply grateful to Jan Thompson, Carl Yorke, and Lawrence Friedman for their support, moral and otherwise, in writing this story; to Lynne Anderson for her usual superb work in producing the manuscript; and to Jon Malysiak, Jill Nuppenau, and Jill Bernstein for their great work in bringing the book to market.

And of course my gratitude abounds for the generations of American law teachers whose fine companionship and sense of theater made this story possible.